Under The Gypsy Moon

The Land Of Thee

CHAPTER 1

THE GYPSY MOON

She was a wild creature—never meant to be tamed.

There was a lot she hadn't yet known on that night, and a lot she had forgotten. She didn't know who she really was—that she was never meant to be captured, stifled, or tamed. She didn't know that she *had been* captured, stifled, and tamed. She didn't know that she had a light inside of her burning bright as fire, and a beast ready to break free—not yet, that is. But on that night she felt something different, something pulling her—from within or without—she wasn't sure.

And then, she saw it.

Her toes hit the top of the dunes. She gazed across the sand and the water, and she saw it. The dark sky at the water's horizon glowed hot—blazing red and bright orange—a fire rising from the sea and burning into the sky. She knew that this was no fire at all. This was something perhaps more dangerous, more forbidden.

She'd never seen it in all her life, or as far as she could remember, that is. For, all she knew or could remember were in the tales she had been told.

It was late in the night on this night, somewhere between midnight and the time of night that flirts with mystery and intrigue. In that strange hour, it was only her and the beckoning of a rising forbidden moon. The horizon going up in brilliant flames—she decided.

She was ready to give in to the call of the Gypsy Moon.

She stepped forward, knowing that she was breaking the rules—moving with knots of excitement accompanied by the taste of anxiety in the back of her throat. She looked over her shoulder, wondering if she was being followed, if they were going to stop her. She took another step and turned her focus back around, her face colliding with the tips of a fleeting wing, as something flashed past her and she slipped over the edge of the dune, but caught herself at the top.

She lifted herself up and turned to see what she thought was a bat until she heard it caw. Crows at night were strange, she thought, watching in confusion as it disappeared into the sky. She brushed her hair back with sandy fingers and started toward the moon. She was on her way somewhere, but she didn't know that, not yet.

She ran across the flowers of the sand, the beach rose, the goldenrod, the prickly grass, and whatever else lurked on the tops of the dunes at night. Her eyes set on the strange, soaring moon calling to her.

Warm and wet with the dew of the sweet hour and the spray of the salty ocean, she ran to the crashing waves. Picking up speed, running faster, getting closer—reaching for answers to questions that she didn't yet know she had. For the first time, she was answering the calls of the peculiar night.

She was answering the calls of the moon and breaking all the rules.

The Gypsy Moon was forbidden, you see, and perhaps a little dangerous, some may say. With that in mind, she stomped deeper and ran faster into the night. Watching the sky flood bright with the light of the forbidden moon, the corners of her lips curled into a grin. For it was on this night that she wanted what was deemed forbidden—she was curious about what was so dangerous.

She was a creature of the Wild, after all. But she did not know that, for she had been tamed for quite some time.

But a lady can only be tamed, and pushed and pulled for so long before something inside of her decides to break free and she remembers who she was always meant to be. Be it a wild woman or a bird or a beast or a beaut or a brute—the beast within will only grow louder until it is released—the light will only grow brighter until it's all that is seen.

She could feel, on this night, that there was something inside of her she needed to release. There was something inside of her on this particular night, that felt different from the rest. This night was like no other night, you see, and the Gypsy Moon was like no other moon she'd ever before seen.

It was the brightest moon that ever filled the sky—three times the size of any other full moon you've ever seen or have imagined. And it only ever appeared without warning—at times only once a year, other times up to eight or thirteen times. And there were those strange times it would appear for three-hundred and thirty-three nights out of the year. At times it held the fiery glow of a thousand plus three suns, and had been known to leave a lasting burn on some—those who ever dared step into its light, that is.

Now *she* was daring to, for the first time. She was rising into the night alongside the forbidden and dangerous moon—the moon she'd always been warned to steer clear of, to hide from. But unlike the tales she'd been told, she did not feel scared, she did not feel burned by its light.

Rather, she felt compelled to get closer to it. To run faster. The closer she ran to the strange rising moon, the better she felt and the stronger her urge grew to go faster and further. She was getting closer. She was getting warmer. There is no looking back now, she thought.

She ran in the middle of a night that was like no other. Just her and the rising moon and the top of the damp dunes. Perhaps a coyote or two, she wondered, and a strange crow flying around. She ran faster as the light of the moon rose higher above the horizon. She was hungry to know more, to learn the truth of that forbidden moon after all the tales she'd been tricked into believing.

Many tales of that mysterious moon made their rounds through many moons, for as long as she could remember. Talk circulated from folk to folk of folk going missing under the Gypsy Moon—never again to be seen. It was condemned for the strange happenings that seemed to follow its lead. People often behaved wilder under its influence, some would even say crazy, depending upon perception. Beliefs became hazy, and blurry, and tended to blend.

Some would say that many a man had lost his marbles through his dance with the Gypsy Moon. Others would say many a man had found his marbles through that dance. Sometimes people appeared to flip upside down, so to speak, depending on who was looking. You could blame it all on the Gypsy Moon, or you could call it a blessing, depending upon perception.

Now she was caught in its spell, but she didn't know it. She was captured in the rapture of this lunar enchantment. But she didn't know what it meant to be captured in the rapture. She didn't know that she was in the hands of the wild, wild moon. All she knew was that she'd stumbled upon something she had always been told not to stumble upon. Perhaps this was an accident. Perhaps there are no accidents.

Perhaps it was magic stirring in the air, or the fever of a collected conscious. Whatever was stirring, she felt the pull of what had always been banned—running through the prickers amongst the creatures of the night—ready to give in to it. Ready to surrender. No longer would she surrender to everyone else's tales and warnings of such a beautiful miracle in the sky. She was surrendering to the moon now. Surrendering to herself, giving in to herself.

She wasn't going to be told what to do any longer. She wasn't going to follow the masses and hide from the glorious moon, not for one more heartbeat. She wasn't going to let anyone stop her this time. She wasn't going to let anyone tell her how to be scared, or what to be scared of. And she certainly wasn't going to pretend to be scared of the Gypsy Moon anymore.

What's so scary about a moon, she wondered. She'd decided she was ready to find out. Or perhaps the moon had decided that for her, long before she had.

Perhaps the moon knew that she was never meant to be locked up, tied down, or overlooked. She was, indeed, a woman of the Wild—meant to be free. And deep down she knew it. She longed to be free, again. She longed to be wild, again. Though, she did not realize that was what she longed for. She only knew she longed for something that she felt she'd lost. And now, she thought, was the time to find it. This, she thought, was the night.

She did not realize she would no longer allow the ennui of a lost culture of lost creatures settle into her bones, and sway her into forgetting who and what she really was—what she'd always been and all the parts of her that had been tamed.

She was tired of being tamed. She was exhausted from being told what to do, how to live, what to eat, how to dress, what to say and what to read, where to work and how to love. She was through seeing things the way other people wanted things seen. She was through believing the things other people wanted her to believe.

That's the way to kill a fire.

Her brain was burnt from living to the ticking of everyone else's time. She was tired of doing everything according to how everyone else wanted things done.

She was tired of living how everyone wanted her to live—tired of living a life made up of other people's dreams and fears.

Now she was turned off by all the rules, rules, rules. She wanted to break those rules. She was ready to break them, and there was no better time than now.

She was ready to live, and there was no better time to live than now—under the Gypsy Moon.

She reached the other side of the dunes and pulled off her gown. Standing at the top of the sand mountain, enthralled by the giant, tangerine moon rising above the horizon, bleeding color into the night that surrounded it—she stared at the commotion in the sky, naked and breathless.

She darted down the steep sandy banking—running to the secluded midnight ocean that shared the glow of an orange moon. The water called her name with each new beat of her feet.

She was ready to live, and there was no better time to live than now—under the Gypsy Moon.

The moon pulled at her curiosity strings with every new breath that flooded her lungs. She kicked up bits of beach with each march forward. Getting closer to where she'd longed to be—where she knew she belonged—wherever such a place was.

Escaping into the howling of her own heart and soul—she was escaping into the howling of the night. Running into the arms of the unknown—running into the comfort of the darkness of the night. Feeling freer and more alive with each step closer to the waves hitting the shore and the sizzling of the moon blazing into the sky.

She was ready to move the way flames moved. She was ready to dance the way winds danced. She was ready to crash the way waves crashed. She was ready to live, with the intention of following the beat of her heart, for the very first time.

You see, she really was a creature of the Wild. Though, she hadn't yet known that. How could she know she was a creature of the Wild, if she couldn't recall what a wild creature was? Perhaps she had known a wild creature or two. Perhaps, somehow, she had forgotten.

She only carried memories of the things that everyone else always wanted her to see and believe. Perception is everything.

She was ready. Ready to dance naked under the dangerous moon and the stars. She was ready to break free from the chains that had kept her from the light of that magic moon. She was ready to taste the milk of the moon. Run with the wild. She was ready to let her hair down, as they say.

For, what is the point in having hair, if not to let it down as you please?

She ran down the hilly dunes and through the sand. She ran away from coyotes only looking for one thing from her. She ran away from the conversations that no one enjoyed. She ran away from the ticking of time and the day-to-daying. She ran away from the black and white and boring. She ran away from what she felt wasn't all that life really was. She ran. She ran across the sand, closer toward the water and the warmth of the rising moon.

When she reached the water's edge, the fire in the sky had nearly risen completely above the horizon. Hovering just above the water, the moon dangled from the sky, taking up space within the darkness like she'd never before seen. She and the Gypsy Moon were emerging together, rising into the night in sync.

The waves had stopped and the water was a crisp mirror of glass, reflecting the forbidden moon and glistening stars. She took a deep breath, staring at the Gypsy Moon as it soared before her, and upon her release, the moon fully emerged over the horizon in the night sky.

Bright, fiery, tangerine. Bigger than any anomaly in the sky, and warmer than a hot summer's day—it was as bizarre as it was beautiful. She stood before it—the tips of her toes at the water's edge, her skin bare and glowing in the light of the Gypsy Moon. The bridge of moonlight upon the water stretched between her and the lunar marvel.

She studied the sharp lines of iridescent froth, as she pleaded before the water. It flirted with her toes as she stepped into its abnormal warmth, slinking down like she was melting into a bath and the arms of a familiar love. She sighed, feeling herself becoming lighter, her worries lifting. She swayed with the glassy water, and for the first time, she basked under the bright light of the Gypsy Moon.

She washed the warm sea over her shoulders and face, opened her arms and floated atop the water. Resting over the calm sea, letting it carry her—for she had always put her trust into the sea. Most others found it odd to place trust into the unpredictability of the ever-swelling ocean and the hands of the forces of nature—having to release all control and just trust. Perhaps this was the reason.

To her, the water was a confidant. She had been running to the waves for as long as she could remember. In fact, it was one of her only true memories. For comfort, for joy, for balance—it was a place to put her salty tears, in exchange for a deeper understanding. She'd always felt better after telling the ocean all of her secrets and fears, worries and heartaches.

So she lay on the mattress of the sea and let herself get carried away. For she knew she was in the hands of a trusted friend.

Above the embrace of the ocean, she looked up at the sea of stars and the Gypsy Moon growing brighter as it pulled her where it pleased. She'd never felt more content than right there in that moment, under a blanket of twinkling stardust, floating in the arms of the night, under what some would call a magic moon or a dangerous moon, depending upon perception, that is.

She looked beyond the moon and the stars, into the deepest darkness of the skies, where all the mysteries and all the answers reside—in the unknown. She whispered her secrets into the night, all that she was wanting, all that she was hiding, all that she was longing for. She spoke to the twinkling twilight and let out all her pieces for the milky skies to carry away.

The moon had climbed higher and perhaps gained a few hundred pounds. She stared into the belly of the fire in the sky, remembering the tales she was told of the misfit moon.

"Only a girl with stars in her eyes can see the Gypsy Moon arise," she reminded herself of one such tale.

But a tale is just a tale, is it not? Or perhaps a tale was so much more under a moon with a glow so hot—a moon that perhaps has only been seen by the likes of beasts and babes and gypsies and queens... and her.

"If the saying is so... then I must have stars in my eyes?" She let that thought play with her imagination for a moment, or two, or three, all the while drifting with the soft swell of the sweet sea—watching the stars play with the light of the moon, tasting the salt of her forgotten memories, letting the briny water wash over her face.

"So, is it true? Only a moon-gazer has stars in her eyes? Only a girl with stars in her eyes can see you rise? I must have millions..." She floated with her words, letting them sink in deeper, but how deep can words sink when one is floating under the light of a magic moon?

"I'm not scared of you, like I'm supposed to be. I don't think I am, anyway..."

She dipped her head under and swam and spun in the water before once again floating on her back. "It's probably scarier for those goons hiding away from you. Why do they do that? Why do they want me to be so scared of you? Is it true? Will I lose my marbles if I dance with you?"

The stars twinkled and the moon shined brighter as she continued, "Do I even *have* any marbles to lose? I feel completely lost already, how could there be more to lose? I don't even know who I am..."

Naturally, at times when she would talk to the night, she'd wait to hear her response in the silence of the passing of time. But tonight was different for her. Tonight, she could not feel the passing of time. Tonight, she had no concern that any time would pass at all. Tonight, she was conversing with the forbidden Gypsy Moon, and things were only just beginning.

No one was there to stop her. No one was there to tell her where to go or what to do. No one was there to lure her around with tricks and treats for her heart. It was just her—just her and the moon, and the water, and the night. And whether or not she knew it just yet—she had no desire to let her fire be smothered any longer.

She wanted to know who she really was.

So she stayed where she was, wherever it was that she was. She rested atop the glassy water mirroring the mysterious sky, floating and drifting under the guidance of the Gypsy Moon. She basked in the arms of the warmth of the moon—her eyes reflecting into the heavens, as falling stars streaked across the sky—more than she could begin to count.

"Only a moon-gazer has stars in her eyes..." she whispered to herself, floating further into the wild unknown, under the pull of the Gypsy Moon.

Chapter 2

THE LAND OF THEE

She opened her eyes in the light of a brand-new day. No longer was she floating on the glassy sea under the midnight sky. Seafoam rushed over her naked body that lay on soft, white sand. She sat up, letting the warm water wash over her lap, and spent a moment or two in a morning daze, looking out to the waking of the new day.

The sky was unlike any morning sky she'd ever gazed upon—the colors slid through one another—layers of gold, yellow, blue, and pink dripped like paint from the highest heights of the Heavens. Stars still streaked across the sky, floating and falling above her, but they'd multiplied by hundreds or thousands. A rippling sea of diamonds floated above her.

But what was most peculiar, she thought, was the Gypsy Moon still shining bigger and brighter in the breaking of the day. Not only larger and brighter than the night before, but with a fire raging ten times more—blazing like a thousand suns in one. The sun, though, was nowhere in sight—perhaps because the moon took up so much space in the sky.

There were no clouds passing by—only stars floated through the new day's sky. She was lost, mystified—emotionally entangled waking up in a place such as this. She was bewildered at the sight set on display for her, but thrilled at the beauty of this unfamiliar place as it took hold of something inside of her—something that did, indeed, feel familiar.

Although she was coated in confused wonderment, she was pleased to be waking up in a whole new place. For that's just what she was looking for, whether she was sure of it or not. She was searching for a place that felt like a space that had been missing from within her. And this place certainly felt like a place that she'd always known, yet had not known—like a reoccurring dream that she never once had.

As she looked around, she came to the conclusion she'd washed up on an island—although, most everywhere is an island in the bigger scheme of things, depending upon perception, that is.

The calm water splashed over her lap as it collected the colors of the strange sky blending into the fresh air of this new place. The air smelled of sweet sunflowers and fresh oranges, lilies and lilacs, lavender and warm, fresh pie.

She wondered where she was. But she couldn't wonder too deeply, for how could she wonder where it was that she was if she'd never before been where it was that she was?

She stared out to the horizon as the slow morning tide washed back and forth over her bare feet and legs. Pink blended into blue, and blue danced with gold, and the stars twinkled, and fell, and flew. The moon radiated a glow like the amber eyes of an owl, or the orange juices of a tangerine, sometimes like the blazing of the sun. Everything was moving and alive and changing before her eyes.

Trees and brush, and robust greens and flowers crowded out from a forest that overlapped the white, sandy beach. Thick vegetation crawled out to the sand from within the deepness of the woods. She sat on the coastline of a swollen forest that was drenched and glistening in green, under the most peculiar light of day and the Gypsy Moon.

She heard the drumming rhythm of a heartbeat coming from deep within that wild place. The distant sounds plucked at the strings of an infinite flame still ablaze somewhere inside of her. But she questioned what she heard—perhaps she was only hearing the beating of her own heart, or perhaps she was only hearing things within the confines of her mind. Is that not where all things that are heard reside?

The side of her face and body were painted with white sand, her hair messy and everywhere, and a mist in her mind fogged the very few memories she had. There was a cloudy feeling that she could not shake within the wonderment of how she'd washed ashore of a place she did not know, without any recollection of drifting so far, and furthermore—where it was that she was.

"How many stars must I have in my eyes, to be seeing all of *this*…?" She closed her eyes and took a long deep breath before opening them again, brushing the soft sand from her face.

She looked over her shoulder at one of the lone trees on the beach, and saw her gown draped over one of its branches. She looked around and behind her—she couldn't find an answer as to how that gown got there, and she didn't feel like sitting there any longer, analyzing such things at a time like this.

She got up on her feet and walked over to the tree. She grabbed her gown and slid it over her sandy head, brushing the sand from the rest of her body as the gown slipped into its place.

She felt strange. She felt confused. She felt lost. But mostly she felt new—she felt excited. An excitement that hadn't gripped her in any time that she could remember, an excitation that existed on the wings of butterflies that she could not see, but could feel coming to life inside of her.

She looked down at her feet immersed in the pure white sand, contemplating her next move. Her toes tinkered with the softness of the shore, her lips curling. She was soft and slow in her contemplations. In a place such as this, it is easy to become distracted by such simple pleasures as soft sand and, oh, say, butterflies.

She slipped her hands in the pockets of her gown, twiddling her fingers and thumbs as she twiddled her toes in the sand. She felt the foldings of a paper at her fingertips and pulled a note out from her pocket. It was marked with a 'Q' or a 'B', she wasn't sure which, as the letters were scribbled atop one another. She unfolded it and read from it,

"Welcome to The Land of Thee,
where things may seem
how you choose to see,
where darkness
lights up mystery,
and all the pathways
that you seek.
Where the wild ones
live free,
and the child
sends you off to sleep.
Where the..."

She studied the words on the wrinkled paper—wanting to dissect each line, each sentence, each letter married into each word. But she couldn't. She couldn't make any sense as to what she was reading as she was reading it, why she was there reading it, or how it could have even gotten into her pocket. And before she could finish, a big, black Crow snatched the note from her fingers—flashing its bright blue eyes at her.

"Hey!" she called to the bird and chased after her note. And in her pursuit, she thought she heard the Crow chanting the words she read as it led her astray—or led her on course, depending upon perception, that is.

"Welcome to The Land of Thee... Welcome to The Land of Thee..."

This not-so-cawing of the Crow was very odd in and of itself, but what was strangest to her was not that the blue-eyed-bird chanted the tunes of her riddle, but that the bird had a voice that sounded familiar—the voice of a woman, a familiar wild woman perhaps.

Her bare feet barreled through the sand as she kept her eyes on the black-winged beast that continued to tease her. She ran after the bird until the beach met with the wild and protruding forest. She pulled the curtain of dangling ivy and green to the side, and stepped through the thick veil of the trees—into the lush unknown. She did not realize that she'd slipped into the Wild.

As she made her first tracks into the other side, a glowing mist swept through the air of the woodland, a foggy shimmer poured through the cracks of the new forest. The hazy sparkling mist—the dust of the stars—floated in the air and showered the life of the land.

The forest sparkled in saturation with the rich overflow of the most vibrant florae she'd never imagined. This was unlike any other forest she'd ever stepped into, unlike anywhere she'd ever been, yet it continued to feel strangely familiar.

Familiar, like she'd been there all along. Though, this feeling was opposed by the certainty in her mind that she'd never seen such a place in her life. Still, something inside her felt right at home there. Something inside her told her she was right where she belonged.

All the different trees were larger than the next, most covered in moss, everything layered and dripping with the golden dew that moved through the air. The light of the sky had brightened, still dancing in the colors fed from the Gypsy Moon. The tide of the sea of stars was high, she felt their shimmer grow closer.

The forest floor was a carpet of moss and she moved across it with timid steps. She walked as if not to wake a sleeping giant, slowly making her way deeper into the forest, one tip-toe at a time. She looked around with a curiosity that was exciting and yet soothing. A curiosity that she felt was leading her into the deep unknown, but really this curiosity was leading her into herself.

Softening into the forest further with each gentle step, eventually her tip-toeing turned to firm footsteps on the cushiony moss of the Wild. And just as she got most comfortable in her footing, she heard the calls of the birds off in the distance. She stopped and stood with both feet sinking into the ground.

She held her breath, listening closely to the birds and their song, but she couldn't make out the direction of their singing. She shifted her gaze to the sky and the glistening tops of the trees around her, but she saw nothing.

Nothing but pristine, glitter-soaked treetops, and a painted sky that was forever changing. No musical birds. That is, until several darted down to her, seemingly from nowhere, whipping past her, spinning her around—or leading her to spin herself around—in several circles before her butt hit the ground.

The birds sang with delight as they flew away, "Welcome to The Land of Thee... Welcome to The Land of Thee... Welcome to The Land of Thee..."

"Ooh, you birds!" she huffed. Her heart raced with the fleeting flush of fluttering butterflies darting around like the Crows. She stood up, brushed off her backside, and chased after the pestering black birds.

She searched through the thick trees, but the birds were nowhere in sight. She traveled deeper into the land of the largest trees and golden mist and unfamiliar familiarity. She tried to grasp everything she could see, but she was having trouble believing her own eyes. One should never doubt their own perceptions, depending upon perception, that is.

She climbed over fallen trees and over rocks. She got lost in a maze of trees entangled within one another. Spider plants marched down branches, moseyed along the trees, crawled across them like creatures. An uneasy grip took hold of her, and she ran farther away from the creepy crawlings across the old limbs of trees.

She ran toward every caw of the Crows, continuing to look over her shoulder at the strange, marching plants. When she turned to look ahead once again, she ran face-first into a kaleidoscope of a thousand butterflies. Each one was no larger than the size of her thumb's fingernail. Their wings shined gold, like the shimmering dust that fell from the sky and covered the trees.

There were at least eight-hundred and eighty-eight of the fluttering flies, perhaps as many as thirty-three-thousand of them, and she was caught and frazzled in their flutter. She flailed her arms as the butterflies fluttered their wings all around and in front of her. They flew into her gown and pockets. They flew onto her shoulders and in her hair and face. They flew into her nose and ears, and kissed the lashes of her eyes.

They even flew into her mouth—the butterflies fluttered past her lips as she tried to rid them from everywhere else on her body. She'd swallowed maybe a hundred, maybe eighty-eight, or perhaps only twenty-seven fluttering butterflies, and the rest flew away.

She heaved and huffed on the ground, trying to release whatever she'd ingested. With her hand over her mouth, she gulped, accepting the fact that she'd just taken down a swarm of butterflies for breakfast. She dropped her chin down and looked to her chest and stomach—she could feel the wings of the butterflies fluttering down her throat and flying into her stomach, where they settled. Or more so made themselves at home.

She stood with butterflies in her stomach, and she heard it again, "Welcome to The Land of Thee..." cawing out from the distance. She ran. She ran to the cawing of the Crows with a sea of butterflies in her stomach.

She ran after the Crows for the most part of the day. Wherever she ran, the Crows continued to tease and fascinate her with their song from great distance. She kept after them—she was not going to give up on her chase.

She wanted that paper of hers, she wanted what was swept out of her hands. She wanted to know why she was there in this wild place. She wanted to know what this wild place was, and she wanted to know why the Crows seemed so very strange. But the more she ran toward their caws, the farther they seemed to sound.

She grew exhausted from hunting down what she wasn't even sure she was searching for. She approached an ancient tree that stood taller than the rest, its roots above the ground almost as high as she was. She sat on the moss and leaned her back against the cradling of the tree. The butterflies eased their fluttering wings and rested there with and within her.

Nurtured by the roots in the strangeness of a familiarly unfamiliar forest—wondering, admiring, confused, enchanted, studying the beauty before her—admiring the golds and blues and pinks, and falling stars of the sky. The stars had grown close enough to nearly touch the leaves on the tops of the tallest trees.

Was she lost, she wondered. Would she find her way, she wondered. Her way where, she questioned. She looked to the mysterious sky with questions in her eyes, more questions than she had the night before. "Where am I...?" She yawned, her eyes drifting into slumber.

CHAPTER 3

THE GYPSY OF THE NIGHT

S he was falling in and out of her dreams.

A prickling upon her skin sent shivers through her sleep. She batted at her arms and legs only somewhat consciously—eyes still closed, her mind still wandering within her sleepy figments. She tried to hold onto her slumber for just a bit longer, but when she felt the tickling itch rise upon her neck, she opened her eyes and woke up swatting. Dozens of glitter-dusted spider plants marched up and down her body. She screamed, kicking her legs, and they scurried and disappeared faster than she could jump up onto her feet.

Perhaps they were harmless, she thought, after a few deep breaths and heart palpitations. They were quite cute really, she thought, after a few more sighs, and chills down her spine. She stood up from the roots and brushed off the back of her legs and gown, trembling.

She could tell that several hours had passed, but she wasn't sure how many several it had been. The colors of the sky were different. Milky purples and deep blues blended within amber hues, and the stars fell closer.

Perhaps it was night, she wondered.

She wasn't sure if she could tell night from day or day from night any longer. She felt lost and a little crazy, but a part of her felt more alive than ever. A part of her was thriving in this forest.

She examined the darkness in the gaps between the trees, freezing her focus at the lights shining in the distance through the dim thicket of large trees. She wanted to see what those lights were lighting. She did not want to be caught up in the darkness as the sky aged into the night. She looked around and ran for the lights, dodging tree limbs and jumping over roots, before she was spit out to a path of warm golden sand, that sparkled like the glistening of the tops of the wild trees.

The amber lights shined upon her, and shined a spotlight on her shadow. It was darker than she'd ever noticed it to be. You see, in the Wild the dark is always darker and the light is always brighter.

She studied the strange darkness that met her at her toes, staring until her eyes pooled with their own tides. And through the ocean within her starry eyes, she watched her shadow begin to move. It did not lawfully mimic her presence as expected, for she stood completely still as it came to life.

"No... " She shook her head, quick to talk herself out of what she was seeing. "It's not real... " she assured herself. "My... my eyes are playing tricks on me.... it's these crazy lights...." She disregarded her shadow, chalking it up to just that—tricky, tricky eyes and strange, wild lights. But, you see, eyes do not play tricks, and everything is made of light.

She shifted her focus from her shadow when she heard the cawing of a Crow far in the distance. She had to find them. She studied the path laid out before her—the lights floated overhead with no strings attached, illuminating the path and guiding the way. They glowed like pieces of the Gypsy Moon. Perhaps they had been sent from the moon.

She walked along the path not knowing where she was going, or where she was.

"Where darkness lights up mystery..." she tried to remember the words of the note as she walked along the path, "and Crows and shadows make you go crazy..." she improvised a bit. What more is a girl to do when she's found herself in the Wild, but to reinvent the words of her missing note?

As she continued rehearsing her new renditions to the wild forest, she heard the cawing again, followed by the sound of a woman singing the same words somewhere amongst the trees. She slowed her steps for a few heartbeats, looking through the dark gaps between the trees and up to the sky. Seeing nothing, she picked up her pace.

"Where darkness lights up mystery... And I've *definitely* gone crazy..."

She paused again, certain this time she heard whispers on a breeze that was not there. She whirled around, peering high and low. Once more, the echo of a voice—a woman's voice—danced through the air.

"Hello...?" she called out, unsure whether or not she wanted to hear a response.

She heard nothing, not a single peep. She looked around to the forest of trees, relieved to have not received any response. She continued down the path—or perhaps she continued up the path, depending upon perception, that is.

"Maybe I'm losing my marbles like they said would happen..." she pondered to herself as she walked along and again heard laughter upon her inquisitions. She paused once more for another moment, standing vulnerably still in the milky darkness of the lit-up, sparkling night. "Hel lo...?" she called out again. "Helloooo?"

But still no answer.

"Maybe I'm dreaming..." She didn't believe that to be true even before she spoke the words. Upon this particularly foolish analysis, she heard a lady's voice whisper with the trees.

"No... " came the voice. "No, no, no... " She looked over her shoulder to the party of trees, but didn't see anyone or anything in the darkness and the depths of the forest.

"Okay. That's it. It's true. You really *do* lose your marbles when you dance with the Gypsy Moon..." She heard more laughter in return. She looked over her shoulders.

"Is someone following me?" she called out. "Hello...?"

She waited for a response, but still didn't get one. She looked all around. "Who's out there...?" she called to the trees and the wild darkness, her voice louder than before.

This time she was expecting a response. She wanted a response. She was nearly demanding an answer from the dark of the forest. She was apprehensive, what with being somewhere in which she didn't know where somewhere really was, but that slight apprehension was overlapped by the wanting and needing to know.

You see, she was not in the Wild by coincidence, for, there is no such word as such a word as that. *Coincidence*, that is. Perhaps there was indeed a reason for her being there in the Wild, and perhaps it would be in her not yet knowing—in her wanting and needing to know, that she would find what that reason was.

She waited for a response from the trees or something beyond the trees, as the butterflies of her belly tied themselves in knots. For all she knew up until then was that she was alone in that wild forest, aside from the Crows and the traveling spider plants, and such creatures of that nature. And although she wanted a response, she wasn't quite sure what to expect.

"Boo!" the voice whispered over her shoulder, sending chills up her neck.

She spun around, but no one was there.

"Missed me!" The voice breathed over her other shoulder, and through her hair.

Again she turned, finding no one.

"Now you gotta... " her hand was cradled into the warmth of another, "twist me!" She spun into the draping fabric and arms of a blurred face, and was sent whirling and twirling toward the trees. Stumbling over her own toes upon her near collision with the trees, she fell to the ground. She sat up, looking to see who had just sent her spiraling into the wood.

A woman, strangely aglow—almost as bright as the lights above the path, walked toward her with a hand offered out.

"Hi, Butterfly!" The woman had a smile that wrapped around her face, and eyes that glittered like diamonds, like stars.

*A woman, strangely aglow—almost as bright as the lights above the path,
walked toward her with a hand offered out.*

"Hello..." Who is this creature, she wondered. "Have—have you been following me this whole time?"

She was mesmerized by the appearance of this woman, but she studied the creature warily. She'd been told tales of such crazy women who'd lost their marbles—perhaps this was one of them, she wondered. She did not take the woman's hand.

"*Following?* Ha! I wouldn't say it quite like that... I'd say it more like this—"

"Like what?" She stood up and brushed herself off without taking her eyes off the woman creature.

"Follow, I did not. I have awaited your arrival. And.... well, I cackle at your denial." The wild woman spun with laughter, the rippling fabric of her gown flying behind her like a wild breeze.

"You knew I was coming?" She took half a step back from the spinning woman.

The woman stopped spinning. "You see, I say—I'll say it more like this—I've awaited your return to dance our sweet tryst, this little rendezvous, that, of course, was insisted on by you." The woman flicked the girl's hair.

"I have not insisted on any sort of a tryst with you! I've never even met you before..." She readjusted her hair the way she'd had it.

"Such a silly thing to say. I say, you see, you've appointed this meeting here with me." The wild woman waved a hand in front of the girl's face.

She glanced over her shoulder quickly. Should she try to run? Where would she even go?

"I can see you don't remember such things.... and *that* was your very reason for conducting this meeting!" The woman clapped.

"Don't remember such things? No, I just, that wasn't me—you must have me mixed up. Really, I don't know you..." She retreated another step from the woman.

"Oh, Butterfly, you and I—we met many moons ago, and right now you act as if it isn't so, but soon enough you'll know." The woman stepped closer. "Soon enough, you'll know what you need to know. Soon the haze will clear and you'll know just why you're here. You've got it all stored, up in there..." The woman tapped the girl on the side of her head.

"What? *What* have I got stored up in here?" She tapped her own head. "And—and who *are* you?" she asked the woman, and took two more steps back.

"Who are *you?*" the woman asked.

She found herself lost within the woman's question, unable to find words for an answer. *Who was she,* she wondered. She didn't know.... She couldn't remember.

"Yes, it seems you have forgotten... "

"How would *you* know what I've forgotten?" the girl snapped at the woman.

"Oh sweet Butterfly, you wouldn't be here unless you were starting to remember... " The woman tapped at the girl's temple.

"Remember *what?*"

"Well, *slowly* starting to remember, that is... " the woman corrected through a chuckle.

"Remember *what!?*" She raked her fingers through her hair and pulled on the ends.

"Who you are, Butterfly."

"Who *I* am? Who are *you?*" The girl asked the wild woman, wondering why she was still entertaining this crazy creature. She needed to catch up to the Crows. She did not have time for such riddles and rhymes and silly conversation.

"It's not of topic now—you'll figure it all out." The woman turned to walk the path.

"I've lost my marbles, haven't I..." she asked herself under her breath and watched the woman walk on, wondering if she should run the other way, or follow along.

"Oh, no. No, no." The woman spun back around. "You haven't lost your marbles just yet... Oh, but certainly you will." The wild woman winked at the girl. "Upon our revered rendezvous and rapture, you'll capture moments from your mind that have been lost in time... time,

time, what is time?"

"Lost in time?" Was she in the company of a crazy woman? Perhaps she should have turned the other way and run when the woman was not looking.

"Is it not just a melody that plays in your mind?"

"*Time?*" she asked, trying to follow.

"Ah, yes. And so it is. I say I see, I see I say—you have so much to see along the way..." The Gypsy spun around once more.

"Along the way? Along the way to where?" She shook her head and hands, backing up. "I really think you've got the wrong girl." She turned to walk the way she came, but froze when she realized she had no idea where she was going.

The woman cackled like a laughing gull.

"What's so funny?" She turned around. "I'm really not joking. I mean really, *who* do you think I am?"

"Who do *you* think you are, Butterfly?"

"I... I..." She couldn't find the words to who she was. Did she even know who she was? Had she ever known?

"You are *ready.*"

"Ready?" Ready for what? Whatever it was she was ready for, she wanted to know. She found herself too curious to pull herself away and run from this strange wild woman, intrigued by what the creature may have known.

"You're ready to know all that you've always known, and yet, *that* is something that you don't even know!"

"I *don't* know! I don't know *what*?" She stomped on the ground.

"Oh, no, no—you *do* know, you just don't yet remember. Now, don't lose your temper." The woman stepped closer. "This is why, you see, you brought me to you and you to me."

"Why?"

"For the memory of what never dies, imprints across space and life, the fire burning deep inside... " The woman spun herself closer toward the girl. "Don't you not see?"

"I *don't* see…" She was completely lost within the wild creature's words.

"Oh my, Butterfly, you're all wrapped up in your confusion—"

"Confused! Yes, very confused!" She sighed and dropped her shoulders, relieved that perhaps this woman was beginning to understand her.

"Confused is what? You're confused about confusion. And confusion, sweet Butterfly, is a mixed-up, mingled-up potion of round-about thoughts and notions—spinning, spinning, going, going, never stopping, never slowing." The woman spun three more times.

"It's even more confusing the more you try to explain things to me," she sighed, feeling lost once again.

"I will say it more like this, look Butterfly, you're confused, yes?"

"You're kidding…" She rolled her eyes.

"Well, I love laughter, I do, but here, we're speaking of you… and yes. Yes. You're a bit confused. But, see Butterfly, a confused butterfly is a butterfly who wants more than she is ready for. And for now you are simply ready for this *coeur à coeur,* before your tour." The woman grabbed the girl's hands.

"*Coeur à coeur*…? Tour? Tour of what?" She pulled one of her hands back and tried to turn away, but the woman yanked on her other hand.

"*Coeur à coeur*… my heart to yours! Confusion is a great start, a steppingstone to clarity—the thing that leads to questioning. Then, answers are found lingering, where you're least expecting them…" The woman yanked on the girl's hand once again.

"I—"

"Curious to know how to get a quicker answer?"

"Yes…?" She was certain she was.

"Forget about the question! Quicker comes the lesson!" The woman laughed.

"Forget?"

"The only way to remember is if you first forget, get it yet?"

"I wish I got it, I really do…" she said in slight defeat, looking down at their clasped hands and wondering if she should try to pull away.

But despite this woman clearly having lost her marbles as they say, the girl was beginning to feel her trepidation vanishing. She felt lost by the woman, and at the same time, she felt familiar—found, in a way. She was confused. Bewildered. Mesmerized. But no longer was she scared. She was almost certain of it.

"Well, had you not forgotten, we wouldn't be here, happily reminiscing! Now, pay no mind to your entangled thoughts you're thinking, and move forward with me, without resisting!" The woman pulled her forward along the path.

"Move forward to *where?*" She reached her free arm out behind her—unsure what she was hoping to grab onto—as the wild woman pulled her along.

"I can say it more like this… " the woman looked to her as they walked, "you're *here*, Butterfly. That *is* what *is*. So there is no better tryst than a tryst such as this. Even when you get spun into a twist… *that* will be as good as *this*." The woman spun the girl under their linked hands and pulled her along.

"I'm here… that is what… *is*." She wiggled her fingers to see if she could slip from the wild creature's grip, wondering if she even wanted to. And when she almost did, she stumbled over her own footing and squeezed the woman's hand even tighter to hold on.

"It is time, is it not?" With that sweet segue, the woman grabbed hold of the girl's hands, still looking into her eyes.

"Time? For what?" She looked at their cradled hands.

"Time, time, what is time? Is it not just a melody that plays in your mind?" The woman laughed in the girl's face, and led her forward to continue walking the path. She walked hand in hand with the wild woman, as the wild creature delved into her like they'd always known one another.

"So, come, come. We'll continue ahead, *ahead!* It is naturally time that the Wild get fed!"

"We're going to feed the Wild?"

"Well, if that is how you wish to say it, though, *I* wouldn't say it quite like that, I'd say it more like this—it is simply certain for she who is hungry to devour each hour set forth." The woman pointed forward.

"What's this…?" She was lost within the words of riddles and rhymes.

"What's what? Hours and minutes? Time, time, what is time? Is it not just a melody…"

She cocked her head to the side, a confused smirk bent across her lips. "You're quite hard to follow," she told the woman.

"Which is why I've grabbed your hand. Do you understand? See—follow, you must not, but devour, oh, you must devour every little drop!"

"You're a special kind of woman, aren't you?" Or just crazy, but she didn't muse those thoughts aloud.

"It is so. One thing you will come to know—the words from which my lips speak are always true and right. So, sweet Butterfly, shall we speak of the glory that makes the moon so bright? Or shall we speak of the creatures that sing in the night? Or are you curious how burnt wings of a bird take off and take flight?" The woman spun under their chained hands.

"You know about the birds?" She was curious to learn whatever she could about the Crows.

"My, my, Butterfly… are you a bird?"

"Clearly, I'm not…"

"Clearly, how so?" The woman held up their linked arms and flocked them like wings.

"What do you mean how so?" She looked down at her body, which was clearly in the form of a girl.

"How do I know that you are not a bird?" The woman studied her closely.

"Well, look at me, just look at me!" She pulled her hands out from the crazy creature's.

"Mm, yes, I see! And… who do you believe Thee to be?" The woman spun the girl under their arms once more.

But after her spinning was spun, everything halted once again when she realized she had no memory of who she really was. Her footing froze but the wild woman continued along the path, pulling and nearly dragging the girl along, until she remembered to move her legs.

Who was she? She still couldn't remember. All she could remember were the tales told to her in that place she had escaped. Tales like, *a girl is nothing more than silly written words.* Or *a woman who laughs and roars is a woman who shall be scorned.* And, *the ones aglow most bright are the ones to truly fright.*

"I... I..." She realized the wild woman was quite bright. "Wait—who are *you?*" Should she truly be in fright of this woman? "Where did you—"

"Where did *you* come from, Butterfly?"

She blinked, fumbling upon the throws of a question she was not sure how to answer. "Well I..." She wrinkled her forehead, darting her eyes across the ground. "Last night I... I was floating, and—"

"I know where you came from. You need not tell me so. It's you who doesn't yet know what she already knows." The woman stopped them in their tracks, and faced the girl. "I am called the Gypsy of the Night. Like the moon." The woman shined brighter, and so did the moon.

She looked at the woman—Gypsy of the Night—and at the moon in the sky. The falling stars had fallen closer, gravitating toward the wild Gypsy, who continued to speak in rhymes within a soft glow. The strange Gypsy sauntered along, dancing and clapping.

"Come along, Butterfly, join me, join me. We have places we have to be." The Gypsy winked at the girl.

And without being pulled, she followed the wild woman on her own, hoping it was the right choice as they drifted further along the path, deeper into the thick of the wild forest.

CHAPTER 4

TEA FOR THEE

*I*s this why they said to stay away from the Gypsy Moon?

She followed the Gypsy deeper into the wild, wild forest, following the golden path of sparkling sand. *Is this what happens when you lose your marbles,* she worried, as they pedaled past the trees—the Gypsy pulling her along as if they were flying. If she didn't know any better, then she would have thought they were. But a creature who doesn't know who she is, doesn't know any better, or any worse.

"Where are we going?" she asked. "Where even are we?" Why was she even here?

"Oh my. Sweet Butterfly." The Gypsy slowed their pace. "Perhaps you are *here.* Perhaps you are *there.* Perhaps this world is your world, perhaps this world is a wild world. Perhaps you have found yourself in the Wild that lies *between* worlds." The Gypsy spun herself in and out of the girl's arms. "Perhaps a world is just a word, and all of everything exists in between. The letters of course, or the gaps, or the scenes."

None of this makes sense. This woman would have been condemned back where she came from, she was certain. "I don't think I belong here..." she mused hesitantly. "I should probably go back—"

"Back *where,* Butterfly?"

"Back to..." Back to where, she was unsure. Back to the place where she'd forgotten who she was? Back to the place she'd run from, the place with all the rules and fear and forbiddances—no, she didn't want that. Perhaps this place wasn't so bad, even as she trembled with unease. It was certainly better than that place she came from.

"*Here,* is where you belong, Butterfly. Far from the march of the many or few, *this* is the march of you. At times you'll be flying, sometimes singing or crying, and best believe you'll be dancing and falling too..." The Gypsy tended to open up her lips and let the words pour out without having to stop and think as she spoke. You see, she was the Gypsy of the Night—she spoke in rhymes and sometimes riddles, but she spoke the words of the Gypsy Moon. She spoke the words of the wild night. She spoke of the unknown of what's to come, and her words were always right. And after a few words had fallen from her lips, she'd speak the rest with even greater confidence. For, the Gypsy spoke the words of the truth that lies in the darkness of the night, the truth that always lingers in plain sight.

"I'm still not quite understanding all of this, you know... I'm just... so confused..." The girl shook her head. She had long since forgotten how to hear such truths.

"Yes, I know, Butterfly, but, really—confusion? Still? Why mix yourself up with such a word? And you think you're a bird? What's the big deal?"

"Bird?" It was barely before the word fell from her lips that a crew of Crows split through the gap between her and the Gypsy—their feathers grazing across her neckline and flapping in her face. The birds flew circles around them, singing "Welcome to The Land of Thee... welcome to The Land of Thee..."

"The birds!" she called out after they flew off, spitting glitter-drenched feathers from her mouth.

"Yes! Yes! Yes!" The Gypsy clapped and snickered and bounced about and spun around in a sweet frenzy.

"That crazy flock of Crows keeps doing this to me!" She slammed her foot on the ground, still spitting. "And they have my note!" She scraped her hand over her tongue.

"You can say that their flying together is a flock. Or that it was a murder. Either way, you're right to say, they are, indeed, a little bunch of hoarders." The Gypsy rubbed her gown onto the girl's tongue, and the girl pushed away.

"Stop! Stop that!" she yelled at the woman, but as she yelled she realized that the feathers and sparkle-dust were gone from her mouth. "Oh..." She touched her fingertip to her tongue once more. "Oh... thank you... I think..."

"Butterfly, you needed my help. I delivered." The Gypsy shrugged her shoulder, winked, and dropped her now shimmering gown back down to the ground. "And there they go, a wild flocking murder of Crows. *Where* they go, now wouldn't you like to know!" The wild woman flung up her hair and arms and laughed into the sky.

"Yes!" she yelled over the woman's laughter. "Yes, that's exactly what I'd like to know!" She would beg if she had to.

"Well don't you know?" the Gypsy asked as they continued walking along.

"Don't I know? Know what?"

"Don't you know about the Crow? A flock is a mock of a Crow, a murder is a miter. The Crow isn't always what it seems, it is whatever you perceive... However you perceive the Crow to be, you see?" The Gypsy cawed like a Crow, and the girl flinched. "The Crow has a light so bright that it ignites a fire that burns deep inside. You have this too, sweet Butterfly."

"I do?" She looked around herself, to see if she was aglow like the wild woman.

"And in this place, a light so bright—it cannot hide. Here, you will find the secrets of the night. And in a murder, there are many. Secrets, that is. No, no—Crows. In a murder there are many a miter of Crows. Don't you not know?"

"Do you always talk like this?" How was she supposed to find any answers from a creature like this? But perhaps she wasn't so bad after all. She wasn't something to be feared, just a bit strange, she hoped.

"I'm not sure I follow, Butterfly. Now, listen—a flock is a flock. A murder is a murder. A miter is whatever comes your way. A miter is whatever I say. I say, they are all the same, same, same. You see?"

"I—"

"What's the big deal, Butterfly? Why ask why, Butterfly? It's only a word, they're all only words. Words dancing like girls in the world. Words, words... each meaning depends upon how you view *your* world, this world, or that world. Depending upon however bold or however tame, it's what you make of a word, that gives it the life it gains."

She played with this thought inside her baffled mind as the Gypsy rambled on and they wandered along the path under the light of the night. It's what she makes of a word, that gives it life, she thought. Perhaps this same idea applied to the Gypsy too, and the strange forest. Perhaps she should try to view things... differently. Perhaps she'd been thinking and seeing through the same kind of eyes as the people and place she'd run from.

"Now, Butterfly, let's eat pie!" The Gypsy grabbed the girl's hands and pulled her off to the side, down a different path that appeared and lit up according to their presence.

They came to a dining area set under a canopy of glistening trees and stardust. The large stump of an old tree was surrounded by seating made of moss, covered with every different kind of pie you never would imagine. Pies towered on top of pies on top of pies, adorned with a dusting of sparkles. Not sprinkles, no, sparkles.

The Gypsy pulled her to the table, and they sat before the pies on top of pies. The Gypsy first dug into the tower with her fingers and hands—the guts of pies spilling onto the crusts of the pies and onto the stumpy table. Fillings oozed from pies of every color, and colors that you've never even seen or heard of, or ever would imagine. Imagine imagining a color you've never before imagined?

"Devour, Butterfly! Devour this wild pie!" The woman tapped her shoulder with a messy handful of pie, offering it to her.

She held out her hand, and the Gypsy dropped the pie into it, and laughed as it splattered everywhere. "Thank you..." She brought the pie to her nose, smelling it first.

"Eat, Butterfly! Eat the pie!" The Gypsy smacked the bottom of the girl's hand, smashing the pie into the girl's face.

She pulled her hand from her face, licking her lips and flicking her hand upon the table, glaring at the Gypsy through her pie encrusted eyelashes. "What did you do that for?" she yelled at the Gypsy—angry for being startled, angry for being slapped with pie—wondering why this woman was the way she was.

"You were taking much too long, Butterfly." The Gypsy grabbed the hem of her gown and rubbed it over the girl's face.

"Stop! Stop!" She began to push the wild woman away, but then she remembered when the Gypsy wiped the feathers from her mouth. She was helping, she reminded herself, and let it be. She was thinking that perhaps she was beginning to feel more comfortable with the woman, the wild, wild woman. Even though she also often felt infuriated with her.

"There you go, Butterfly." The woman dropped her gown back to the ground as it blended colors with the pie that it had just wiped—shifting to a new gown, before her very eyes.

"Thank you..." She watched in amazement and confusion, as the woman's dress became a completely new color, the color of pie.

An old tarnished teapot and two teacups sat on the table beside the tower of pies. The gold leaf etching on the teacups gleamed in the moon-light from above. They were decorated with golden cats of different sizes—some jumping over and under the moon, some playing with stars. She stared at the cup as she slowly reached for a handful of pie.

"Yes, eat, eat!" The Gypsy reached between the towering, now *leaning* pies, picked up the teapot, and poured the tea into the cups.

"Oh my!" the girl gasped when the tea came out from the spout—glowing much like the Gypsy, much like the moon. "How..." The bright light of the liquid radiated with the rising steam as the warmth cascaded into the teacups—the liquid light taking up space in the darkness of the strange night.

The Gypsy glanced at her, chuckled, and placed the teapot down. The wild woman handed her a cup of luminescence, and together they clinked their cups under the nightlight of the Gypsy Moon, atop cushions made of the softest moss. Just as the girl brought the cup to her lips, the Gypsy started off with a toast.

"Chip, chip, cheers! Let us meet fate, let's enjoy our *tête-à-tête*." The Gypsy clinked cups with the girl once more.

"*Tête-à-tête?*" she asked.

"Your head to mine, my head to yours... a little like our *coeur á coeur*." The wild woman held her cup up to the sky, as if to cheers with it as well. "And to your return to this wild, wild place!"

They almost sipped from their cups, until she slipped on the Gypsy's words and interrupted. "What do you mean, *my return?*" Why did this crazy woman think she belonged there?

"Oh, Butterfly." The Gypsy placed her cup down and with her pie-coated hands, squeezed the girl's cheeks much like a nana, or meemaw, or noni would. And this, she was not expecting, but could not back away from either. The woman's hands relaxed on the girl's cheeks and cradled her face. The glowing lady, sitting right beside her, stared deeply into her eyes, and said, "You and your starry eyes... holding all of the stars, just like the sky."

"*My* starry eyes? Stars in *my* eyes?" She looked into the Gypsy's diamond eyes, and up at the sky. "You mean... like how the saying goes?" She looked to the Gypsy, waiting for an answer.

"Don't you know? The stars of your eyes, they are aglow. You may not know, but you will, Butterfly. You'll remember me and then you'll fly, you'll travel far and meet the stars." The Gypsy slid her hands off the girl's face, and clinked their cups back together. "All of it you'll know once you let go, Butterfly."

"Meet the stars? How is that even possible? How is *any of this* even possible?"

"How is anything ever possible, Butterfly? Can you answer me that?"

the Gypsy asked.

"Well, no I—"

"Exactly. And besides, what's the point?"

"The point...?"

"In trying to figure out why this is like this, and that is like that. Why not simply let things act how they act?" The Gypsy clinked their cups once more.

"Well, I wasn't going to stop anything from acting how it acts." She shook her head. How could She? She was but a girl. A lost and confused girl, at that.

"Oh, but you could have. Often if you look too hard, what you see can disappear before your eyes. The harder you try." The Gypsy sailed her arm to the sky. "And even so, had you not, if you cannot halt a thing from acting how it ought, what then is the point, sweet Butterfly, in trying to figure out why?" The wild woman clinked their cups once again. "Cheers, Butterfly."

She pressed the teacup to her bottom lip and she sipped her first sip of that hot, glowing drink, on her first night in that strange wild place.

"Oh!" She pulled the cup away from her lips and studied the glowing liquid with surprise. "What is this?" She wasn't sure of the tastes she was tasting, but whatever it was, it agreed with her at first sip.

The Gypsy laughed. "A potion made of cosmic commotion. A potion made from the blazing milky ocean, of the sky above." The Gypsy held her cup to the sky. "A brew made from pure light and love. A sweet tea of moon milk and honey, and many other things in between." The wild woman clinked and cheersed once more.

She sipped another sip. It tasted of a taste that you've surely never tasted, though a taste that would ring true with a tastebud or two. Perhaps it was slightly sweet, like honey or syrup, or cereal drenched milk. Perhaps with a hint of tangerine and lemony zest. Perhaps thick and creamy, but with a dash of savory, salty brine.

"Wild tea, Butterfly, tea for Thee! This one is a special batch, brewed specially for you." The Gypsy winked at her.

"For me?" She swallowed hard, suddenly worried that perhaps this tea was a trick... perhaps even poison.

No, she told herself, *no.*

"Oh yes, Butterfly, it's quite generous indeed. You'll see."

She looked at the cup in her hand—the radiant tea swirling around inside the walls of the porcelain, glowing in her hand as if she were holding a lantern. She held the cup higher and studied the gold-etched cats, noticing that some of them had turned into Crows. She brought the cup closer to her eyes to examine it at large. What is going on here? Am I losing my marbles, she worried.

"Can I ask you a question?" she asked the Gypsy, still staring at the cup.

"Of course, I'm sure it is one of unnecessary concern, but that's for me to discern. Go on, recite."

She looked at the Gypsy slightly offended. "What's with the cats and the Crows?"

"Cats and Crows, and you and me—are we different or the same? Cats and Crows, and me and you—are we wild or are we tame? Crows and cats soar and purr under the Gypsy Moon." The Gypsy purred, and then cawed like a Crow. "Do you? Soar and purr, too?"

Before the girl could muster up an answer to the Gypsy's questionable question, the crazy woman grabbed a handful of pie, and stuffed it into the girl's mouth. The girl pulled herself back and attempted to intercept the Gypsy, but the Gypsy moved much too fast in the face of shoveling pie. She wiped her mouth and chewed quickly, staring at the crazy woman, wondering how such an odd creature who could be so maddening could start to feel so comforting, so familiar, in a world where nothing made sense.

The girl's face was too full of wild pie to answer a Gypsy's question. But even if her face wasn't full of any pie at all, she wasn't sure how to answer most questions asked by the Gypsy who was wild, wild, wild. So, perhaps it be best to keep her mouth stuffed full of pie, grateful the Gypsy stuffed it for her.

"Butterfly, of course you do." The Gypsy answered for her.

She swallowed hard. "You mean soar and purr? I do?" Crust and juices spewed from between her lips and teeth. What did it mean to soar and purr? She wanted to find out.

"Ha! Cheers, Butterfly!" The Gypsy ignored the girl's inquiry. "Now eat!"

They dug their hands into the tower of pies and pulled out the warm fillings. She tried every kind of pie set before her on the table. She scooped away at their insides with fruity fingers, filling her face with every flavor. The colors tasted accordingly, the sparkles sprinkled on top tasted of a sugary sweetness that perhaps only the moon and stars could create.

She was a child at a birthday party, and the party was for her. Perhaps she was soaring. Perhaps she was purring.

"Cheers to you and your dance with the moon, may it bring you answers soon." Again, about to sip from their cups, the Gypsy continued once more, "And to *you*, of course! Here's to you, the starry eyed one-of-a-kind!"

They clinked their cups and she washed the pie down with a large gulp of the wildest tea, wondering what it meant to have stars in her eyes. She scooped up another handful of pie and buried it past her lips.

"Yes, yes, eat, eat, you'll need the energy to keep on your feet, Butterfly. You're here to feast and to be fed, like the wild, like I said…"

"Here as in…?" she asked with a mouth full of pie. "As in The Land of Thee…? Where's…" she swallowed, "where *is* here?"

"You don't listen very well, do you?" the Gypsy asked. "Still you are here rambling inside of your contemplations, getting stuck on a word of situations. You're here, Butterfly. Just be, Butterfly. You'll see. You'll see, Butterfly."

"I just… I want to know what I'm doing here…"

"Beginning. You are beginning. Remember? You're *here,* and *there* is *there,* and the quickest way to get *there* is to be *here.* Here leads to there. So enjoy here. Enjoy the ride, Butterfly." The Gypsy clinked cups with the girl.

"I think I'm beginning to enjoy myself..."

"And even in the darkness that lurks in the night, even then you'll be alright." The Gypsy nodded to her.

"The darkness?" Should she be worried?

"An individualized thing, it tends to be... like most things seem to be, though not ever, really," the Gypsy explained in her Gypsy way.

She stared at the Gypsy, studying this familiar yet strange creature, wondering if she would ever receive a straight answer from the woman.

"At times, one must trek through darkness, to remember all they truly harness." The Gypsy grabbed the girl's chin. "Tell me, Butterfly, whatever will you do with those stars in your eyes?"

"Why do you say that I have stars in my eyes?" she asked while staring into the diamonds of the Gypsy's eyes.

"Well, don't you?"

"Well, I don't know. *Do* I?" She thought of the saying she'd always heard.

"Well, Butterfly, you tell me. How do you think you got here? Don't you know the story?"

"I know the story that only a moon-gazer has stars in her eyes, but I'm not sure I even know what that means..."

"Oh, sweet Butterfly, that's not how it goes! Simply put, you've forgotten. But this wild tea, here, will flip the switch, or perhaps help you see things a little bit flipped. Each sip that goes down will help to remind you..." The Gypsy clinked their cups and they drank.

"Remind me of *what,* though?"

"Let us cheers to you, Butterfly," the Gypsy ignored the girl's question, "for bringing us back together again, even though you haven't a single clue in your head!"

"Hey! I'm not clueless, I'm just... confused..."

"That's perfectly alright. See, eating pie, sweet Butterfly, is much more fun for everyone than confusion is, for anyone. Now we feast, we toast and clink." They clinked their cups. "Now, repeat this please, after me—the Gypsy." The Gypsy stood halfway up from the table and curtsied. "The Gypsy of the Night, that is." She sat down.

"Why are you called the Gypsy of the Night?" she asked, ignoring the woman's instructions.

"I bring things to light that no one else sees in the darkness of the night. I am... a messenger of sorts. I recite what must be told." The Gypsy sipped her tea. "And so as it should, then so it must. Dawn comes after dusk, and in between is the darkness of the night. I'll say it quite like this—all darkness melts into the moon, once again becoming bright. Everything returns to light." The Gypsy cheersed to the moon.

"Everything returns to light..." She melted into this concept, wondering what it meant, enjoying the wild woman's riddle.

"And on the topic of all things light—you'll discover, meek or might, dark or bright, you are the one who turns on the light." The Gypsy and stars pulsed brighter.

"I turn on the light... what does that mean?" She wasn't sure what it meant, but she liked the sound of it.

"Perhaps that's been forgotten, but it wasn't all for nothing. All will be remembered, you'll see."

When would it be remembered? When would *anything* be remembered? This wild woman insisted on telling the girl how much she had forgotten, but she never seemed to mention what it was the girl had lost.

She wanted to know. She needed to know.

What was she supposed to remember? What had she lost?

CHAPTER 5

WILD OR TAME

"Now, Butterfly, repeat after me."

"Repeat, *that*?"

"Repeat *this*... the shadow's the saddle, the seat in which..."

"The shadow's the saddle, the seat in which." Why was she repeating rhyming riddles? Even though she did not understand the riddles, she liked the ways of the wild woman, so she humored her.

"The ticking and talking and clocking chimes switch..."

"The ticking and tocking and clocking times which..." the girl parroted, or so she thought.

"Listen, listen." The Gypsy waved her hand. "I'll finish..."

And so the Gypsy recited:

> *"To light up the night with a light so bright*
> *In the between that is seen in seas and scenes...*
> *See, seeing is perceiving, perceiving is believing,*
> *and believing is a cocktail of words and reasons...*
> *A fleeting feeling, subject to shift like seasons,*
> *that's what we tend to do—*
> *shift and search, and dance and move...*
> *And if you listen to the answers that come to you,*
> *and move and groove where they lead you to,*

where wild and light, and shadows so bright
speak in tongues of truth...
in lieu...
of what the Tamers told you,
then you will find what you're searching for.
And even more—
you'll rise and soar
and land right where you were before...
But see, in that world where the tamed are scared,
where words are often used for fear,
they told you lies and kept you there.
Kept you blind so you wouldn't stare
into the light that brought you here...
And here you are, in between
memories and moments and dreams,
wondering what all these words mean...
Words are the cords and swords and birds and lords of the story.
And if for you, the story is worry,
then worry one will, without all the glory...
But if perhaps your story is wordy with little woes or worry,
then the words of your story will be perfectly purely
spilling and splashing and getting you moving.
Moving in the sense of your mind,
where your words are the wheels,
the wheels are your sign
with words of what you choose to say...
Or if you choose to stay...
Whatever you say, say it certain
and in your own way.
Whether for a coeur à coeur or tête à tête,
the words you choose are yours to use.
Use the gibberish from your lips
in whichever way that you wish...

> *But do know, Butterfly, that words are like this—*
> *words and scenes and schemes and dreams,*
> *mean only what you choose them to mean.*
> *So, here, here, listen clear—everything is in the air,*
> *like the floating stars and glowing moon,*
> *everything here is up to you,*
> *what you see, what you know and what you say...*
> *You decided long ago that we would meet here today.*
> *Now you decide the game you play,*
> *the way you play, and the pace you take.*
> *You decide the words between lines,*
> *you decide the pace of space and time—*
> *Time, time, what is time?*
> *Is it not just a melody that plays in your mind?"*

She stared at the woman and tried to swallow all the words she'd just been fed. What does it all mean? The pace of space and time, had this woman lost her mind?

Or had the girl finally lost hers?

Who were the Tamers, what did they lie to her about, what was the truth? She wanted to know. She needed to know. She sipped from her tea, ruminating over the words of the Gypsy.

"Cheers," the Gypsy pulled the girl from her thoughts, "to The Land of Thee, perhaps it is the land of dreams and schemes and wild, wild things."

"The land of dreams and schemes and—?"

"Whatever land you want it to be." the Gypsy assured her.

"What does that mean?" Somehow she was becoming more lost with each passing breath, and yet feeling more at home. "What exactly is The Land of Thee?"

"Oh don't you not know? This Land is where you begin to see that you are the light, and you are the key. The land where tea for Thee is poured to drink, and the wild beast breaks free. The land where your light shines so bright, you can finally see."

"What *beast?*" She shuddered.

"And to the fiery light within! Now again we must begin—feast!" Again, the Gypsy ignored her question. Though, she was beginning to care less about asking questions and to care more about... enjoying just being there, in that strange place, next to that strange creature.

Together, they scraped up more pie, synchronously shoveling it into their pie-holes. They continued to mutter words and stuff their faces full of sticky sweet pie. They talked of—rather, the Gypsy did most of the talking, per usual. But she found comfort in that, you see, in a place so strange and new, and on a night quite unlike any other—she found comfort in the peculiar embrace and riddling rhymes of the Gypsy of the Night. She found comfort in the peculiar embrace of the *wild, wild, Wild*.

Indulging in the warm, fruity sweetness and the wild, milky tea, they laughed deep into the night with bellies full of pie. They slipped on their words and loosened their movements, everything becoming more fluid as if they'd become intoxicated off of the night. Or perhaps it was the wild pie. Or perhaps it was the potion of cosmic commotion and pure light and love. Or perhaps it was the Gypsy Moon. Or perhaps it was the wild amalgamation of it all.

The falling stars drifted above their heads. The Crows sang in the distance. The darkness of the night danced with the light. Things flowed more freely than before. Things were becoming lighter in the forest—by weight, by sight, by feeling, by light.

Everything felt softer for her. Her muscles, her face, her shoulders, her mind, her breath, her heartbeat—felt fluid, felt new. She felt the warm current streaming through her veins. She felt the heat and the light of the fiery moon pumping inside of her. Her fingers and hands floated and danced with the air.

The butterflies swam up and down, and swayed around and around—making her feel as if she were traveling over hills while sitting swayingly still. Her heart beat to the rhythm of this wild place. She felt excited. She felt free. Perhaps, she thought, she felt more like the Gypsy. Perhaps she felt more like herself.

She looked at the Gypsy as if she'd always known her, but she didn't know why. "You seem so familiar to me…" she admitted in between the woman's stories. She enjoyed listening to the Gypsy's stories—stories in rhymes, rhymes in riddles.

"I should certainly hope so…" The Gypsy poured more glowing tea into their cups and they held them up once again. "A toast! A cheers! To you and to you, and to I and to I!"

"Cheer—"

"And the night of the light that was just right for your sight. To all that you see, and all that you might. Sweet, sweet Butterfly, with eyes so starry and bright!" They clinked once again, and sipped long, fulfilling sips. "And now to our feast! Cheers to our feast set forth for Queens! A feast set forth for wild Babes and creatures and beasts!"

They each took several more sips from their tea and scooped up another handful of pie, clinking them together like cups and shoveling the handfuls into their mouths—dribbling cherries and berries and all sorts of fruits from their chins, and wiping it away with their arms.

"Toast! Toast!" The Gypsy held her tea back up. "As I said before, there are many wild teas and moon milk drinks, but this tea is the tea for Thee, it was made for this night, for you to toast with me. Now, drink up, buttercup! Soon the eve will slip into dawn, and in that way, this night will be gone."

The girl stirred her fingers in her tea, wondering what it was she was supposed to remember. She licked the glow from her fingers and wiped the rest on her gown as she took a large sip. When she pulled her lips away from the cup and looked up, she saw it wasn't the night that was gone—it was the *Gypsy* of the Night that was gone—vanished.

"Hey… where—"

"Cheers!" She smiled as if to halt her laughter from getting loose when she heard the Gypsy far in the distance.

She did not mind that she was alone deep in the night of the Wild.

Perhaps she would have minded before. But *now* was not *before*. Now she was feeling differently. Now she was seeing differently. Now she was deeper in the Wild, in the unknown, in the Land of Thee.

"Wild or tame?" she asked herself in a whisper, looking at the cats and Crows of her cup. She slunk down deeper against the plush moss, taking a deep breath in and letting out a long, delightful sigh which sent her deeper into the cushion. "I'd like to be wild… but I think I've been tamed…"

She stood up from the table with her teacup in her hand. She looked up to the sky. "Hey!" she yelled to the moon and stars. "I don't want to be tamed! Have I been tamed? I don't want to be tamed! Do you hear me? I want to be wild again!" She trailed off for a moment, her voice softening. "I want to be…" she paused, gathering her mixed up thoughts, "me? Again?" She tossed her confused questioning into the night and studied the changes that moved in the sky.

The colors above her grew brighter. She thought she'd like to find a better view of the release of a new day. She walked away from the table of pies, and—keeping her cup of tea—continued along on her journey—wherever it was that that was. She stepped across swollen moss until she found herself dancing in and through the forest, much like the Gypsy had.

Butterflies danced inside of her to the rhythms of her heart and the beating of the Wild. She felt like water as she moved along—liquid and free—spreading across the air and floating within it, being carried and swept away with it.

She was no longer attached to anything—rather, she was *connected* to *everything*. She was free, dancing in the center of it all—the trees, the stars, the breeze, the moon—under the wild lights of the mysterious transition between twilight and dawn.

She tasted the sweet stardust in the air, and felt the electricity of a thousand atmospheres. Something inside of her was awakening, coming alive again. She heard the beating of the drumming of the wild forest. She *was* the beating of the drumming of the wild forest.

Swaying and tip-tapping to the music of the Wild and the music of her mind, through the ever-expanding path of the strange forest, she shimmied and shook through the maze of trees. She was being pulled by the call of the Wild and strange. The call of the Wild and the moon pulled her forward, beckoning her along the strange path, whether she knew it or not. She was right where she belonged—wherever it was that she was.

She paused for a moment and sipped from her cup. It tasted sweeter than all the other sips before this one, and each to follow would be sweeter than the last, of this she was certain. This concoction of cosmic dew and ethereal honey that had dripped down from the Heavens now dripped past her lips. She decided it was no poison at all.

It was more delightful than the salty ocean on her skin, and the sweaty sweetness of the summer air. Better than syrup dripping down a warm, salty shoulder. Better than a sun-baked orange. The taste lingered on the tip of her tongue, and perhaps it always would.

She sat on the ground, and lay on the forest floor where the moss was many shades of green. The beach sand streamed through the forest like a river. She slipped into the rapture of the Wild and swam into the essence of that sweet, wild potion. She studied her surroundings—the greens, the dancing and waking of the forest, the movements in the sky, the dripping of the glistening dew, the sparkling of the brightest and closest stars anyone had ever seen—she studied, and swallowed, and devoured it all.

The sky was moving into lightness before her starry eyes. The Gypsy Moon was still resting as big, bright, and warm as before. Perhaps bigger, brighter, and warmer in the early morning sky—lighting up the new day like sunshine.

As the day became day, she watched the wild sky dance according to the whispers in her mind and what must have been the pull of the moon. She looked to the land of trees and vivid greens, watching them come to life. She saw the breath of the trees, and heard their rooted laughter. She watched them dance with the magic of the forest, the magic of her. Their branches stretching and intertwining with one another, waking up with her and the brighter morning light.

"I think I like it here..." She relaxed into the surface of that peculiar place. And just as she'd softened and slipped deeper into the forest and herself, the murder of Crows flew overhead.

"Welcome to The Land of Thee... Welcome to The Land of Thee..."

Within seconds, her bare feet were back on the ground, chasing after those wild black birds once again.

Chapter 6

THE WILD COYOTE

S he chased after and hunted for the Crows until the sky's colors grew brighter into the dewy morning. She ran after them whenever they flew high and far, and rested whenever they'd rest. She didn't know where the birds were leading her, but she knew she'd follow them until she found her note. She couldn't help but think that piece of paper had all the answers for her—answers to the unknown, answers to all of this—whatever *this* was.

She had unfinished business, and perhaps she also had business that was only just beginning. She really had no way of knowing what business was her business, finished or unfinished, if she couldn't find that riddle-ridden rhyming note. She was driven by the thought that its words could tell her what she was doing there, in that familiarly unfamiliar wild place. Or perhaps that piece of paper could explain how she ever got there, or even how to get out of there. She wondered if she was even quite sure she would *want* to get out of there. Where would she go, she thought, and why would she want to?

She knew the note stolen by the Crows held answers she sought to questions that she didn't even know she had. She knew the note kept secrets that she wanted to know. Like what she was doing there, or perhaps even who she was. And at this point, that's what she seemed to care the most about.

As she and the birds traveled together yet apart, they sang the song of the Wild. The stars fell and floated closer to the ground, sharing that wild space with her. The stardust played with the sweet zephyr of the newest day, softly and slowly distracting her from her chase with the birds. When she realized she'd lost sight of the Crows, she followed the guidance of the stars instead, hopeful the stars would lead her back to the birds.

She was led to a path of orange sand that closely matched the tangerine of the moon. When she hit the sand, a cat walked out from the trees and crossed to the other side where it changed from white and the many shades of dark, to black and the many shades of light. She watched with disbelief as it walked under the brush and leaves. She walked to the brush, crawling under to get to the other side.

A soft stream flowed at the edge of the brush and leaves. The cat stood at the edge of the stream, and she stood beside the cat. Both of them watched as a basket floating atop the water approached the edge where they stood. Inside the basket lay sleeping cats, cuddled and intertwined, sleeping and purring, stretching and twisting—filled to the brim and nearly overflowing. The cat beside her jumped into the basket and the rest of the cats adjusted to make comfortable room for their feline friend.

She heard a jingle, like the jingling of bells, and the basket of cats slowly drifted away from her, as if it were being pulled by an invisible line to the other side of the stream.

She wanted to follow the basket—she wanted to know who pulled it. At times one does not realize the many different chases their curiosities can lead them into.

She walked across a slippery log with her arms out to the sides, the water at her ankles splashing up to her knees. She jumped onto the ground when she got to the other side, but the basket of cats was gone—nowhere in sight—her sight, that is.

She walked on that side of the stream now—past the trees and tall grass, searching for Crows and cats—being lured even deeper into the Wild. She tip-toed and pressed her soles through the thickness of the forest until she found herself standing in an open field of wildflowers—or *wild* flowers—depending upon perception, that is.

She stirred with the sweet fragrance that stirred through the breezes of the soft air. She twirled through the many acres of flowers and spun with delight. The stars glistened. The flowers flourished. And, so did she.

The flowers grabbed hold of her ankles and toes as she walked through them—hugging and greeting her in the morning light as she passed them by. If she stood idle for too long, they would climb up her legs as if they were ladders and pull her down to the ground. And that's exactly what they did.

As soon as she lay atop their wildness, the flowers softened around her body, nestling around her. It didn't take long before she was rolling herself around in the garden like a wild animal. Stretching, laughing, rolling on the ground, she sprawled out over flowers that hummed the song of the morning. She was like a cat in a garden of catnip—milking the warmth of the morning as if it were a hot bath. Purring like a Queen, a Queen of the Wild, a Queen of the wild flowers. She had a fever of elation, a wild fever.

Cradled by the meadow of blossoms, she stretched her arms out far and looked up at the ever-changing skies once again. She was busy being swallowed up by the magic and strangeness of the forest. She was busy soaking up everything in that moment—the smells, the flowers, the colors, the stars, the warmth, and the beating of her heart. She was starting to feel the very first symptoms of becoming unfettered—a sensitivity set forth by the wild, wild place she was in.

The beginning stages of finding oneself becoming unfettered can be as much exciting as it is exhausting at times. She yawned with a sigh and smiled. She rolled over to her side with tired eyes, curling up into herself and the thick blanket of wild flowers. She closed her eyes and smelled the flowers as they formed into the shape of a flowery teddy bear.

As she started to fall into a deep sleep, she was startled by the sensation of falling through the sky. She flinched and kicked her leg in her sleepy oblivion. She stretched her leg out further to the side—sprawled across the field of flowers as if it were a bed made just for her.

She twiddled her toes as they rubbed against something soft and furry, like a warm, shag carpet between her toes. As the carpet began to undulate and move the way lungs move when taking in air, she realized she was not alone in that bed of wild flowers, after all.

She jumped onto her feet in fear before feeling another breath of that being. It took her a moment to figure out what type of creature it was—that hairy beast on the ground. It was a coyote. She'd been resting in arm—or leg's—reach of a coyote, on a bed of wildflowers. This was no regular coyote, this was a giant coyote.

She froze in her fear for a moment, plus several moments more, unsure of what to do. She'd never been so close to such a large beast before, as far as she could remember. She stood above the sleeping coyote, eyes watering, not blinking, breath shallow and stifled, and she stared at him.

After becoming fully saturated in the sweat of her disbelief and distress, she stepped back several erratic steps. Upon her reversing, she tripped over the trap of entangled wild flowers. Her back slapped the ground and the flowers did not hesitate to lather her fallen body. She sat up before she was completely consumed, and brushed the flowers off her. When she stood—the Coyote was awake, staring at her with his mesmerizing eyes of two shades—one blue and one gold.

"Good mornin'," he greeted her.

She didn't say a word. She *couldn't* say a word. She wanted to be polite to this scary beast of a creature, but she had no words.

All she knew in that moment was fear and an elevated heart rate. All she saw in that moment was the tunnel vision of a giant Coyote, greeting her in the strange, morning light.

"Well, what is it?" he asked as he ate from the bed of wild flowers. He was calm for a coyote his size, or for any coyote of any size. But still, she remained silent. "What ya so scared of?" he asked.

As if he didn't know.

The Coyote was awake, staring at her with his mesmerizing eyes of two shades—one blue and one gold.

Again, she stood there—aloof in her own fear, frozen and tense. "Alright, alright. Listen, girl, I get it. But if ya don't start talking," still chewing away at the wild flowers, "how ya ever gonna know?"

"Ever know what?"

"Ha! There it is! There she is! Ah, I knew ya had it in ya."

She covered her mouth as if she'd blurted a big secret, and muttered past her hand, "I... I think I should go..."

"Go? Go where? Where ya gotta go, Girl? Ya just got here. Ya got somewhere ya gotta be all of a sudden?" The Coyote licked his lips. "We got a lot work to do."

She blinked. She realized he was right. She really didn't know where she was going, or where she was, or where she would go in such a moment as this, to escape from such a coyote as this—a coyote larger and smarter than most other coyotes. And who's to say that if she did walk away from this giant beast that he wouldn't stop her after three or four steps and enjoy a breakfast feast?

"Hmm?" He waited for an answer, taking his time as he got up on all fours. He stood nearly as tall as a horse, and had a coat so shaggy she could get lost in it. Like a coyote in a lion's mane—his thick coat dressed his body like a king.

"I really don't think we should be talking..." She took one shaky step back.

"Well. Rude. What did I do to ya?" He took one step closer.

"Well, so far nothing, but you're a giant coyote, and that's all I need to know."

"'At's right. I suppose ya do know that about me, don't ya? I'm a coyote. And I know you're a girl, so what. What's the big deal?" The Coyote wagged his tail.

"Well... yes I am a girl." And what does that matter? "But I'm *not* a coyote—I don't attack or eat people..."

"Says who?"

"What do you mean, *says who?* I'm not the coyote here, that's you!"

She took another step back.

"Well, ya got me there... ya figured me out. Now let's go—I've been waiting for your company." He yawned, flashing his teeth—the sight that motivated her to dart away as fast and as far as she could. But the Coyote was obviously much larger and faster than she was, and he was quick to follow after her.

She raced through the flower field, looking back at him as he hunted her down in an almost leisurely manner. Why wasn't he running after her? The confusion set in as heightened fear. He had a trick up his sleeve, she knew it.

The wild flowers clung to her ankles and toes, weighing her down, slowing her every step. The floor fell from under her feet, changing shape—sloping down. Her feet pedaling faster beneath her until they couldn't pedal at all. Her legs slid from her, she slid down the hill, falling to the ground with a hard thump.

She stood up before the Coyote could catch up to her, and dashed deeper into the thick of the wild green trees.

She peeped over her shoulder every other breath to see the Coyote getting closer.

"Hey Girl, come 'ere, I ain't gonna hurt ya."

Her heart almost leaped from her mouth as he called out to her and she tried to conceal her heavy breathing. She dipped behind a monstrous tree and planted her back against its bark, trying to catch her breath as quietly as she could. She was sweating—she was shaking—her heart was racing. Could the Coyote smell her fear? She peeked out from behind the tree to see if she'd lost him, but he was sniffing his way to her, right on her track.

She curled her arms up to her chest and spun around to face the tree, pressing her forehead and body tightly against the mossy bark, trying to become one with it, desperately hoping that he did not see her, and that his sense of smell was just the worst. But it didn't take long before the Giant Coyote was on the other side of her tree.

They were both winded. She found herself standing and waiting on the other side of the tree, unsure of what the beastly creature may do. Her beating heart had never been so close to the adrenaline of such a beast before. Well, a beast cloaked in a fluffy coat of fur, that is.

"Girl, please. No need for such a show. Just trust me." The Coyote licked the tree, breaking the timid ice first.

"*Trust* you?"

"Trust me."

"You just chased me through the forest, and you want me to trust you!?" She barely moved her body from its tight hold.

"Oh, and that's all you're going off, huh? That's your judgment of me? So I chased ya, so what? You're great in a good game a chase. I was just warming ya up."

"Warming me up?" She flinched with offense.

"Plus, I'm no different than you, ya know—getting a good chase outta this wild place."

What he said made her pause in her fright and think a little deeper. After all, he was right. He'd chased her into the forest just like she'd been chasing after the Crows this whole time. And she was nothing to be scared of, was she, she wondered. She was not chasing after the Crows to attack and eat them, she was chasing after them because they had something she wanted, and she was curious about them. Perhaps, she thought, that's why the Coyote was after her, perhaps she had something he wanted. Perhaps he was curious about eating her for brunch, she reminded herself.

"But... but I know about you coyotes..."

"*You* coyotes? Ya know about *us*, coyotes? Have ya noticed, girl, I'm all alone? There's only one a me on this side a the tree. I'm the only coyote here, talking to ya." The Coyote bit off a mushroom from the side of the tree.

"Oh yeah?"

"'At's right."

"Well... how do I know you don't have a pack of your friends just watching and waiting to attack me?" She softened just enough to look over her shoulders and peek behind her.

"Well, ya don't know that, I don't think. But I know."

"I know too, I know what you coyotes do." She wanted to believe he was not nefarious, but she knew about coyotes. "Most of you hunt and kill, and eat your prey... is *that* what you're trying to do to me?"

"Oh? And why do ya think I'd do it to you? Have ya seen me do the things ya say I do? Maybe you've seen other coyotes do these things, but ya don't see me killing ya right now, do ya?"

"Well, no—"

"And I very well could now, couldn't I?" The Coyote stuck his nose closer to her side of the tree.

"I—" She wanted to run.

"And I ain't, am I?"

"Oh, please! Please, don't!" she begged.

"I ain't gonna, Girl. Do ya really think *I'd* do that to *you*?"

"Well, I've only just met you, I have no idea what you would do—I haven't seen you do much of anything other than sleep and chase me..." She shuffled her feet, but knew she could not escape him.

"'At's right. So how do ya know? If all ya seen me do is sleep and chase, how do ya know that's what I'm all about?" He stepped a little closer to her side.

"I've been told." She scaled along the tree, creating a dance between the three of them.

"Oh, ya been told? Do ya always believe everything everyone tells ya, Girl?"

"No, I—"

"Ya oughta not do that," the Coyote instructed.

"Well, Everyone in their right mind is scared of coyotes...." They continued to dance around the tree.

"And are *you* everyone, Girl?"

"No, I am not *everyone*, Coyote..."

"No, ya ain't everyone, Girl. And am I every coyote out there?"

"No, but—"

"Are ya in ya right mind, Girl?"

"Of course I'm in my right mind!" She froze their dance.

"Who's to say which mind's a right mind, heh?"

"It's, I'm, you—"

"See, there? Well, then, what do ya have to say for yourself?"

"I don't—"

"Shh... say nothing, Girl, except that you'll do me the honor of showing me your trust. Do me the honor of walking by my side for a moment or two. Maybe you'll like it. For, I haven't hurt ya like the other coyotes have, and I ain't gonna." He stepped closer.

"But how will I know you're telling me the truth?"

"Right... Well, the answer's very simple, see. You, Girl, got nothing to lose. You'll come with me and you'll find that you could trust me all along, or you'll end up being my prey, as you say, knowing that you were right, after all. Either way, ya win. And, so do I." The Coyote licked his chops.

She didn't find much comfort in his answer as she stood behind the other side of the tree. But the Coyote was very persuasive, you see. He was a smooth talker, weaving words around the women of the Wild, charm dripped from his jargon and teeth. It was an art, really, a beautifully mastered art. Or perhaps it was the natural characteristic of a giant, wild creature. Comforting endearment was the measure of his grand presence.

He certainly did not seem like other coyotes. She was beginning to think that perhaps he wasn't all that scary, after all. Perhaps he was only joking, when he said she'd be his prey. She was beginning to think that maybe he did seem honest. Maybe she really *could* trust him. But she wouldn't know unless she gave it a go.

"Well... I suppose I could use the company getting around in this forest for a little while...." she admitted through chattering teeth.

"Me too, Girl, me too." The Coyote walked to her side of the tree. They looked at each other—he looked a little less frightening to her now. Her shoulders dropped down, her face softened, her heart beat simmered

as much as it could. He nuzzled his long nose under her arm, and perhaps a friendship of opposites would begin... or continue.

CHAPTER 7

THE WILD JUNGLE

S he and the Coyote walked through the forest of trees and tall grasses, on moss and sand. At first, they walked quietly together, not saying many words, getting used to the feeling of one another, getting used to the rhythm of the other one's walk.

"Why are you out here all alone, anyway?" she asked the Coyote. "Shouldn't you be leading a pack or something?"

"Girl, I'm neither a leader, nor a member of the pack ya thinking of," he told her. "And, I ain't alone. I am what I am. I is what I is."

"I really wasn't trying to be rude..." She bit her lip.

"'At's alright, Girl, it's okay. I know what ya saying, Girl. I'm a coyote, as ya see with your own eyes... and maybe a pretty big one to ya. All ya know of me are scary stories, and, I don't mind." He held his chin up. "'At's why we're walking together right now."

"It is?"

"And, Girl, maybe you're the leader at the head a the pack, did ya ever think a that?"

"But..." she lifted an eyebrow at him, "I'm not a Coyote."

"But I am, 'at's right?"

"Well, you're much larger than any coyote I've ever seen... you're even too big to be a wolf…"

"I ain't a wolf," he clarified.

"Maybe not, but what kind of coyote is *bigger* than a wolf?" she asked.

"This kinda coyote."

"Oh, I'm sorry…" She chewed her lip.

"Ain't gotta be sorry." He looked at her, half his face lifted in a smile. "Don't be so uptight, Girl. The point is to just relax. Sit back. Enjoy. Stop being so sorry and worried. Just… be."

"That's it?" Sit back and relax? Just be?

"'At's right. Hop on my back if ya want to, take a load off… enjoy the fresh air." The Coyote halted and knelt down. "Go on Girl, hop on."

She was not sure if she should take the offer. Perhaps it would be best to keep on her own feet for now, just in case. "Oh, no—no thank you… I'm okay walking."

"Alright, Girl. This big old back ain't going anywhere," he stood up, "it'll be here when ya need it."

"Thank you…" She studied him as they continued their walk. Did she trust him? She was beginning to. But back in the world she had escaped, the world that she was used to—no one would ever be so friendly as such creatures she'd already met in that wild, wild place. Was it a trick? Or was it real?

She carried on with him, holding onto the belief that she could trust him, while contrary thoughts rested in the back of her mind.

"We should fill our bellies, Girl." The Coyote sniffed at the air as they walked.

"Well, if you're not like *other* coyotes, then *what* do you eat here?"

"Well ain't that a funny question, heh?" The Coyote chuckled.

"I just mean," her cheeks crimsoned, "because, you're so…" She looked at his gargantuan body.

"I eat whatever I want, Girl… I eat a lot a this," the Coyote chomped on the tall grass at the edge of their path and continued walking, "I like to snack on it, during my morning stroll." Grass hung out the sides of his mouth as he continued, "whatever I need to be eating, is what I be eating, Girl. I eat what the Wild feeds me, which most a the time is just what I want, not *always* what I want, but *always* what I need, when I need."

"But what if you can't find what you need?" Like a stolen note, or the birds who took it...

"Impossible. Ain't no lack of nothing in the Wild." The Coyote paused and itched the back of his ear with his hind leg while standing, and they moved along. "Everything we need comes to us. Just gotta have a bit a faith, Girl."

"That's all it takes, huh?" she rhetorically asked through her skepticism, but wanted to believe it was so simple.

"'At's right, Girl. Now, how my teeth looking?"

"Your teeth?" she asked, cocking her head.

"Ayep. This grass gets my flossing done for me too. Keeps the teeth clean and sharp. What a ya think?" The Coyote flashed his sharp smile of pearly whites.

"Um... dazzling!"

"Why thank ya, Girl. How 'bout yours?"

She flashed her smile his way and asked past her teeth, "what do you think?"

"Good, good... could use some grass, I think."

"Oh, really?" They laughed through their teeth as a Crow flew overhead and dropped a clam in front of their feet for the Coyote to eat. He ate the clam in one gulp, shell and all.

"See? The Wild always provides," he said, licking salt from his lips. "And what you been eating, Girl?"

"Me?"

The Coyote sniffed at her. "Aha... I thought I could smell pie!" He lapped his tongue across the side of her face. She wiped her cheek and looked at him, a surprised confusion upon her face. "It was fruit. From the pies," he casually said. "It's gone now."

"Thank you...?" No one back from where she came would have ever behaved like these strange creatures in this strange place. And although it was odd to her, she also found great comfort in it.

"Anytime, Girl." He licked the top of his nose. "Welcome home, by the way."

"Oh—I... I'm not really from here..."

"Not from here! Ha! Girl, this is The Land of *Thee*."

"So I've been told." She sighed. "But I'm not even sure what that means or how I even got here, or what I'm *doing* here, or what I *should* be doing here..." She shook her head and kicked a rock.

"There ain't nothing that ya *should* be doing." The Coyote batted at the rock when they walked past it. "Should ain't nothing but a blurred word."

"A blurred word?" she asked. "What's a blurred word?"

"A blurred word—it's a word of confusion and delusion... a word with no meaningful meaning except a lack a certainty."

"I don't think I follow..." But she wanted to.

"A blurred word hints at a lack of self, Girl. A dumb word full a fear, unease, un...certainty."

"Oh... So I *should not* use the word should?" She smirked at the Coyote.

"You are funny, Girl." The Coyote chuckled. "But ya don't need to worry 'bout the *shoulds* and *should-nots*. You'll get all them answers that ya seek, you'll see. So, just relax. No worries, Girl. No worries."

"So, I *should not* worry..." Together, she and the Giant Coyote laughed.

"Worry—also a blurred word."

"Why worry?"

"'At's right, Girl, 'at's right."

They walked in silence for the next many steps. It was a comforting silence which was not silent at all. They listened to the sound of their footsteps, the sound of the trees waking with the day, the sounds of the creatures in the forest—the sounds of the new wild day in that wild place.

"So, Girl, what do ya *think* you're doing out here, as ya say, all alone?"

"That's a hard question to answer..." But one that she desperately wanted the answer to.

"Perhaps it was a trick question."

"What was the trick in the question?" she asked.

"Tell me, do ya remember your arrival?"

"Oh…" She thought for a moment. "Not really. All I remember is that I was running through the dunes, and then… I saw the Gypsy Moon…" She looked to the moon. "My *first time ever* seeing it!"

"Ya sure 'bout that?"

"Oh, I'm sure. Where I'm from, it's forbidden."

"That ain't where ya from, Girl. Believe me."

She slowed their pace slightly and scowled at him. "Don't you think I would know a little more about where I come from than *you* would? You don't even know me…"

"Sure I do, Girl." The Coyote let out a chuckle. "And I like ya. You play a good game."

A good game of what? She watched the Coyote stroll ahead of her, as she almost came to a complete stop in the path. How did the creatures of this place know her? She wanted to believe them, but all she had were the memories of the world she'd once lived in, the world she'd escaped. How could these creatures know her if she didn't know them, in a place she'd never seen before? The worries from the back of her mind began to creep into the forefront—was this all a trap?

"Come on, Girl." The Coyote looked back at her. "Go on with your story… ya saw the moon, yep…"

She snapped back into the moment and caught up to the Coyote, reminding herself to just relax. "This time I broke the rule—"

"Broke the rule, did ya?"

"I didn't want to hide anymore, like everyone else always does."

"Hide from the moon? Impossible. That there moon sees everything, there ain't no hiding from that. And if the moon wants ya, it'll get ya. Ain't no hiding."

"Well, after I saw it, something changed. Something happened. I'm not sure what." She put her hand to her forehead. "I went in the water,

I was floating... and then the next thing I knew, I woke up here..."

"Maybe that's how ya got here... ya let yourself float."

"I'm not sure what you mean..."

"We all float, but most tame creatures tend to hold themselves down, forget their gift of buoyancy." The Coyote kicked a rock to her. "Ya stopped holding yourself down. Ya stopped holding back. Ya gave in."

"I gave in..." She kicked the rock back to him, proud that she'd given in.

"'At's right. Ya let yourself float. And now you're floating wherever ya please."

"I'm not so sure about that..." She sighed. "I don't even know where I am right now. So how can I be going where I please?"

"You're walking with me in The Land of Thee," he reminded her. "Always going where ya please, Girl, even if ya don't know it."

"How can I be going where I please, if I have no idea where it is that I please to be going?"

"Girl, you were floating to get here, to get somewhere, even if ya didn't realize. And that's how ya got here. And now here ya are." The Coyote reached to the side of the path and swallowed another mouthful of grass. "And you could still be fully afloat now, if ya just stop holding the rest of yourself down."

Had she been holding herself down? And if she had, how could she lift herself up? Perhaps if she allowed herself to float a bit more, she'd find the pesky Crows and her stolen note. She wanted to stop holding herself down. She wanted to float. She wanted to fly. Perhaps she couldn't, because she'd been tamed. Had she been tamed?

"Stop thinking so much. You overthink." The Coyote continued. "Thinking too hard, thinking too much. You're *here* now. So be here. Enjoy it. Float with it, Girl."

"You make it sound so easy..."

"It is... and yet here ya are, making it so hard for yourself. But it ain't, you'll see." The Coyote glanced at her and continued, "Revelations take time, as they say, especially when ya been tame for so long."

"Tame?" How did he know of her contemplations? How did he know if she'd been tamed? And was he right?

"Not so much anymore. Eh, you're getting there. But for now here ya are, with me and the sweet breezes of the Wild. So, take a load off," he instructed. "Relax. Enjoy." He ate a flower from the edge of the path. "Hey, maybe ya wish to be floating wherever the wind takes ya, heh?"

"Maybe... I'm just not sure how the wind took me *here*..."

"Does it matter so much *how* ya got here? Or does it matter more that you *are* here?" he asked her, still plucking flowers from the side of the path with his teeth. "Do ya like it here? You enjoying yourself?"

She reflected on her short time spent in that wild place so far, still asking herself if she'd been tamed. "Oh... I do. I do like it here..." she thought about the strange sky and stars, the creatures and Crows, "it's... like nowhere I've ever been." And yet it still felt familiar somehow.

"Oh, but ya have. But besides that, ain't that all that matters—that ya like where ya are?"

"Is it? I mean, I *do* like the way I feel here..." she admitted through her confusion.

"Well, then ya oughta not care 'bout anything else. Except if we're ya walking to keeps feeling good. All this floating and walking and seeking is one big journey, Girl, and the only thing that matters is that you enjoy that journey, 'cause it's yours to enjoy."

"But... things are not always going to be enjoyable," she argued, wondering how any creature could be so naïve in thinking that everything is perfect. "How can everything always be flowers and rainbows without sorrow or despair or things going wrong?"

"Ah, now that's not what I said." The Coyote looked at her with raised eyebrows. "You're always gonna trip on the path. Always gonna have to get back up. Not every path is gonna be filled with, how ya say, *rainbows and flowers,* no, but every step of every path will be a steppingstone to where you're going. And there's a great deal a beauty, a great deal a serenity, in knowing that. So, Girl, are ya? Are ya enjoying the journey?"

She thought about his words. She thought about her journey, playing back the many bizarre, yet liberating moments that led her to *that* moment—walking there with that Giant Coyote, through the wild and strange forest. "Yes... I am. I am enjoying my journey."

"Even when the journey gets a bit bumpy and rough, enjoy it for what it is Girl. Them bumps are getting ya where ya need to be."

His words settled into her as she walked beside him, over every little bump. Perhaps the Crows were getting her where she needed to be. Perhaps the Giant Coyote was as well. She was beginning to entertain his philosophies—to enjoy her journey no matter how strange, to relax and just be, float with the sweet breezes of the Wild—or at least the thought of such things.

She enjoyed the company of this peculiar Coyote now. He was candid and blunt, yet sincere and delicate in the way that he spoke. He carried himself with strength, bravery, and oblivious confidence. Yet, he was carefree and goofy, relaxed but aware. A boyish charm, topped with the charisma of a wise and gentle man—he was giant, but harmless. She felt a conviction within her heart that she could trust him. Just like he'd told her. Regardless of the worries falling farther to the back of her mind, she felt that he was safe. He was honest. He was real.

He was familiar, like someone she'd already known. Or like several people she'd already known. She felt safe around him. She hadn't sought a source of security, even though she had many fleeting fears since she'd arrived—but now she was soaking in the protection and guidance that he naturally exuded. He was a warrior—a gentle and vulnerable, yet mysterious warrior that seemed to care for her as if he'd always known her.

Not only was he unlike any coyote she'd ever come across, or unlike any beast she'd ever known—he was unlike anyone she'd ever known, in a way, and in the same way, he was like every man she'd ever known. It was as if there was already a place for him within her heart. Somehow she could feel him in the reverie of her yore.

She walked alongside him in a quiet confident comfort, in a strange, wild forest that was ever-evolving.

"Do you know the... Crows?" she asked the Coyote.

"Birds of blackened char and mystery, 'at's right, Girl, I know 'em."

Her heart skipped a beat. She'd found the right creature to get her where she needed to be going. "Oh!" She skipped between her steps. "You know where to find them?"

"Girl, I know the way to the Crows." The Coyote chuckled. "So do you."

"What do you mean?" She'd been after them since she got there—if she knew where to find them, then she'd know where she was going.

"Nothing's ever missing, lost, or outta reach, Girl. Ya just gotta... listen, follow the feeling, have some faith."

She listened to the rhythm of their footsteps along the path. "So... where are they? Where are we going?"

"We're gonna find them Crows for ya. But understand, Girl, journeys ain't ever traveled in one straight line, and speeding, well now, that just ain't advised..."

"No speeding...?"

"Not if ya wanna enjoy the ride. We tend to travel in circles, Girl, and we gotta take our time... soak it in, let the wind push our tails..."

"Tails...?" She was sure he meant sails, and was more curious about his other words. "What do you mean we travel in circles?" It certainly did not seem to her that she was simply circling around.

"'At's right, 'at's what we do. Round and round. Making the same stops here and there, without so much as knowing it." The Coyote smiled at her and continued, "'Cause depending on how your eyes are seeing things, the same stops look different each time. And when ya arrive, you're always different than previous times. As we revolve, we evolve, Girl..."

Was she revolving? Was she evolving? She'd like to think that she was.

They walked together through the misty moss forest—not in a straight line, rather, in a circle of sorts—as she'd learned from the Giant Coyote. The day grew warmer and the moon grew larger as they traveled deeper into the Wild—where the bounty of the trees and lush greens had expanded ten times more. Tropical flowers and tropical trees mingled with that of the woods. The stars buzzed faster, the breeze blew wilder—where were they?

"Um... Coyote?" She looked over her shoulders at the many changes taking place in the forest, or wherever that place was. Were they still in the forest? "Where are we?" she asked as they came to a rickety old bridge, her voice almost lost behind the babbling of a rainbow stream rippling at least a hundred feet below.

"The Crows, Girl," The Coyote reminded her as he stepped onto the bridge.

"Oh, yes, that's right... I know..." She contemplated stepping onto the bridge, but what if it crumbled out from under her? And where would it lead her to? "But where are we? How come things are different?" She brushed her fingers through the marriage of thick, green fern and palm leaves. "Everything's changing..." She did not step onto the bridge.

"Ayep, Girl. Things they are a changing. Little change a scenery is good for ya." The Coyote flashed his colorful eyes at her from the bridge. "Now c'mon, you'll be fine."

Everything was always changing. But she would be just fine. She wanted to trust that she would be just fine. After all, what was the worst that could happen? Might she fall?

She filled her lungs, holding her breath as she stepped onto the bridge. Her legs shaking, her knees weak, her heart pounding to escape her body—she gripped the tattered ropes holding up the bridge and moved forward. The water below her calmed as she released her breath with a gasp, and she felt her fears rise from her as if they'd been pulled by the skies.

"Perceptions always change, Girl, depending on what ya believe." The Coyote's claws clicked as he led her across the bridge. "We're getting closer. Digging deeper, Girl. We're checking out the jungle."

Perhaps the jungle and the forest were both equally wild, and equally just as different. Perhaps the jungle and the forest were the same, and it was all a matter of perception. Her perception was perceiving her surroundings looked wilder, thicker, brighter, greener, lusher. Everything was expanding. She felt at least thirteen to twenty-one degrees warmer, and perhaps a little lighter.

By the time they met the other end of the bridge, she felt refreshed. As if she had breathed a thousand and one new breaths. She was ready. She was ready for more.

They roamed through warm lagoons of bright blues and greens, splashing and crashing their bodies down. Stars drifted, and fell, and followed them – blending with the water and lighting up the entire bath. She and the Coyote swam after the falling cosmos—never succeeding in their catch. You see, wild stars were a peculiar creature—bright yet opalescent, and either falling, or floating, or fleeting, or following, or frozen in motion, or flying most of the time. The stars were alive. The water was alive. *They* were alive.

They trudged out of the water as the stars lit up like fireflies in the strange light of the day—where the pinks danced with the golds, and the purples danced with the blues, under the fiery brightness of a swollen moon. They watched the sprightly twinkling lights, walking together atop dunes of white and purple sand—the Coyote chasing after a star here and there, digging his nose in the sand, playing with the day.

After many hours—whatever hour a wild hour was—of traveling in and out of the wood and dunes of the forest, her legs grew tired and she gave in to the Coyote's offer for a ride. He knelt down and she climbed on as if he were a horse, since he was the size of one. From then on she would ride a little ways then walk a little ways—the Coyote ready to carry her whenever her legs grew tired.

She reflected on her decision to walk with this giant beast, as she traveled deeper into the Wild beside him. Had she made the right choice? So far, it felt like the right choice. The farther they traveled together, the deeper her comfort and trust in him grew.

The farther they traveled together, the denser the land became. They were in the thick of it now—in the thick of the Wild, that is. The air grew warmer. The zephyr grew heavier. The Wild amplified more with each breath. Perhaps she did too. And perhaps it was because they were in the jungle—the Wild Jungle. Perhaps the Wild was eternally expanding. Perhaps *she* was eternally expanding. Perhaps it was a synchronized act of expansion.

She slid from the Coyote's back and walked alongside him with her hand on her chest, feeling the beating of her heart. She heard the drumming of the Wild once again. The wild rhythm of her beating heart. The Wild's rendition of her beating heart. The sound grew louder with each step deeper into the Wild Jungle.

"Do you hear that?" she asked the Coyote. "The drumming... the beat?"

"Oh, yeah, Girl, yep, I hear that."

The path through the jungle was much like the path of the forest, as it seemed to manifest itself according to the moment. She didn't know where this new wild path would lead to, nor did she know where *any* path would lead to. She did not know where the jungle would lead to, nor did she know where the *forest* would lead to. But she was enjoying her time spent figuring all of it out, one step at a time.

The Coyote halted their momentum in the overgrown jungle, and plucked two fresh mangos from a tree. She had grown hungry, and wondered if maybe he'd read her mind. She looked at him and his two different eyes and wondered if he was reading her mind about him reading her mind.

"Mango?" he asked her as the mangos hung from his teeth.

"Please."

They ate the extra-large mangos in the middle of the verdant path, letting sticky fruit juice drip down in a mess. They laughed at each other with their mouths full and oozing. But then she froze and furrowed her forehead.

What was that sound?

She looked at the Coyote, who reached for more mangos in the tree, unfazed by what she heard.

Had she really heard what she'd heard? She squinted her eyes and leaned closer to the sea of fresh vegetation. She heard it still, this time clearer.

"Wait!" she demanded. "Didn't you hear that?"

"Hear that what now?" The Coyote dropped three mangos from his mouth.

"That sound! The people! I thought I heard voices..."

"Mmhmm. The sound a Babes."

"Babes?"

The Coyote ate up all three mangos in one gulp. She realized that it didn't faze him one bit—the sound of Babes in the jungle, that is. Whatever Babes were. He was more focused on eating than anything else at this time. He was a Giant Coyote, after all, you see. You could imagine how famished one must get on any old day.

What was a Babe? She did not know. But something inside of her was begging her to find out. "Can we go?" she asked with slight hesitation.

"Go where?" The Coyote licked the juices from his chops.

"After the Babes... I mean, to the sound of the voices..."

"Oh, sure, Girl. We can go."

The Coyote ate three more mangos and insisted that she, too, eat at least one more, before they took off after the sound of Babes in the jungle.

CHAPTER 8

THE SOUND OF BABES

She ran with the Coyote through the thick and winding wild of the jungle, scurrying along the slim path. They hustled closer toward the sounds, the calls, the beating of the drum. With each step forward, she heard the wild echo of her heartbeat more clearly. Soon she would be approaching the sounds that had been calling to her.

Through the large trees, the stardust, and the thick banana leaves in the sparkling jungle, all she heard was the wild drumming, the laughter, and the songs of Babes becoming clearer—the pull more demanding. The closer she came to the beckoning calls of Babes and their beat, the more aware she became of the beating of her own heart, and the feeling of a fire burning within her, and the tugging of a wild beast ready to break free.

She rode atop the Coyote's back up hills of knotted jungle roots and slippery, sweaty moss. They traveled through wet, salty caves—dark caverns where light hid and shined in certain corners. They moseyed under hot, shimmering waterfalls, across rotted wood and jagged rocks—each step taking them closer to the sounds of Babes.

When they came to a steep stairway of chipped stone and saturated moss, the Crows flew past them—soaring above the stairway and toward the sounds she was searching for. She hopped off the Coyotes back and darted up the steps as fast as she could.

"The Crows! My note!" She wouldn't let them get away this time. Would she?

"Slow down, Girl!" The Coyote ran after her as she raced up the steep stairs.

"Beast!"

Who said that?

A blue-eyed Crow flew over the edge of the top of the stairway and darted down toward her.

She flinched and tucked her head in fear, slipping down the stairs. Hitting each jagged edge and continuing to slide down the slick moss—she tumbled until she hit the side of the Coyote's body, planted across the stairway to catch her.

"You okay, Girl?" The Coyote looked over his shoulder.

She coughed. "I'm... I'm okay..." why was that Crow calling her beast and flying at her? They already had her note, what more did they want? Wasn't *she* the one chasing after *them?* She rolled over and slowly sat up on the step, adjusting her gown and poking at the scrapes on her knees.

"May I, Girl?" The Coyote licked the wound until it was not only clean, but completely healed—gone—vanished. Not a blemish was left on her skin. Not a single ounce of pain, anywhere on her body. She looked at the harmless giant beast that had befriended her, happy to have met such a loyal creature in that wild place.

"Thank you." She wrapped her arms around the Giant Coyote and squeezed him in a hug.

More Crows flew above their heads, cawing in a way that many a murder of crows would not caw at all. They cawed in a way that women would caw—perhaps in a way wild women would caw.

She and the Coyote watched the Crows head toward the sounds of Babes—flying in from different directions, then disappearing in their retreat to wherever the sound came from.

She got back on both feet, brushed off her hands, and the two of them persisted. Through the tangled wood of the jungle where the lavish greens and overgrown leaves create walls and curtains and canopies—they trail blazed through the glistening drapes of the jungle—losing sight of the birds, but never losing the pull of the sound of Babes. She felt further unfettered with each step that she planted on the ground.

She was digging deeper into the Wild, where all hearts beat faster, where the light inside shines brighter, the shadow gets trickier, and the beast, or beaut, or brute within gets closer to breaking free.

She and the Coyote had been pioneering through the congestion of that wild place for several, or perhaps many hours of the day. But time was becoming a bit of a blurry focus for her. How could she ponder the ways of time at such a time as this? Time is of no essence when entrapped in the seduction of one's inner-workings. The ticking of clocks holds no value, when the Wild knocks upon the door.

As sweet sweat dripped from her brow, she felt herself getting closer. She and the Coyote came to a large grove of trees, where parties of spider plants moved to the sounds of the Babes. Pedaling through the trees, she caught a fleeting glimpse of the glistening creatures that danced amongst the Crows.

She and the Coyote stood behind one side of a tree, together this time, and they peered out around the other side—to the sight and sound of Babes.

"There they are," the Coyote whispered in a rasp.

"What are they?" She marveled at the sight of the wild creatures. The current of their bliss rolled through her as if it were her own.

"Jungle Gypsies. Babes," the Coyote told her softly. "Wild, pure, untamed creatures. They are Wild ones, Girl."

So it seemed. She gazed upon a tribe of wild women, singing, dancing, laughing with the stardust and sweet zephyr of the Wild—completely free and alive. She stared at them as they flowed and caroused and spun around, each of them covered in the diamond dust and layered in golden light. Their bodies undulated in a fluid dance from head to toe—like water, like wind, like the romantic verse of a timeless sonnet.

They lit up like the moon, the stars, the sun, like fireworks and the brightest lights of the greatest celebrations. They were radiant. They were dazzling. They were divine creatures. Wild creatures of many shapes and sizes, each with hair longer than the next, dancing to the rhythm of their very own beat.

Dark green leaves the size of her own body surrounded the dancing Babes—some of the women dawning only their flesh and the shimmer and light of the day. The other untamed creatures wore skirts and gowns that flowed and rippled like the oceans and the winds. Twisted trees and tall grasses swayed along with them, in the same way that the women moved. Vines and stems and bright flowers swung and braided and blended together, and the golden mist sailed through every gap and crevice.

She watched these majestic creatures as if she'd never before seen another woman—for she hadn't ever seen one quite like this, not one that she could remember, that is. She felt herself come more alive from the inside, watching them sing their songs, watching them celebrate whatever it was they were celebrating, watching the Crows fly and dip through the pack as fluidly as the pack swayed and danced through each other and the stars.

The beauty she saw in these women was not marked in the way they physically appeared. It was not held in the beauty or shape of their faces or their figures. The beauty of these dancing Babes was pronounced in the way she felt when she watched them simply being and breathing, breathing as she was. They had energy—a magic—they had a light that blazed like fire. And as she watched, she could feel the same energy—the same magic—the same light ignite within.

You see, these women had a spellbinding presence that stirred up everything around them. It was evident to her how naturally untamed the women flowed with themselves, with the day, with the stars, with the birds, with the trees, with all of life. In their dance and in their touch, in their every move—there was an effortless harmony, a bewitching rhythm, a symbiotic vibration—all one wave rippling through the ocean, running wild with the beating of their hearts. She had a craving for that.

As she watched from behind the tree, a few—or more, or less—Crows flew through the grove of trees, whipping over her shoulder and diving into the ocean of dancing Babes—where they blended into the mix and disappeared from sight... hers, that is.

Following the flight of the few birds was the whip of the jungle zephyr, sweeping her dress up and her hair in front of her eyes. She spat her hair out of her mouth and rushed to collect it, shoving it away from her eyes and regaining her vision.

She promptly jumped out of her skin with a squeak.

For she was nearly nose-to-nose with three radiant and wild women standing before her on the other side of the tree. She staggered back a step, her spine colliding with the Coyote, who was seemingly unfazed by all of this... and probably hungry too.

"Here from where in which we stand—we, as in this trio of the three of we—it looks the likes in which you've broken free from that place—the place that held you captured in your longing for so long..." the Babe to the right spoke first.

It took a moment for the girl to regain her voice and gather words from her mixed-up mind. But this time she was not as fearful of these new strangers like she first was with the Gypsy of the Night and the Coyote. She was growing more accustomed to the ways of the wild creatures now.

"Captured?" she asked. Had she been captured?

"Captured, yes. And chained to your longing for *here*, your longing for *now*," the Babe on the right answered her.

The Babe in the middle continued, "You know, the feeling you feel—the one you've felt for so long, longing for something that you knew was amiss, but what it was—you just couldn't grip."

"The feeling you've felt, the longing you've lingered in, you just could not place or point your finger on..." the Babe on the left added.

How did they know? How did they know exactly how she had felt, when she could barely describe it herself? "Yes, yes, I have felt something like that... but—" she sighed, "but why do you say I was captured?"

"*Was*. Was meaning you *were*, but oh, you're not anymore!" The Babe on the right continued, "Clearly, you've made your way back! Took you quite a while, but we knew you'd make it."

Knew she'd make it... back?

As if the trio of Babes were a unified creature, they synchronously glanced over the girl's shoulder to the Coyote. "And you've arrived with our favorite wild beast, of course!" The three Gypsies hugged the Coyote as he walked out from behind the giant tree.

"I'm fond a the Babes, Girl. They're good," the Coyote said, a grin stretching his shaggy, feral face. He stepped around the girl only to be set upon by the Babes in a splendid embrace of arms and glittering stardust.

He wagged his tail and rolled on the ground, basking in belly rubs. The girl blinked in surprise. She knew he was a friendly coyote, perhaps—most likely—the friendliest coyote, but she did not expect he'd know the Babes so well. She watched them from behind the tree, and although she trusted the Coyote, for a moment she contemplated—could this be his pack? And just as that thought crossed her mind, his blue and golden eyes locked with hers and she knew—as if he'd spoken to her without any words—he was a good coyote, he would never deceive her.

Besides, she did not feel threatened by the Babes in the way she would have if they were, say, a pack of wild coyotes. She began to realize that aside from a few of her fleeting trepidations, this strange world was not such a scary place. Startling and alarming at times, confusing, yes, but caused her to fear for herself?

No. That was the other world.

She smiled at him and wondered for a moment longer if he knew *everyone* in the Wild, and if *everyone* knew *everyone* in the Wild. She wondered if everyone in the Wild knew her, and if they had been watching her this whole time. It certainly seemed as such.

As she sighed with this thought, the three Babes stood up and looked her way. All she really knew then and there in that wild, wild place, was that these three women she didn't know stood before her with a wildly friendly coyote that she barely knew, yet they all felt like familiar comfort.

She followed the guidance of her friend, the Coyote, and the light burning like fire in her soul. She stepped out from behind the tree and stood before the three Babes that were reminiscent of sunshine.

"Care to indulge in a story?" The Babe in the middle grabbed her hands, sending a jolt of electricity through her as she looked into the eyes of the dazzling women.

"I..." she stumbled for a moment, pulled from her own thoughts, "yes, of course!"

"It's a tale of tall depths and great heights, dark shadows and bright lights. A tale that has already begun..."

"Mm-hmm..." Eager anticipation pulsed in her chest.

"'Tis a tale of what was and what is, and what will be. A story of how certain things are created, how certain things are seen." The middle Babe nodded to the Gypsy Moon.

"Okay..." She bounced her gaze between the Babes.

The ratherish riddling woman to the right added, "it's the story of re-membering your memories... told between worlds, a story told between words..."

The middle Babe continued, "And in this thing—where the unfolding unfolds—your story is told, written and dripping in gold. And there's the story between you and then I, and I between you, and you between we, and us within you." The girl danced her eyes at the three women as the one in the middle continued, "See, though parts of stories can seem singular, everything is always intertwined—the meaning of time, or even the lack, stepping ahead and then stepping back, the dark of the night and the blinding of light, day to night or night to day, the run of the Wild and the hunt of the tame, and—there is always a middle where everything blends, always a beginning... never an end." The Babe grasping onto her hands had her spun in a web of rhymes and words.

The Babe to the right went on, "Here you are, watching your own unraveling before your eyes, watching *you* come back to life, and yet... you haven't even figured it out yet, have you?"

"Figured what out?" she asked.

"Of course she hasn't. After all, she's only *just* found *us*," the Babe to the left reminded the other women.

"What do you mean *I've only just found you?*" she asked the women. "What more do you know?" Did they know she was coming? Did they send for her? Did they know where the Crows had taken her note?

"You've many stops to make in your travels here, and, well, you've only just begun. The journey back after being gone so long can take some time. Revelations take time." The Babe to the left spoke in a common-sensible manner.

"Being gone so long from where?" she asked, wondering if they too, had the assumption that she'd once been in that wild place before.

"The things you know yet not of, you've truly known all along." The woman in the middle looked into her eyes. "The *real* you, your untamed mind, the stars in your eyes, the moon in the sky—have all led you back, to where the truth resides."

"The real truth?" That is what she wanted. That is what she longed for. "Is *here?*" she asked.

"Right here." The Babe in the middle pulled the girl along as everyone in their huddle slowly stepped in unity away from the tree, migrating closer to the glen of Jungle Gypsies.

"Isn't it funny," the Babe in the middle squeezed her hands tighter, "how we conjure scenarios inside of our minds? Whatever we scheme up, whatever we dream up, that's what we get, that's what we find?"

She hadn't realized they had been drifting further from the tree until now. For she felt no more than that she was floating. "It is...?" she asked, shifting her eyes at her surroundings as they slipped through soft and slow steps.

"Oh, you haven't noticed?" The three women, or Babes or Gypsies, settled their saunter and laughed as if they knew something she did not—or still had yet to learn. She was taken aback by their synchronized laughter, though not offended by it. It was endearing. And though she did not find as much humor in that moment as they, she continued to smile and study them.

"Do you trust that you'll find what you're looking for here?" the Babe to the left asked the girl after the laughter had simmered.

She gazed into the unknown which was the entirety of her surroundings. Would she find what she was looking for? Was it here? When she looked to the ocean of dancing women, she noticed there weren't any crows flying or gliding in the midst of them. Completely gone from the picture in her eyes—they'd vanished—but where? They'd vanished—and without notice. But how, she wondered. How could they have vanished without her spotting the flight of a single one? She pondered and stared at the mesmerizing tribe of women, wondering how she'd lost the Crows once more.

"Well," she peered through the dance of the other nearby wild creatures while answering the trio of Babes, "I was... we were, looking for the Crows—"

"Need not tell us what it is you seek to find," the Babe who cradled the girl's hands interrupted her and yanked on them, bringing the girl's attention back. "If it is to be sought then so it will, if it is to be found, then you will find it."

"Sometimes you could be staring right at the thing you're looking for, without even realizing it..." the Babe to the right told her, still laughing.

"Perception is everything." The Babe in the middle held the girl's hands higher. "Now, are you ready?"

"Ready?" she asked.

"Ready," the Babe asserted. "Ready. Not in question, nor in doubt. Speak the words you've always known, from your veins and your heart and your bones, speak out loud with certainty the only truth you've ever known. Not through language, but through Soul, let *yourself* know what you've always known."

"*What* do I know...?" She wanted to know. She wanted to know what it was she'd always known. What was her truth? Who was she?

"Certainly and for starters, you must know that there is no question in your word," the woman to the left explained.

"Which word?" She was trying hard to follow. These were Jungle Gypsies, as the Coyote had told her, and much like the Gypsy of the Night, these wild women spoke circles around her.

"Are you *ready?*" the middle Gypsy inquired.

She looked at the woman that gripped her hands. She stared into the stars of the Babe's eyes, or perhaps she stared into the reflection of her own eyes, or the reflection of the skies. She knew now, there was no question in her word.

"Ready." And ready she certainly was—for what, she did not know.

What she knew was that it felt right floating with those Babes.

If it is to be sought then so it will, if it is to be found, then she will find it. She thought of what the Babe squeezing her hands had told her. Perhaps she could let go of her concern for the missing Crows. At least for a little while.

After all, in that moment she was far more interested in the glistening glen of jungle creatures and the story that they spoke of, and the music that they sang, and the stars falling from the Heavens, and the Giant Coyote, and the dreamy colors of the strange sky. You see, she was far too *interested* in the Wild to be *concerned* with the Wild.

The Coyote darted ahead to the calling of the Babes, and they welcomed him with belly rubs. She and the three Babes caught up to him and the current of wild women. They, without any hesitation, pulled her into their wave of song and dance in the wild, wild jungle, under the stardust-laced canopies of trees and flowers and the dancing branches and big leaves of all the ancient trees.

The Babes gathered around, hugging her as if they'd always known her, as if they were awaiting her return—encompassing her as if there were an eternal kinship shared between her and them. Had these women known her once before? She was not sure, but she was already beginning to feel used to their games, as if she'd once played them before.

They passed her around to one another through a dizzying dance that started off slow, but quickly grew momentum. It was thrilling to her, at first. But after a moment or two, or three, perhaps four or five—moments were not conceptual anymore—she grew slightly dizzy.

As she spun in their web of spinnery, she saw there were too many of these Babes to count, and she wondered if she'd ever stop spinning in their dance of sweet embrace. She became certain that they'd spun her around and dipped her down to greet the same handful of Babes more than just once.

After the spinning had been spun, the women surrounded her one by one. They sat in the swaying tall grass under the hanging green leaves and golden vines. She followed suit and sat down too, in the middle of a murder of Babes—a tribe of Babes, rather—each one with their dazzling eyes all brilliantly struck upon her.

Chapter 9

THE TAMERS AND THE TAMED

"**D**o you think she knows?"

Nothing more than an innocent question, though it pulled her ears regardless.

Do they think she knows *what?*

She strained to hear an answer, suddenly desperate to know more, but the chatter of wild women conversing all at once merged like a melody of birds chirping and singing in sync. She couldn't make out what they were saying amongst themselves... about her.

"Do you think I know what?" she spoke up.

"What you're doing here..." one of them answered.

"Who you are..." another answered.

And the Gypsies laughed.

"Slowly... she's beginning to see..." another woman spoke in a familiar voice, but she did not see who spoke the words.

"I'm beginning to see?" She looked through the crowd. "I'm beginning to see what?"

The Babes laughed and a few called out, "you tell us!"

Was she beginning to see who she was? She was not sure.

She sat down too, in the middle of a murder of Babes—a tribe of Babes, rather—each one with their dazzling eyes all brilliantly struck upon her.

Was she beginning to see all of the memories she had forgotten? It did not seem so. What was she beginning to see, that she could not see she was beginning to see?

She questioned herself as she beheld the haze of stardust cloaking the misty glistening women. The Coyote, in his enormity, walked through the veil of haze and the maze of glowing Babes, and came to the girl's side.

She put her arm upon his back as he lay by her lap to enjoy an afternoon nap in the glow. She looked at the Giant Coyote in that moment and decidedly thought that she did not want a Wild where the Coyote was not.

"What was it like?" one Babe asked, pulling the girl's attention back to the crowd of wild women. "The world of the Tamers and the Tamed?"

"The *Tamers* and the *Tamed?*" she asked, a chill trembling through her spine that fleeted with a grim screech in the sky. She jerked her head up to find strange, dark creatures, circling too high for her to discern whether they were Crows or... something darker. "Are those Crows?" she asked, squinting her eyes at the sky.

"Vultures..." that familiar voice clarified.

Other Babes gasped and whispered to one another. "Vultures... they've already come..."

The butterflies in her belly fought for an escape.

Who were the Vultures? Her breath grew shallow, her shoulders tightened. Her heart raced at the sound and sight of them. But why? They were just birds—she did not know them. But she felt an aching nagging within her, warning her that those Vultures were there for her. They wanted her. They were after her.

She wrestled with the thought of running, though she did not know *what* she would be running from, or *where* she would be running to. All she knew was that she could not stop shaking at the sight of those Vultures.

"What are they?" she interrupted the glen of whispering chatter with shaky words. "Why are they here?"

"Pay 'em no mind, Girl." The Coyote briefly lifted his chin from his slumber, his eyes remaining shut.

Easy for a Giant Coyote to say.

She was beginning to wonder once more, whether or not she had been tamed. Had she *really* been tamed—and by whom?

"They're hunting..." the familiar voice spoke up, "as Vultures do."

Hunting as vultures do? That sounded innocent enough. Perhaps she was only fooling herself into fear upon following the guidance of a trembling spine. Though, you see, one should never ignore such guidance.

"How brightly there, from where you came, does the moon glow?" A Babe from the sea of Babes absorbed the girl back into their bubble of questions and stories and never-ending riddles.

She looked to the strange, bright moon, only to find that the Vultures had moved on. She sighed, dropping her shoulders and releasing her jaw, feeling lighter and melting more comfortably into her seat upon the Wild floor. She smiled at the Gypsies, who awaited her answer.

"Oh..." She gazed at the moon once more, in awe of its size, its light, its guidance. "Our moon back there... is not like yours is here..."

"Ours *is* yours!" The Babes, of course, were speaking of the moon.

"How so?" she asked, and reflected on the moon from where she came. "In the sky that *I* know, back from where I came, the moon is not always full like this, or this *large*... or this *color*... nor does it shine all through the day like it does here..."

"Because it is fake," that familiar voiced Babe asserted. "Had they ever a chance to dance with the Gypsy Moon—"

"Oh, no, they couldn't—it's forbidden," she told them.

"Oh?" The familiar voice asked, "And how do you explain your dance with it then?"

She had broken the rules. Would a Tamed one break any such rules?

"I broke the rules..." she admitted, realizing that perhaps forbidden was a blurred word after all. "I was always warned to never go near it. I was not to look at it, not to even think of it..."

The Babes commotioned in an uproar with one another, many of them shouting, "Tamers! Tamers!"

"Tamers?" There's that word again. A word that had her questioning herself further in this wild place. Had she been tamed? The more she asked herself, the louder the answer became—screaming at her from the depths of her mind. But it was not an answer that she liked.

"Go on, go on…" the Babes insisted, ignoring her question.

She frowned, digesting her words before they met the sound of day, "They'd told me…" she swallowed the heaviness of her fragmented revelation and continued, "if I ever saw the Gypsy Moon, I'd lose all the marbles in my mind… like others had…"

"Tamers!" Babes called out.

"Marbles!" other Babes cheered.

"So sad for all those Tamed ones. They've never seen true light," one Babe said.

"The only true moon is the Gypsy Moon," the familiar voice spoke. "That other one is a fake, to keep the Tamed ones tame."

She had *lived* under that moon in the land of the Tamers. Had it kept her tamed?

"A fake moon?" she asked. "What was it I was looking at all those nights then, up there in the sky?"

"Certainly *not the* light that *you* ever made! Nor the light from which you came."

"Not ours either… light, that is. No, no, what you saw was the work of the Tamers," another Babe explained.

"Why do you keep saying that word—*tamers?* What does it mean?" She wrinkled her brow, struggling inside of her hope that it did not mean what she thought it meant.

"Oh, you know them *very* well. Better than any of us!" one Babe said.

"You're the one who was just there, why don't you share?" another Babe insisted.

"We'd love to hear!"

"I don't know what you want to know…" And what could she possibly tell them? The tales of terrible women who roam the world untamed and marble-less? Had all the tales she'd ever been told been tales of such women as these Babes that she sat in the center of? Had she been lied to for as long as she could remember? She was beginning to see the probability of such luck.

"Perhaps we already know all we need to know, seeing that you no longer know what you've always truly known, what you used to fully know," that one particular voice chimed back in. "And though you still know all you need to know somewhere deep inside, the Tamers did a good job keeping it locked up to hide."

The girl brought her hands to the sides of her head, wondering how she could ever unlock the hidden secrets within her mind. Or wherever it was that her deepest memories were stored.

"So, you just continue with your story," the voice continued, "how you came to *find* the Gypsy Moon..."

"Well..." she took a deep breath and placed her hands into her lap, "like I said, I never saw the Gypsy Moon before... I wasn't allowed to. But then..."

"Yes? Then?" The women were eager.

"Then the other night..."

"Yes?"

"I finally got away..."

"And?"

"I just had to..."

"Yes? Yes?"

"I felt something inside of me..."

"Your beast... Your fire... The Wild..." the women cheered.

"And there it was, the Gypsy Moon," she stared into the moon and continued, "I'm not sure how it happened... I was at the right place at the right time, perhaps? No," she chuckled, "perhaps the moon was calling me home..." she shook her head and looked down, "I accidentally washed up... *here*." She did not yet know that such things as accidents did not exist.

"Accidentally?!" the Babes quacked. "What is this?"

"The *word?*" she asked, unsure what they were unclear about.

"Such a thing does not exist. There are no accidents," another declared.

"Then what do you call..." she scrambled for words, wondering how she could have possibly landed in such a strange place that was perhaps a whole world away, "what do you call me ending up *here?*"

"Meant to be," one Babe answered.

"The rendezvous we've been awaiting!" another added.

"What do you mean?"

"What's meant to be, will always be. There is purpose in... *everything*," a Babe explained, "every step, every breath, every wild wander... all of it is for *something.*"

"From the blink of your eye, to the thoughts in your mind. You are concurrent, you are rippling—everything has reason," that familiar voice from the crowd answered her. "You are in everlasting cahoots with all of existence, you know..." and continued, "Accidents do not exist."

"Accident... now *that's* a blurred word, Girl," the Coyote mumbled in his afternoon nap as if he were talking in his sleep.

"Ah yes, the meaning of words is a frivolous thing. A word can only mean what you want it to mean," the familiar voice added, "you see, words are worlds. They hold a great deal of meaning, but only once you've felt and seen them. When it's that time in your ride for you to decide what certain things mean to you... you'll see that a word can mean the world, or a word is just a word. It is up to you to make an entire world out of just one word, and *you* have made an entire world from all your words."

"My words?" she asked. "Which words?"

"The words you wrote!" one Babe called out.

"What words I wrote?" But what about the note? *Those* were the words she so desperately wanted to know about.

"You paved the way for your return, you wrote the words, here in this world," another said.

"I'm telling you, really, as much as I like it here, I've never even seen this place until now!" She knew there were things she had yet to learn, as every creature she'd come across in that place had made it quite clear. And although she felt found in a strange way in this familiar place, she was persistent with her denial. To admit that she was from this wild world that she had no recollection of, would be to admit that she had been tamed, and that everything she had always been told was a lie. You see, when one's eyes begin to open to the true light, it can be blinding and at first full of fright. To let go of what you were always told was right... Well, you see, revelations take time. She continued, "And as beautiful as it is, I am completely lost..."

"*Lost!*" the Babes responded in a rumbling chuckle.

"Well, I don't know where this place even is, or how I ended up here, and I don't know the way to go... to go..." she pursed her lips and scrunched her forehead, contemplating her journey forward, "wherever it is that I'm going... so, yes... I'd say I'm as lost as lost can be!"

"Listen here, you are never lost, but if at times you think you are, just remember," the familiar voice spoke from the crowd, "it's never too hard to find yourself again. You just have to look, and listen. See, if you truly were lost as you think yourself to be, certainly you wouldn't be here, with the Babes of which are we. You always know the way to go, deep down, you always know. You wouldn't be right here, right now, if you didn't know where to go. And if, for some reason, you think you've gone the wrong way, simply stop, and turn around, and make it right again. Though, how can we say if any which way is ever the wrong way?"

"Oh! The shadow is out!" One woman pointed toward her.

She looked over her shoulder to her dark shadow undulating within the tall grass. Not only was her shadow much larger than she, but it was, like before, not sitting as she was sitting—it was standing—standing tall. She stared into the darkness that stretched out from her body, watching it sway like the wind in its unpredictability, peering at it as if it were a stranger.

"I don't understand how this is happening..." the girl admitted, regarding her shadow and perhaps every strange thing in that wild place.

"The objective is not in trying to understand such things you don't quite understand," the familiar voice of the unseen Babe told her. "The objective is to enjoy the not understanding of such things you don't quite understand. It is really quite exciting in this way, is it not?"

"Well, I'm not quite sure I even understand *that*... but I'm trying..."

"There is no rush, you know. Everything will unfold. Everything *is* unfolding..."

"That's what happens—everything unfolds as you unravel," one Gypsy added. "And soon you'll be a beautiful unraveled masterpiece!"

"Oh, *thank you*..." She tugged her hair back.

"No, *thank you*." Many Babes responded.

"For what?"

The wild women rolled in laughter. "For the light!"

"What light?"

"Oh, sweet starry eyes, you are just like the moon, you're shining so bright!" The Babes laughed more.

"You are the brilliance of all things alive, and the light that reveals every dark line," again, the familiar voice spoke out. "You are *all* of the light, and the dark mysteries in the night skies. You are the spark that ignites each flame, and the blinding light of every new day."

How could she be everything that voice told her she was? Perhaps they *did* have her mixed up with someone else. "That's... very nice, thank you... but why do you think I'm all of those things?"

The Babes laughed at this remark of hers.

"*We* see your light—which *you've* forgotten how to see for yourself—though, you still see it here, in everyone else." The same voice continued, "You've seen your shadow, too—which you haven't yet accepted, but you certainly can't deny." The voice pressed on, "So now tell us, will you deny the fire you feel within you where all of it resides?"

She knew the feeling the voice spoke of. She felt it that first night she saw the Gypsy Moon atop the dunes. The night she broke all of the rules and honored her fire inside. She pressed her hand over her lungs and belly, feeling the heat from her fire that blazed deep within her.

"Do you feel the beast within?" another Babe asked. "The one that's trapped inside, ready to break free?"

Was that what she felt when she first awoke in that wild place? The drumming and the beating of her heart, the pull to the sounds of Babes—was that her beast trying to break free? She dropped her gaze to her body, placing a warm palm upon her chest, wondering how much of herself she had lost.

"Don't worry, don't be shy. We're all beasts, all of us alike," a Babe pulled the girl from her thoughts. "We're all wild... your wild has just been trapped inside for a long, long time."

"My wild has been trapped inside?" Perhaps, if she had truly been tamed, she could still find her wild somewhere deep inside.

"That's how you got here..." another woman continued, "you heard it knocking, knocking to break free."

She *had* heard it knocking. She knew she had. Perhaps she *was* on the right track. Perhaps she was on her way to where she was meant to be.

"You heard the call of your moon, the roar of your beast, the sizzle of your fire... you started to remember..." a Gypsy explained.

"Remember *what?*" She knew she felt her fire and her beast. She knew she had unresolved memories and that she had most likely, at one point in time, been tamed. But she did not know much more than that.

"That you're a wild one, just like us!"

"With a caged beast waiting to break free!" added another.

"Well, how do I let it out?"

The Babes laughed in turn to her question.

"You've already begun to," the familiar voice told her.

Had she? Had her beast begun to break free? She wanted to break freer. She wanted to break so free that she could feel it. That she knew it. That there wasn't a single doubt about it.

CHAPTER 10

HER NOTE

"**Y**ou've made it..." a Babe said, "right where you belong..."

All of her fears had pushed so far back to the darkest depths of her mind, she slowly began to embrace herself in this wild land—this land that she decidedly agreed in that moment, was right where she belonged and needed to be. "Thank you for having me..."

"*Having you?* Ha!" The Babes chuckled once again and a few of them synchronously said, "We came together, you and we, just as it was written and meant to be."

She quietly gasped at the words of the Babes, intrigued to know what was written about them, and her. Had they written her note? Had they received their own notes?

"We are concurrent and rippling with all things, you see. That means you too, especially here, in the world of in betweens." The familiar voice continued, "Every movement, every motion, every notion, assists in the fate of all things..."

The girl adjusted herself, wondering if she'd subsequently shifted life's fate with her subtle movements.

"You're a part of the ripple, the ripple which is everlasting, and flowing in the ocean of all things in commotion." The voice told her. "You'll understand this greater down the line."

"I really do hope I will..." The girl smiled, feeling warmer in the middle of the jungle Gypsies.

"Wild a thing, is it not?" one Gypsy asked. "To find yourself back in this place that you think is so new to you?"

She thought about the Babe's confusing question—why was every creature so dedicated to the idea that she'd been there once before? Had she been tamed? And had she had to have been from that wild place in order to have then been tamed?

As she asked herself these questions, the sound of ruffling feathers smacking about erupted from deep within the glistening glen of Babes. Wondering what the commotion was about, she peered through the realm of wild women that sat before her like a forest of wildflowers—luminous Gypsies sprinkled over every spot she gazed upon—until she found a spot where there was not.

She saw black feathers flying up from a gap within the ocean of women. The ruffling stopped. She squinted her eyes and leaned closer toward the Babes.

"The Crows," she whispered, and a murder of Crows flew up from the glittering glen, laughing like ladies and passing something from beak to beak.

"My note!" She gasped and jolted onto her knees. She watched as they quickly flew over her head and disappeared into the sky—laughing and handing her note from bird to bird the whole time.

"Thieving beasts!" she shouted at them.

The tribe of wild women gathered in cheer and howled in laughter at her forthcoming of bewilderment. It seemed to her that they were laughing not at her, but laughing as if they were in the presence of comedic brilliance. As if they thought she had told a joke—but she wasn't joking. She was uncertain if she should feel offended by this laughter or if in fact she did say something that was looking to be laughed upon. And after a moment or two, the laughter softened.

"What do you find so rude and strange about the Crows? Perhaps you'll find you're not so different," that known voice asked.

"They stole from me the second I got here!" she answered over the muffled chuckles that still rambled through the swarm of Babes.

"The Crows do not steal," the voice told her.

"That was *my* note they just had!" she explained, as if they didn't know.

"And *why* does this irritate you?"

"It..." she thought about her note, trying to remember *any* of its words, "it has answers for me..."

"Perhaps *you* put that note in your pocket..." one Babe shouted in laughter.

"How would I—" She shook her head. "Why would I..."

"Welcome to the game," the familiar voice laughed.

"What do you mean—*what game?*" she asked.

"The meaning of most things is up to you."

"What if it's a trick?" She thought about the Crows, darting her eyes to the sky and back to the Babes. "Like you say—a game?" She hadn't thought of it like that before. "What if the Crows have been leading me astray on purpose?"

"But look how far you've come, chasing after those birds and those words and that tiny piece of paper!" one Babe exclaimed. "Isn't it *worth it?*"

She reflected on how far she'd come, and then she remembered what she saw before she and the Coyote had stumbled upon the Babes. "You know, I thought I saw the Crows here with all of you..." she flew her eyes across the sea of Gypsies.

"Your chase for the Crows led you to us." The familiar voice of the unseen Babe who incessantly chimed in continued, "Perhaps it could be a trick, but how will you know if you never give in?"

That Babe, whichever Babe it was, was right. Perhaps the Crows were leading her astray. Perhaps they were even slightly nefarious for all she knew. But she would never know unless she persisted in her chase. If she had a game to play, it was with the Crows. And she wanted to win. She wanted to find her note.

"Perhaps the Crows are revealing things to you that you are still too blind to see…" the unseen Babe continued. "Sometimes you cannot see certain things until you are no longer looking… Often when we look too hard we become blind to what we're searching for."

She thought about those words from that strangely hidden Babe as she looked over her shoulder at her ever-changing shadow. She watched it ripple and sway in the grass until she saw a Crow's shadow fly across the ground to where she and hers were. She looked up to see the black bird from which the shadow was made, but there was nothing. When she looked back to her shadow, that was gone too.

"The Crows are swift, you know," one Babe pointed out.

"I've come to realize…"

"Was that a sudden realization? Most revelations take time."

"She's heard that already, haven't you?" another Gypsy asked.

"I have…" Just then she heard a murder of Crows in the distance singing the song of her note. The Babes sang along in perfect harmony with the birds, and she watched in enthralling confusion.

"Welcome to The Land of Thee… Welcome to The Land of Thee… Welcome to The Land of Thee…"

The Babes sang like birds singing like wild women—laughing and singing and swaying—in celebration, not in mockery. It was mysterious as much as it was pleasing.

"The Crows are many things, Beast. They are not always what they seem…" the familiar voice spoke out.

"What is *that* supposed to mean?" Should she be offended, she wondered.

"You're not here merely for your note…" the known voice ignored the girl's question, "you know that as much as we do. You came here already seeking something… now didn't you?"

She thought for a moment, whatever a moment really was, and knowing that she had run from that other world in search of herself, she admitted, "Perhaps… I may have…"

"Whatever you sought… you'll find that here too," one Gypsy called out.

"You think so?" she asked.

"We know so," the Babes called out and another continued, "You've been drying up for so long… you've come here to soak it all back up."

"Soak what back up?"

"The Wild," they answered her.

"The Wild…" she repeated to herself, feeling the warmth of the words.

"In this wild land, this space between worlds and the very gap between words…" the familiar voice divulged, "At the merging of your light and shadow, all will be revealed—the light, the dark, everything in between."

She did not know what it meant for her light and shadow to merge, she was not sure what one had to do with the other—the light and the dark, that is… not yet, that is. At this point, she was a bit blurry on what it was that she knew or did not know at all. She was not sure if they had told her a story, or if she had told them a story, or if any stories were still being told.

She was confused, although perhaps seeing and thinking more clearly. She was curious. Sitting there among the wild women, feeling like a flower budding out from the earth in a meadow full of vibrant ones—blooming in their presence. She was more alive than before. She felt her heart racing alongside joy, and her skin dripping with the sweet, happy sweat of the moment. She was on fire under the influence of a tribe of brightly burning fires.

"Ready?" the women asked her.

"Ready…" She stood up with the rest of the wild women, without a question in her word.

Lavish amounts of exotic fruits dressed an old moss shrouded tree that lay across the jungle floor. She walked alongside the Coyote and the Babes to the tree of fruit that she was certain was not there when she'd arrived in that dwelling place of Gypsies. They devoured every fruit of the jungle without ever getting full. The Babes were as messy as they were graceful—eating and feeding themselves the bounty of the land—letting the juices drip down their necks and collect into their ucipital mapilaries.

She danced and fed herself fruit, at times a fleeting Babe would take her by surprise and pop bites of citrus past her lips while passing by. This was the same for the potion being passed around from dancing Gypsy to dancing Gypsy.

They shared a carafe made of iridescent glass, with an elixir inside that tinseled like the stars. Like liquid stars, she thought. But how? She was certain she did not know, and yet she did not bother trying to understand, for, it was quite exciting in that way. You see, she was just beginning to enjoy the not knowing of what she was not yet knowing. She was enjoying not knowing that she was enjoying what she did not yet know. She was enjoying the way she was seeing things at the moment, with her starry eyes.

The women danced around the girl, sharing the potion of liquid stars with her and their beastly friend. The Coyote readily lapped it up, as any giant beast would. And although she wondered if it would be in poor judgment to follow the guidance of a creature giant within a sea of Babes when it came to potions and such things, she was curious. She wanted to know what such a potion made of stars would taste like... and what would it do?

It was the sea, a sea made of sugar. Notes of salts danced across her tongue, and every other sip lingered with an aftertaste, rather, an after-feeling—or perhaps an after-knowing. Soon she thought that perhaps she, too, was starting to feel as wild and free as the tribe of Gypsies, or Babes, or women seemed to be.

Perhaps she was starting to feel as wild and free as she was really meant to be.

They were not only wild and free, these women. They were a kin of real women—a family of sisters—kindred souls. Their love for one another was as vivid as the colors of the jungle and the Gypsy Moon. They were the women who turned each other's lights on and helped each other shine brighter than the stars in the sky. The women who were sacredly bonded together in a pack in this wild, wild, place. A pack of wild Babes lifting each other higher, higher, higher.

These were the women who howled in the light of the moon in the night, and called out and carved out the shadows of the day, and bellowed at the call of the crashing of the waves. These women *were* the crashing wave.

They were a Wild Tribe of Gypsies, or Babes, or *wild*, Wild Women. They did not just live in the wild jungle, they *were* the wild jungle. And if they were in the forest, they were the forest too. If they were swimming in the ocean, then their molecular structure matched that of the water they rippled with. They were the wind, the rain, the storms and all of the rays of light. All that they touched, perhaps they became, or perhaps it was the other way around. Wherever they were, they embodied, or perhaps that was vice versa as well.

They reflected all things, and all things reflected them.

There was no jealousy between these women. No judgement. No competition, no comparison. No animosity. They were animals, yes. They were living majestically in the energy of all things that have ever been—in the light and the dark and everything in between. Authentic women—living in the energy of the stirring commotion of creation. Wild women—undomesticated and fully alive, hand in hand with the forces of nature, the forces of themselves, the forces of the Wild.

They were the watchers, the knowers, the nurturers, the preservers, the lovers—all dancing with the pull of the moon, the Gypsy Moon. And, so was she.

Chapter 11

THE RAIN DANCE

The wild night was upon them.

The skies wandered into the darkness of a night oddly lit with color and light—the snowflake-stars glinting brighter in the light of the moon. The trees shook off dustings of star confetti as their branches swayed and intertwined with the rhythms of the women of the night. Perhaps the trees had always been alive in such a way. Perhaps the trees started this dance in the first place.

She'd spent what felt like forever with these wild women and the Giant Coyote. *Dancing, drumming, feasting, emerging, unfurling*—becoming more alive with each breath in the wild, wild jungle. She let herself be tossed around by the magic sweeping through the air. She let herself be pulled by the mysteries of the moon, while she danced so freely under the spell of its glow.

She was right where she belonged, she told herself. And these women were her sisters. She did not know how, but she knew—these women were her sisters—they shared a fire in their soul. And perhaps that wild place really *was* something to her. Perhaps there was a reason these wild creatures and this wild world felt strangely familiar, and everyone seemed to know her.

She would know more once she found her note. She would find her note once she was done dancing the night away with these wild

Babes—she had time, she told herself. Surely they would take her to it in the morning—they had to know where it was, she thought. She could trust them—she could feel it. She'd get to the Crows in no time.

"The words say that when such the time as this does come, to get to the beach and run, run, run." A Babe danced circles around her and continued with more riddles, "Ignite a fire from our lights within... see if you remember again!"

Together, the Babes shouted into the night, "OWE-OWE-OWE! YEE-YEE-YEEW!" and grabbed the girl's hand, leading her to two entrances within the wild greens and leaves.

She pulsed with enticement as she stood before two paths and a wild Tribe of Gypsy Babes. *Get to the beach and run... see if she remembers again,* she replayed the words that the Babe had just spun a web around her with. *The words say that when such the time as this does come...* Which words? She studied the Babes, wondering if they'd received a note too, wondering if there was more to her note, wondering if her note was a part of a bigger story.

She wanted to know what that story was.

"Think you're ready to rollick?" one Gypsy asked the girl.

"Oh, yes..." Although she was pulled from her contemplations, she was indeed ready to rollick, whatever that meant to a wild Tribe of Gypsies.

Collectively the women roared together, "YEE-YEE-YEEW! YEE-YEE-YEEW! YEE-YEE-YEEW!"

As the Babes cheered on, the familiar voice whispered through the girl's hair and breathed into her ear, "You're not the only one who was sent a note, you know." The girl shivered as the voice continued, "Ours was written to us long ago... as was yours, Beast."

When she turned to see who the Babe was, a slap across her cheek forced her face to whip to the other side.

"*Hey!*" She grabbed her face and slowly turned her focus back toward the Babes, glaring at them through bewildered eyes. "Who slapped me?!" She yelled at the women, one palm to her cheek, the other facing out as a shield—a shield that she held up higher when the entire chain of Babes began laughing. "Why are you laughing?!"

"It wasn't us... but we know who it was!" One Gypsy pointed to the girl's shadow on the ground, as it danced a victory dance.

"You!" She screamed at her shadow as if it were something separate from her, and indeed it acted so—desperately calling her attention—behaving so... wild in the Wild. It kept her on her toes, even if she didn't know. It was her dance partner, whether she was dancing or not. The more she studied and became aware of it, the more it came to life.

"Who do you think you're talking to?" A Gypsy asked.

"That's what I'd like to know..." she said, studying the strange movements of the darkness that seeped from her.

"Then ask for what you're seeking, have faith it will come to you—your wish granted, needs met, questions answered—" One Babe walked over to the girl and continued, "when the time is right, it will always be ready for you, if *you're* ready for *it*."

The women gathered around her and grabbed her hands once more. Her shadow vanished in a flash. Her hands in theirs, they walked down the sandy path next to the path on the left. A chain of Babes rambled through the path of the night and the Coyote trailed along at the end of the line.

"Let's continue our celebration of your delirium!" the Gypsy in front of her cheered.

"My delirium?!"

"Mm, which, by the way, is fleeting." The Babe went on, "All things fleeting must be celebrated accordingly. Delirium has never lasted forever, but the celebrations always will."

"But..." she scrunched her face, certain that she was not anything more than slightly confused, "but I'm not delirious..."

"Oh, *of course* you're not, you're just..." the Gypsy behind her softened the blow, "not yet aware of what you truly know. A little rain will help!"

"*Rain?*" She was still adjusting to the vague, riddling ways of the wild creatures. What did rain have to do with anything? Could rain wash away her tame? She hoped it was so easy. Perhaps, she thought, it could be.

"Get you out of your drought." The Babe behind her continued, "It's cause for *celebration,* really…"

"My drought?" A drought is *not* something worth celebrating. But these women were so cluelessly carefree that they did not think in terms of logic such as she. And perhaps that was the biggest reason for her to trust their guidance.

"You're not so ready for rain if you're still hung up on the drought, now are you?" another Babe asked.

She ran down the line within the chain of Babes. Realizing with each pounce upon the sand that although she may have been tamed, she was indeed on her way to reclaiming her wild. She was about to find out who she truly was once and for all. She was about to learn all of the answers, she knew it.

"Celestial showers up ahead…" the familiar voice called out from the Babe chain, and the girl looked to the ground and over the shoulders of the running women before her, searching for her shadow, as the voice continued, "The story gets told as the Wild unfolds. Wild skies and roots will thrive as wild winds sing and dance. Now, watch the Wild break your tamed trance."

Anticipation laced through her. She was on her way back to her true self. Her trance would be broken. And although she wasn't sure what that really meant, she knew she wanted it more than anything. She would run with these Babes for however long it took to be wild again.

The path led them to the calm sea sparkling in the bright night. The moon in its enormity hovered above the glassy water—its reflection taking up all the space in the mirror of the ocean. Its light, blazing in the sky, poured glitter onto the soft ripples of the moon-mirrored sea—the glinting, rippling rays greeting them as they met their destination.

The chain of Babes held up their linked hands and looked upon the moon.

"OWE-OWE-OWE! YEE-YEE-YEEW! OWE-OWE- OWE!" the women bellowed out to the moon, and the Coyote howled alongside them.

With their hands still clasped, the Babes kicked their feet through the sand, jumping up, laughing and frolicking like children—or animals, or beasts, or wild women. As the wild women stomped and kicked up the warm sand, dinoflagellates lit the ground aglow—saturating the sand in fluorescent blues that spread under their toes and across the surface of the beach.

She watched the sand soak into the many different blues and glisten like ribbons of tinsel around their feet. She had seen so many wonders of the forest, and the jungle, and the Wild, but the next thing always seemed to top the last. Every moment, every encounter was thriving in even more magic than the seconds leading up to it. She looked at the traveling plankton and, releasing all of her reservations and fears to the Wild, belted out her loudest, "YEE-YEE-YEEW!"

Once the entirety of the beach was cloaked in the brightest bioluminescence, the wild Tribe of Gypsies turned their chain into a circle at the edge of the water. The plankton within the circle cleared away, and grew brighter outside of their chain and all along the sands of the beach, starting at their heels.

"OWE-OWE-OWE! YEE-YEE-YEEW!" the Gypsies called out, shuffling their feet in the sand and dancing around the circle. She followed their lead, keeping up with their relaxed pace, which gained more momentum with each new bellowing of the Babes. The rhythms of their movement took over, spinning into a fast frenzy, creating a breeze from their whirling bodies—their hair flying behind them in the warm of the night. The Coyote ran his own circle around them, howling with all his might.

As the Gypsies stirred up the Wild, the glow of each of them mingled into the center of their circle. They circled faster and the fire within them burned brighter—spilling out from them, and igniting into the center. She watched as she spun into a dizzying trance—wondering if what she was seeing was really what she was seeing.

A fire made from the light of Gypsies burned brightly in the center of their chained circle. They danced around their blazing hot creation that they alchemized from the fire in their souls and the warmth in their hearts, and she wondered, did she help make that fire too? Did light pour out from her while she was so focused on the light of everyone else?

She did not allow her inner inquiries to slow her down. Frolicking around the Babe-made fire, she chanted with the wild women into the night and into the moon, into the fire, and into her soul, "Welcome to The Land of Thee... Welcome to The Land of Thee..."

She danced and stomped like the indigenous woman that she was, gazing upon the magnificent moon as it swelled before her eyes. A ring of fire circled around it, hugging the massive moon—mirroring the glowing Gypsies that hugged the brilliant bonfire.

She laughed herself nearly to tears, as she remembered one of the tales she'd always been told by the Tamers and the Tamed—*beware, for when you see a ring around the moon, a wild woman will lose her marbles soon.* She reveled in the realization that perhaps *she* was that wild woman in that tale told by the Tamers. She never understood what that tale truly meant, and though she still did not yet know what it meant to lose her marbles, she knew she would find out.

The glowing plankton and the stars in and out of her eyes shined brighter than before. The milky night's sky dipped and danced much like the wild women did. The Gypsy Babes called out to her and to the moon, to the skies, to the winds, to the rains, to the Heavens, to the cosmos and the creatures, to the commotion of all creation, and to themselves. They called out to the Wild.

"Welcome to The Land of Thee... OWE-OWE-OWE! Welcome to The Land of Thee... YEE-YEE-YEEW!"

The more they shouted, and stomped, and danced into that night of beautiful enchantment, the more she could feel herself opening up and becoming anew, or old version of herself. Louder with each shuffle around the fire, she heard the cawing of the Crows, the distant barking and roaring of animals, the cats' meows. Everything in the Wild danced and sang along to the sounds of Babes, the trembling of their soul-fire, and the excitement of another night under the Gypsy Moon.

She felt the pull of that excitement and those vibrations. She felt the pull of the words of her song. She felt the pull of the night, the pull of the moon. She felt the pull of the stars, the water, the plankton, the salt and sweet breezes. She felt the pull of the Wild. She felt the pull of her soul.

"Welcome to The Land of Thee... Welcome to The Land of Thee..."

The women opened their ring around the fire and walked their Babe-chain to the very edge of the water—embers flying off their backs and shoulders and the ends of their hair. Lined up before the sea, standing tall and hand in hand with their toes dipped in the warm water's edge—they looked to the endless horizon as it blended into the glow of the Gypsy Moon. As they raised their arms and linked fingers in celebration to the Heavens, a heavy rumble of thunder shook the ground beneath them.

The rumble rippled up through the Babes and shook the beach and the water and the waves. The ocean bubbled with excitement as droplets of the sea began to pluck up and rise into the sky. The Babes waved their arms to the Heavens—cheering as more droplets fell up into the sky like rainfall in reverse.

The rising raindrops passed the falling snowflakes of the stars, as one fell up and the other flew down. She watched the water of an ocean rise before her eyes one drop at a time, as the familiar voice called out to her, the wild women, the Coyote, and the many creatures of the wild night, "Now, Babes, it's time we rise to this long-awaited occasion. Time to put more pieces together, and begin to figure out the equation. As the words were written, it's time to dig into the depths of the dark and unknown. Time for the contrary skies to be shown." The moon grew brighter, and the ocean's raindrops fell up faster as the unseen Babe continued, "And for *you* to remember what you have always known. Time to reminisce over such a spell of dryness, and welcome the first drop that drips into rain. You'll win, or have the Gypsy Moon to blame... first, we begin with a game..."

"A game?" she asked, glancing around at all the Babes, searching for her shadow amongst the women and their reflections.

"Mmhmm, oh yes!" the Babe beside her answered. "Time to move forward, gain more momentum... slip into the soil like a mist and a monsoon, to get back up and lap up the milk of the moon."

She wasn't sure what any of those words meant to her, but she was surely intrigued. Gain more momentum to where? To her note? "Ready..." And she certainly thought that maybe she might have been.

Most of the ocean's water had lifted nearly all the way up into the sky—perhaps hidden within the dripping colors, perhaps swallowed up by the moon. The sea for as far as she could see was a shallow puddle now, and as soon as the Babes let out a harmonious cheer to the Wild, every last drop of sea-rain was plucked up by the sky, sharing space with the glowing Gypsy Moon.

On the naked sea floor, all she could see were endless miles of glassy glowing gypsum stretched out before her and all of the Babes. The ocean rested in the sky, and the sky's reflection rested on the ocean floor. The salty gypsum of the sea floor was a mirror to the night's sky—perfectly reflecting the dripping colors and falling stars and the bright Gypsy Moon without a single ripple running through. As if there were two moons in the sky—her eyes could not see where the horizon of the sea floor ended and the infinite starry skies began.

"Tag! You're it!" She was pushed from behind by that Babe with the familiar voice. Was it her shadow? When she looked over her shoulder to see who it was, no one was there—not even her shadow.

Every last salty Babe ran onto the glassy sky-reflecting sea floor. Their game had begun. And she, as the tagger in the game, ran onto the ice-like ocean floor and began her chase.

The wild women scattered about in all different directions. She watched as they fluttered, and skipped, and twirled, and ran on the slippery sea-flat with stars falling all around them. Their bodies moved above and below as they traipsed across the invisible line that divided the sky from the ocean-flat. A perfect mirrored image—everything that was,

was twice as much.

The women still shined just as bright after releasing so much of their light into the fire—perhaps collectively they were as hot and as bright as the moon. Their garbs and gowns and bare skin swayed—soft and radiant. Their hair and shoulders glittered aglow, coated in the dust from the falling stars. They must have looked like fireflies from afar, like little night sprites.

After some chasing and attempted missed tries, she tagged a Babe's shoulder. They laughed on the wet sea-ground and twirled each other around before the sprite took off to tag another. She ran in the real and reflected parade of wild Babes and floating stars—running and playing a game of tag in the middle of an eternal sky.

They laughed from their bellies. They howled with joy. They ran through the shallow puddle of salt and gypsum and stars, and they tagged each other. The Coyote rested on the beach with the fluorescent plankton—looking out at the nearly dried-up sea of night sprites—howling in harmony with them.

She felt as if she were a part of something—there on that sea floor running around with all of those Babes. She felt as if it were something big. She could feel the expansion of something inside of her, and the expansion of something all around her. Or perhaps she could feel something returning—coming back to life and growing—from somewhere deep within. Whatever it was, she was a part of it. She was a part of all of it.

Through her running and laughing, and splashing and tagging, and howling and twirling, she'd spotted her reflection in the glassy sea floor. She paused her prancing in her playing to study the image of herself mirrored back at her—her shoulders and hair coated in the glinty dust from the falling stars. She smiled at the image of herself, for she liked the way she saw it. She looked familiar. She looked happy and joyful. She looked warm and bright. She looked found and not lost. She looked like she was home.

She laughed at her reflection as if she'd found a long-lost friend. She put her hands on top of her head and shook her hair around, watching the reflection of the shimmering stardust shake out and shower around her. Her cheeks lifted higher. She looked around the reflected image of herself to see if her mysterious shadow was out and about, but she did not see it this time. She saw the stars falling all around her. She saw the moon shining in her starry eyes. And she saw the darkness of the night and the infinite skies. But she did not see her shadow... unless, perhaps, her shadow was well and alive in every ounce of darkness and hidden answers in the skies.

As she stood in the middle of the ocean, looking down at her reflection and that of the sky, she felt a drip drop onto the crown of her sparkling head. She looked up and just as she did, she felt another wet drop drip onto the tip of her nose. The drop dripped down the space between her nose and lips—the space that perhaps was created for moments as this. The drip dropped down over her upper lip, where it slid to the seam of her lips. She tasted the sweet salt of the sea. The ocean, still being held by the sky, was slowly releasing its rain.

After she felt the drip of the salty raindrops, she looked ahead and saw a Babe darting towards her with an arm out ready to tag. The butterflies in her belly leaped up as she ran. The raindrops dripped a few drops more. The wild Gypsy Babes continued playing the game on the slick sea-floor as more raindrops fell from the ocean in the skies.

The Gypsies splashed in the ever-growing puddle—bellowing in bliss under each new refreshing drop of the ocean's rain. Their toes tapped onto the wet surface of the salty gypsum sea floor that mirrored the night and the rain. They continued to call out, "TAG," and, "YOU'RE IT," and, "YEE-YEE-YEEW," and the sea-drops fell down faster with their growing gratification.

She was thriving and alive out there in the middle of the sea—running and jumping and being. There was no one to tell her no, or that it was dangerous. No one to tell her to be afraid and hide away. There was no one to stop her.

Her hair and gown were soaking from the rain and clinging to her skin. Her cheeks as high as could be and beginning to hurt. She was replenishing under the rapture of the ocean's rainfall. But the water collecting on the sea-floor was noticeably rising, the sea had reached up to her knees, and it was beginning to fill up faster as the rains came heavier. Still, she played on, and the Babes played on with her. They splashed and kicked water at each other as it rained down. They danced and twirled one another under the sweet salty showers. Dripping, soaking, jumping, splashing, tagging, laughing—the Babes played on. And then, she felt a tap on her left shoulder.

"Tag! You're it!" Just as she was tagged, the ocean in the sky came pouring down so hard, that she could no longer see anyone. Raindrops crashed to the waves like thunder. She was it.

The ocean quickly filled and swelled back up. She and the Gypsies were right in the center of it all—being pulled by the crashing water. The waves were wild and rippling. The sea swept them up and carried them atop its wild surf as it swallowed up every drop dripping down from the sky.

She could hear the Babes still calling out, still bellowing.

When the water pushed her close enough, between crashing waves, she spotted the other women, still laughing and splashing, and soaking up the salty rain as they floated, or swam, or let the water tug at them. She wondered if this was their plan all along. She looked to the beach, and wondered if the Coyote was still there.

The rains came down heavier than a monsoon, so it did not take long for the last drop to fall from the sky and fill the ocean back up to its entirety. And when it did—the rain stopped—but the surf remained stirred up and turbulent. The Babes made their way closer to one another and linked fingers until every Gypsy held another one's hand. Now the swell of the sea would sweep them away to their next destination... wherever it was that that was.

She traveled hand in hand with the Babes, either at the end of the line of the chain, or the middle of it—the details in that made little to no difference. You see, each spot in line provided a similitude, as either spot in the line was sure to lead her somewhere.

They rode the waves past mountainous trees and glittering walls of stone—the Gypsy Moon following along the whole way. From what she could see in between jerking and splashing in the water, they were traveling at fairly high speed toward one of those large stone walls. The wall reflected light from the stars and the moon, and was so massive that she could see no way around it—they were heading straight for it.

She knew that the other Babes must have been seeing it too—but not a single Babe seemed to care. As they surfed across the intense ripples of the waves, they started chanting once again, "Welcome to the Land of Thee... Welcome to the Land of Thee..." She wondered if the swell of the surf heightened at the sound of the Babes.

Their approach toward the stone wall picked up speed—she was certain they'd collide. But before she shut her eyes in fear and preparation, a bolt of lightning struck the wall—opening the door to an illuminated waterfall.

She realized the Gypsies knew all along—they were not about to crash into a stone wall. And although she was nearly drowning in their excitement, she was more than hesitant with hers. As she frantically prepared to fall into the unknown, the rest of the Babes called out with glee. They'd almost reached the entrance to the drop, and her fear—which is merely a blurred word—was trying to take the lead. But, you see, fear cannot take anything that it has not been given.

One by one, the line of linked Babes dropped down and disappeared from her sight—their joyful calls rising up as they plunged down. Soon it would be her turn. Before she reached the crest, she thought of letting go and grabbing onto the side of the wall to stop herself from being pulled down by the water. But where would she go from there? Eventually she'd have to let go, and face whatever awaited her below. She thought of how far she'd already come, and if she can do such things as befriending a coyote, then perhaps she could also slip down a waterfall, and maybe be alright.

So she surrendered.

She slipped over the brink. Her body fell fast through the salty soaking slide. She couldn't hear the Babes anymore, she was surrounded by the sound of the rushing waters dumping on top of her and all around her. The butterflies in her stomach flew up to her chest. She had a fleeting thought that maybe they'd break free. They did not.

The further she fell, the running waters parted into cascading streams, warm air washed over her, and she realized she was no longer outside. A diamond-laced pool of the color and shine of the dinos, waited below to catch her.

She plunged through the water and sunk through her bubbles and the bubbles of other Babes. The water was hot—as hot as she could stand. She emerged from her submersion in the feverish pool and when she gasped for air and tasted the waters that dripped from her lips, she tasted a sea that was salty and sweet.

Her body floated effortlessly. When she realized she was still in one piece, she called out with the rest of the sprites scattered in the hot tub in the bellowing chant of the Babes. The calls echoed back and rippled the water that held them. They'd been swallowed into the belly of a sea cave.

The cave walls were dressed in what looked like thousands of strings of lights—lights the size of pinheads, reflecting the blues of the pool she floated in. Scattered within those lights were crystals of tangerine—glowing icicle formations larger than each Gypsy, reaching up or down or out to the sides.

Every time the cave echoed the Babe's calls back to them, a wave of brighter light rippled through the many strands of blues. The tangerine crystals sang along with the sound of all things in vibration. Those sounds slithered up and down her spine—sparking something inside of her back to life.

She looked around at this brand-new oasis—the steam rising from the hot, glowing pool, the waterfall towering in front of her, splashing her with sweet salt, the strange lights and crystal-like formations all around—and she slapped the water and howled with laughter. She did not resist—she'd trusted the fall. And she was okay. She was better than okay—she was alive and just beginning to open her eyes for the first time in a long time.

She sighed inside of a smile. "I think I'm going to like it here with you Babes..." And she, like the rest of the Babes, relaxed in her buoyancy. She gazed through the top of the sea cave and felt the Gypsy Moon looking back at her. Her smile grew perhaps as bright as the moon or the stars, and she let herself float in the hot luminesce pool.

CHAPTER 12

MOON-MAKERS

She floated through the Babes like they were a school of sparkling sea sprites, and she was one of them. Some of the wild women floated as well, letting their hair drape atop the surface of the water as they gazed at the twinkling lights. Others splashed the hot water over their shoulders. Some swam or played under the waterfall. And as she looked around and swam through all the Babes, she noticed there were less of them in the pool than she saw drop down the waterslide.

She wasn't sure if anyone else seemed to notice, or where those other Babes could have gone, but before she could investigate, a Gypsy sprite splashed next to her, catching her attention. The Babe spit water out from her mouth like a fountain, before dipping backwards and splashing down into the water. The Babe bursted back up and pointed to the Gypsy Moon.

"Look at that..." The Babe nodded to the moon. "You're fascinated by it, aren't you?"

She looked up at the blazing fire in the sky. "I am."

"You know, they say the belly of the moon shares the heart and soul of the moon-maker."

"Moon-maker?" She looked at the Babe and the Babe nodded. "What's a moon-maker?"

"A maker of the moon."

She stared at the Babe, and stared at the moon. "How can a moon share a heartbeat... or a soul?"

"How can anything exist *without* sharing those things?"

Again, she looked at the Babe, and back at the moon. "But, how... why—*how* could a moon be made?" she asked, certain that one of them had to be confused and hoping it was not herself this time.

"How is anything made?" the Babe asked back, and answered, "Light!"

"Light?" she asked, and thought perhaps she'd heard that before.

"That's right. *Everything* is made from light."

"Then how is there a moon-maker?"

"*Everything*—that includes me and you, is made from light. So we, too, *make* the light. Always where it's most needed."

Another Babe swam past, "Skies will open, skies will speak, with rains that fall from tears she weeps..." she chanted.

The girl frowned. "What does that—"

"You know, some would call *us* moon-makers, I'm sure, where you're from... and we *are* moon-makers, but we're not *THE* moon-maker," the Babe beside her continued.

"No... I've never heard of that until now... back where I'm from they call you things like Gypsies, or crazy women who lost their marbles..."

"You can call us that, if you'd like," another Babe swimming past interjected.

"Gypsies? Or crazy women who lost their marbles?"

"Sure! It's got a great ring to it." Another Babe popped up from the water. All of the women were listening now, even those near the waterfall.

"Do you go by any other names... here? Do I call you moon-makers? Babes?"

"You can call us Babes," one Babe answered.

"And Wild Women," another suggested.

"You could even call us Gypsies, if you'd like..." another Gypsy called out, and all the Gypsies laughed as the cave echoed, the lights rippled, and the icicles of vibration chimed and shined.

"And why are you called Gypsies?" she asked, unsure what was so funny.

"We're gypsum creatures," a glowing Gypsy answered.

The cave of glowing crystals lit up brighter as she asked, "Gypsum creatures?"

"Creatures of the gypsum, some would say..."

"Who would say?"

"Mostly those who've sought to tame..." The Gypsies looked at each other, and up at the moon.

"Tame... *you?*" she asked the Gypsies, but they answered with only smiles.

"See, they called us the creatures of the gypsum, because we glow just like these guys!" A Gypsy swung upside down from a cave crystal like a monkey from a tree, and dropped into the pool.

"Oh... that's gypsum?" she asked.

The Babe next to her nodded. "We landed in the dunes of Sparkle City among the glowing gypsum..."

"Landed?" she asked. The Gypsies smiled at her inquiry but didn't answer. "Sparkle City? Where is Sparkle City?"

Again, her question went unanswered.

"And it appeared that we and the gypsum were very much alike... can you see it? They say it's in our glow..." The Gypsies laughed as the gypsum crystals chimed and shined even brighter.

"Oh... I see it alright, I certainly do." She did.

"And we see it in you!" the Babe beside her squealed and dipped under the water.

But she was not glowing, from what her eyes could see. So what were they seeing? "See what?"

"See just what you are," the familiar voice echoed in the sea cave.

She wanted to know what she was. And she wanted to know where that voice was coming from. "And what am I?" As soon as she asked, all of the lights went out. Everything went dark, even the light of the Gypsies themselves. All she could hear were the heavy fluttering and flapping of wings. All she could see was the slick glare of black feathers in every direction. As she tried to peer through the thick chaos of their fluttering flying, one Crow flew in front of her face.

They locked eyes, and she realized that this was no ordinary crow—this was the Crow she'd come face to face with before. Those beautiful bright blue eyes, that familiar voice.

"Perhaps you are a wild Beast..." The Crow left her with those words and flew away in a flash. The rest of the birds followed to the top of the waterfall, where they flew out of the crystal cave that was once again aglow with the gypsum and the creatures of it.

"Alright Babes, let's follow," one Gypsy said.

"Follow? How can we follow them?" she asked.

The Babes looked at her with assured smiles. "Come on." They waved her over and dipped their heads under water.

"*Where?* Wait!" She dipped under but didn't see them. She came back up from the water and looked all around.

"YEE-YEE-YEEW!" they called to her, and she spotted them poking out from behind the waterfall.

She called back to them and threw her body under the water, swimming to the waterfall. When she got to the other side of it, she saw a bright stream that flowed through a dark tunnel within the cave. She swam with the Babes to the stream, and once inside the tunnel, the course of the water pulled them along.

The cavern walls around them were smooth and rounded. The further she traveled through the twists and turns, the walls lit up in all colors—shifting in hue as the Babes propelled forward. From yellow, to gold, to tangerine, to red, to purple, to blue, to greens of every kind—as if the walls of the cave were electrified by light and by color. She watched all of it pulse through the tunnel with her.

The lights of the tunnel and its changing colors shifted to the dripping colors and falling stars of the sky—where the Gypsy Moon shone. She was back outside. They'd been released into a small lagoon surrounded by sand and big leaves on lush trees. She looked at the Gypsy Moon, wondering if it had grown, as the Giant Coyote dove into the water and swam circles around her.

She splashed around with the Coyote and the Babes, feeling like she'd returned home from a long journey—unaware that it was not over. The algae lit up once again, the trees swayed, and the wild ones stayed in the warm lagoon splashing and soaking and playing until it was time to go—whatever time a time like that was.

She and the Babes were still sparkling with the dust of the dinoflagellates. She laughed like a girl winning in the game of joy. She ran between the trees and sandy dunes with the rest of the Babes, chasing after the stars and the Coyote. The dino-dust dripped down their skin and retreated back to the beach.

The women linked hands once again, running their chain through the path in which they came. Laughing. Howling. Roaring into the night. Leaving glistening footprints in the sand. Stirring up a balmy breeze from their movement and vibration.

The Coyote howled alongside them, as they collectively darted through the jungle. She looked back at the beach and saw that the well of the sea was still filled to the top, without a trace of a single drop ever being lifted into the sky. She lifted the corners of her lips and looked ahead in her run with the Babes, under the lights and the magic of the night, and she did not look back again.

They returned to the trees and flowers now painted heavier in the stardust of the Wild, just as they were. The warm zephyr had built up only slightly—the trees glowed and swayed that much more. She and the Gypsies howled into the rest of the night and danced like wild women dance. They danced with their toes in the tall grass and their head in the stars.

She was in love under the light of the moon and the stars and the Gypsies. She was in love with that moment and all of the moments surrounding it. She was in love with those beautiful women. She was in love with that curious and large yet loyal Coyote. She was in love with the magic of the forest, the magic of the jungle, and the magic of the night.

She was in love with the Wild. But mostly she felt love for herself. She felt true love within herself.

More alive inside her body, her mind, and her heart than ever before—every cell within her danced with excitement—trillions of cells shining bright like the trillions of stars, and lights, and dinoflagellates that flooded the night. She felt the warmth of her veins flowing with pure life through her body. She felt the vibrations of the ground below her feet. She felt the very vibration of her own thoughts.

She was seeing through her starry eyes in a different way—a way that she was unsure of, but a way that she liked. She buzzed with excitement and thirst for every consequent moment.

It was as if she was just beginning to live, to really live. This feeling was familiar to her, this feeling of unconditional love, of being alive. These feelings of liberation were already alive somewhere within her. She felt the butterflies flying through her, and she liked it. She liked how all of this felt. She had a new taste for life upon her tongue. She had a new taste for herself. She was thriving atop the rapture of the sweet, sweet enchantment of the wild, wild, Wild.

She danced into the sweetness of the night with her newfound sisters. She felt like she'd known every one of them forever. She felt like the festivities of the night had been swallowed by the infinite skies. It was as if time had stood still while she and the Gypsies caroused the entire evening. Though, she didn't really know so much about time anymore. For how could she know much about time at such a time of timelessness? The days and nights seemed to blend together and she couldn't quite recall how long she'd been in the Wild. Nor did she really care.

But perhaps in terms of time, it was the ticking and talking of time turning to dusk, when the tribe of Gypsies felt tired and complete, pleased with their everlasting ceremony. Some Babes rested their heads on another's lap, others lay in the trees, some lay under the trees, and a handful of Gypsies slow danced into their dreams. They were quiet, relaxed, soft, and melting into the deep darkness and the magic of when night flirts with the thought of the day.

She lay in the tall grass with her heavy head resting on the sleeping Coyote. Her head rose and dipped with the slow rhythm of his breath. She lay there in the middle of the jungle with tired eyes, wondering about the stars and the moon and what sort of strange happenings would take place when she awoke from her nap. But before her lids dropped down, she saw something out of the corner of her dreamy gaze.

A little body pranced around the meadow of scattered wild women, making stops to each sleepy Babe. She sat up to catch a clearer glimpse of this parading creature. She realized it was a little girl—a child skipping from woman to woman, Gypsy to Gypsy, Babe to Babe, sprinkling a sparkling dust over their tired eyes and laughing. The little girl creature headed her way.

"Hi!" The little girl had a smile too big for her face.

"Hi, there..." She looked up at the shoeless child who swayed side to side with her hands clasped behind her back.

The Coyote woke with a yawn and wagged his tail at the sight of the little girl.

"Coyote, my Yoti!" The child laughed and rolled on the ground as the Coyote covered her in coyote kisses. "Good Yoti. Good Yoti!" The little girl sat up and fixed her flower crown around her messy hair, and leaned against the Coyote who had already settled back into the grass and started eating it.

"You know each other?" she asked, realizing that it was a moot question as she figured at this point everyone knew everyone in the wild, wild, Wild... especially the Coyote.

"'At's right..." the Coyote mumbled through the tall grass.

"I love this big Yoti!" the little girl blurted inside of rambunctious laughter.

She couldn't help but follow the unwavering guidance of the little creature and lose herself in laughter as well. You see, this little girl was delightful in every way and quite contagious. The two of them laughed together and the Coyote continued to eat the grass.

"I *knew* you would love it here!" The little child played with her nightgown of not just one color, but of every color—colors shifted through colors with each word that the little girl spoke. Much like the tunnel, it shifted through every shade of every color, right down to the blues. From ocean-blue to crow-eyed-blue to the blue of the pool and the lagoon, to any and every color of the Wild that she'd so far seen. The dress changed like a chameleon—so fluently that it was almost undetectable. Depending upon who was looking, this could certainly be overlooked.

"You... knew I would?" she asked the girl slowly, moving past her amazement. Had *every creature* in this place been waiting for her arrival? "What... what are you doing out here in the jungle?" She looked around at the sleeping Gypsies and silent trees.

"What are *you* doing out here in the jungle?" The little girl poked her in the nose.

"Hmm..." She smirked at the child. "Do you know how late it is?"

"What does that matter?" The little girl smiled and shrugged, because really, what did that matter?

"Well, I guess you *do* have a point..."

"And I can do this too!" The little girl spun around in circles and the colors of her dress followed along—swirling around the child until she was swallowed by pure color, spinning in the night.

She sat there, mesmerized, hypnotized, as she watched this little girl creature spin into a small tornado of a rainbow of colors. Nearly frozen in awe, her eyes sparkled at the sight of this magical being who brought to life new color in the night's sky. She watched colors move and dance, made from the likes of a little girl.

She continued to watch as the colors of the whimsical whirlwind showered back down to the grass, and standing before her once again was the little girl, fluffing her colorful nightgown.

"Did you like it?!" the child asked.

"Like it? I *loved* it!" She clapped for the little girl as the little girl clapped for herself as well, and not one of the sleeping Gypsies were disturbed. "That was wonderful! That was brilliant! How did you do that?!"

A child skipping from woman to woman, Gypsy to Gypsy, Babe to Babe, sprinkling a sparkling dust over their tired eyes and laughing.

The child and her oversized smile swayed from side to side.

Her hands pressed together, she let out more laughter. Laughter was the little girl's answer to everything.

She too, laughed along with the little girl.

The child softened her laughter and whispered, "Is it bedtime now?"

"Oh, are you tired?" she asked the child. "You can sleep here…"

The little girl laughed wildly at this. "No, no, not *me*, silly! *You! You*, silly!" The child laughed louder. The Coyote chuckled through his feast of grass and flowers.

This, of course, meant that she too was again swept into this spell of laughter cast upon her by the magical little girl. You see, this little girl was quite catchy, quite catchy, indeed. Her laughter was like medicine. She was a curious little thing, strange but sweet.

"Me?" she asked the little girl once she caught her breath.

"You!" the girl insisted. "You, silly! Sleep, silly, sleep!"

"Why?"

"'Cause, tomorrow's a big day. So you're gonna need a big rest!" The girl laughed.

"Indulge in a little R-n-R, Girl. Rest is good," the Coyote spoke past sleepy eyes and grass in his teeth, and he stretched and lifted his hind legs. The little girl crawled onto his back as he stood up, and they looked down to her in the tall grass.

"Sweet dreams…" the little girl whispered to her from atop the Coyote's back.

When she looked up, the child sprinkled that sparkling dust into her starry eyes before she could blink or resist. She drifted back down to lay on the jungle ground.

"What about tomorrow?" she asked them.

The Coyote looked down at her with his dazzling blue and gold eyes, and before she lingered into her dreams he quietly told her, "Girl, you're going somewhere, even if ya don't know it yet." And he took off into the jungle of trees with the little girl on his back.

She watched them ride into the darkness of the night until they were out of her sight. And there, in the middle of the wild jungle—under the flowers and leaves and trees, and the glow of the strange moon, in the midst of the tall grass and the magic of the night—she fell into her sleep like the rest of the tribe of slumbering wild Gypsies, and her breath carried her into her dreams.

CHAPTER 13

THE CONTRARY SKIES

She woke with her head in the tall grass, still feeling elated from the night and the day before. She felt elated, yes, as well as unscrewed, unhinged, unsettlingly unleashed. She was in a bit of a daze, foggy yet free. She woke with the feeling of a thousand questions and answers on the tip of her tongue, all of which she could not find the words for.

She knew much more than she did before, but in all of the details she could not quite recall. So many of her inquiries were so close to almost seen. This presque vu, or tipping of the tongue, was a trait of the tangled becoming untwined—the wild and strange tricking of the tangled and tamed mind that's beginning to unwind. She knew that something was ready to unfold from her lips, but what she didn't know was that this inability to place a finger on the words in her mind, this presque vu, was a simple sign of a huge breakthrough. You see, at times like this—times of breakthroughs and revelations—the brain tends to jog rather than run, for matters of protection.

She rolled onto her back and looked up at the ever-changing morning sky.

She lay under the sparkling dust-covered trees that swayed with a slight breeze swiftly traveling through the air—a breeze that she could feel from the tall grass rubbing against her cheeks. She watched it dance with the strange stars and glistening flowers and leaves, and she lay there, trying to remember her dream that she'd just awaken from. But everything felt foggy or far away, like her mind was traveling in a distant place. You see, the pull of the Wild is perplexing indeed, and this can lead to foggy delusions of perceptions of forgetting, when in fact she was in the midst of truly remembering. And in her mind of memory, she could not tell the difference between her most recent dreams and how she'd slipped into her sleep.

She sat up and watched the mist move through the new day. She saw the flowers, the leaves, the trees—the beautiful star-dusted swaying ones, the ones just waking to the morning, the old ancient ones. She saw the empty tall grass stretching out before her. She saw the falling stars. But, she saw no Gypsies. She saw no Babes. She saw no Coyote.

She stood up, her heart nearly choking her lungs. She looked up at the trees to see if anyone hid in the branches. Everyone was gone. She spun around. She walked around. She looked behind the trees. There were no signs of celebration, no Babes and no Coyote. It was just quiet.

She looked at the ground and at her dirty feet and toes, wondering where everyone had gone. Why hadn't they woken her up before going wherever it was they'd gone? Perhaps they did, she thought, and she couldn't be woken. She wondered again if that little girl was a part of her foggy dream, or if the Coyote was off in the Wild, running with a child on his back. That thought created a perfect picture inside her mixed-up mind, and her lips curled at the delight of such a vision. But still, she was confused, and quickly the curl of her lips reversed.

Things felt different. Things *were* different. There was a shift in the air—a heavy shift. Like the dense movement before a storm. This, too, was a familiar feeling.

She walked to the two paths and took the one on the left. Perhaps the Gypsies were simply enjoying a morning swim. What a lovely way to start the day, she thought. Everything in the skinny path on the left was calm and quiet. Like the calm before the storm.

The further she walked down this path, the taller became the greenery around her, and darker turned the colors of the sky. She had an uneasy feeling, as if she were a stranger to this newly darkened wild world. This path did not look familiar anymore. The starry mist of the skies turned to a foggy grey, a swift mellow darkness.

Perhaps she'd taken the wrong path, she thought, wanting to turn around but having nowhere to go, as the path was closing behind her and congesting all around. The only bits of that wild place that she could see were just barely the brights of the greens of the trees, and the lights of the stars that floated and fell and disappeared before her.

No longer could she see the Gypsy Moon. She couldn't remember the last time she hadn't seen it. She had no idea where she was. Though, she supposed, she had never known where she was.

You see, it's quite difficult to see where you're going when you're so used to looking with your eyes. She'd stretch her arms out in front of her, to try to clear out a window through the compressed fog, and take a few or two more steps forward. She wasn't getting anywhere fast, except more upset.

You see, when a creature has been tamed for so long, the path to liberation can be quite wild indeed. The path can be bright. The path can be dark. Sometimes the path may feel close to impossible to get through. All sorts of feelings can erupt on a wild path, and all sorts of things can unfold.

At that moment, on the foggy path on the left, many things began to unfold. She began to lose the motivation to go forward on that dark, wild path at all. She started to feel uncertain of that whole wild place. Perhaps she did not belong there after all.

"Where am I even going?" she asked herself. There was no response from the Wild, not one that she could hear, that is.

The darkness of the morning settled in deeper now. The wind picked up and grew louder. The dark became thicker. The fog grew denser. Her pulse jumped at every ruffling leaf. Her steps slowed, a cold sweat tickled her nape, and her eyes darted everywhere, lingering on every shadowy hollow and twitching fern. The darkness pressed in on her, further cutting her off from the sky and the moon.

She wondered again where everyone else might have gone, and why they left her there. She wondered again where she was now. And she wondered again where she was going. With each new wonderment she mixed into her mind of confused memories, she found that she had no answers for herself. With each new worry taking up space in her mind, the weather brought along more darkened dimness in the skies.

The sky grew dark like night—not like a night under the Gypsy Moon, no—like a night with no moon, no stars, no lights, no life. She was saturated in the soaking wet heavy fog. The trees and leaves had closed in on her. She heard thunder roaring in the distance. Bright bolts of lightning lit up the dark haze.

The elements stirred all around her in an angry torrent. The wind slapped her face as it came ripping through harder, faster, and stronger with each new gust. It screamed at her, and she wanted to scream back. She jumped as crashing lightning hit the ground near her feet, and jumped again when it struck a different spot just as close. Fear flooded her mind, fed by the unpredictable conditions. Or perhaps the conditions were feeding off her mind.

Heavier winds came cursing and spun her around. She stumbled to find her balance. Lightning shattered through the fog, striking the ground beside her, knocking her to the cold, wet ground. Thunder hollered at her and convulsed into the Wild. The Wild threw a wild, wild tantrum.

"Leave me alone!" she screamed into the darkness as tears slipped from her eyes. She tucked her head into her knees and stewed in her anger. Her heartache. She had been stranded by friends who felt like home. Her sisters. Gone, without a single word. How foolish of her to think they were leading her to her note. They'd left her. Alone. To face a storm all by herself in that strange place.

She cried. And she cried. And she cried.

And what she did not know, what with her head tucked tight into her knees, was that the more she cried, the closer the rains came. She listened to the wind howl between her sniffles and tears, and heard the Crows cawing, only cawing—cawing in that strange way of theirs.

She pulled her head up from her knees and looked toward the sky, desperately wanting to see the birds—desperately hoping to see a familiar friend, or at least a familiar face. But she did not see any birds when she looked up at the sky. What she received instead was the first raindrop from the wild Heavens. It splashed onto her cheek and rolled down her face, and was followed by another drop, and another, and another, until the rain was pouring over her, and she could not open her eyes.

She dropped her head into her dirty hands and wiped her face. She jumped up and ran through the forceful winds and hard rain in search of refuge, her cold feet slipping and sliding across the mud. Not sure what she was doing or where she was going—she was just going. She peered straight ahead and raced as fast as she could—feeling like an animal caught in the storm, sprinting to shelter, fighting for survival.

Another violent gust of wind collided with her, knocking her to the sloshy ground. She slid down the path that had become a mud-slide. She slid unwillingly through the fog. She slid through the rain, through the thunder and the lightning, and the disappearing stars. She slid at the discretion of the mud and the hills, and the twists and the turns of the Wild.

She screamed at the Wild as it pulled her along and carried her where it pleased. She wanted to scream at the Gypsies, or at least ask them why they'd deserted her. They felt like sisters to her, sisters that she'd always known, all along. But now she did not know what to think. Now she questioned who these Babes really were, and if they were nothing more than nefarious creatures. But her heart sank as she dwelled over such a notion, for she knew deep down that it was not true.

They felt like family, like they knew her inside and out, and she knew them the same. She sighed. Abandoned, alone again. Sliding through the tight wild path, and she couldn't believe it. Perhaps she could, she just didn't want to. How, she wondered, could she have felt so high, high,

high one moment, and so low, low, low the next?

She'd spent the previous day and night celebrating in ways that opened her eyes to what she'd never known. She'd been swallowed by the love of soul sisters. But where were they now, she wondered as she slid faster. Now they were gone. And she was alone, crashing and splashing deeper into the Wild like a drop of rain, separate from the rest. That is, until she came to a sudden, hard stop, crashing into a dark wall of damp roots and moss.

She felt the mossy walls around her and realized that she was in a root cave provided by a Giant tree. She pressed her back to the wall and slid down it, wrapping her arms around her knees. Outside, the wind and the rain pounded down in a vicious cacophony.

She couldn't stop thinking about the Gypsies. Although the roaring of the storm was distracting, all she could think about, all she could ask herself was, *where did they go, and why did they leave?* She realized perhaps the rains came at her expense. But she couldn't understand why.

She stared out at the dark day and the mud washing by, and listened to the storm as it barked at her. She played with her sad toes in the muddy ground. She crawled over and poked her head out from the cave, looking up at the sky to see if it had cleared in the least.

It hadn't.

She sat on the cold ground and moved her position around. She thought about the Gypsies, the Crows, the Coyote. She thought about the note. She questioned the moon and the stars and all the creatures of the Wild. She questioned herself.

She sat and shifted and wiggled in her anger and grief until it devoured enough energy from her. Her eyes grew heavy and her vision foggy—she began fading in and out from seeing and dreaming. She was slipping out of the messy, muddy moment and drifting into sleep. That is, until she was startled. Not by the thunder or the rain or the lightning, but by a different sound.

She rubbed her eyes and looked to the entrance of her shelter. For a moment or two, she saw nothing, and sank further into her feelings of defeat. But then at the sounds of sloshing through the mud, her eyes opened wider. A whisper of familiar laughter seeped into her cave, and she perked up higher. She saw two little legs run past her cave, followed by four large furry ones. Her brows lifted and her belly flooded with warmth. The sloshing feet came running back her way, and all six legs stood in the puddles before her shelter.

The Coyote ducked down as he walked in, but the little girl didn't have to. The child held a large cup of glowing tea in both hands and skipped to her, splashing tea over the brim of the cup, and taking a seat beside her. The Coyote took a few steps toward her and stood by her feet for a moment before he shook the rain and mud from his coat like a wild animal does—unintentionally or intentionally—showering both her and the little girl. The child laughed at this, and she laughed with the child. The Coyote knelt down by her feet and lay his large head over her cold toes.

She looked at the little girl and the Coyote as tears rippled over the glass of her starry eyes. The blustering sounds of the angry storm seemed to soften and fade in that moment, or perhaps she'd decided not to listen to them. She released a sigh of solace, relieved to be near familiar faces in the dark. And because of this, and the fact that all sorts of feelings can erupt on a wild path, a few tears fell from her eyes and ran over her cheek, dripping down to her chin and gathering in her ucipital mapilary.

The little girl held up the tea, "Warm up?"

"Thank you." Her cold hands took the cup of liquid light from the warm hands of the child.

"You're welcome." The little girl wiped away her tears. "Girl, don't cry. It's all going just right."

She felt those words slide into her soul and swell inside the crevices that needed them most. Those five simple words spoken by the little girl hit her more potently than any other words spoken by any other creature. You see, in a world of words, and the gaps that lie there in between, any word can be felt and seen, depending upon how one perceives. Perhaps, in that moment, those were the only five words she needed to hear, or see.

She and the child stared into each other's eyes before the child burst into laughter and crawled to the Coyote and began picking the bugs out of his fur. This tickled him quite a bit, and he rolled with laughter.

She relaxed and sat back, softening into the new warmth within her new shelter. She drank her tea and watched as the little girl picked and plucked and tickled, and the Coyote laughed and kicked his legs. But her mind fell back to thoughts of the Babes, and the happenings of the night and morning.

"Can I ask a question?" she asked.

"Girl, you can do whatever ya please," the Coyote answered.

"Where did everyone go?" She needed to know, perhaps because she was more relaxed, perhaps because she was not yet relaxed enough.

"Whataya mean?" The little girl paused their play and looked up at her.

"Last night I was with everyone—celebrating, dancing... but this morning the Babes, you guys, *everyone!* Everyone was gone. It was just me... alone. Left to face this storm by myself..."

"By *yourself?!*" The girl looked at the Coyote in delectable disbelief.

"Isn't that how you found me? By myself?" she asked, pointedly.

"But you're never by yourself, silly!"

"But..." She looked around at the dark cave.

"Maybe you ain't seeing it just yet, Girl, but it's true. You ain't ever alone, Girl, not ever," the Coyote chimed in.

"Well, I've felt very alone..." she admitted.

"Well, don't, Silly! If you were alone, you wouldn't be keeping dry under here!" The little girl swung up her arms, looking around at the tree-root-cave-shelter.

"What do you mean...?"

"The trees are alive too, ya know!"

The child was right. She'd been seeing the trees come to life since she arrived in that wild land. Perhaps, she thought, she was not *completely* alone.

"And without them, you'd be stuck in the rain. See!" The little girl looked at the Coyote and then back at her. "Not alone, Silly!"

"'At's right, Girl, you ain't never alone..." the Coyote agreed.

"Plus you gots us, and your true you, and the moon, and the very light that made you! You're in everlasting cahoots with the conductor of it all, ya know!" the little girl squeaked and laughed.

"But... why did everyone leave without me?"

"Maybe 'cause this part's just for you," the child hinted.

"This *part*?"

"Of your journey, Girl," the Coyote answered.

"It's *all* for *you!*" The child's eyes widened. "That big old storm out there, this cave... even me and the Yoti!"

"The confusion, the clarity," the Coyote added.

"It's *all* for you, Silly!"

"All of *this?*" she asked, unimpressed. "All the cold, wet rain and the storm that sent me flying on my butt... *that's* all for me?"

"Mm-hmm!" the little girl answered with a smile that swallowed her face.

"But... why? I don't want it!"

"*Do too!*" The child poked her on the nose. "Maybe they left you to face the storm, 'cause the storm was only *meant for you*."

She thought about what the child was saying as she sipped the hot, glowing tea, and asked, "Why? *Why me?*"

"You're the one that needed it!" the little girl insisted.

"You were the only one meant to experience it, Girl," the Coyote told her. "It's a part a your story. Your journey... your adventure." He flashed his gold and blue eyes at her in the dark cave. "You're getting where ya going. And all this mess that happens in between makes ya who you are, takes ya where ya getting to, reminds ya who ya always have been. You just go where the wind takes ya, Girl. And thrive in the thrill of it all."

It's all a part of her story, her journey. This obstacle would lead her to where she needed to be. She wrapped her head around that. But why did it have to be so hard? It's all a part of her story. Why did her story have to be so challenging? Perhaps it was the challenges that would make her story what it would be. Perhaps her story was already written in her note. Although she came around to what the Coyote and the child were telling her, her discouragement fractured her viewpoint.

"Everything seems... so... hard," she sighed.

"Oh no, Girl, you're just getting caught up in your tired mind. It's only hard if ya make it that way." The Coyote sniffed at the cool air wafting in from the opening of the cave. "You keep worrying yourself and getting all caught up in fear. Blurred words, Girl, remember? They got nothing on ya."

Had she been making it harder than it actually was? She did not think she could make things any harder than they were, but she had never asked herself the question either. Perhaps she was only making things harder for herself—holding on to her anger, her fear, her loneliness. But it was so hard to let go of, and so easy to hold onto.

"Girl, there are times in your life, along your journey, when it's good and sometimes necessary to walk alongside the masses in motion, and at other times... it just ain't."

"Look at the bright side, Silly! The rains came, so now you can grow!" The little girl jumped up and stretched her arms out as if to imitate the blossoming of a flower, and the flowers of the child's crown blossomed in size.

She stared at the little girl, wondering where she came from, where she belonged. "You're a special little girl out here in this place, aren't you?"

The little girl smiled and plopped herself to the ground, looking at the Coyote in delight.

"This one right here is the Wild Child," the Coyote introduced the little girl.

"Hi there, Wild Child, I'm..."

"You don't need to tell me, Silly! I already know!" the child interrupted her and snickered. Then the child leaned in closer. "You need to get ready, you know!"

"Ready?"

"Mm-hmm!" The little girl showered that sparkling sleepy dust over her eyes and said, "You need rest... you're on a journey going far!" The child embraced her in a hug and kissed her on the cheek and whispered, "I know who you are, and I love you very much."

She slithered down the wall and watched them step away from her. She slipped into her sweet slumber, induced by the Wild Child, in the shelter of her tree root cave. She drifted nearer to her dreams as the child of the Wild and the Giant Coyote walked back out to the stormy, wet path. And before she was fully afloat in her dreams, she heard the Coyote say as he walked further away, "Just remember, worry and fear will dim them lights, Girl."

CHAPTER 14

THE WILD CHILD

She awoke in the tree root cave from a short sleep and a long dream. She had hazy dreams of riding a carpet made of wild fur and flying to a higher place among the stars within the sky—wherever it was that that was. She dreamed of kittens pawing at stars. She dreamed of the stars in the eyes of a cat that she'd never before met. Or perhaps the eyes in her dream were her very own eyes. And the stars in the sky, those were hers too. You see, dreams are funny in that way—they can mean a million things, like riddles and rhymes and the words a bird sings—if you dig too deeply—you might overlook what it actually means.

She lifted herself from her half-fallen slumber and sat up tall again in the damp dark root cave haven. She felt slightly lighter—slow and groggy—but lighter. It was hard for her to be sure, again, if the Wild Child was a part of her dreams or not. The two seemed to blend—the child and the dreams, that is.

She was a bit blurry and light-headed, and rightly so—for how could she not be light-headed in the slightest after dreaming with her head so high up in the stars? These are symptoms of a mind of materializing memory, connecting the dots from what used to be, only not yet entirely consciously.

She rubbed her hands over her eyes, and looked down at the half-full, depending upon perception, cup of tea. It was still aglow. She lifted the cup and brought the cold porcelain to her lips, sipping from what she expected would be a now brisk, but satisfying drink—though to her delight, it was still hot, warming her from the inside out. She held the cup between her hands and looked ahead at the small entrance of the root cave.

The colors had moved from grim to slightly brighter. It was still dark compared to most other days she'd spent there in the Wild, but it was lighter than before. She could hear the rains softening, becoming lighter, quieter, friendlier, still present, still falling.

The wind still blustered, but had exhausted almost all of its cries, and it was settling into a calmer blow. She heard a faint blast of lightning and thunder in the distance occasionally. Things were shifting. You see, in the Wild, the only tangible constant is intangible change.

She contemplated her next move. She'd woken with the newfound motivation, or the inspiration, to go forth once again, wherever forth, forth was. Perhaps it was the sleep, or the simmering of the storm, or the tea that fed her this re-incentive to continue forward. Perhaps it was in the realization that she made it through the storm. Whatever it was, it graced her with a feeling that she would be okay, and that everything was going just right.

She was ready. She was ready to ramble on.

She wiped her hand across her cheek, painting more mud onto her face. She finished the rest of her hot tea. Clutching the handle, she crawled forward, making her way out from the damp tree root cave and into the warm, light rain and the slippery moss.

She thought to herself, standing under the mizzle and looking around at the wet Wild—that it wasn't so bad. She could handle a little rain. She could handle a little wind. There was nothing scary about any of this anymore.

The elements weren't screaming at her or pushing her around like they had before. And if they still were, she wouldn't cower again like she did the last time. Perhaps she was stronger than the weather.

The fog had nearly entirely lifted, and she saw the forest, adorned with only subtle dressings of the jungle. The stars shimmered brighter the longer she looked around at her somewhat familiar yet unfamiliar surroundings, and began to float and fall once more at their own discretion. The wind was nothing more than a slight breeze. The fog continued to drift away and return with the glistening mist that she'd grown to love. The swollen Gypsy Moon lit up through the lifting of the stormy conditions.

The more she looked into the wild, wild, Wild, the better she felt. The better she felt, the brighter the skies shifted. From that desolate darkness back to those dreamy skies of pinks, golds, purples, and blues, she was returning, once again. She was becoming, once again. She was evolving, once again.

She looked up at the Heavens, and with the drifting stars all around her, she breathed in deep the fresh air and smiled to the skies. The rains fell soft over her face, just as they did before, but this time it felt different. It felt new. She smiled wider until her lips parted and the rain hit her teeth.

She opened her arms with her empty teacup in hand, letting the rains cleanse her. Standing under the showers of the Wild, she felt brand new again. She felt ready again. She spun herself around and kicked her feet in the puddle of mud that held her.

She was an animal, standing in the middle of the stirring elements. She was aware of the conditions around her, and she was ready to make her own. She was a creature of the Wild, after all. She was a wild, wild, wild one.

"Thank you. *This,* I can handle..." she said to the moon and sky. Perhaps she'd defeated her fears once again. Though in the Wild, she couldn't help but to have this lingering suspicion in the back of her mind that there was always someone or something watching her. Listening to her. Her only response was within the whispers of the settling breeze.

"It's all going just right..." she reminded herself. She moved forward with her chin up, and her teacup open to the sky to catch the falling rain. She attempted to balance the cup atop her head as she walked along, but after several tries, she gave it a rest so as to keep the cup from smashing to the ground. She wondered if teacups *could* smash into tiny pieces in that wild, wild place—or if anything could.

If something drops to the ground of a wild place that no one's ever known, then would anyone ever know that anything ever broke?

She immersed her curiosities about such puzzling laws and divine compositions as she walked along with a deeper sense of awe and wonderment. She had begun to realize that she was unaware of many things from where she stood. It gave her great pleasure at the thought of indulging in the unknown.

She was remembering once more... remembering little things. But little things always lead to bigger things, all in good time.

"Welcome to the Land of Thee..." She heard the Crows in the distance and as she gazed to the skies for them, their song turned to cawing cries.

Her stomach dropped. Heat flooded her cheeks. Vultures screeched, sending alarm through the Land, and a chill through her spine. The stars trembled. She followed the trail of trembling stars to where the Vultures flew—high above in the depths of a dark unknown.

A murder of Crows flew out from the canopy of the treetops and darted to the heights of the skies where the Vultures took up space. Cawing like angry, wild women with nothing to lose, the Crows did not back down. The Vultures vanished without hesitation. The Crows quickly resumed their singing, and flew frighteningly fast into the unseen.

She knew that she could not keep up with them at such a pace as that, so she did not bother to try, even though her legs shook with the adrenaline of spotting them... *and the Vultures.* Who were they? And why were they there? She shivered in her unease, questioning whether the Vultures were hunting *her* or *the Crows.*

She listened to the Wild for an answer, but only heard the strange silence of the aftermath of the feathered confrontation.

In that silence a song from somewhere within her soul reignited in the forefront of her mind. The words came to her from somewhere between the light of the moon and her mind. She sang to herself in a soft whisper:

> *"Don't you get glum,*
> *when you're missing the sun,*
> *and the rain's been beating you down.*
> *Don't you feel blue,*
> *when all you can do,*
> *is listen to the silence of sound.*
> *Please don't you worry,*
> *you're not in a hurry,*
> *what you need will always be found.*
> *Just look inside you,*
> *to all that is true,*
> *and see love is always around..."*

She moved on, toward whatever conditions lay ahead, singing her lost song that had so swiftly flowed back into her memories. After only a few steps, she paused when she heard the laughter of several creatures in the distance. She walked a little faster toward the sound and heard it again, followed by the strangely feminine cawing of Crows. She ran.

She slid around a sharp corner in the path and froze at the sight of the Wild Child flying a few feet off the ground—the Crows holding the child's arms and being her wings. The child was laughing, but was she alright? Were the Crows nefarious, or a friend to the little girl? They seemed to know each other... enjoy each other.

The Crows brought the child to the ground. This time she knew—it was not a dream—that magical little girl was real, as real as real can be, really real indeed.

Keeping her eyes on the Crows who flew circles above the Wild Child, she waved to the little girl with both arms flailing, rainwater sloshing out the sides of the teacup she still held in one hand. The little girl excitedly waved her arms as well—the two almost an absolute reflection of each other.

"Bet you can't catch me!" The little girl ran further ahead and the Crows followed in their flight.

She caught her breath, drank from the cup what was left of the collected rainwater, threw it down to the ground, and chased. And she chased. And she chased. And she chased.

While she chased, many things took place. Like tripping forward into mud puddles with her face. And slipping in the mud more times than not. But she laughed at those things, and she laughed quite a lot. Whenever she fell or when she slipped, she couldn't help but care a little less each time. She was having too much fun being caught in the rain as the chaser in her chase. She'd found the Crows, and she was going to win in this game. Her heart was pumping, her butterflies fluttering, her lips curling. She was playing. She was alive.

You see, after falling in the mud and then climbing your way out, it really is much more rejuvenating to play than to pout.

She spent the day chasing after the Crows and the Wild Child. The birds flew just high enough above the little girl. Through the puddles and the mud, and the moss and long grass of the wild forest, she followed the child but kept her sights on the birds at all times. Did they have her note?

They ran up and down the dunes of purple sand, making sand-angels, the little girl keeping out of reach so as not to be tagged in the chase, the Crows waiting in the trees. They splashed in the water streams and the soft friendly rain. The Wild Child led the way, the whole way, in this little game.

She got lost in the thick of the tall and tangled trees, lost in a wild land, running in a chase across wooden bridges over sparkling streams. She followed the Crows. She followed the child. She climbed to the tops of the trees and balanced across their entwined branches—the spider plants joining in on the chase when she ran across their residence.

She was no longer worried. No longer worried about finding her note and the Crows, as they were right there in front of her nose. And although they remained steadily out of her reach, she would find a way.

Alive and feeling, seeing, playing, chasing, exploring. She was exploring the Wild. She was exploring herself. She was going to get her note. And that was no such thing to worry about.

The rain had settled to a drip here and a drop there, and the day had become brighter again. The Wild glistened ever-so brightly like before the storm, and quickly grew warmer. The stars were free and beaming bright—falling, chasing, dissolving.

She ceased her momentum when she had nearly come to arm's reach with the child along the path. She watched the Crows as they conjugated together under the arms of the little girl, becoming her wings and soaring her into the sky.

"See you soon!" The Wild Child laughed from the skies as the birds carried her off swiftly.

She gazed up at the child, and the Crows getting away. There was no way she could follow them like that. She watched them disappear. She let them get away. They could have had her note. She was so close. She kicked a rock.

"Don't you get glum..." Her song popped into her head and she took a deep breath. She reminded herself that everything was going just right. She would find her note. She would find her note.

She had to find her note.

The colors of the sky danced a soft dance—dripping with gold, and pink, and blue and the tangerine of the moon—like paint swimming in a bucket. *That* is how she liked to see the sky, she thought, without a single Vulture in sight, and nothing but bright beautiful colors in the sky. She looked up and took in a deep breath of the refreshed, wild air. She breathed in the sweet smell of honeysuckle and lavender and jasmine. The fragrance of the flowers was so strong, she could taste them.

She walked through a maze of large, sparkling, dripping in gold, old trees to follow the knowing of her nose. She came upon a wild meadow of goldenrod and blue and purple flowers fenced in by large and potent bushes of honeysuckle, jasmine, and lavender. She swam through that sweet scent, feeling the warmth of a thousand butterflies coming to life within her, and the awakening of the bliss of her entire molecular make-up. She walked forward with her bare feet into this beautiful, blissful meadow.

She plopped down in the middle of the flower-filled field and was about to rest her back against the ground when she heard rustling in the bushes a few feet away. She lifted herself and looked toward the sweet smelling suckles. She stood up onto her feet. She was ready in a serene and only slightly alarmed way.

To her relief, the Coyote walked through the fence of flowers into the unkempt carpet of yellows and blues and purples. He ambled over to where she stood, holding her teacup in his mouth, rainwater splashing out the sides.

"Is that for me?" she asked.

The Coyote walked it over to her until his snout hit her shoulder. She grabbed the teacup from his mouth with one hand, and pet him with the other. She sipped, and kissed the top of his head.

They sat together in the field of flowers as she drank from the cup of nectarous rains with a certain satisfaction. And although she only saw a few sips-worth in the cup, as she drank, the liquid did not stop pouring out. It was bottomless wild water. She drank until she was fully replenished.

"Thank you!" She wiped her mouth with one hand, and put the cup down on the forest floor with her other.

"I figured you'd enjoy that. Ya require a certain amount a fuel when running with the Wild Child... and them birds." The Coyote seemed to know what he was talking about when it came to the Wild Child, and the Crows... and most things, really. "Now, tell me, Girl... was that storm so bad?"

"Oh..." she smiled at the Coyote and looked down, "no... it wasn't so bad at all."

"'At's right, Girl. You can make it through any storm that comes your way."

"You think so?" she asked.

"I've seen it, Girl. Look, ya made it all the way back here. Now, *that* is really something."

"*Back here...*" She mulled over the words. "Everything here feels so...

familiar. I just wish I could remember..." She looked to the Coyote. "Why can't I remember?"

"On account a them Tamers messing with ya memories, sucking the wild right outta ya."

"They did *what!?*" She had slowly been coming to terms with the notion that perhaps she had once been tamed, but it ripped at her heart to hear it put so bluntly. To fully acknowledge that she had been ravaged of her true self was perhaps scarier than the Tamers themselves. She was appalled to hear that such taming could have happened to her, that her wild had been stolen from her, and that she was only left with a faint feeling of it, and not a single memory. She looked down, and combed her hands through her hair.

"Well, it's alright, Girl. Ain't permanent."

"*Ain't permanent?! What* ain't permanent?!" She lifted her head and looked at him.

"All the memories, Girl, they're coming back to ya," he said with an assuring tone. "You'll remember everything in no time."

"Maybe once I get my note..."

"Just relax, Girl. It'll all come to ya," the Coyote comforted her. "Keep playing with us wild creatures, and you'll be good to go, Girl. Solid. Riding the waves, enjoying the ride. Taking one thing at a time. That's how we cruise, right? 'At's the whole point... Enjoy, Girl, enjoy."

"But how can everything just be enjoyed, when not everything is entirely enjoyable?" It was certainly not enjoyable to accept that she had been tamed.

"You're thinking in hard terms. Ya need to go softer, Girl. How are you to say that not everything is enjoyable?"

"What about real, true sadness? How can I, or anyone, *enjoy* heartache and pain?"

"There's beauty there, Girl."

"How?" she asked, desperately wanting to find a way to forget that she had been tamed.

"Now listen, Girl, ya ain't ever gonna know what a good time is, unless ya had a bad one to compare it to. And ya ain't gonna know what a bad time is, unless ya had a good one. I told ya before, and I'll tell ya again. Not every moment is gonna be the most joyous, ain't no way." The Coyote paused and smirked at her. "But every moment will indeed get ya a step closer to where ya going. And there's a whole lotta comfort and joy to be found in that knowing, Girl. A whole lot."

She thought for a moment before she spoke. "Like being stuck in the storm? It led me to this chase... with you and the Wild Child..." She slipped back to her thoughts for a moment. "If I hadn't gotten swept up by the storm, then I wouldn't have found you at the tree root cave, and I wouldn't be here with you now..." She had fallen into a slight revelation.

"'At's right, Girl. Ya didn't like it when you were in the thick of it, but look at ya now. Further along on your journey. Stronger, too."

She wrapped an arm around his shaggy fur coat and pressed herself into him.

The Coyote looked at her starry eyes and she looked into the blue and gold of his. And then he spoke of other more important things, "Ya gotta try some a these wild things, Girl," he spoke of the goldenrod on the ground that he ate away at.

"Is it better than the wild flowers, you think?" she asked him.

The Coyote chuckled and chewed, "now, I don't believe I'd say one such a thing was better than any other such a thing. They're all... things. Offering a different taste."

"I suppose I could try a taste..." She plucked up a bit of goldenrod and gave it a chew.

"Ya like it, Girl?"

She spit the chewed-up goldenrod onto the ground and wiped her mouth. "I think you might like it more than I do."

"Girl, what do ya really wanna say?"

She laughed. "It's absolutely disgusting!" She spit several times more.

The Coyote laughed with her and chewed a little more. "You are funny, Girl. You are funny."

"You're pretty funny, too, you flower-eating Giant." They sat in the silence of the whispering winds that had calmed from the storm.

"One thing I learned about ya, Girl... Ya like a good game a chase."

She chuckled, realizing that he was right—this game of chase with him and the Wild Child, and even more so her chase with the Crows, warmed her soul, as if *that* was what she had been longing for.

"There's a reason we do the things we do and like the things we like, Girl." The Coyote sniffed at the sweet air. "For the Joy. The thrill of it."

"Everything we do is for the thrill of it?"

"And the joy. See, we wild creatures like feeling good. That's all we're ever looking for, it's all we're ever chasing."

"That's it? Ever?"

"Why do ya go to the places ya go to? For the thrill of it, Girl, the joy. Why dance with Babes in the middle of the ocean? 'Cause it *feels good.* Why chase the Crows or the child or the Wild? Why fall in love, Girl? Why do anything at all? The thrill of it. The joy it brings ya. The way it makes ya *feel*." The Coyote ate more goldenrod and continued, "Even if sometimes it hurts ya—ya know it's worth it, for the joy." He swallowed the bitter flowers. "What else thrills ya—now *that's* something worth seeking, Girl."

"Perhaps that's an answer I'll find on my journey forward?"

"There it is, Girl, you got it."

She still wasn't sure what it was she was getting, but she was excited to get it.

"You are, Girl, ya sure are. You're getting it, 'at's right. And it'll be the thrill a your life. Walking your circles, going along just fine." He nudged her shoulder with his snout. "Ya always got your light, Girl, but every now and then ya might find yourself in the dark."

She had already found herself in the dark in that wild place. Was there more darkness to come? She looked to the skies, ensuring there were no Vultures circling overhead.

"'At's alright. Just be careful, now, Girl. You'll be alright, just be careful."

She scrunched her face in concerned bewilderment and looked at the

Coyote. She wanted to know what she was to be careful about. He was talking about the Vultures, he must have been. Or perhaps he was talking about the Tamers.

"Ya need both, ya know, Girl, the light *and* the dark. Ya need 'em both. To grow. To survive. Come to know *that* and everything is cause for celebration. Everything is worth enjoying, Girl." He took in many more mouthfuls of goldenrod, eating the flowers like a beastly animal. "Even when you're stuck in a storm.... or getting pulled by the current."

She looked at him while he continued to stuff his mouth full of weeds, like any giant coyote would. With yellow spit spraying out from between his teeth, he looked at her again and said, "Now, you got a whole lotta chasing to do... Let's catch up to that Wild Child before she gets too far... I'll beat ya!"

And just like that, the Coyote stood up and took off running, leaving her at the end of the line in a chase of three.

"Well, hold on! I'm coming!" She ate a little more of the disgusting goldenrod, stood up, stuffed some of it into her pocket and took off running after the Coyote and the Wild Child and the Crows and her note—barefoot through the wild meadow of beautiful weeds.

Chapter 15

THE CAT LADY

She'd been playing catch up in her chase for quite some time now. At times she'd run to catch up, and other times she'd walk to catch up. She never did see the child or the Coyote or the Crows up ahead, but she held onto a fragile faith that she would. She had no doubts about it at the time, although she was becoming more aware of the changes in the sky.

The sky was darker—the colors painted within it drifted deeper into the tones of shadowy blues, milkier ambers and hotter pinks. Stars fell and floated above her like snowflakes, but they'd multiplied by perhaps a thousand, or a hundred *times* a thousand, or a thousand times infinity. The shimmering gold dust of the stars sparkled brighter in the darkness of the dusk and the light of the Gypsy Moon.

The day had grown to that very particular time in between the light and the dark. You see, anytime between light and dark, and dark and light is a very particular time indeed—any time of this time is a time of ins and outs, a time of lifted veils, a time of in betweens, a time of everything. And by this particular entwined time, she had been at the end of the line of the chase for many, many hours.

But what was time, really, at this point? What were hours? How could such a thing as time still meander in her mind at such a time as this? Time was not of much concern to her anymore, at this time, that is.

Once the pinks turned into purples, and the deep blues shifted deeper with dusk drifting into night, she found herself at a fork in the road. Rather, a fork in her current gold-glistened path. She stood before the two new paths, looking to the one on the left, and the one on the right. She was perplexed, standing there, watching as those wild amber glowing orbs of light switched on one by one, lining the strips of the two paths that stretched out before her.

"Which way do I go? Which way would *they* have gone... ?" She paced back and forth, chewing on some of the disgusting goldenrod from her pocket.

She wondered and pondered and chewed and paced, analyzing with many parts of her brain, which way the Crows and the Wild Child and the Coyote would have taken and why. Were they working together? Were they all friends?

She did not know what each path would lead to. Though, she never knew where any path would lead to before walking down each one. She did not know the Wild like *they* knew the Wild. She did not know the Wild at all. Perhaps she did, somewhere deep inside—though she was still unaware of the many memories within her soul and mind.

She stood there before the two paths, wanting to know what each one would lead to. How could she choose a path if she did not know where either one led? Perhaps the choosing did not matter if the knowing was unknown.

"Which way.... is the *right* way....?" she continued to question herself while pacing back and forth in the dark light of the strange new night and glaring up at the sky.

"Oh, what if I pick the wrong one? And I get lost and never find them?" She paused. "I *am* lost." She sighed. "How do I know....?" She pleaded to the sky and the stars, and the Heavens and the Gypsy Moon, "Show me a sign or show me something.... show me *anything*...."

There she was, standing in the sparkling stardust of the fresh, dewy evening, seeking answers that she never knew she'd seek. Her starry eyes gazed above as the falling, floating stars lit up brighter than she'd seen before—perhaps in response to her pleas, or perhaps it was just a tease.

Either way her attention had been caught. The soft, wild zephyr flew forth in a wave of wild warmth, and carried with it the voice of an old woman.

"Who is it that you pray to? Who answers your calls? Are *you* not the one who answers your calls?"

She heard the jingling of bells, and saw the dark shadow of a body walking out from the trees. She took a few steps back into the night.

"Are *you* not the one who holds all the answers?" An old woman walked out from the shadows with bells on her fingers and bells on her toes. "Are you not the one who holds the key to the answers that you seek... all that you shall ever seek? Just listen, my Dear, listen... and you'll hear."

The woman stood before her, holding a purring cat under the light of the Gypsy Moon, in front of the fork in her current path. Dozens or maybe thirteen plus seven other cats surrounded the old woman, and now surrounded her as well. This was a woman just as intriguing as the rest—but unlike the rest. She came with a clowder of cats, a flock of furry feline followers. You see, in the Wild, where nothing has been tamed, there is a distinct connection between the feline and the fem.

"How.... how come I didn't hear you nearby?" She was wary of the old woman, but not enough to question whether or not she should run. She had not need to run.

"Well, my Dear, you're so busy over here worrying about what to do and where to go, which way is this way and which way is that. Anything could have happened and you may not have even noticed." The Cat Lady had a face that looked cherished and happy and full of life and wrinkles. Each wrinkle told a story, and each one gave the impression that she was always smiling. Perhaps she *was* always smiling. She was much tanned, as if she had been loved and burnt by the sun, or perhaps the Gypsy Moon, for over a hundred years. It was not a dull, charred burn—in fact, she was glowing.

The cat jumped down from the glowing woman's arms as the old woman swept the girl into a walk of circles—circles that she did not

Each wrinkle told a story, and each one gave the impression that she was always smiling.

realize this Cat Lady had led her in.

"You worry over nothing? You fear the unknown? Getting hung up on things that you don't even know?"

"Well, I'm just not sure which way is the right way... " she answered with soft defense.

Another cat climbed onto the back of the old woman and rested atop her shoulder. And as they continued to walk in their circles, a few other cats chased the woman's long white hair that just barely touched the ground. A stranded braid here and there or colorful strings of yarn dangling from a few wooly dreadlocks were most intriguing sources of play for the smaller kittens.

"My Dear, who is to say if this way or that way is which way? Who is to say which way is the right way? Who is to say if the right way is not different each day?"

"I...." She wasn't quite sure how to answer the woman's question, or questions. Or if they even were questions at all.

"Let me ask you a question..."

Another one, she thought.

"Do you believe that one path will make you happier than the other path?" The Cat Lady halted their circling and pointed to the two paths before them.

"Is one path better than another path, my Dear?" the woman spoke softer now. "Do you seek happiness? Joy? Warmth in your heart, regardless of the path that lies before you, regardless of the path that you shall choose, my Dear?" The woman, now holding another cat in one arm, placed a warm hand upon the girl's shoulder.

She thought about the woman's question before she answered it. "Well... yes, I do." She slunk back into her thoughts, looking down at the bells on the old woman's toes. "Isn't that what most everyone wants?" she asked the woman.

"Does it make a difference, what most everyone wants?" the woman asked. "Or does it truly only matter to you, what you want?"

"I..."

"And what *do* you want? Is it happiness and joy?"

"Well, yes, I suppose ultimately, it is…" The note. The note. The note.

"Then perfect, my Dear. That is all you will ever need to be sure of," the woman assured her. "You'll get where you're headed, if what you seek is true." The woman laughed only with the lines on her face.

"Well, right now, where I plan to be headed is whichever way the Crows went… and the Wild Child… *and* the Coyote… But I'm not so sure which path that is…"

"Ah, see here, my Dear, perhaps you will never find the birds and the beast and the girl if you wander down the path you presume would be their choice."

"What do you mean?"

"You're going about it all wrong. See Dear, you can't get anywhere you're heading, by trying to follow in some other beast's footsteps. You'll always know the right way to go if you just stop, and listen. Have faith, Dear, you'll get there. Simply breathe, and listen, Dear… then, you'll know."

She was not following in another beast's footsteps, she thought. She was trying to find her note. She breathed. She listened. She heard the Cat Lady continue.

"For starters, Dear, I can tell you, listen clear, and you'll always know which way to steer." The Cat Lady pulled the girl in closer as they stared out to the unknown. "There are two ways to be sure if the path you choose is the right path for you…"

"Yes?"

"How you feel when picking the path you pick, and how the path you picked gets you feeling." The old woman threw her head back and laughed.

"Oh…" She gazed upon the possibilities of each path ahead, thinking about how her current path had her feeling.

"Are you enjoying it?" The woman led them into a soft pace in front of the fork in the path.

"Well, yes, I am. I'm enjoying myself… on *this* path. It's very… *inter-*

esting here, in this place, and quite confusing. From time to time..." she peered at the dark sky, "it has been scary..."

"See here, Dear. Who is to say that baffling distractions and frights in the night are not inherent pieces of the perfection of your journey? Your path. Your story. Your masterpiece, Dear?"

"Perfection? I certainly wouldn't say everything's been *perfect*." Her eyes darted back to the skies.

"Perfect! Ha! My Dear one, perfection and perception are one of relative nature, you know." The old woman chuckled and sighed. "You understand so much more than you give yourself credit for, do you know this?"

The girl's eyes paced back and forth to the woman's dazzling ancient eyes.

"No, that's right, of course you do not, if you already knew *this* then you, well you would know..." the Cat Lady stifled her words as if she'd said too much.

"I would know what?"

"Ah, revelations take time, Dear." The woman held captive the girl's eyes.

The girl sighed. She had heard that already.

"Yes, I'm sure you have, Dear." The woman's cats rubbed against their legs, getting lost in the old woman's gown that dragged further to the ground than her hair. Real wild flowers blossomed from the gown as it followed behind the Cat Lady—mimicking her body like a shadow. "See here, sweet Dear, have you ever noticed that you've never before seen the light of day without first seeing the darkness of night?"

"Is that how it goes?"

"They dance around one another, the light and the dark, that is. There is a deep-seated contrast forever stirring in the air.... whichever path you choose, the contrast of light and dark will also be there. See, Dear, there is not *one single path* which does not contain both light *and* dark." The old woman adjusted one of the effortlessly draped shawls of beige that hung from her small, but strong shoulders. "So, will you enjoy it when you see it, Dear?"

"Enjoy what... exactly?"

"The contrast of all things that leads to everywhere you're going, and everywhere you need to be." The woman halted their pacing.

"Oh, um... I'm not so sure... maybe?"

"Very good, Dear."

She looked down at the Cat Lady's cats, and the bells on the woman's toes. She wondered if the basket of cats she saw on the water was the Cat Lady's basket of cats.

"Yoo-hoo?" The Cat Lady grabbed her attention.

She shook herself. "Oh... yes?"

The Cat Lady, whose ears were dressed with feathers that poked out like earrings, looked into the girl's eyes and leaned forward, resting their foreheads against each other.

"It is in the dark, sweet Dear, where you find your true light. When you get stuck in the dirt, Dear, is when you find your true strength and power. When you're lost in the dark, stuck in the dirt, or out in the cold, what do you do? You get yourself out with the help of your light and a higher you."

"I do...?"

"It's true. See, Dear, you have to get through the dark and the dirt, to come out the other side, and when you do—you are even more... *you*." The lady snickered and continued, "All my life, I have watered the most beautiful wild flowers, flowers that grew from the tiniest of seeds, starting from just a speck in the ground, having to make their way up through the dark, cold, heavy dirt, in order to reach the light. In this case that I say, the dirt could be the perfection of it all, Dear, depending upon perceptions, of course." The Cat Lady laughed and squeezed her hand, and whispered in her ear, "And both of those paths have dirt in them somewheres."

She looked into the squinty eyes of the Cat Lady, whose smile was as innocent as a child's and as wise as time.

"But if it is joy that you seek, then it simply does not matter where the dirt lay," the woman added.

She gazed into the woman's all-telling eyes for another moment, and looked down at the cats rubbing against her legs, and flopping onto their bellies beside one another. She looked at the paths before her, took a deep breath and sighed in relief.

"It is all up to you," the woman reminded her.

She looked at the old woman, then ahead at the two unpredictable paths, stepping forward. She breathed and listened, as the Cat Lady had advised. She heard the sound of her breath. She heard the whispering breeze. And she thought that perhaps if she listened… exhaustively, she would hear the cawing of the Crows.

"I think I've made my decision," she declared. But when she looked over her shoulder, the Cat Lady was gone. She looked at the ground—the cats weren't at her feet anymore, or behind her, or flopped over and purring on the path. Without a jingle from a bell, without a single cat's meow, they disappeared just as fast and mysterious as they'd appeared.

She shook her head in confusion, she spun around in search of the old lady and all her cats, but she saw no trace of any of them. This wild way of parting was becoming all too familiar to her. She decided not to get hung up on how strange it all was. For, she was getting quite used to the strangeness of this wild, wild place. Perhaps she was growing quite fond of it as well. Perhaps no one ever said goodbye, because perhaps no one ever really left her.

She turned and faced the fork in her current path, sweeping her hair behind her ear. She was ready. She'd made her decision, and she walked forward with it now in confidence. She took the path on the right.

Or perhaps it was the one on the left.

Chapter 16

THE CHOSEN PATH

The path of her choice lit the way as she moved forward, free from fear. The orbs of light lined up and lit up the new lane like they had on the paths of the nights before. Like clockwork and friends that never fail—the lights were there, still switching on one by one, showing her the way. Or leading her astray. Perhaps she was showing herself the way—her own way. Or perhaps her feet were following the footsteps of a long-lost memory.

Perhaps she was the same as the light—lighting up the path just as the lights did every night.

The stars shined brighter, still descending from the ever-changing darkness of the night's sky and falling closer to her within the showers of the stardust. She attempted to reach for the stars, but each time she tried, they would either move out of reach, or disperse into shimmering dust before she could snatch it. She wondered if the stars would always be out of reach. She hadn't yet thought that perhaps the stars were only playing games with her. Perhaps she could reach all of the stars she wanted to—it just depended upon the angle in which she was reaching. You see, realizations such as this take time, and perhaps that is what paths are for.

This path, like the ones before, woven with sand and moss, and the trees and their branches that swayed with the rhythms of the night and the rhythm of the new path of her new choosing. She looked to the many trees as she walked, wondering if every tree grew taller on each new path. It was hard to be sure of such things, as the Wild seemed to be forever changing right before her eyes.

More stardust-drenched spider-plants crawled over each other and marched across the branches. The creeping crawlers dipped down from the trees like spiders on silk linings. The trees, as well, were lathered in the shimmering dust of the stars. Sometimes she'd remember that she too was being showered with this sparkling dust, so from time to time she'd brush it off her shoulders, and every time she'd wished she hadn't.

The moon, still on fire to its core, still shifting through the shades of heat and almost blindingly aglow, swelled ten times more with each passing second—although what were seconds at a time when time flies? Were they just a part of the rhythm that played in the pull of the night? The pull of the moon?

The Gypsy Moon followed her along this new path of her choosing, just as it had through all of the rest. They kept an eye on one another with each new step, down each new path.

She paused briefly when she heard something moving within the trees. Perhaps it was only the roaring of the butterflies from *within* her, or the grumbling of her stomach, as she couldn't recall the last time she'd eaten. She stepped forward and stopped again when she heard the jingling of bells. She looked over both shoulders and into the woods, but she did not see the Cat Lady.

She moved along, until her feet fumbled over a cat that darted out from the woods, as it swatted around a little glass ball. The cat kicked it between her feet and over her toes, and batted it up the path, before climbing the closest tree. She had seen this cat before—it was the cat of black and the many shades of light. It walked across a low branch and stopped to lick its paws. Before her starry eyes—the cat shifted—from black and light, to white and the many shades of dark.

She stood, bewildered and staring at the cat. She blinked. She rubbed her eyes, but that didn't change a thing. The cat of white and dark rested its body down, draping its arms and legs over the branch. She took in a deep breath, wondering how much more strange that wild place could get. She continued forward, looking up at the now sleeping cat as she walked under it.

She stopped at the cat's toy on the ground. She knelt and picked up a dirty, old, scratched marble. She looked at the marble, and looked back at the cat in the tree. She had heard a thing or two about marbles in the past, but she didn't know a whole lot about cats. She stood again and tossed the marble down, for after the sleeping cat's slumber.

She walked furthermore with the tumbling grumbles of her belly, contemplating the strangeness of those wild creatures in that wild place. Everything was so different and always changing. Things were not always as they seemed. Things were how she wanted to be seeing them. She came around the corner of the path and when she saw its harvest and the adornments showered within it, she thought of the Cat Lady's tale and said, "Oh, certainly there was dirt on this path... and some really great seeds!"

Arrays of fruits hung from trees, and rested within the congestion of large vines and leaves. With more steps forward came more endless choices of fruit. Perhaps this particular path was so filled with fruit because it was the path of her choosing. Perhaps this path was so abundant with fruit because this was the path that could bear such a harvest. Perhaps it was because she was hungry and shade-shifting cats are a sign of good fortunes ahead. Or perhaps this path of her choosing was becoming so abundantly filled with fruit because she was hungry and in need of such a thing.

"The Wild always provides..." She remembered what the Coyote had told her. He was right. The Wild provided for her when she was in need. She didn't even have to ask.

This fruit was unlike ordinary fruit—this fruit grew under the light of the Gypsy Moon, and was larger than any other fruit, or food, she'd ever before seen. She plucked purple plums from the edge of the path—purple plums the size of her head, at least. Red juices poured out and ran down her jawline. She ate the fruit in at least one hundred bites, or one hundred plus one hundred more. She rambled on down the line.

She pulled a nectarine the size of the Coyote's head from a tree and it dropped to the ground, pulling her down with it. She knelt and dug her teeth into its flesh, biting into it like a wild beast. This was enough to feed a whole pack of giant coyotes, she thought. Perhaps she was eating at it just as they would.

She continued along the path plucking and picking and pulling from the harvest of the wild, wild forest. She filled up on an unfathomable amount of cherries that could feed a king, or perhaps thirteen kings plus all of the Cat Lady's cats. But her favorite were the tangerines. One of these was as big as a crow. She ripped the skins off and took large bites, sucking out the juices as more dribbled down to the holding spot of the dip in her neck.

She foraged and ate while her bare feet guided the way. Her arms were full with the holdings of tangerines and plums and cherries, and she hummed her song and strolled along. She did not notice the fat bumblebee buzzing circles around her… that is, until he buzzed in front of her face.

"Got some good pickings here!" he buzzed.

She shrieked and jumped back, dropping all of the fruit.

"Now don't go getting in a tiffy, I'm not buzzing about you, I'm buzzing about your grub." The bee buzzed around the fruit as she picked it up from the ground.

"Oh, is this okay?" she asked, and then she offered, "You want some?"

"It's a nice-looking spread, I dig."

"Was I allowed to take it?" She stood up with her fruit. "I was just so hungry…"

"*Allowed?* You're in The Land of Thee, Honey!" he reminded her.

"You can have some… " she offered again.

"Why thank you, but I got what I need all around me. There's plenty of everything, everywhere... for everyone," the Bee buzzed. "You're welcome."

"Thank you... ?"

"I helped prepare that meal for you, ya know. You like it?"

"Oh, yes! You did!" She took a bite from a piece of fruit in her arm to show her appreciation. "Thank you, it's wonderful!" Fruit bits spewed with her words.

"There's a good menu here, laid out for you. Do you think it's the path?" The Bee landed on one of her fruits.

"Do I think *what's* the path?"

"You think it's the path that makes the menu?" With that question, the fat Bumblebee buzzed away.

She thought about his question as she stood there in the new path, puzzled. She repeated it out loud, "Do I think it's the path that makes the menu...?" But she did not have an answer to her question, for how could she have an answer to such a question that she couldn't quite comprehend?

The Bee buzzed back again, as quickly as he'd buzzed away, and in front of her nose, he asked his next question, "Or is it you that makes the path *and* the menu?" Again he buzzed away, without first taking her up on her offer to share some fruit.

"Is it me that makes the path... and the menu? What does that mean?" she asked herself, still unable to dissect the first question and certainly unable to dissect the second.

She lowered her body and her fruit and she sat on the path for several moments, eating the rest of her feast. She ate the tangerines, then the cherries, and then the plums. After she was done, she licked her sticky fingers and lips. The grumbling of her stomach had settled and she was now filled with the sweetness of the wild new path. She was content, inside and out, and she stood and continued on her quest.

With the comfort of a not-too-full but certainly satisfied stomach, she was in no rush to get anywhere in particular. Although, there was really nowhere in particular that she was aware she was getting to. She was pleased with the conditions of this new path. Even though there were no signs of the Wild Child, the Coyote, or the Crows, she felt at ease. So she walked with leisure and joy and a stomach full of natural zest.

Every so often she thought she'd heard the call of a cat's meow, or the cawing of Crows, or the hooting of owls. Although she was aware of those sounds in the distance, she wasn't paying much mind to the distractions of this night, not just yet. She was far too busy now—indulging in the satisfaction of her dinner, walking down a beautifully lit path with a swelling sense of freedom. She was swelling, much like the moon.

> *"Don't you get glum,*
> *when you're missing the sun,*
> *and the rain's been beating you down.*
> *Don't you feel blue,*
> *when all you can do,*
> *is listen to the silence of sound.*
> *Please don't you worry,*
> *you're not in a hurry.... "*

She danced with a soft wild breeze, singing her way down the path. The stars danced above her head. The dust showered her. The Gypsy Moon watched over her.

"Oh, I do love this song.... " a new voice spoke out from the forest.

She stopped in her tracks and looked to the trees. An angelic white owl sat on a branch, staring into her soul.

"Did you say something to me?" she asked the Owl.

"Oh Darling, that song of yours, it is so lovely."

"Oh, thank you... "

"No, *thank you.*"

She tipped her head to the side, examining the Owl.

"For choosing this divine path. And here we are, meeting at last." The Owl shook up its feathers, and continued, "I fancy we could have happened upon one another regardless of the path of your choosing. But, now... that's neither here nor there. So do tell me, are you enjoying yourself?"

"Well, yes. Yes, I am. But why is that so important?" she asked.

"The name of the game, Darling." The Owl explained, "The objective is joy. You're the only one on the board, Darling. You wouldn't ask someone if they're losing, would you?"

"No..."

"No, of course you wouldn't. You would ask someone if they are winning. So, are you winning?" the Owl asked.

"How, exactly, do I know if I'm winning?" She wiped cherry from her chin with the back of her hand.

"Ah, my Darling. Reflect on the objective. And then you find your answer." The white Owl spread its large angelic wings, and flew to where the girl stood, pausing before her face. "Keep singing your song, Darling. I will come to listen every time. Even if you do not see me..." The Owl flew off into the night.

She watched the wise bird fly away until it was out of her sight, and continued down the path with slower steps.

"Don't you get glum,

when you're missing the sun,

and the rain's been beating you down.

Don't you feel blue,

when all you can do,

is...."

"Listen to the silence of sound!" A squeaky bat flew beside her.

"Oh! You startled me!" She jumped out of her rhythm of walking and fumbled over the side of her foot. She peered at this strange Bat after she settled. "So... you know the song?"

"I know things, Babe."

"Oh....?" She wasn't sure if she wanted to laugh with this bat or swat him away.

"Oh, I know things. Listen here, Babe, I know a thing or two, lemme tell ya...."

She waited a few seconds before insisting, "Go on, tell me..."

"Listen, ah, I know a little bit a this... I know a little bit a that. I know this thing, that thing, and the other thing. I know things. I know a thing or two," he clarified.

"Oh." She blinked at him. "Like my song... how do you know my song?"

"I told ya, I know things."

"Have you been following me?" she pried.

"Ha! Listen, Sweetheart, don't get a big head, here, alright?"

"What? No, I'm not saying that, I just mean, it seems like all you wild creatures *know a thing or two* about me, and it's, well, it's..." She couldn't find the right word. Frustrating? Confusing? Slightly alarming?

"Well, ah, listen there, Sugar, don't ya get glum when, ah, you're missing the sun, there, alright?" he reminded her.

She laughed, and felt lighter.

"Besides, we go way back, so, uh, yeah, I'd say I know ya, Babe! And I gotta say, right now I'm liking your other half much better."

"My other half? Who's my other half?" What does he mean?

"Way more my speed, if ya know what I mean."

"I have *no idea* what you mean..." But she needed to know. "Who's my other half?"

"You mean the other half that stayed here, waiting for your return? Geez, Babe, is your head on straight, or what?"

She glared at him, fighting the urge to swat him away, and desperately wanting to know more of what he could tell her.

"Don't answer that, no need to answer that. I can see ya got your head on straight alright. Maybe a little *too* straight! Ha!" The Bat laughed.

Do not swat the Bat. Do not swat the Bat. Do not swat the Bat.

"Listen, Sweetheart, I'm no blind bat, mm-kay? I call 'em like I see 'em."

"You're kind of rude..." She was becoming more than perturbed.

"Uh-uh. I ain't rude, Sugar-lips. I'm right. Now, word around the

Wild is you dig this place, huh?"

"Well, yeah, I, uh—"

"You uh—you uh—you sound funny, Toots."

"*What?!*" She stopped walking and the Bat flew a circle around her.

"I heard that fat Bee told ya about the menu, huh?" he asked.

"Oh, the menu..." She was still unsure what that meant. "You mean like the plums and the fruits and the things I was eating before?"

"No, I don't mean like the plums and the fruits and the things you was eating before," the Bat teased. He wasn't the friendliest bat, but he was cheerful in his own way, and talkative, with a fast city-bat accent. "I'm talking big. *The full menu,*" he said slowly as if to spell it out for her.

"Oh..."

"Hey, I don't know the rules a the game, Babe, and I don't care, but I tell you what—if I wanted to, I could see the full menu right here and now...." The Bat tightly closed his eyes and flapped his wings fast to pause their pace. "BOOM, done, did it. Full menu."

"I don't get this...."

"C'mon. Close your eyes. Whatever you can imagine, Toots, whatever it is. We're not just talking food here, I mean *everything*. Whatever ya got in there." The Bat poked the side of her head with his nose. "Ain't like it's something new. Listen, Babe, you've been placing orders left and right..."

Had she? The Wild did show her that it would provide for her when she needed. Had she been placing orders without knowing it?

"Order it up. Whatever you want, Babe, it's on the menu. It's all there, plain sight. Place your order. Boom. Bingo. Bango. Baby. Oh, and, ah, delivery is as easy as you wish, Babe." The Bat flew ahead of her and out of sight.

"Place my order, huh? Whatever I want? *What do I want...*" she asked herself and walked and wondered. "I want to find the Crows and get my note back... Is that on the menu? Maybe then I'd know a few things, like... who am *I* to be in a place like *this*... "

The Crows flew over her head, singing as they past her, one of them holding her note in its claws.

"My note!" She ran after them. "Give me back my note!" she yelled at the Crows, watching their flight in the sky, wishing she had wings.

She shrieked and froze when she heard the eerie screeches of Vultures trail behind the song of the Crows. Her heart fell to her stomach, alarming every last butterfly, as she searched through the stars in the sky for the Vultures. She saw nothing but stars, but she had the unshakable feeling that the Vultures were watching her, hidden just out of her sight and awaiting the perfect moment to capture her. She pedaled as fast as she could toward the Crows that had almost gotten away. For she wanted her note, but perhaps she also did not want to face the Vultures alone.

Her feet dragged as she chased after the birds and her note. She ran up and down the hills of the path, slipping around each turn, going as fast as her tired feet would allow. But her feet came to a screeching halt when she watched the birds fly past the Wild Child jumping on a bed made of moss, and the Coyote asleep at the end of it. A canopy of ivy draped over the bed like a picture from a dream.

You see, this wild place had a wild way of resembling dreams—dreams that had never been had—dreams that had longed to be had.

She ran to them, overwhelmed with the kind of excitement a child would feel. The Crows vanished into the night's sky, but that was alright in that moment. She'd found the Wild Child. She'd found the Coyote. She'd found a bed. She knew the Vultures would not hunt her while she slept beside a Giant Coyote.

Perhaps all of this was on the menu. Perhaps she had placed her order.

She pulled herself up onto the tall bed and the little girl jumped into her arms. The Wild Child squeezed her, and she squeezed the child a little tighter. She felt a swell of tears flood to the surface of her starry eyes, and when she lifted her cheeks a little higher, a warm tear rolled down.

The Coyote shimmied over and nuzzled his nose between the two of them—greeting her once again and covering her in kisses. The three of them cuddled together in the mossy bed that was perhaps made by the magic of the moon or the forest, or the magic of the Wild or her mind, or perhaps it was made by the magic of a little bit of faith.

Before they fell into their slumber, the Wild Child squeezed her hand and kissed her cheek, and whispered into her ear, "Sweet dreams. I love you, you know."

CHAPTER 17

THE PULL OF WATER

Something in the early warmth of the morning pulled her out of her dreams. She scrunched up her face when she felt a flick and a tickle upon her nose. She lifted her hand to swat at whatever had pulled her from her slumber, but when she opened her eyes, she was face to face with the glowing Gypsy of the Night. The Gypsy, with a smile as bright as the morning light, continued to tickle and poke her nose with a black feather half the size of her body.

"*Bom dia,* sunshine! Good morning, Butterfly!"

"Good morning..." She blinked and rubbed her eyes and swatted the feather from her face, before she fully realized who she was waking up to, "Gypsy!"

"And how now, how was your sleep? Was it soft and sweet or more so, was it hard and deep? Did you dream in the arms of the stars, and travel to however far be far?" The Gypsy poked herself in the nose with the feather. "Tell me Butterfly, did you sleep okay? Did you sleep just fine?"

"I—"

"I will tell you, Butterfly, and I will say it more like this—"

"However you wish..." She rolled her eyes and scooped her hair behind her ear.

"Mm, yes. It may be said that sleep is a matter of another world in another time." The Gypsy leaped up and continued on about time. "Time, time, what is time? Is it not just a melody that plays in your mind?"

Through the stars in her eyes and the glistening haze falling from the sky, she looked up at the Gypsy and smiled, recognizing the bliss pouring out from this wild creature. The wild woman plunked down at the end of the moss bed and tickled the girl's feet with the black feather. She laughed, and kicked, and rolled around, until she sat up to the realization that the Coyote and the Wild Child were gone. Where did they go this time? A faint laughter from the distance of the realm of tangled wood sailed across her cheek and past her ears. She knew they were somewhere, not too far.

"You just sit, Butterfly. You just sit and rest. Yes, yes, yes!" The Gypsy flicked the girl's forehead with the feather. She flinched.

"I wish you wouldn't do that," she hissed through her teeth.

"So, now, do tell me, did you dream?" the Gypsy asked.

"You want to know if I dreamt?"

"Yes please. And every detail, every tease. See, Butterfly, a woman can dream and a woman can scheme, but only a wild one knows what that means," the Gypsy rambled her rhymes within the scheme of riddles.

"*I* don't know what that means. Does that mean that I'm not wild?"

"Butterfly, you do so know the meanings of such things. Now, are you?"

"Am I what?" She stretched her arms and legs on the bed, trying to avoid the feelings of frustration that can come with conversing with the Gypsy of the Night.

"Are you wild, or are you tame?"

"Oh..." She sat up. Had her wild returned? "I want to be wild again, but..."

"But?"

"But how do I know if I'm wild or, or if I'm still tamed?" She bent her knees to her chest and wrapped her arms around them.

"Perhaps a wild Babe never asks if she's been tamed, unless the taming has already been done, and she has not yet come out of the spinning that was spun." The Gypsy flicked the side of the girl's head with the feather.

The girl sighed and rested her chin on her knee, paying no mind to the flicking of the feather. That was not what she wanted to hear. She wanted the Gypsy to declare her as wild once more... even though she knew that the Gypsy was right—she was not yet unspun from the taming that had been done.

"Now, now, don't get down, Butterfly!" The Gypsy tickled the girl's face with the feather until she lifted her head and squirmed around on the bed. "A tamed one is still a wild one at heart. And you being here, well, that's just the start..."

"The start to what?" She adjusted herself on the bed.

"To reclaiming your wild. Finding who you were before."

"Who I was before I was tamed, right?"

The Gypsy nodded. "Before you were tamed, Butterfly."

"How will I know if I'm finding who I was before, when I don't even know who I am now? How do I know I'm on the right track when I still feel so lost sometimes?" she asked the Gypsy.

"Ask yourself this—are you here right now?"

"Yes...."

"Are you the cat's meow?"

"Uh..."

"How did you get here? Did you scratch at the call of the Gypsy Moon?" The Gypsy scratched at the moon. "Or let me put it more like this, did you wish to be swept into her swoon? Or maybe I might say, I say I see, I see I say—do you see the swooping has already swept you?" The Gypsy flung the feather around in the air and shook her head. "No, no, no... perhaps, Butterfly, all you need to do is look all around you."

"Look all around me, for what?" she was once again becoming mixed up in the webbings of the Gypsy's words.

"To see what you need to see. That's the easiest thing."

She was not awake enough for these riddles.

"To see what you need to see, to receive the answers you need to seek. Look all around you, to see within you." The Gypsy combed the feather across the girl's eyelids. "Wild or tame, it'll be told throughout this day."

She looked to the ancient trees and the golden stardust glistening in the filtered moonlight of the early morning forest.

"Looking outside, Butterfly, is looking within." The Gypsy poked the feather at the girl's heart. "What's inside is outside and what's outside is in. And *here*, like I said before—nothing can hide—not the shadow, nor the changing tide. And the light, ha, the light would never even try. *Here* is where all is revealed, *here* is where we lift your veil." The Gypsy used the feather to brush the girl's hair from her cheek. "So, Butterfly, if you're still trying to figure out where you stand in your game of wild or tame, listen to this place—it calls your real name."

"My *real* name?" She wanted to know what that was. What was her name? Who was she? Was she wild yet, or still tamed?

"That's right, Butterfly. Who you really are... the you that you forgot." The Gypsy tickled under the girl's chin with the black feather. "Now, about your dream..."

"But—"

"Your dream, Butterfly, your dream!" The Gypsy attempted to tickle the girl's chin once more.

"It was... interesting... " She swatted at the feather. "I was on a boat..."

"Mm, yes, a vessel afloat... continue..." The Gypsy threw her arms in the air and tossed the feather into the Wild.

"And all around me... birds, big, beautiful birds..."

"And the colors of them were?"

"The colors? They were almost blinding. Bright white and glowing..." She looked to the sky.

"Glowing bright birds, Butterfly, you don't say. Silly me, of course you do! I just heard you! And these birds, you saw how they flew?"

"How they flew?" She had trouble understanding the meaning behind most of the Gypsy's questions. "They flew everywhere. All around me. And, oh, they were beautiful...."

"Beautiful, you say? Tell me, Butterfly, did you find their beauty in their flight or did you find their beauty in their glowing light?"

"I..." She found herself in the throes of another wild Gypsy inquiry and got lost in the memory of her dreams. "I can't say whether it was one or the other—I guess it was everything about them. But the strangest part is—I felt like I was flying with them too..."

"Do you still think that you do?"

"Think that I do... *what?*" She shook her head and continued on. "Then all the birds flew toward an even brighter light... like the Gypsy Moon. Almost blinding. But it was strange—*stranger,* it was blurry, hard to see..."

"Yes, Butterfly. Depending upon where you are in your path, there are times when the light will be trickier to perceive," the Gypsy revealed.

"Well, it was just a dream." She shrugged her shoulders, furrowing her brows at the Gypsy.

"And what's that to mean?"

"*It was a dream,* that's why it was bright and blurry. It was just a dream..."

"Ha! Just a dream! If it was this way in your dream, who's to say, Butterfly, that it is not what it means?"

She looked at the Gypsy, frustrated with her questions. "Would you like to hear the rest?"

"Yes, oh, yes!"

"The birds turned to black, all of them. And then one of them flew right at my face and pecked at my nose..."

"Oh?" The Gypsy leaned in closer. "And?"

"And then I woke up. And it was *you!*" She smirked at the Gypsy, who clapped and laughed at the climax.

The rhyming woman slid from the end of the bed and ducked out of sight. "Here, here, here, Butterfly." The Gypsy rose with a platter of a tower of pies that stood perhaps as tall as both of them combined. She placed it onto the bed, and climbed up again and sat down. The tower of pies towered between the two of them and leaned from side to side.

Every kind of pie you could imagine, and every kind you could not, stacked and piled atop each other—the warm fillings spilling over the crusts, just like her last tower of pies, except this time the tower was twice as tall. The Gypsy reached her hands behind her back and pulled out two glowing teacups atop saucers, and placed them beside the tower of dribbling juicy pie.

The girl wondered how or where the Gypsy could have pulled the teacups from. But then she realized that it was the Gypsy—there was no point in questioning the Gypsy, as there would be far too many questions.

"Pie for morning thought! What do you think, Butterfly? Have you a thought to say for this day? One marble for a dime, if you give me your time," the Gypsy sang as she stood up and cut through every layer of the pie tower with her hand, plowing through at least twenty-seven or thirty-one, layers, that is. The insides bled with every color of the rainbow and then some. Juices slid to the Gypsy's elbow and dripped onto her rippling gown, seeping into the airy fabric and fusing with it—becoming a gown of a new color once again. "It is alright if you wish not to tell. Remember, Butterfly—I am the Gypsy of the Night, I see all of everything, whether in or out of sight."

Did that mean that the Gypsy was always watching her? Knew her every move? "What do you see... when you look at me?"

"I see all that is light, and all that is dark," the Gypsy revealed. "I see all that is and ever was. I see the dawn of all time and the dusk of infinity. I see the true you. And I see the true me. But what I see can only be seen by me. So, sweet Butterfly, what I see does not matter in The Land of Thee..."

Who is the true her? She did not ask. She watched the Gypsy slap a sloppy piece of pie onto each of the saucers that held the glowing tea, and she grabbed the sticky plate when the wild woman handed one to her. She wanted to ask who she truly was, but bit her tongue, knowing she would not receive a clear answer—one that would be clear to her, that is.

"Thank you." She watched the Gypsy lick her hand and arm clean of pie, and wipe the rest onto her gown, which, like before, seeped into the fabric, renewing the gown once more.

They smiled at each other as they synchronously dove into their pie, feeding themselves with their fingers, eating their breakfast atop a bed made of the softest moss, under the brighter light of the day in the realm of buzzing stars, tasting the melting flavors of fruits that had become jammed-up-jelly fillings between crumbling crusts. She ate as if she'd never eaten, placing the saucer down and diving directly into the tower with her hands.

"I do hope you're ready for this day of all days..." the Gypsy spoke with a mouth full of pie, and she somehow did so gracefully.

"Why? What's happening today? What's the occasion?" She licked the filling from her fingers.

The Gypsy placed her sticky hands onto the girl's cheeks, smiling at the girl as if she were a little child. "You are so sweet." Then the woman grabbed a fistful of pie and stuffed it into the girl's mouth without any warning, and reminded her, "There is always an occasion, Butterfly."

She looked at the Gypsy, swallowing down the pie, waiting for an actual answer to her question.

"Oh, well, Butterfly, you see, I say—the moon schemes with the movement of things, but not such schemes in which you may think—like the schemes of a wild woman or a creature or a Crow—no, no—the moon speaks to you... did you not know?" The Gypsy devoured more pie.

"I... I'm not sure I've heard it speak to me..." She thought back, trying to recall any conversations she'd had with the moon.

"Ha!" the Gypsy roared. "Oh it's been speaking to you the whole time, you just didn't realize that's what you were hearing."

She looked at the Gypsy, furrowing her brow in confusion.

"Oh Butterfly, the moon spun you into a dance at first glance, a glance that was never glanced by chance—as chance is a slur to kismet circumstance," the Gypsy reminded her. "The forgetting of who you are led you to wonder and look to the stars, and today you just may get as far as far is far. You ran, you chased, and led yourself back to this place." The Gypsy laughed. "And today, you'll get even closer to your fate."

"How do you know?" And what does that mean? She wanted to know. She wanted to know if that meant she would find her note. Did the Gypsy know where her note was? Perhaps the Gypsy knew where the Crows resided.

"It all began, Butterfly, when you were plucked from the ennui of out there, and spun between worlds in here..." The Gypsy plucked at the air. "It's only a matter of time—time time, what is time..."

"What... *what* is only a matter of time?" What was going to happen? Perhaps this was the day the Gypsy would take her to the Crows. Perhaps this was the day she would find her note.

"Oh, Butterfly, you've seen how things can be. Look around, Butterfly, you're in The Land of Thee!" The Gypsy hopped on the bed, chanting, "Welcome to The Land of Thee... Welcome to The Land of Thee... Welcome to The Land of Thee!"

She peered up at the Gypsy. "You sound like the birds... The Crows." She wondered about the strange woman and her connection to the Crows. "You sounded like the Crows for a second..." She looked to the darkness within the trees, hoping to spot one of the black birds.

"Do you still search for the Crows, Butterfly?"

"I'm searching for my note." She licked the pie from her hands and fingers.

"You mean your note of words?"

"That's usually what a note would consist of..."

"What's a word but not a bird? Words are birds who can't be caught." The woman reached behind her back and pulled out another black feather. "Words fly through space and life, they soar through minds and travel time... time, time, what is time?"

"Gypsy?"

"Mm, yes, it's me." The woman stabbed the feather into the air.

"Where did you get that feather?"

"This feather?" The Gypsy shook it in front of the girl's face, just close enough to graze her nose.

The girl swatted the feather and nodded.

"Here," the Gypsy slid the feather behind the girl's ear, "you keep it."

She adjusted it, wondering where it came from, and who this Gypsy that she was so fond of, really was.

"So, any plans today?"

"Maybe I'll find my note..." She broke off a piece of crust and nibbled on it.

"Oh sweet Butterfly, you've already found it! Haven't you been listening?"

"Of course I've been listening..." She wondered briefly—had she been listening?

"Then you'll know what I mean if you don't already. Remember, Butterfly, revelations take time! Time, time, what is time? Is it not just a melody that plays in your mind? And in between, well—*that's* the very best time!"

"In between?" She was trying so hard to keep up.

"In between—it's the dance you prance within your journey. The jive you jiggy along your way. The wanting to know the unknown, and enjoying not knowing the not yet known. Having the faith that you already know what you need to know, and then stepping into what you've always known—*that* is the in between that leads to such epiphanies, and the in between is the most wondrous of things." The Gypsy pulled another feather from her back, and tapped it back and forth on the girl's shoulders.

"So, are you saying the journey is the best part?" She attempted to catch the feather in between taps.

"Yes Butterfly! You're getting it! Though I should say it more like this—you mustn't forget—your journeys, your adventures, your stories... are eternal. You will forever be chasing, wanting to know of such things you do not yet know, but things you do truly, deeply know." The Gypsy waved the feather like a conductor orchestrating its masterpiece.

"As long as you enjoy the not knowing of the not yet known, and have faith that you'll always know what you need to know, then your journeys will be ever-flowing—they will be ten-fold. So the journey is the best part, yes. As well as every journey after that." The woman sat down. "And the journeys, well, they are *now and always*, so the best part is... *always!*" The Gypsy clapped for herself. "So? So about the Crows!"

"Oh, yes! *About the Crows,* please..." Would she forever be chasing the Crows?

"You know the Crows, you know," the Gypsy told her. "You've always known, Butterfly. Yet your knowing is not yet known, for, you've always known all there is to know, you know? Don't you not know?" The wild woman stirred the feather up in the air. "Well, see, *that* is the in between."

"What is?"

"All of this! All of this you see! *This* is the in between—the not yet known and the journey here to seek... " The Gypsy paused and peered at the girl with excitement. "Butterfly, your newfound knowing of the unfolding—these new parts you have partaken in, have been most won-drous for your return indeed, but I think I'll say it more like this—'tis the sweetest *thus far,* for you have not yet tasted the stars, sweet Butter-fly." The Gypsy stood up and danced around the tower of pies as they followed her—leaning from side to side.

"Taste the stars?" She huffed her words through a mouthful of pie, eyebrows teasing her hairline.

"And learned a thing or two..." The wild woman chuckled. "Like what you've always known to be true... The real you that is you." The Gypsy poked the girl's nose with the feather. "And all the memories that will ensue...."

"*Which* memories?" What were all these memories she was still sup-posed to be harboring? Everyone kept telling her she would remember... but when would the remembering start?

"You'll learn soon enough, Butterfly, you'll see. You'll see the sky ripple like the sea. You'll travel through the dark and the light, Butterfly. Through words and time. Revelations take time... time, time... what is—"

"What is time?" She interrupted the Gypsy. "What do you mean I'll travel through dark and light, and words and time?"

"Time, time, what is time?" The Gypsy threw her feather high up into the sky.

She looked to the Gypsy's feather as it disappeared into the colors of the sky, and saw that the Gypsy Moon had grown larger. The stars had grown brighter and multiplied by many. The shades of the day moved like the sea. She stared into the colors and into the ripples. Into the unknown. She studied the stars above, right out of her reach. She heard them buzzing, she heard them singing. She felt the heat of the moon and the energy of the wild place.

"Your feather, I can't see—" She tore her eyes away from the sky, only to find herself alone again. She was only slightly surprised to find that the Gypsy was gone. "Poof. Every time. Just like that." This was becoming a regular occurrence. She was expecting to receive her goodbyes in this way, at this point in the Wild, that is. She took another bite, or two, or three of pie, and stuffed some pieces of crust into the pocket of her gown. She stretched one last time in the bed, and slid down like a little child.

She stood on the warm, dusty sand of the path and took a few sips of the warm drink that resembled sunshine—or Gypsy Moonlight in a cup. She examined the detail etched into the porcelain—upside down trees, and birds flying over the lip. She looked inside the cup where more birds were engraved, and she drank the rest of the tea to see the bottom. The birds inside the vessel formed into words spiraling into the question: 'A girl can see when she's spun around, but can the girl see when she's upside down?'

Was this a message? From the Wild, perhaps. Or from the Gypsy, she thought. She was unsure if she was truly being asked this question by a teacup in the Wild, or if these were the teacups the Gypsy shared with all the guests of that wild, wild place. She looked to the bottom of the porcelain, puzzled.

After a moment of pondering the perplexities of such a question, something told her it was time to move forward and not time to look into empty teacups trying to decipher what they could mean. She felt warm from the hot drink. She felt ready. She wasn't going to get held up by the not-yet-knowing of such messages.

She placed the cup onto the bed and walked away, continuing on the path. After eighty-eight steps into her ever-unfolding journey, she came upon the Gypsy's big black feather. She stood and stared, wondering where the Gypsy was plucking such large feathers from. She knelt and picked it up, shoving it into her pocket like a sword, and marching forward on her new path.

"Don't you get glum,
when you're missing the sun..."

"And the rain's been beating ya down!" The Bat nearly flew into her face, before flying circles around her. "Hey Babe, looks like you're growing some wings!" The Bat flew off and she pulled her feather out from her pocket. She turned around, waving it at him, and saw the bed that she'd slept in and the tower of pies that she'd eaten from, and the teacup she'd just held in her hand had all vanished. As if none of it was ever there to begin with.

Peculiar, the way everything seemed to be. Or didn't seem to be. Always appearing through thin air, and always vanishing in that same way. She was confused, but she was enjoying the feeling. She was settling into it. She did not get hung up on such things that she did not want to get hung up on any longer. She turned around and moved on, sweeping her feathered sword from side to side, clearing the imaginary veil as she walked through it, and not looking back. There was no need to look back. No time to look back.

Time, time, what is time? How could she not have time when she didn't know what time it even was, or what *time* really was. There was no certain time she had to arrive at any certain place. Not in the Wild, anyway. Wherever she was, was right where she was meant to be. And wherever she needed to be, she would certainly find herself there.

She walked and wondered where she might end up. Not where she would end up in the next hour, or the next several hours, and maybe not even tomorrow. But she wondered where all of this would lead her to, in the long run of things—in the big picture, in the future. And she thought, well, what even is the future, and when does it begin? And how long does it last? And when is the future considered to be the future? And can the future actually ever be considered the future, and therefore, does the future ever really come? And if not, what are we all waiting around for the future for?

Perhaps the future is in the next day, or hour, or the very next moment. Perhaps, she thought, the future was right now. She let her thoughts carry her away as she walked with the golden, misty morning. Or perhaps she let the morning carry her away as she walked with her thoughts, it all depends upon perception, you see.

She watched the trees wake and stretch their branches, beginning their day by intertwining their arms. The green and glimmering spider plants crawled through the forest, branch to branch. She wasn't sure if the greens of the Wild ever slept—she always saw them moving about.

The golden, sparkling rays of moonlight showered the path and weaved through the trees. The trees serenaded the morning with soft whispers. The stars buzzed with the sound of the memory of children laughing. The moss and sand caressed her feet and toes. She looked at her dirty feet and smiled, thinking of the Cat Lady and the bells on her toes. And with that thought, she heard the sound of bells jingling in the distance. But as soon as she heard it, it stopped. She thought her ears were playing tricks with her. She had yet to realize that ears do not play tricks.

Shadows, however—certainly do.

Her ever-expanding shadow stretched out from her like the morning stretched out from the breaking of the dawn. She stood and stared, watching it morph in its shape and size. Her darkness—shown by the light, had her tangled in a trance of bewilderment. It breathed like her body breathed, but it moved with a mind of its own.

She gazed into her darkness as it moved this way and that, putting on a show for her while she stood frozenly still above it. She stared until her eyes grew glassy. She stared until a rambling gust of wind swept past her, carrying her shadow along with it. On the ground where her shadow had been displayed, she saw a black feather resting in its place.

She looked up to the sky expecting to see a Crow passing by. But she saw nothing. She picked up the feather and twirled it in her fingers in front of her face while she let the birds take up room in her mind's empty space. She placed the new feather into her pocket beside the Gypsy's feather and continued on her path.

She came to a rickety, wooden bridge that stretched across a shimmering stream and divided her current walkway. The stream, like most things in the Wild, seemed to come from out of nowhere. But there it was before her—holding the rippling reflections of a glowing, sunshiny moon.

The current of the stream was soft and calm like the gold morning. She paused before crossing the bridge, looking into the water and searching for her reflection.

The water moved slow and free, calm and inviting.

She reminded herself that the future was now and she had nowhere else that she needed to be. She wondered if right where she was, was right where she needed to be. She slipped her gown to the ground and stepped into the water.

It was warm as a bath. Like the waterfalls of the jungle. Crystal clear and sparkling, like her eyes. She smiled into a deep breath and immersed her body under the warm water. She bathed and she floated. She splashed and she swam. She softened into the comfort of the hot, wild bath as stardust dripped from the skies and rained over her and the ripples of the peaceful stream.

"Don't you get glum...

hmm.... hmm.... hmm.... hmm...." She melted into the sounds of her song as the sound of the rippling water heightened. The current was quickly picking up.

Remember, in the Wild—the only constant current is change.

She felt the shift take place within the water, but before she could do anything about the changing of the tides, the stream was pulling her along. The current was pulling her song, her words, her morning, her mind, and her body along with it wherever it pleased.

Within seconds, she was moving faster within the ripples, and trying as hard as she could to fight it. But her fight was not as strong as the current of the stream—the current of the conditions of her current path. She was on a wild and unexpected ride at the discretion of the water. But she would not surrender. She would not give in.

She tried to push against the pull. She struggled to swim back upstream and grab on to passing rocks. She wrestled to get back to the source, the bridge, the path of her choosing... and her gown. But she continued to get swept further away—and at a radical pace—no matter how hard she smacked her arms and legs against the tide to fight it. Her head dipped in and out of the water. Panic gripped her, and swiftly swept her away with the stream.

"Yoo-hoo! Darling...."

She flipped her focus up to the sky and saw the wings of the white Owl soaring above her head—flying at the same speed as the current.

"It is such a lovely song you sing..." the Owl said.

"Um, a little help, please?!" she begged frantically.

"Oh, downstream, Darling, downstream."

"What?"

"Stop fighting the forces of nature. Just go with the flow and enjoy the ride. Perhaps it will bring you somewhere you want to be." With that message, the Owl turned around and flew back the other way.

She had nothing to lose. She was being pulled by the stream, and her help had just flown away. She heeded the Owl's advice. She put her trust into the water like she'd always done before. She let the stream sweep her away. She gave in, and the ride became less daunting. She surrendered. She surrendered to the pull of the water. She surrendered to the pull of the Wild, unaware of where it would carry her.

CHAPTER 18

THE NEW PATH

She'd spent hours, or several hundreds of moments, or multiple thousands of seconds, being taken away by the arms of the water. After such time, and through the changing of the colors in the sky through the developments of the day—the meandering stream finally dropped her off to a moss drenched shore, with a rocky landing.

This part of the Wild was like no other part she'd yet seen. You see, every part of the Wild was like no other part she'd yet seen, or remembered.

She opened her eyes, the left side of her face planted into the terrain of moss and sand-sized beach stone. She rested with her breath, blinking and twinkling the stars in her eyes. She looked out at her surroundings as much as she could from where her body rested. She realized she had reached her new destination, which was wherever the stream wanted her to go—wherever the Wild wanted her to go—wherever the Gypsy Moon wanted her to go—wherever her light and the fire inside wanted her to go.

She indulged in the uncomfortable comfort of being washed up on the precarious shore. Her arms spread out onto the sharp edges, her knees bent. The land lovingly embraced her. She felt grateful to be alive.

She pressed her palms and fingers into the coast of weeping moss and pebbles, and pushed herself up on her feet. She stood dressed only in the sting of new scrapes and burns from being dragged, or pulled—depending upon perception—by the current, and from being washed upon a shore of an infinite number of tiny rugged stones. Her bare feet stood on the slippery moss and puddles of pebbles. Naked and dripping wet, her bones cold, her skin warm.

She looked down at her footing and at the rocks and at her toes. She grinned until her cheeks swelled over her eyes. Although she stood in the dressings of her vulnerability, she was happy. She was happy to be alive after being swept away by a mad motion of the wild tide. She was relieved to have her feet planted on the jagged ground.

"I made it out alive..." She sighed.

She stood on the slippery shore and looked out at her surroundings—at this new part of the forest that she hadn't yet seen. Mountainous trees hugged the strange beach—a clearing between them provided a path into the fresh new forest. She heard the path call her name. She felt the path pulling her in.

She stepped toward the unknown of the forest as glinty glares from the ground gleamed at her eyes. Many steps inward and she was standing on a shore of washed-up marbles, some shimmering and shining in the Gypsy Moonlight of the day, but most of them were dusty, flat, old. These marbles on the Wild floor led her mind to stir with the many tales she'd once been told.

You see, many a man had been said over the course of many moons, to have lost their marbles much too soon when dancing with the Gypsy Moon. Perhaps, she thought, these were their missing marbles.

Would she lose her marbles, too? Perhaps she already had. She was not sure if she wanted to lose her marbles or keep her marbles. For she did not know what either one meant.

She knelt down and picked up a foggy yet gleaming marble, the first one that caught the attention of her starry eyes. She rolled it between her fingers, staring into it—still bright and shining from the inside, but scuffed and dirty on the outside. She wondered if anyone ever came looking for their lost marble, and if it was the one in her hand.

She studied the marble, her spine curled to the stars. A blindfold from the skies fell over her head and eyes. She dropped the marble and pulled the veil from her face, seeing that it was her gown. She scrunched it into her hands and looked up to the sky, where she caught a glimpse of the white Owl flying away.

"Thank you!" she called out to the Owl as it flew past the veil of the mighty trees.

She rang out her hair with the gown, and flung it behind her. She wiped the water from her arms and legs, took a deep breath and stuffed her face into the gown—her head in the comfort of her hands and garment, she freed a roaring sigh of release. After several more such breaths, she slipped the gown over her head and looked at her toes.

She picked up the foggy, glistening marble and held it between her fingers once more, looking to the inside. Although it was old and rough, she saw the reflection of her eyes within it, shimmers of the stars in her eyes glistening through the faded glass.

"Stars in my eyes...." she whispered to herself through a gasp of trifling disbelief.

She was beginning to see things that she couldn't quite see before, like the shimmer of the stars of her own eyes. Perhaps her shift in perception was due to the pull of the Gypsy Moon. Perhaps it was due to the pull of the ever-changing trails, or the bumpy ride of the stream. Perhaps it was due to her strengthening faith that all was going just right. Or perhaps it was simply due to how she was choosing to see at this point in her journey.

She laughed faintly at the marble and the sight of the stars in her eyes, and dropped the little glass ball into the pocket of her gown. She was ready to move forward in her current future.

She was ready. She was certain. She was not looking back.

She stood and brushed her hands across the bottom of her gown and headed for the path before her. She stepped over puddles of fogged-up marbles toward her new destination—wherever it was that that was. For she did not know the significance of what she was walking into. Not yet, that is. But regardless, she was ready.

Lathered in the heat of the Gypsy Moon, she marched on faster—compelled to keep going, to see how much closer she could get.

She stepped off the beach of moss and marbles, into the new path she'd been sent to by the Wild. She walked between soaring trees. She stood in the entrance of her newfound road, staring up at the greens that reached into the depths of the sky so high that their tops were a thing of mystery.

She peered through the stitches of trees with the wonderment of a child. The world that held her was so expansive—forever growing, forever becoming.

She spun in circles, watching the branches in the sky twist with her. She gazed up in her blissful astonishment until her neck grew tired and she had to look down to accommodate her spinal comfort.

Not only did the trees live with their heads in the sky and the heavy showers of stardust, but the stars were bigger, the greens were brighter, the lush lusher. Perhaps, she thought, things grew faster here, in this part of the Land of Thee.

She walked through the entrance of the tree-pillared-path. Her feet and knees weakened under her as the ground and all of her surroundings began to shake. A monstrous roar rumbled behind her, sending a fearful tremble to her core. The shaking abruptly stopped. She placed her hand over her chest to catch her heart, and slowly turned her cheek and looked over her shoulder. Her heart dropped before she could catch it. The entrance to the path was gone. The trees had closed in on her. She was fully encapsulated in that new realm of the Wild.

She wondered how it was possible, but quickly remembered that most things in the Wild didn't seem possible, and yet, they were. The Vultures screeched and her eyes darted to the sky, but they were nowhere in sight. She ran toward the trees where the path's entrance once was.

"Welcome to The Land of Thee..." A single Crow flew down from the towering trees and soared past the girl, just above her head, holding her note in its claws.

She froze her momentum and turned around, watching as the Crow flew deeper into the path. She leaped forward before it disappeared into the unseen and continued her chase.

A stray marble here and a missing marble there began to show up along the path during her chase. Certain marbles would catch her eye—whether it was their shimmer or their shine—if she felt compelled to grab one, she would try to pluck at the ground while in motion, dropping the ones she'd captured into her pockets as she ran.

At each winding turn on her path, lay mountains of more marbles. She ran through an obstacle course deep in the Wild, dodging heaps of marbles left and right, every other step. She whipped around a wild turn and crashed into a mound of marbles, fumbling atop its peak and spreading them across the path.

Slipping and sliding to lift herself from the chaos on the floor of the path, it took her several tries to get back up onto her feet. But when she did, she did not run. For the Crow had escaped from her sight. She reminded herself that everything was going just right—she would catch up to the Crow right on time.

She let herself be slow. She let herself have faith that she was right where she needed to be. She looked up at the trees and the Heavens above, showing her face to the showers of stars. The further she walked, the taller things grew. The blades of grass, the leaves of the trees, all emerging—growing before her eyes and coming to life. She was a small creature being swallowed up by the wild, wild, Wild.

There was no turning back now. So she did not. She would not. She had no such intentions. She was being pulled by the strange Gypsy Moon and the even stranger Crow. She was being pulled by the beast within. She was beginning to break through. She was beginning to break free. But she did not realize this, just yet. For how could she see that she was in the midst of breaking free when all she was choosing to perceive was the tallness in the trees?

She sat on a low branch and leaned her back against the tree, letting her legs dangle over the sides. She reached into the pocket of her dirty gown and pulled out a pie-crust crumb that she was pleased to find was still there. She didn't think the Owl would eat from her pockets, but she thought the crumbs would have fallen out during the gown's travels.

She parted her lips and plopped a buttery bite of crust onto her tongue. Within seconds, the Crow—the size of two crows plus one and with the largest wingspan a wild crow could have—swooped past her face and landed on a nearby branch. She caught herself from falling, never taking her eyes off the bird, consciously calculating, as if she'd just found a lost pet who needed snatching. The Crow looked at her from where it stood on the nearby branch, unfazed and unimpressed.

"Hey!" she blurted to the bird in a lapse of patience, and watched, defeated, as it took off deep into the sea of trees. After all this time, she had finally gotten close enough to catch the bird, and she let it get away. How could she have let it get away. She needed to know where they were always flying off to. What were they hiding, aside from her note?

The bird was too fast and too far gone to follow. She knew she couldn't catch up. She slid down from the tree branch and carried onward, hoping she'd cross paths with the Crow again.

She reached for another pie crumb from her pocket, and as she felt around for it, she recalled how quickly the bird had appeared the last time she'd pulled a piece out. She wondered if the Crows had been traveling very close to her, if they'd been following her, watching her. She thought that if the Crow had come so quickly for her crumbs the first time, then surely it would again.

She stopped in the path next to a pile of missing marbles—the toes of one foot dug into the sand, the toes of the other squishing water from the moss. She pulled a piece of crust from her pocket and looked through the trees and up to the sky. As she brought the pie to her lips, the Crow appeared from within the darkness of the distant trees.

"Crow!" The thrill of having enticed a Crow allowed her to pursue the type of impulsivity that could scare one away again. But it was not scared. It did not flinch or fly away—it landed on a low branch ahead of her.

She pulled another piece of crust from her pocket and threw it on the ground between her and the Crow. The Crow cawed the kind of caw a wild woman would caw, and dived down to the path and pecked at the pie crust, glaring at her with eyes of the clearest ocean.

The Crow finished the crumbs of crust from the path floor and looked at her for more. She broke off another piece, and threw it before the bird had a chance to fly off again. But this time the Crow did not care about the crumbs on the ground. The bird watched her.

"Why do you chase us, Beast?" the Crow spoke in that familiar voice that she'd heard many times before.

"You... it's... it's *you*. *You* have my note..." Who was this bird?

"How can you be so sure?"

She wrinkled her forehead and lost herself in baffled frustration.

The Crow walked closer toward her, flashing its blue eyes into her soul. She was reluctantly eager about this fortunate tryst—this *tête-à-tête* with the black Crow. Even though she'd longed for it, she was filled with the angst of the unfolding of this highly anticipated encounter. For when you find what you've been chasing after for so long, sometimes you forget what you were chasing after in the first place.

"How, Beast, can you be so sure?" the Crow asked again.

"I was there! You snatched it right from my hand!"

"And so it is *I* that you chase?" The bird hopped closer, and she stumbled back two steps.

"Yes—no, I—"

"Do you even know what you're really looking for?" The Crow hobbled closer to her.

Of course she did. She crossed her arms. She was looking for her note.

"You sought before you even got to this place, Beast, before you found that little letter. You've been searching for a long time."

"How do *you* know what I was doing before I got to this place?" Her impudence overruled her words.

"Such questions are unnecessary. You would not have come back here if you weren't in that other place—looking for answers." The Crow pecked the ground and ate a worm.

"For the last time, I didn't come *back* here! I've never been here! Why does everyone keep saying that?" She knew that place felt familiar to her. She knew the creatures felt familiar. She knew there was something about that place that she had to be tied to. But she wanted her note, and that pesky Crow was driving her mad.

"It is foolish to ask a crow questions for which the answer is already alive and well within you," the Crow stepped closer, "though, perhaps it is not. To ask a Crow a question is the same as asking Thee." The Crow tilted its head.

"How is it the same? We are not the same! I don't know where my note is or what my note says, but *you* do... I don't know what I'm doing here, but *you* do..." She flung her arms to the sky and dropped them to her sides in defeat.

"As do you, Beast. You know exactly why you're here."

"Yes, you're right. I *do* know why I'm here. I'm looking for my note that you stole from me so that I can find out why... I'm here." She dropped her shoulders. "I don't even know how I got here to begin with." She kicked a marble.

"You were searching for it."

"How would *you* know if I was searching for it?"

"You've been searching for a long time. Your chase for us is not for finding words of a hidden note. Your chase for us is for finding something else, something much greater that you've been seeking since you left this place."

"Left this place? I'm still here, aren't I?" Her words were as short as her patience.

"You left long ago. And got caught up in that realm of time—tired time, and Tamers," the Crow revealed.

"Oh, here we go again with the Tamers. Is that where I'm from—the land of Tamers who messed with my mind?" At the moment she was more furious about the Crow who seemed to be messing with her mind. She rubbed her forehead and disheveled her hair.

"You still don't even know where you're from, Beast. You don't even know who you are... or who I am to you. How do you know I am not a

Tamer?"

"Are you?"

"I am not."

She rolled her eyes. "Do you have my note? Can I just have it, please?" She held out her hand.

"You still think that's all you want?"

"I *know* I want it." She dropped her hand.

"There is so much more that you seek, Beast."

"Well, then tell me what that is, instead of playing all these games with me... "

"A good game is always fun. Unless, of course, you are a sore loser."

"I'm not... " She shuffled her toes in the sand.

"Do you think you'll know what you've found when you find it?" The Crow took one step closer, and she took half a step back. "Perhaps, Beast, you've already found what you've been looking for," the blue-eyed bird stepped closer, "perhaps you never lost it? Will you know you've found it when you find it?"

The Crow observed her contemplations, and before she could muster up a thought for an answer to at least one of the bird's questions, it flew away. She stood in the new path—dirty feet above the sand and moss, starry eyes looking up at the sky—watching the bird fly further and further away.

She repeated the words of the Crow over again in her head. She wondered, what *was* she really looking for? What was she seeking, there in the Wild? A way out of that place? A way deeper into it? Or just a simple piece of paper with some words on it?

Once the Crow had disappeared into the distance of future skies, she continued on the path. The path continued to become more congested with clusters of marbles. What were those marbles really doing there on the path? What was *she* really doing on that path?

Deeper down the wild road, marbles nearly covered the path in its entirety, interrupting every step she took. She had to go slow, stepping on and over marbles and catching herself before tripping or slipping upon one or many.

It was when the path had become entangled with intertwined vines that she couldn't find her footing. Instead, she'd found herself stumbling through the obstacles of a new path—if every step she took was not calculated and accurate, she could slip on the marbles, or get tangled up in vines, vines that were beginning to slither to life like snakes.

A shiver crawled up her spine as she tried to weave through the workings of the wild trap, and avoid stepping on a snaking vine. It seemed like one hurdle after another, and she wondered if perhaps this wild place was always playing tricks, playing tricks on her. Perhaps this wild place was a place of wild games, and it was playing games with her.

"Are you winning?" she asked herself in the greatest Owl impression she could invoke. But before she could answer her own question, and perhaps because she was paying much too much attention to where she was stepping, she caught one foot between two slithering vines. She slipped—she tripped—she hit the ground and became intertwined with the marbles and vines.

She tugged on her legs to slip them from the grip of that moment, but she could not free herself—she was too caught up in the makings of a wild forest. She panicked in a less than mild manner, and the vines responded by clustering closer toward the warmth of her body.

She yanked and pulled with discomposed caution, but the vines would not budge. The more she tried, the more strenuous it became. The Wild had a hold on her. The forest held its star player.

The vines grew feistier and gripped tighter as her frenzy took control. She felt sick to her stomach—her palms slipping with sweat.

With the vines grazing on her anguish and becoming more lively, the ground below her began to move with the commotion. Marbles bounced up from the Wild floor like angry bubbles in boiling water—some hitting her arms and shoulders upon their descent.

She squeezed her eyes shut in anticipation of getting hit, and yanked harder on her leg. One vine swatted at her hand as she tried to pull away, and the rest took over. They gripped themselves around both of her legs.

She looked down at herself in the grip of the wild vines and screamed.

She had stepped into a trap—a trick—an ambush—a seduction.

Her body grew hotter. Her brow dripped with sweat that fell into her eyes and blurred her fearful vision. Her anxious mind and beating heart raced against each other. She tried to shimmy her legs, but they barely budged within the clutching of the vines. She scrambled to wiggle her feet out of the trap, but the more flustered she became with each shake and wiggle, the tighter the vines fastened their grip.

She felt hopeless. Defeated. Captive on the ground, in the middle of a path she did not know, knocked down once again. The Crow had gotten away. She'd been forced to a new path by way of a forceful stream. She'd come this far, and now she was trapped in the hands of the Wild. But she would not give up. She would not be trapped without putting up a good enough fight.

She floundered on the ground and pulled on the surrounding vines to slide her legs out from their hold on her. But when she tried this, the vines quickly tightened and hauled her up from the ground and dangled her above the path. She hanged upside down, in the grip of something wild.

She had been captured. But who set the trap?

CHAPTER 19

FLIPPED UPSIDE DOWN

Her dirty gown draped over her face as she hung upside down from the vines. She attempted to pull the gown back down—or up—over the rest of her parts and away from her face. But after trying for so long, she dropped her tired arms in defeat and let them dangle like the gown and the rest of her body. She grumbled with all of her aggravation, and perhaps with the hopes of receiving a response.

Suspended by her lower half, she was getting a different view of the wild place, whether she thought she wanted one or not. A new view that was slightly obscured by the dangling of her dirty gown, but she knew where she was without having to pull her dress from her eyes. She knew that she was hanging in the middle of the wildest place she'd ever been, and she knew that she was dangling at the whim of that wild place, but she didn't know why.

She swung soft and slow in the breeze, hung out like dirty laundry, wondering why—why she was there, upside down, hanging by her ankles. How would she get herself out of this trap? Who did this to her, and how close by did they dwell. Or was it just a wild game in that wild place?

Was she sent there, to that strange wild place, to be the brunt of all the tricks and games? It seemed to her that she was relentlessly getting caught up in the messes of the place. And *this* was one mess, and trick, and game that she did not want to be dangling in for much longer.

She took a deep breath and curled her spine up toward her feet as best as she could, trying to pull on the vines and loosen their grip. But wild vines who live like snakes were much stronger than her fingers. Their grip did not loosen upon her tugging, rather, their grip grew tighter around her legs. She slapped and punched at the vines as they squeezed her until she felt like she could pop, but when the vines proved they had no intention to surrender, she gave up fighting and dropped the rest of her body back to dangling.

Her gown dropped over her face as she heard a cat's meow calling from below. Her eyes moved to the top of her head and she looked down at the path. The cat of white and the many shades of dark sat beneath her dangling body, meowing at her and moving its tail from side to side.

She smiled narrowly as she felt a slight tinge of relief flow through her from her toes to her head. The cat of black and the many shades of light sauntered along behind it, and was followed by another, and another, and another, and her smile grew twice the size.

"Perfection and perception, my Dear...."

She pulled her gown from her eyes and looked to her side. The Cat Lady rested on a lofty branch of an ancient tree, holding one of her cats. The lady lost herself in laughter as the tree quickly became covered in climbing cats.

"Hi... " she interrupted the woman's laughter.

"Hello there, sweet Dear."

"Hello... " Didn't the old woman see she was hanging there, clearly in need of help?

"Are you enjoying yourself, Dear?"

"Enjoying myself?!" She was offended by such a question at such a time as this.

"Yes, are you?" The Cat Lady stroked each cat that climbed past her.

"Are you *kidding?*" She flung her arms out.

"It is a simple question, not a joke. Although, I could tell you a joke, Dear, if that's what you're wanting."

"Can't you see me?!" She flailed her arms around, which brought her hanging body to a subtle swing. "Clearly, I don't need any jokes right now!"

"Oh yes. See here, sweet Dear, my vision is quite perfect."

"Then you can clearly *see* that I'm hanging upside down!"

"Oh yes, yes, I certainly can. Although, Dear, I wouldn't say you're *hanging upside down*, as you so gracefully put it."

"Oh, no? Really? Then what would you call *this?*" She flailed her arms with more vigor, swinging herself harder.

"I would call it what it is..." the woman chuckled, "the part of your path where perceptions tend to... flip." The old woman shrugged her shoulders and laughed some more.

"Well, *obviously* the view's quite different from where I am." She was not impressed with the old woman's answer.

"Through your adventures, Dear, of finding your true joy, views tend to change. Rather, they evolve. And that is all."

"That's it? That's all?" She punched her gown out of her face and gathered it in her hands, pinning it tight to her sides.

"What more do you want to hear, sweet Dear? You did not want a joke..."

"*What more do I want to hear?*" Was the old woman serious? "For starters, I'd like to hear that you can help me out of this mess!" she pleaded with the Cat Lady.

"You are not in need of helping. There is no mess."

"What do you mean? Look at me!"

"Yes, Dear, I see. You can simply call this the dirt of the path. We both knew it had to be somewheres," the Cat Lady reminded her.

"But I'd at least like to be *standing* in the dirt, if there had to be dirt somewhere!"

"Oh Dear, you're *standing in it,* all right."

"I'm *not* standing," she muttered under her frustration and dropped the gown over her head.

"What do you imagine the dirt of the other path to be like?"

"The only thing I can imagine right now is getting down from here!" she yelled through her dress, the blood rushing to her head feverishly. She had the sinking feeling that this Cat Lady might not help her at all. Her pulse raced through her panic.

"Oh, Dear, Dear, sweet, foolish girl. Seeing things from a new perspective is necessary at times."

"Says who?"

"Are you not still here? *Here*, in this fresh fate that's never before been? *Here*, seeing it all unfold before your eyes? You are *unraveling*, my Dear. And you *get* to be *here,* right *here,* seeing all of it, with a brand-new view that you have no choice but to recognize." The Cat Lady held up a cat and kissed it in the space between its eyes. "Your journey has not changed course, my Dear. It is still the same one. And this, right here, is a very big part of it. Just like flowers in the dirt, Dear, you'll get through this and find yourself some light. Now, what makes you think this is so bad?"

She hung upside down, her face hiding under her gown, her body dangling by the thread of the wise woman's words. She did not know what to say. She did not have an answer for the woman. She knew what was so bad about hanging upside down and the blood boiling in her head, but she wondered if perhaps she really would find her light in that situation.

Was there a reason she was hanging there? Was it getting her where she needed to be? She was not sure how far she could possibly get while hanging upside down unable to free herself. She pulled her gown away from her eyes.

"Oh, Dear... you *are* in need of a joke."

"I'm not in need of any jokes." She rolled her eyes.

"Oh yes you are, Dear. A joke is just what you need." The Cat Lady whispered into the ear of one of her cats and laughed a wild laugh.

"No it isn't," she hissed at the woman, but then looked to her with remorseful eyes for doing so.

"How can you be so sure?" The old woman smiled over the layers of smiles upon her face, paying no mind to the girl's attitude.

"I need help, you know... not jokes," the girl spoke softer, but still wanted to be heard.

"Jokes are more helpful than any other such thing your mind could muster in this moment, Dear."

"Jokes will not get me right side up." She sighed.

"In fact, they will, Dear. Laughter has the power to change all things. A little laughter from the belly can go quite a long ways, Dear. I can tell you, I have been what *you* call upside down in the Wild many, many times. And look at me now—I am right side up!" The Cat Lady laughed wildly at herself, and continued in her laughter, "But who's to say what's right side up, anyway? Perception, perfection..."

Upon the woman's last word, a murder of Crows flew over them in the sky. The Lady and her cats didn't seem to notice or care, but *she* did. She pulled her gown further from her face and watched the birds pass her note from bird to bird. She whipped her body around, reaching up and curling her spine toward the Crows. They dropped her note, and it grazed her nose on its way down to the path.

"My note! My note!" She dropped her arms and peered at the ground, wishing she could reach the note.

She watched as one of the Cat Lady's cats sauntered over to the note and plucked it from the ground with its mouth.

"My note!" she begged the cat as it ambled up the tree to where the Cat Lady sat. The old woman took the note from the cat, and combed her hand across the cat's back.

"My note! That's my note!" she called to the old woman, hoping the lady would hold onto it for her, or read it to her. But instead, she watched as the Cat Lady snickered at the note, as if she'd read nothing more than a funny tale, and tossed it into the breeze.

"No!" she screamed, watching as the Crow caught the note in midair and flew with the rest into the distance, singing the song of The Land of Thee.

"Why did you do that?!" Her voice trembled. Her body shook. Her eyes spilled over with tears, which dripped over her forehead and to the tips of her hair.

"Do you fear the Crows, Dear?"

She sniffled. "I... I..." She wiped her eyes and face with her gown. "I don't *fear* them... I don't think." She sniffled once more. "I just don't... *understand* them." *Or this crazy Cat Lady,* she thought.

"They intrigue you?"

She held her head in her gown, soaking up the river of tears that spilled from her eyes. "Oh, yes..." she sobbed. "They intrigue me, alright." She took a deep breath and sighed.

"And why do you suppose that is?"

"They... have... my note!" She couldn't be more clear.

"Your note, Dear?"

"The one you just threw back to them!" she screamed. She felt like a wild animal caught in a trap, wanting to lash out and howl.

"Which one is that?"

She took another deep breath, her tears being replaced with infuriating frustration. "When I washed up here, in the... The Land of Thee... I found a note in my pocket... And I have no idea what it says, other than those words they keep singing—"

Welcome to The Land of Thee, Dear," the Cat Lady greeted her. "What are those words to you?"

"I'll never know! You could have helped me with that!" she huffed in defeat. "Instead you gave the note right back to the very same Crow that stole it from me in the first place!"

"Oh Dear, the Crows do not steal."

"They do! They did! One took it right out of my hand!"

"Oh, no, Dear, the Crows do not take," the lady argued.

"But they did! Right from my fingers! One of those Crows snatched it from me!" She pointed to the distance of the sky where birds dwell.

"No, no, Dear, the Crows do not snatch."

"If the Crows do not steal, take, or snatch, then what do you suppose they do?"

"The Crows do many things, Dear."

"Name one thing they do that does not involve theft." The girl pursed her lips and gazed at the Wild, dodging her eyes from side to side, looking to the land as if it were an enemy.

"The Crows deliver, Dear. They recite," the woman told her.

"They deliver and recite *what?*"

"What you are seeking." The lady pulled a cat off the top of her head.

"They have not delivered or recited anything to me..." She rolled her bloodshot eyes.

"How can you be so sure, Dear?"

"I've only spoken to *one* of those Crows, *once,* and it did not recite a thing!"

"How do you know that's what's for certain?"

"How do I know?! I only *just* met one of them, down there on this path." She waved to the path and the gown dropped over her head. She pulled it to her hips and added, "And believe me, it certainly wasn't reading me my note!"

"That is your perception, Dear. You see, the Crows change often. They are many things..."

"They are thieves, is what they are."

"No such thing. They deliver. They recite. They show. They create. They mimic. They unravel. They reveal."

"Well, I'm still waiting for the big reveal..."

"Take a look around, Dear. She, who hangs upside down." The woman plucked a cat from her shoulder and laid it on her lap.

"Look around? While I'm upside down?" Her anger clouded her ability to understand the words of the wise woman.

"What better time to look around than when you're hanging upside down, Dear?"

"What am I supposed to look around for, *from here?*"

"Look around, see what you see. Listen to the sounds, the sounds of the Wild. The sounds of the Crows. The sounds of your Soul. It's all here, waiting for you to notice. Look. Listen. Watch. It's all around you..."

Although the Cat Lady spoke only words of wisdom, she was too deep in her discontent to feel and truly hear them. But words have a way of lingering in the back of a mind until they are needed.

"What is it that you say you seek to be revealed, Dear?"

"I want to know what I'm doing here..."

The Cat Lady laughed, running a hand over the spine of the cat in her lap. "Dear, you and I both know what you're doing here... You're what you call, hanging upside down, no?"

"Very funny." She dropped the gown back down.

"A joke is always conducive, Dear. Here, in The Land of Thee—"

"You mean the land of tricks and games," she murmured through her gown.

"Where vines dangle from the trees, and pull you up by your dirty feet," the Cat Lady recited to her cats.

"That's a little rude, you know." She pulled the gown under her chin. "Making up rhymes about me while I hang here in front of you."

"I am making no rhymes, Dear. I am simply reciting." The Cat Lady cocked her head. "It doesn't sound familiar to you?"

"No. I don't think so..."

"Realizations take time, Dear. Revelations take time."

"Time, time... what is time?" she sighed within her best impression of the Gypsy of the Night.

"Very good question, Dear. You're catching on. See, sometimes a flip of the view is all you need. To see what you need to see. What you've been longing to see."

"I long to see my note," she spoke within another sigh.

"And here you are and yet you doubt yourself. Seeking is enough... after that you watch. You listen. You ripple with the current, Dear." The Lady motioned her hand and arm like a wave from the ocean. "Just have faith. You are in The Land of *Thee*—all will be revealed. Whatever it is that you seek is *already* being revealed to you, Dear."

"How do you know that?"

"How do I know? Oh Dear, that is how it works. Sit. Watch. Listen. All will be revealed..."

"I can't sit..."

"Yes Dear, you're right. Hang there. It will all unravel before your eyes."

"Okay... I'll wait right here. I won't go anywhere," she muttered through sarcastic teeth.

"Oh Dear, you *do* like jokes." The Cat Lady chuckled under her breath.

"I think I like anything better than hanging upside down."

"Enjoy it while it lasts, Dear—not everything remains the same. Rather, all is destined to change."

"Easy for you to say."

"Yes, it is. I do find, Dear, that when I speak, my words flow quite fluently." The woman laughed with her cats.

She watched the old woman laughing, and wondered to herself, is this something she should be enjoying? But she remembered that *should* is a blurred word. She wondered if there was something she was missing here, something she was supposed to be learning, something she wasn't seeing. She looked through her flipped view at everything around her and below her. What was she missing? She could not see past her current circumstance.

She took a hard blow to the middle of her back. Her body swung forward as the air escaped her lungs and she gasped for breath. Her eyes raced from side to side. She'd been shoved by what felt like a howling gust of wild wind... with hands.

She tried to keep her swinging body frozenly still, but that was quite a challenging feat while attempting to regain full function of her ability to properly breathe.

"Oh, Dear." The Cat Lady laughed.

"What?" she begged. "What was it?" She panicked.

"Oh nothing, Dear, nothing. The shadow's out, that's all."

She released some of the tension from her body and coughed. "My *shadow?*" Here she was, hanging upside down in the middle of that Wild place, and her shadow had the audacity to push her around. She wanted to fight back. Her arms lashed out, trying to defend herself against the ghost of darkness. She was angry. Angry at the Wild. Angry at her shadow. Angry at everything. She didn't want to be pushed around anymore.

The shadow circled around the girl's hanging body and shoved her once more.

"Stop!" she screamed at her shadow and it grabbed hold of her shoulders, settling her body back to center. She glared at her darkness, wondering why it was playing such games with her, teasing her, taunting her. Her shadow pulled on the tip of her nose. She swatted it away until it soared up to the sky, where it disappeared.

She rubbed her nose, scowling up at the sky. Charred black feathers fell from above and floated past her face. Her eyes followed as they drifted to the ground and turned to ash. What was this place trying to tell her? What was her shadow trying to reveal?

CHAPTER 20

THE BURNT CROWS

She studied the ground, where the black feathers were nothing more than ash. She knew the Wild was trying to tell her something, trying to make her see. But what did it mean?

"What do you suppose you'd do, if you weren't all caught up in these vines?" the Cat Lady asked as if she did not see the battle that had just taken place between the girl and her shadow. "You'd be chasing after the birds."

She knew the old woman was right, but she did not respond.

"You know that is true, Dear." The old woman laughed robustly as several more laugh lines appeared on her face, and remained there.

She sighed in response and pulled the gown over her legs as far as she could.

"Tell me, Dear, have you ever had to chase after light in order to find it, in order to see it?" the Cat Lady asked and answered, "No. And... this is the same for the Crows, yes?"

"What do you mean?"she asked the woman.

"You do not have to chase after the light, in order to see it..."

"But what does that have to do with the Crows?"

"Oh, Dear." The woman sympathized with the girl in a single smirk.

"At times, a creature stirs mad—chasing after all it does not understand, in order to understand it. It is only when the chasing halts, that the creature can truly see. You see, Dear?"

"So you're saying the Crows are like the light?"

"Oh, yes Dear, very much so. The Crows *are* the light, yes, as much as they are the dark… and many other things." The Cat Lady examined the girl. "Much like you, my Dear."

"What do you mean, *like me?*"

"Oh, Dear, clearly you don't have to chase down darkness to find that you have a shadow, do you?"

"Did you *not* see what just happened?"

"Yes, Dear, your shadow. It's a part of you—it follows you wherever you go. And," the woman whispered to her cats, "it often has a mind of its own." The lady laughed more.

The girl peered at the woman in the corner of her eye, wanting to know what the lady had just told her cats, knowing it pertained to her.

"You don't go chasing around your shadow, just like you don't run about in search of light, correct?" The Cat Lady continued, "And the reason you don't go searching for those things is why?" The woman paused for a brief second before answering the question. "Because even though you may not see it right before your eyes, you trust that it must be somewheres…"

The girl looked to where the trees soared into the great heights of the sky, wondering if the Crows were up there, watching her, wondering if her shadow was up there, looking down at her.

"Dear, we chase to know the unknown. To find answers to unnecessary questions—"

"Unnecessary questions?" She was offended. "I think asking what I'm doing here is a pretty good question!"

"It is not in the answers you seek that make the difference in your story—it is you. It is what you're *truly* chasing, deep down, Dear. And so, that is the question," the Cat Lady held up a cat and asked, "why does *anyone* chase after anything?"

"Why doesn't anyone *help* anyone?" She flailed like a fish caught on the line, furious that this woman had not yet helped her down.

"We chase because of joy, Dear," the lady ignored the girl's flailing inquiries. "We chase because of love. Those are the things most everyone seeks—that's all anyone has ever been chasing. Present company included, upside down or right side up."

"Really, what I'm chasing after is my *note*." As she said the words, she felt her own disbelief. Was she simply chasing after the words of her note? She knew she certainly was, but was there more she was searching for? More she was chasing after? She was chasing after herself. Searching for who she truly was. Was that all laid out in the note? She would not know until she held it in her hands once more.

"Sure you are, my Dear," the woman chuckled.

She sighed, pushing the thoughts from her mind and focusing once again on her current circumstance. "So, are you able to help me, here? I mean, clearly I've halted my chase, what with my being wrapped up in vines and all..."

"Yes, Dear, you have halted your chase. And it is when you stop chasing, that you begin to see more clearly."

"Actually all the blood is rushing to my head and my vision is getting a little fuzzy..."

"Blink a little, Dear. Just blink a little."

"Maybe I should just keep my eyes closed," she muttered under her breath.

"Why shut your eyes, Dear? Is it time for a nap? I've slept upside down more than once or twice, and I can tell you, Dear, it is a thing worth trying. I will not oppose if that's what you wish to be doing at this such time..."

"No, I don't wish to be napping." She rolled her eyes and dropped her arms.

"You close your eyes to not see what you see?"

"Exactly."

"Oh Dear, why? Everything you're seeing, like it or not, is everything you *need* to be seeing, Dear."

"How can you say that?" She glared at the woman.

"Everything happening here and now is just what you need..." The Cat Lady held up two cats and whispered to them, "if she's truly looking for what she *says* she's looking for..."

"Why would I need *this?*" She slapped her gown around and out of her face.

"Oh, Dear... it will all be revealed."

She sighed.

"Answers, Dear, they're all around you... And what's more... *You're* all around you." The old woman held out her arms and hands, showcasing the Wild for the girl. "Everything that you look upon, Dear, you are alive in. All that you seek and all that you see... is alive in you."

The Crows cawed like women roaring in the distance. She listened until she could no longer hear them, wishing she could break free and run after them.

"You and the Crows, my Dear... Would you like to hear a story?"

"I'm not doing much else," she grunted.

"Good, good. Now listen, the Crows are many things, my Dear, and many more things beyond that. They fly through words and time." The Cat Lady flocked her arms to the sides like a bird flying. "Upon their wings you can see the darkness that lurks in the night. But if you look a little deeper, you will see they are also carriers of the light."

The birds did, indeed, fly through words—the words of her note. But how were they carriers of light? She had not had the chance to look deeper and find out.

"You can find the answers to life in the shapes of feathers and on the backs of wings. Now, are you ready for the story, Dear?"

"More ready than I'll ever be..."

"Much more than many moons ago—before the moon lit the sky—wild Gypsies fell with the stars and roamed the land like wild birds. Like wild animals. The Wild was a part of them, and they were a part of the Wild..."

"Did you say before the moon lit the sky?"

"Listen Dear, listen... Days came when the wild Gypsies of the land were sought after and hunted—"

"Why?"

"The Gypsies were wild creatures—they were untamed."

"And they were hunted for that? For being wild?"

"See, a wild woman is a powerful woman, Dear... a wild woman is, well, everything. She is a connection to truth, a conductor of sorts... stirring the winds whichever way she pleases, adjusting the light to make things just right..."

She wanted to know—was *she* a conductor too?

"The wild Gypsies were hunted in the night in order to be tamed..." the Cat Lady held up one of her cats and spoke to it, "to cage their beast within... and dim their burning light."

"Why were they hunted in the night?"

"Remember Dear, the women were beautifully bright creatures and there was no moon to shine over them in those nights..."

"Where was the moon?" she asked, squinting her eyes at the moon that filled the sky.

"It had not yet been delivered. Listen Dear, listen..." The old woman waved her hand at the girl. "There was no moon, no moon in the night's sky, and so the Gypsies were hunted in the dark in order to be tamed... and do you know what they did Dear?"

"What? What did they do?"

"The wild Gypsies grew wings and they flew, Dear!"

The girl looked at the wild old woman as if she were crazy.

"They turned into birds." The lady snickered.

"Birds? How?"

"It is the Wild, Dear. The Land of Thee, always has been. And these untamed women, they were everything... conductors, Dear... remember?" The Cat Lady blew kisses into the air to some of her cats. "A wild woman who has not been tamed can do anything."

Was she one of those wild women? She needed to know. Could she do *anything?* Perhaps if she could do anything, she'd not be hanging upside down.

"The Gypsies wanted to make the hunting harder for the Tamers." The Cat Lady continued, "But see, Dear, when the Gypsies shifted from one thing to the next, they were strikingly more aglow than the thing they were before..."

"Aglow? Like the Babes and—"

"Mm. Yes, Dear... they glow, quite bright."

She studied the softly lit-up old woman.

"They became birds of white feathers that shined as bright as sunlight..."

"Why did they shine so bright?"

"You see, Dear... the Gypsies, like the sun and now the moon, had a fire burning inside. A light that could not be dimmed, a fire that could not be tamed... too bright not to shine and be seen. Like you..." the Cat lady said those last two words under a breath.

"What? Like me?" She thought back to when the Babes told her that they could see her light. How could she be aglow? If she truly were, surely she would see it.

"All things within shine forth, Dear." The Cat Lady shined a little brighter. "Their light was brilliant, especially that very first night... but that meant that the Tamers could see them even better in the darkness of the night now. So, they devised a plan..." the old woman laughed a wild roar up to the moon and continued, "One dark night, the white-winged wild women flew up to the sky, as high as a flying Gypsy could fly. To the Tamers, they looked like what the tamed would call shooting stars... shooting up..."

She thought back to the shooting stars she had seen the first night she found the Gypsy Moon.

"The Tamers watched with dim eyes... disbelief it was to them. They did not know *what* they were seeing... There it was, Dear, in the sky... The Crows lighting a fire above the wild night. They flew circles in the sky—their fire, their light, poured out from them and burned brightly amongst the stars. They created the Gypsy Moon, Dear." The Cat Lady pointed to the moon.

"They made the moon?" *Moon-makers,* she whispered in her mind.

"Just like that, Dear." The Cat Lady snapped her fingers. "They flew high into the sky and around and around in circles. Fire and light from the Gypsies poured into the darkness of the sky."

She examined the moon, thinking about the fire the Gypsies conducted on the beach.

"They flew together, fast," the woman's eyes lit up, "high above the Tamer's eyes. Round and round... and round and round..."

"Tamers..." she whispered, staring at the Gypsy Moon. It was them. She knew it. They were the wild beasts who set her up in this trap. *Tamers...* they'd come back for her. But when did they ever capture her in the first place? When did she lose her wild?

Vultures screeched in the distance. She shuddered. She was actively being hunted in someone else's game of chase. She needed to escape.

"Oh, Dear, don't you worry about those pesky dark-dwellers." The Cat Lady cawed to the Heavens. Her caw echoed through the skies, rippling across the stars and sending the sounds of the Vultures into silence. "Needn't worry about that for now."

She felt a small weight of relief rise from her hanging body. Perhaps the crazy Cat Lady was helping after all, in her own wild way.

"You've many more other things to mind, anyhow." The woman chuckled. "Now, back to the story... The Tamers watched the birds of light bring to life that hot, glowing bulb that you look upon in the sky. It was that night, Dear. That was the night that the Gypsy Moon came to life."

"What happened next?" She was eager to learn more, about this wild place and the Gypsy Moon. Perhaps it was the distraction of the story, or perhaps it was that she was beginning to flip her view, but she had forgotten she was hanging upside down in those moments. She only felt free, as if she were floating. Perhaps what she was learning, was vital to her growing.

"The wild women were not done. They knew they had the Tamer's gaze. They spun their web, they cast their spell, they played with fire in the sky. But then... their cosmic creation had became so hot that their brilliant white feathers caught flame from their fire in the sky. Their feathers burned to a crisp... they turned pitch black." The woman picked up a black cat, "Isn't that right?"

She thought about the feathers that fell from the sky and turned to ash. She looked to the ground at the feather's ashes and she looked to the Gypsy Moon. She asked the Cat Lady, "If that's how the moon was made, why isn't that how it *always* looks *everywhere* in the sky? Like the place I came from—" she corrected herself, "the place I escaped before... *returning* here..." The word slipped from her lips without a single thought.

"Listen here, sweet Dear... the moon was born as it is, the Gypsy Moon. Born from the fire and light of the Gypsies. It burns bright like this always and forevers, everywheres. Though, if you have been Tamed..."

"What? If I have been tamed, then what?" She knew she had been Tamed, but she did not know what that meant for her or how it fully effected her. For how could she know what was wrong with her *now*, if she couldn't remember what was right with her *before?*

"It is simply a matter of when you choose to see it through clear eyes... when you choose to see it for what it really is."

"How do you *choose* to see it that way?"

"Perhaps, Dear, it's when you feel your fire burning inside, your light switch itself back on..."

"What happens when you see the moon, the Gypsy Moon, through clear eyes?"

"You tell me, Dear... you tell me..."

"Oh..." She looked to the moon, and back to the lady. "So, what happened after they made the moon?"

"Yes, Dear... their bright feathers turned to black, matching the dark of the night. This made it much harder for the Tamers to track and tame them." The old woman nodded her head in approval.

"What happened to the Tamers?"

"Oh Dear. The Tamers and their dim eyes... upon seeing such wild sights with their foggy eyes, some of those Tamers lost their sight. POOF! Disappeared due to their own fear. And, of course, they *all* lost their marbles."

The marbles. Like on the path. Like from the stories... But was that a good thing?—To lose one's marbles...

"That night marbles fell from the skies and from the Tamer's minds."

"Are those some of the marbles down there?" She looked and pointed to the marble cloaked path.

"Oh," the old woman laughed, "yes, Dear."

"How do *marbles* fall from the sky and people's minds?" She couldn't help but think that perhaps this was another sort of riddle.

"You see, Dear, the stars up there," the Cat Lady waved her arms up to the sky, "they want nothing more than to see all of us creatures shine. So when the time is right, they pluck pieces of themselves from the sky and send them down here, to the creature in most need of fresh thought and eternal memory."

"Fresh thought and eternal memory?" That is just what she needed. She needed to remember. Perhaps she needed marbles from the skies. But would she need to lose her own? She wondered who put the marbles in her mind that she'd been juggling all this time. "How do I get marbles from the skies? And... how do I get *these ones* out of my mind?" She shook her head, slightly surprised when didn't hear any marble cries.

"Oh, Dear," the woman howled with laughter, "you need to cry!"

"Cry?" She was certain she had done enough of that already.

"When tears pour out from a Tamed one's eyes and blend with the Wild or drip from the skies, then, Dear—those tears harden into marbles... the kind you've been kicking around all over this path right heres." The Cat Lady sniffed at the marble-laced path and her cats. "Those marbles, when they fall from your mind, they will be no more—they won't be yours to keep anymore."

What would it be like, once her mind was free from the marbles that had bogged it down for far too long?

"And those ones from the skies, Dear, you'll find those at just the right times." The old woman squished her face into the belly of a cat in her arms and placed it in her lap and continued, "When the stars see that you are ready, they will send you fresh thought, fresh light, and all of your eternal memories...

"Memories across space and life..." she reminded herself of what the Gypsy had told her. "The memory of what never dies."

"Mm, yes, Dear, that's right. The stars drip their pieces of infinite wisdom through the skies and down to the Wild, where they harden into glinting marbles, and hide—waiting to be found at just the right time." The woman laughed until the tree she sat upon looked as if it were smiling too. "Pieces of the stars, my Dear, sent down as gifts of celebration for the wild creatures, and the Gypsies, and the beasts... and for the Tamers, whose marbles were lost, but those down there," the lady nodded to the path, "they can keep."

"Why a gift for the Tamers?"

"They just needed new marbles, Dear... fresh thoughts from the skies to fill their minds."

"Did they use their new marbles?"

"Oh, no, Dear, no... remember, they'd gone blind. It is much too hard to find your new marbles when you've scared your own sight away and insist on living in the fear of your own mind."

What if the same was true for her? Would she become too blind, too scared to find her marbles from the skies?

"Now, just remember, Dear, if ever you see marbles falling from the sky, you'll know somewheres some Tamers or a Tamed one, also lost the marbles in their minds."

"What happens if a Tamer's Tamed one loses her marbles?" She could not bare the thought of never getting her new marbles. She was certain now, she had to lose her marbles. Perhaps that was how she would get her wild back.

"Then no longer is she tamed, Dear…"

She wondered if she'd lost any of her marbles since being there. "What about the Gypsies who made the moon? Did they make it back down to the Wild?"

"Oh…" The Cat Lady paused and pursed her lips, as if to hoard words she was not ready to recite. "Most of them, Dear, most of them."

"Most of them?"

"Most of them flew back down to the Wild together, yes. Though, there was one who stayed in the sky until the moon was complete, as bright as bright can be. A true moon-maker, that one—she stayed until the belly of the moon was all done."

"What happened to her?"

"She fell from the sky after pouring all her light into it, and…"

The murder of Crows flew overhead, softly singing their song, interrupting the Cat Lady.

"I will tell you what happened to the rest of the Crows, Dear—the Gypsies, rather. They flew back to their wild land to be free in the night under the new light of their Gypsy Moon, where the fire of the wild creature burns brighter than any light at all."

"But I still don't understand… if the light burns so bright in the moon, why can't other people see it and this wild place all the time? Surely *someone* would be able to…"

"One can only get to The Land of Thee, Dear, when she listens to the calling of her inner beast, feels the fire in her belly and her light switch on… only then does the veil lift between worlds…"

"So, are the Gypsies I met—" Were they the Crows? Did they have her note? Is that why they left her alone in the jungle? She thought back to her time with the Babes. She remembered how strange it was when she saw the Crows in their glen, mixing and mingling and disappearing within them. They were all connected. They were the same.

They had her note.

"You'll understand soon enough, Dear. Revelations take time. But that's just it." The woman laughed within a laughter that she was already laughing. "That's just what you're doing here."

"*What's* just what I'm doing here?"

"Unraveling, Dear, you're unraveling."

"No..." She shuffled her hands in her dress, remembering once more that she was still hanging upside down. The blood still boiling her brain. "I'm pretty sure I'm still hanging."

"You're becoming, Dear. Your beast is breaking free, your fire being stoked, your light shining brighter." The lady opened her arms up to the sky.

"Are you sure I'm not being trapped... perhaps by Tamers...?" Perhaps by Vultures? Perhaps they were working together? She was not sure what to think anymore.

"Oh, no, no, Dear, that has already happened for you. This is quite the opposite."

"*This* is the opposite?" How could this be the opposite? She *was* trapped. Whatever had *already happened for her* was clearly not over yet.

"Yes, yes, Dear, this is the opposite of that, Dear."

"I want to believe you, but how can I? I'm tied up by vines and hanging upside down well above the ground."

"This is a part of the unraveling, Dear. You cannot unravel without first becoming raveled, can you?"

She did not respond, as she did not want to admit that perhaps the Cat Lady was right.

"See, Dear, sometimes you need to get lost in the dark in order to see the light. You'll get to where you're going, Dear... you mustn't worry... You've gotten this far, haven't you?"

"I've gotten this far... and now I'm hanging upside down."

"Yes Dear, you are hanging. You are here. You perhaps are too distracted to hear everything clearly. But you will. You see, my Dear, everything always gets better from here," the Cat Lady spoke through more laughter.

"Are you certain of that?"

"Oh, of course, Dear, without a doubt. You, Dear, are here for a reason." The woman pulled a cat from the top of her head and placed it in her lap amongst the others. "And you are eternally in cahoots with the greatest conductor of all..." the old woman laughed again, "don't you know?"

A loud rustling came from the other side of the woods. She looked to the trees and saw them shoving around in the distance.

"You don't need to chase any longer, Dear..." the Cat Lady told her, "just watch as it unfolds. You're in a wild place now. You are here—breaking free in The Land of Thee... the Wild will take care of everything..."

She looked toward the Cat Lady, but the woman and all of her cats were gone. She rolled her eyes—she was not surprised.

"The Wild will take care of everything... hmph." She spoke through the grinding of her teeth, "I won't hold my breath for that." She wiggled her legs and punched the air and released a roar of anger. The rustling in the trees roared back at her, and grew closer from the thick of the wild forest.

Chapter 21

THE COLOSSAL OCELOT

The rustling in the trees pushed her heart past its limits and into her throat, mingling up with the many mixings of her mind. She swayed, not softly or swiftly from the vines—but frantically back and forth, forth and back—trying to wiggle her way from their tight hold. Still, the harder she tried, the tighter their grip became, her fingers and hands shaking as she pulled at the vines. She tugged, trembling and sweating, looking over her dewy shoulders with a wrinkled brow and panicked breath.

The noise in the wood grew louder—she knew by the sound that whatever it was, it was going to be large. Larger than the Giant Coyote. The Coyote was really quite large. She shuddered. What was creeping up on her in those wild woods, what could be larger than a Giant Coyote in this wild place? A lot of things, she thought, and she didn't like what her mingled up mind was coming up with.

"Tamers..." she told herself, certain she'd been found. How could they tame a girl they've already tamed, she wondered, looking down to the path, and up to the sky, and everywhere in between. They'd caught her. She knew she'd have to fight, however she could. She watched and waited with shallow breath and piercing thoughts, but nothing happened.

She gave up on tugging at the vines. She let go. She let her body hang, her arms dangling. She felt the blood rush back to her head. She felt the release of strain rise from her pendulous arms. She wanted to wake up from this nightmare. She let her gown dangle over her face, and she closed her eyes. She tried to take in several deep breaths, but she could only feel tightness taking over her chest. She sighed. The Owl's voice popped into her head.

"Are you winning?" she asked herself in a shaky whisper and she started to sing, "Don't you get glum, when you're missing the sun..." in a trembling, hushed voice, in the hopes of attracting the Owl to come and save her.

Halfway through the verse, the Owl swooped past the hanging girl's body, spinning her around. The bird perched itself on top of the vines that held the girl and shook its feathers. Looking down at her with its large, glowing eyes, the Owl said, "Oh, Darling, I *do so* love that song."

Although she was twisted upon the arrival of the Owl, she felt her fears releasing as she spun. When the vines slowed and brought her back to a soft sway, she lifted her gown from her face and looked up at the Owl.

"I knew you'd come!" *Help please,* she thought.

"Of course, Darling. I said I would. But... I am sorry."

"Sorry?" Her eyes watered.

"Oh, Darling, I cannot stay."

"Can't stay?" She choked on her words, swallowing the tears.

"I assume you were calling for help..."

"I am! Please! Please... please save me!"

"I cannot."

"You cannot? *Why?*" It had to be a joke. It had to be.

"I can *not,*" the Owl clarified.

"You can *not? But—but—*"

"Sorry, Darling, not this time."

"Not... this... time...?" It couldn't be so.

"I do love your song, so I will listen from a distance, if you don't mind. I wouldn't want to keep you from your travels."

"Keep me from my travels?" She was desperate. She didn't want to go back to the world of the Tamers. She wanted to stay. She wanted to stay in the Land of Thee, in the Wild. She knew that now, more than ever. "Oh, please! *Please* don't go!" she begged as tears blurred her vision.

"Oh, Darling, we all have places to go. Including you, you know. But don't worry, I won't be far," the Owl reminded her. "I can still hear your lovely song wherever I go."

"But—but what if I'm not winning?" she asked in an attempt to stall the Owl from leaving her. But she truly wanted to know—what if she was not winning?

"What makes you think you're not?"

"Hi, *I'm upside down...*" she could not understand why the creatures in that wild place overlooked such a wild circumstance, and why none of them wanted to help her. "I'm being *hunted!*" She darted her eyes to the rumbling trees. "There is something in the woods and it's getting closer..."

"Oh, yes, there certainly is!" the Owl validated. "Darling, you do not play a game with the intention to *lose,* now, do you?"

"No..." she roared at the bird, keeping her eyes on the trees.

"You play a game with all intentions of winning! Now don't you?"

"This doesn't feel like winning right now..." she whispered to the Owl, stifling her breath.

"Yes, Darling, perhaps to you it does not," the Owl said. "But when we first met, you were right-side-up, with your feet on the ground, and as far as you knew there was nothing large and loud in the woods, and yet you still were unsure whether or not you were winning. Perhaps you needed to get flipped around to see what winning looks like."

"But how could I possibly be winning when I'm... I'm hanging upside down as someone—or *something's* prey?" Clearly she was being hunted, and the hunter was winning. But who was hunting her? Had the Tamers been following her this whole time? Or perhaps it was the Vultures?

"Winning is up to you, Darling, not what *is...*"

"But I'm *stuck* here..."

"Darling, you are never stuck anywhere... unless, of course, you want to be. The constant is always change." The Owl ruffled its feathers. "And everywhere always leads to somewhere new."

She *did not* want to be stuck in that situation she was in. But she was, she was stuck. Where could this possibly lead to?

"You are not hanging upside down forever, only for right now... Until you've learned what you need to learn." The Owl leaned its body down closer toward her. "Sometimes, Darling, we spin ourselves around too fast to solve the riddles of the Wild. Just relax. All will be revealed. Revelations take time. And remember please, do sing your song for me."

And with those last words, the Owl flew off beyond the tall trees to where she could no longer see its white feathers or large wingspan. She kept her gown lifted from her face for another moment or two, studying her surroundings—the tall land of ancient trees, the daunting sounds coming from within them. She dropped her gown back down, and her arms dangled alongside her ears. She felt helpless.

Unsure of who it was that she was sharing her company with, but certain it was no one good, she dangled and swayed as the large whispering movements of the Wild grew closer. Hiding inside her gown, like a child under the covers—she did not want to see what she knew she was hearing. Whatever it was that was making all of that noise, was surely onto her now.

She heard it make its way out from the trees. She tucked her arms under her gown, where her face was still hidden. She stopped breathing for half a moment and listened to the sounds around her, but the sound of her anxious beating heart was the loudest thing she could hear. After a moment or two had passed, whatever moment a moment was, she softened only slightly, as the wicked sounds had ceased. The rustling of the woods had stopped.

Perhaps whatever it was—it was only passing by, she thought. She took a few deep breaths and swallowed. She felt a small wave of relief wash over her. Her body cooled and softened, her heartbeat slowed and became quiet. She lifted the gown from over her eyes with a comfortable level of caution.

But that small wave of relief was shaken away as her gown unveiled what was now standing on the path before her. Her eyes swelled with fear and more tears. Her spine and body tightened as she froze in shock from what she was seeing. She squeezed her sight shut, but it made no difference. When she looked again, it was still there—a cat as tall as the trees of the previous paths stood in the middle of that new path, staring at her dangling body.

The feline looked ready to attack the way a cat attacks its prey. This was no ordinary cat. A cat as tall as some of the tallest trees is no ordinary cat. It was an ocelot... a Colossal Ocelot. The cat stared at her and did not blink with his mesmerizing amber eyes glowing like the fire in the Gypsy Moon.

She did not break her stare with the cat even though she wanted to look away and hide herself. She continued to isolate her lungs, trying not to breathe. She stayed as still as her hanging body would allow—thinking that if she did not move a muscle, perhaps the cat would not attack her.

His stare gleamed deep into her. She became almost hypnotized by him in a sense. She was fascinated by the beautiful and intricate markings of his gigantic body—but she was petrified by his presence and his size. His whiskers stretched out almost as long as some of the smaller branches—brushing across her body with each swift shift of his snout. He was the most intriguing beast she'd ever seen. And the largest beast. And the most terrifying beast. Had he been sent by the Tamers? Was *he* a Tamer?

She dangled there before him as he licked his chops without a single twitch of his eye. He took slow and stealthy steps closer toward her—his amber and creamy cold coat shining in the moonlight of the day. His monstrous and surly body made swift movements in front of her—he took calculated and graceful steps like a wild cat would. She recoiled like a wild cat's prey would. He stopped, licked his chops again, and took two or three small steps closer. She felt an urge to scream or be sick, but she kept everything in. Perhaps she released only a tiny peep.

He circled around her upside-down dangling body, stalking her like she was a tiny mouse, like she was his catch of the day. That's what she felt like. Trying to be as motionless as she could possibly be—hanging in front of him like a fresh slab of meat—she was more than scared, she was more than terrified. Her spine was stiff—her jaw was stiff—yet she was still shaking to her core. Dripping with fear-filled sweat, her breath was short, face red, head hot.

Her hands and fingers trembled as she tried locking them into tight clasps or fists in an attempt to remain stone-cold-still. Her eyes followed as the Ocelot circled and sniffed. The patchwork entanglement of spots and stripes ran down his body—thick, black lines stretched from the corners of his eyes down to his tail. Each time he walked past her up-side-down eyes, her face tightened a little more and her spine quivered. Who was this beast? What did he want?

He paused in his orbit on his seventy-seventh cycle and came back around to her stare. He slithered down closer to the ground—ready to pounce. She could hear and feel the throbbing pulse of her head and her heart, which continued to pound faster and louder. She tried not to look at the giant cat, but she couldn't help it. You see, a wild giant feline really is something to be seen.

The cat batted his extra-large paws toward her. His paws were perhaps double the size of her upside-down body. She scrunched up her face and closed her eyes and wrapped her arms around herself. But, at first, the cat just barely touched her. You see, when a wild cat has caught his catch, he likes to have a little fun first.

He teased her several times with his reaching paws—barely touching her every time. Each time he reached, her heart jumped into her throat a bit more than the last. After some time of teasing—and without any claws and only paws—the Colossal Ocelot batted her body with his more-than-body-sized paws, and she swung to the right like a pendulum. She knew this was coming, and yet she still could not prepare for it. She bent her knees, rolled up her spine, wrapped her arms around her legs, and tucked her head into her body like a ball—or a hedgehog—or a ball of yarn, depending upon perception.

This cat was only just getting started. He batted her around with both paws. She swung back and forth, side to side, and all of the off-kilter butterflies within her were flipped around and upside-down and having trouble keeping up. He was not going to stop any time soon, she could tell. Every time she peeked she saw his entertainment thriving and his momentum picking up, and her dread and fear elevated into her throat. He was having too much fun. He played with her like she was a cat toy being offered by the Heavens.

He swung her faster and harder each time. He tossed her from paw to paw, keeping his large cat-eyes upon her at all times. There were times he'd take a break and let her slow down—she'd think it was all over—but as soon as she'd release the slightest tension—he'd bat at her balled up body again. He had captured, stalked, and was now about to taunt her endlessly—playfully—and joyfully like a cat does when it wins the hunt and catches the prey. She had just made this cat's day.

She grabbed her chest to stop her heart from escaping, and then her stomach, and then her mouth. She could not think straight, her mind was frazzled from fright, her body being batted and spun back and forth and all around and upside down, but she did not cry. She thought that perhaps it was impossible to cry at a time like this. Perhaps the fright of the cat froze the tears within her from ever escaping.

He kept himself entertained for several hours. But what were hours at a wild time such as this? Was there any such time at a wild time like this?

The colors of the sky shifted into the day's end. She shifted into the deeper depths of feeling dizzy and sick. This, of course, is to be expected when you're the object of a Colossal Ocelot's attention. She couldn't handle it any longer. She was desperate for a way out of the grip of the vines and the reach of the cat.

"Oh, please stop!" she shouted out of an uncomfortable impulse. But she quickly realized that she had nothing to lose, so perhaps speaking up would not make a difference in her fate, at this point.

"Stop? Why would I stop? I'm having such fun..." the Ocelot told her.

"I'm becoming so dizzy... I'll get sick..." She placed her hand over her mouth.

The cat stopped batting his paws at her, and sat down. He licked the bottom of one paw leisurely. "Ah, yes. Well, now, we wouldn't want that, would we?"

She swung from side to side in front of his face, wondering what kind of game he was playing. "No... we wouldn't..." Who was this creature playing with her, she wanted to know, and yet she didn't want to know in the least.

"Then we'll take a break." The cat licked his other paw.

She wasn't sure what to think, as she spun around and swung from one side to the other. That's it? That's all she had to do? She wasn't sure if the cat was being deceptive, still playing tricks. But perhaps it didn't matter *what* she thought of the situation, as the situation was that she was hanging upside down at the dismay of the largest beast. He licked his shoulder.

"So, tell me about yourself then, my tasty treat," he teased her.

She didn't say anything. She was unsure how to tell a terrifying beast about herself while she hung in front of him after he batted her around for an entire afternoon.

"Go on, tell me," he insisted.

"*Tell you about myself?*" Of all the things he wanted to poke at her about, this was it? "Are you kidding me right now?"

The cat continued to clean himself, paying no mind to her and her fit she was trying to throw—which only added to her angst.

"*Hello?*" she yelled at the cat.

"Hello."

"You just spent the afternoon tossing me around like I'm some sort of—Like I'm..."

"Like you're some sort of wild creature here," the cat interrupted while she pondered on her words, "in this wild place, wearing the suit of a girl. You wear it well... I suppose."

"Thank you...?" The suit of a girl? What was that supposed to mean? More riddles in this wild place?

"No need to thank me," the Ocelot told her. "I am like you. I am in this wild place, too. But I wear the suit of a cat. I wear it well, yes?"

"Yes..." her swinging body was slowing down, but she wanted to get away fast.

"Yes, I do. And like I said, as do you." The cat purred. "We are the same—you and I. Wild animals, we are."

"So I'm an animal now?" She would not let herself be amused.

"A tiny little rodent of a thing, you are." The Ocelot snickered.

"I am *not* a rodent!"

"Well, you may be a squirmishly small little thing, but we aren't very different—you and I."

"Oh? Are you also swinging upside down from the vines too, or is that just me?" She crossed her arms over her chest, trapping her gown to her body.

"I am not swinging. But indeed, I took part in making the swinging be swung." The Ocelot nodded his head. "We are different, though the same. We are both creatures, wild in nature. Much like everything else."

"I am not a wild creature!" If this is what it meant to be a wild creature, then she no longer wanted it. She changed her mind, feeling betrayed by the concept. "I am a girl who was spit out into this wild place to be tricked and attacked by beasts like you!"

"Oh, in fact it is quite different." The Ocelot could not contain his laughter. "You are a girl, *thriving* in this wild place."

"Perhaps I am a girl who doesn't *belong* in this wild place..." She allowed her discouraging frustrations to cloud her mind. She could not see past the fog of defeat and fear.

"Oh, in fact you do. You very much do. *You* are a creature of the Wild," the Ocelot reminded her. "You are here, aren't you?"

"I am *here*, getting tortured by a giant cat!" she reminded him.

"Ah, yes, shall we throw your pity party now, or later?"

"My *pity* party?! My *pity* party?! You have me *hanging* upside down!"

"And if you have a point to your muttering here, please get to it, you bitter little snack."

"My *point*? My point is we are *clearly* not the same—you and I. You are a big, terrifying, *rude* beast, and I... I am—"

"*You* are what? You are just like me. Different, but the same. "We were sent from the same place, perfectly crafted and created from the same spark, the same light. *We are the same*." The Ocelot lifted his snout to the breeze. "We are different in many ways... but in so very many more, *we are the same*."

He *was* sent by the Tamers, she thought.

"The only true difference between you—little rodent—and I, is that *I* have not forgotten who I am. *You*, however... *you* have been tamed."

"Who are you...?" Fear and skepticism laced her voice. "How do you—"

"Whether you agree or disagree holds absolutely no value to me." The Ocelot rolled his fiery eyes. "Although, we both know you know you've been tamed," he snickered. "The fact of the matter is, a creature whose wild has been tamed, one who has forgotten, that is, like you—little rodent treat—will continue to find herself caught up in contraptions such as this."

"Yeah, thanks to *you*!"

"Indeed, very much thanks to me," the Ocelot agreed. "About time you start showing some gratitude. You're welcome."

"I was being sarcastic!" Her head was throbbing, veins bulging in her temples.

"Rude. You'll thank me soon enough."

"Why would I ever do that?!"

"Because. You didn't let me finish."

"Excuse me? Well then...?" She gestured her hand sarcastically. "Finish."

"You, tasty treat, are being quite feisty."

"I am hanging upside—" She sighed, shaking her head. "Please, just go on..."

"A wild creature, one who has been tamed, will always find a way to slip back into her natural wild ways..." The Cat purred louder. "And *that* is a part in which you could say I take part in playing. You're welcome."

"What does that mean? You're trying to stop me from becoming wild again, aren't you? You're trying to bring me back to them?" Perhaps she did want to be wild after all. Perhaps her mind was all mixed up and being torn in all different directions.

"We are taking each other to places we need to get to, you and I, I... and you."

"We are not taking each other anywhere!" she screamed at him.

"Ah... yes, but we are, you see... the constant constant is constantly change," he reminded her.

"I'm not going anywhere with you!"

"Oh, I am certain, though, you certainly will." The cat rubbed his right paw over his ear.

"No!" she yelled. "No I won't!"

"You will. It is so. And... so it is."

"It is *no!* And... so it *isn't!*" she argued.

"You'll see, treat. I did not expect that you'd have had this all figured out by now. Had you, you certainly would've played a much better game."

Are you winning?

The Owl's voice echoed in her head. What was the meaning of all of these nonsensical games, games, games? The endless riddles. The tricks. She was growing exhausted of the tricky ways of the Wild. Perhaps because she was still hanging upside down. Perhaps because a Colossal Ocelot was incessantly teasing her. Or perhaps one must grow exhausted of her circumstances, before breaking free from them.

The cat yawned and flashed his ginormous teeth. "Whether it is ever realized or not—we, us, you, I, we are all walking each other along the same paths... different, though the same. We—us, you, I—assist in walking each other to the other's destination, commonly without one's own comprehension. Like it or not, it just is so—so let it be."

"*What path?* You've just been batting me around while I hang up-side-down in your trap—in this—this... wild place!"

The cat reached out to bat at her again, just barely touching his captured creature. "Sweet little Birdie, don't you worry about such transitory circumstances."

"I'm not a sweet little birdie. I'm a *girl*!"

"Perhaps to *you*, you are a girl. Perhaps to *me*, you are a sweet little birdie. You call a bird a bird because it flies. Perhaps, then, you are a bat."

"A bat?"

"Hanging there... upside down. Look at you, a tired little bat, collecting shut eye before your wildest travel."

"You're not taking me anywhere!" Even though this place might be crazy, she wasn't going back to the world of the Tamers.

"Or perhaps you are a sloth. Just dangling there, not doing anything at all, a bit lazy..." the Ocelot teased.

"I am no such thing!"

"What *you* are is what *you* see and what *you* see is different to *me*... sweet, little, Birdie."

"Then what are *you*? Are you *not* a monstrous cat?" She tossed his mind-numbing theories back at him.

"I am everything, looking through the brilliant eyes of a majestic, breathtakingly beautiful cat—a *monstrous* cat—according to *you*," the cat huffed. "*You* are also *everything*, looking through the eyes of a... girl," he licked his other shoulder blade and muttered, "or the eyes of a... birdie," and he laughed to himself, "a bat... sloth..." and he laughed a little more.

"I am not a *bird*, a *bat*, or whatever else you say... I am a *hostage!*" she roared. "And this is just nonsense so that you can distract me and eat me alive when I least expect it, or capture me and take me back to that place!"

"Oh my, you birdies and your chip-chip-chirping. You are humorous to me, Birdie." He batted at her again, just out of reach.

"Oh, I am *so glad* you find my discomfort and fear to be humorous," she growled. "And why does everyone around here keep calling me a different name?"

"Little Bat-Bird... perhaps it is because you mean something different to each of those everyones. Each different everyone sees *you* differently." The cat squinted his eyes at her. "For no one can see someone in the same exact light that another someone perceives—we all see things from a different footing within the same light. Therefore, you have been given a suitable name by each of your everyones."

"Will you please just let me down from here, already?" She was far too focused on her current dilemma to pay any mind to the lessons of a large cat.

"Oh, indeed, indeed, I will let you down. All you had to do was ask."

"Aah! You are maddening!" She yanked on her hair.

"Ah, yes, for some, the act of breaking free and losing their marbles can feel quite maddening at times. Ah, but, of course, you'll be just fine, rodent, just fine."

"Losing marbles—" Was she about to lose her marbles? "Please, just let me go. And let me get far, far away from you..."

"I shall, certainly," the Ocelot assured. "You will find yourself far enough to call far, to observe how you feel where you are, when you get there. When you find yourself as far as far can be, then you will see for yourself, Treat." The Ocelot roared with laughter.

"See what for myself?" Was he really going to set her free? Or was this a trick?

"That I am like you, and you are like me."

"Oh, you're still trying to convince me of this?" She smacked her forehead and rolled her eyes.

"I will let you go, as you wish, and you will see."

"So, you'll let me down now?" Please let it be true, she prayed. "You'll let me down and you won't eat me alive?"

"I will let you down, Birdie."

"And you won't eat me, chase me, hunt me, stalk me or kill me?" She bounced her eyes around, looking to the path, the trees, any clearings in the woods—planning her quick get away once he dropped her down.

"I will release you, Birdie. You can see for yourself what is."

"I'm not sure what you mean, but I really would love it if you'd let me down..."

All she wanted was to get down from there, and she wanted so badly to believe that he was being honest with her. Her ankles hurt, and the blood remained at a rapid boil in her head. She was thirsty and hungry and unsure if she could trust this gargantuan cat, but she didn't have any other offers on the table.

"You would like that, would you?" he asked.

"Yes! Please let me down!" she begged.

"See Birdie, I will let you go, but depending upon perception, I may be letting you up, rather than down. But, ah, it is relatively all the same."

"What? What does *that* mean?!"

Before she received an answer to her question, the Colossal Ocelot lifted his larger-than-life-sized paw and batted her so hard that she spun all the way up toward the sky and her legs slid out from the tight grip of the vines. She was free. But she was swatted so swiftly that she flew high up through the night's sky. She was free—and she was flying. The Colossal Ocelot batted her straight up into the Heavens and far, far away, just like she'd asked.

She realized that she was not stopping the momentum of his heavy hit anytime soon. She looked down at the tops of the tallest trees, and down at the colossal cat that looked up at her, laughing. Everything she was just hanging upside down in was getting further and further away...

She was beginning to think she'd never come back down.

CHAPTER 22

THE SEA OF COSMOS

She flew through the skies, feeling the effects of a stomach full of butterflies—butterflies that were unsure whether they were flying up or falling down. Either way, she was quickly growing further away from the tops of the trees and the colossal cat of that wild, wild place, and wondering where she was going, and when she would land. Everything down below was becoming smaller to her starry eyes with every passing second she flew through the starry skies.

Spinning through the dark and brilliant colors, through the floating stardust and the falling stars—she fell up far and flew up fast. She was on her way to where so many of the stars lived—the stars that you've never dreamed of. Or perhaps she was falling up to where all of the stars of your dreams reside.

Through her celestial spinning, she could still see the land and the treetops and the waters of the wild place under her. She could just barely see the Ocelot within the darkness of the faraway trees. The colossal cat looked as small as a bright distant star in the sky. He and his glowing eyes were a small flame glistening in the darkness of what she once knew. She saw him as she spun. She saw that he was, like he had told her—just like the stars. Glowing down there—he was the same as the stars. He was the same as the stars and the stardust that she spun through and up and within.

She realized that everything the cat was saying was real, not a riddle. Everything he was saying was the truth. He was helping her get where she was going. But... where was she going?

She was flying faster—further—and now that wild place was so far away that it too, was the same as the stars. Everything was a distant world, or millions of words away now. Everything that she was so immensely immersed in—everything that was just right in front of her—everything that seemed so important—was now moons of miles away and out of reach, nearly out of sight. Everything that she was so tangled and wrapped up in—everything that she thought was happening—was no longer. Not important anymore. Not happening anymore. Not real anymore.

The only thing that was real now was that she was falling up through the milky sky and spinning through the sparkling cosmos. Nothing else existed. Nothing else mattered. All that surrounded her was all that there was now. And all that there was, was all that she saw and felt.

She spun through the thickest veils of sparkling dusty haze. She soared through dripping hues and layers of lights. She fell up through fluorescent clusters. She fell up through celestial light. She fell up through cosmic darkness. She ascended through empyrean heights. She grew closer toward the bright, fiery Gypsy Moon.

Just as she was about to finally reach the hot moon, she lost the momentum that had her riding straight to the Heavens...

For a brief moment, she was suspended in time—*time, time what is time*—and she reached out a hand, her fingertips almost brushing against the moon.

Her direction shifted.

She began to fall. Quickly. Swiftly.

She watched the distance grow between her and the moon. She began to fall faster, her arms flailing through the winds, her gown flying up to her face. She descended through the skies—through the dark—through the light—through the clusters—through the layers.

Her heart tried to keep up with her fall through the stars, but it rushed into her throat. The butterflies flew to the void left by her leaping heart. Her bones, her blood, everything within her body trembled at the unknown she had been tossed into. Where would she land?

The further she flew through the darkness of the night, the more she realized that she was free from the grips of fearing Tamers or Vultures or suspicious Giant beasts. She was free from everything. Free falling in the arms of the stars. She released all fear that had once clutched her, and hoped that her ride through the color and starlight of the skies would never end. She was back to enjoying the not understanding of such things she didn't quite understand, in a new way.

Perhaps all she ever needed was a push into the sky in order to remember such things. After all, that was the objective, and it was really quite exciting in this way, was it not?

She whipped through the sky. Falling, falling, falling. Stars rushed past her and blurred. Down, down, down. She had surrendered to her free fall, eyes wide open—witnessing the entirety of her downward journey through the stars and the colors and the nearly blinding moonlight.

No fear.

Not now. Not this time.

Time, time—what is...

Splash. Her body slapped hard against water, plunging down into the depths of it. She spun through whichever sort of sea this was, plummeting faster and deeper. That's the thing about momentum—once the wheel is spinning, quickly that way it will go.

Bubbles of glitter churned all around her, her hair and gown swam in front of her face and eyes. Her arms and legs flipped and flailed around with the rest of her body, which created the production of the multiplication of more bubbles all around her. Just when her lungs had almost had enough, she lost her downward momentum and halted her descent. She spun her body back around, and propelled back up toward the sparkling surface and the brighter lights.

She emerged from the water gasping for air. She devoured the sweet air of the starlit sky and slowly began to catch her breath—breath by breath. She slicked her hair back, and wiped her hands over her face and eyes. *I'm back,* she thought, *I made it.* As she pulled her hands away from her face and opened her eyes, she saw that her hands and wrists were drenched in the sparkling luster of the dust of the stars.

She looked down at the water and realized that she had not fallen into a river or ocean in the Land of Thee—she had not fallen far at all. She was still above all the rivers and oceans—she was still above the land—still floating within the sky—immersed in a milky galaxy of diamonds, soaking within the stars. She was still in the cosmos—now swept up and swimming in it, floating within the vastness of the pool of mystery and creation.

She was silent only briefly, looking around at the wonder and the beauty that surrounded her. Her cheeks lifted, her eyes widened, the corners of her lips curled into the corners of her eyes. A buzzing current of electricity streamed through her body, from her sparkling head above the sea to her twinkling toes below. And in that beat, laughter roared out from her belly and her bones.

She knew this place… this place felt like home. She'd found herself in the very foundation of all things, the heart of everything—which she could feel residing inside of her.

She whipped around and threw her head back, cupping her hands around her mouth.

"YEE, YEE, YEEW!"

The Wild call of the Babes. The call of wild women. Of the fire inside of her.

Bathing in the sparkling lights, glowing and glistening as far as her eyes could see, like the dinoflagellates of infinity—she was saturated in the glitter of this radiant water, soaking in the iridescent sea of silver and gold, diamond blues, and fiery pinks.

She steeped in the light of the Gypsy Moon that rested just above her head—just out of her reach—heating her like a hot, blazing sun.

She was still in the cosmos—now swept up and swimming in it, floating within the vastness of the pool of mystery and creation.

She lifted her chin from the warm, sparkling pool and tilted her head toward the hot, tangerine moon that scorched aglow as if it contained the fire and light of the purest souls.

She squinted her starry eyes as her smile grew larger, and she opened her arms to the Gypsy Moon—like a bird basking in the sun. Glinty glowing stardust dripped from her elbows and chin as she saluted the strange light of the sky.

The electricity that pulsed within her amplified with each new beat in her heart. The ripples in the luminous sea rippled through her body—up through her heart, her veins, out through the top of her head, and into the pool of stars and the Gypsy Moon. She watched the ripples flow through everything surrounding her, and everything that surrounded her was indeed *everything*.

"I'm glad I found you that night in the dunes..." she whispered to the moon, lowering her arms back under the water. "Or maybe you found me..." She gazed upon its glow—stretching atop the luminous sea straight to her. She cupped the sparkles into her hands like the bubbles of a bubble bath, watching the glitter pour through her fingers and drip back into the infinite sea of diamonds. "Or perhaps we found each other..."

She took in all of her new surroundings—which were endless—infinite—and ever-moving. Colors swam around her, blending into one another. Sheets of shining stars rippling above her moved synchronously together like a wave within the ocean, like the beating of her heart. She looked back at the moon with a newfound knowing. "This is how you see, huh...? You see... *everything*..." Now, *she* was seeing *everything*.

She stretched out her arms and spun herself around, making a sparkling tidal wave with her body. She laughed up at the moon and splashed at the water. She laughed at herself. She laughed at the skies. She laughed in delight at her phenomenal surroundings. She laughed at the realization that her wishes from the dunes were all being granted, all of this time.

"I think you set me free..."

She bathed and played in the heat and the light. She splashed in the warm, shimmering bath of the infinite skies. She lay back and floated in the sparkles, under the moon. She floated in the middle of nowhere—or perhaps she was floating right in the middle of everywhere… and everything. After all, you see, she'd landed in the celestial Sea of Cosmos.

She was in the arms of the cosmos, now.

She felt the collective vastness of all things, she felt the expansiveness of life, and although microscopic in comparison, she could not help but feel as if she *was* the vastness—the expansiveness of it all. She felt connected to every molecule, every dust particle, every buzzing vibration passing by, swimming in a sea of pure light and love.

She felt the scorching heat of the moon penetrate her sparkling skin. She felt the surging composition of the Sea of Cosmos dancing within each of her cells. She felt herself moving impeccably with the rhythm of the rippling stars… Or perhaps the stars were moving impeccably with the rhythm of her. Floating on the waters of life and creation—her body painted in the sparkling radiance of the cosmos, under the light of the Gypsy Moon—she was like the stars, now. Shimmering, shining, she was the same as the stars.

She reveled in the Sea of Cosmos for hours, hundreds of thousands of seconds, perhaps for several days and nights, and nights and days. But time was not on her mind at such a time as this. Perhaps, at such a time and space as this, time does not exist.

She floated, and swayed, and swam, and bathed, and wondered. She pondered on every strange event that led her to this one—swimming in a sea-bath of stars—floating in the dust of all things. Like that first night in the dunes when she met the moon—here she was again, being pulled by its swoon.

She wondered how she ever washed up on the shore of that wild place to begin with. A curious happening, indeed, though most things do seem strange when you try too hard to understand that which you don't quite yet understand.

After moments of sweet reverie and contemplation, she reminded herself that the objective was not to think backward. No, the objective was to revel in the enjoyment in such things she didn't quite yet understand. It was much more enjoyable in this way, you see. For, when one finds that they are swimming in a sea of stars, was there any point in analyzing the steps one took in order to have gotten that far?

She breathed in the exciting air of the cosmic Heavens, drifting on the current in the moonlight, closing her eyes and letting the moon pull her. Her mind was soft. Her body was glowing. Her heart was open.

She felt the subtle, certain movement of all things, and she felt when that subtle movement shifted into a shaking pulsation. Slowly the jittering vibrations of this wild space flooded over her. She opened her eyes to see the sheets of rippling stars falling to her from above.

She stopped floating and started swimming with trepidation. She looked up and all around. The fast falling light of stars streaking down from the depths of the Heavens shot toward the Sea of Cosmos. There was nowhere for her to go. The closer the blankets of stars dropped toward her in the Sea of Cosmos, the heavier the vibration jolted through her and all that she was enthralled in—all that she was now a part of.

She looked around in a frantic manner, splashing sparkling waters around, aware that there were no beaches to swim to—no land whatsoever nearby. The land she once knew was still moons of miles away, nowhere in sight.

She spun in the water, peering out to the depths of darkness and light, as far as she could see—into the infinite unknown. She entered a state of panic in the middle of the sea of stars. Of course, one should never panic in any body of water, especially in the seas of all creation.

The resonance of the trembling of the cosmos had fully saturated the sea she was engulfed in. The lingering jittering danced with the molecular composition of her body. The rippling chaos of being in the company of the cosmos casually heightened around her... or within her.

Chaos, however, cannot ripple—you see, because chaos—simply put, is no more than a blurred word used for moving pieces within one's world. And much like the shifting currents of a stream, it is far easier to release resistance and move with the forces of nature—the flow of the sea. Let the pieces roll and flow, so to speak, let the stars fall, you see? The moving parts need not be defined. But as you know, revelations take time.

Time, time—

Are you winning?

Even within the greatness of the immense space she was in, she had nowhere to go. She had nowhere to hide. She looked up at the layers of stars above her, and still they looked as if they were going to shower over her, an infinite amount of stars crashing down to suffocate her in a sea of endlessness.

As her concerns over this unpredicted, unknown circumstance grew larger, she allowed her dread and frenzy to let itself cascade. Her body shook regardless of the cosmos' vibrations—she shook at the demand of her trembling mind. The beating of her heart pleaded with her. Worry and fear held a tight grip on her face and any free-floating thoughts.

The bright Sea of Cosmos grew dim. The light of the descending stars started to fade. She could still feel their momentum crashing down toward her, and the quaking of their movement, but she was beginning to lose sight of everything. Even the light of the Gypsy Moon was turning down—the fire inside started to simmer—all within accordance to the worry of her mind.

She thought back to when she was caught in the storm in the Wild Land of Thee. Just like then, the magnificent skies had now darkened from the dimming of her own light. The waters of the celestial sea became choppy, and she was floating in the center of it all.

She *was* the center of it all.

The treacherous current whipped her around like a buoy without an anchor. Her body became tenser with each toss. Her mind and the fluid of her spine overflowed with fear that spilled over the edge of the Heavenly sea. She'd exhausted all of her worries until nearly every glimpse of light within the infinite skies turned down as far as her eyes could see.

The bright fiery light of the Gypsy Moon was barely visible. She swam in the darkness of the night—being tossed around in the roaring current of that darkness—the darkness that she set forth.

She was under the spell of the Gypsy Moon and the Sea of Cosmos. She was under the whim of the infinite skies and the falling stars. She was drowning in the vibration of the fear ripping through the seas.

Or perhaps she was under the spell of her own mind. Perhaps she was under the whim of her infinite self. Perhaps she was drowning in the vibration of the fear ripping through her thoughts.

She looked around as she splashed in the dark waters, but there was nothing for her to see. All she saw was darkness. All she felt was her body slapping down against the seas of all creation. She closed her eyes tight. She tried to escape into a lighter place inside of her mind, but it was hard to focus on anything other than the blurry moving pieces within her current world.

"Don't you get glum..." Her mind began playing her song like a distressed broken record. Repeating lines, playing in the sounds of her consciousness to the rhythm of the wild current that whipped her around harder than any other beast.

"Don't you get glum... Don't you get glum..." The words recited faster with each tug and pull of the Sea, until her spinning head and jerking body whipped against the water so hard that even the lights went out from her consciousness. Briefly, her mind went absent. In the middle of the Sea of Cosmos, her mind went absent. As if the skies had struck her upside the head to knock out the absurdities, her mind went absent.

There she floated atop the Sea of stars and life, without a single worry running through her mind because her mind had been put to sleep. You see, at times of worry and fear and grief, the mind can quickly wander to places dark and deep, and when those times become too steep, the skies—or the Sea—will shut you up, so to speak, to ensure you can sleep. For, with one sleep atop a heavy mind, the spinnings of absurd thoughts subside, and therefore one can rewake with a new and clear mind.

CHAPTER 23

FRESH THOUGHTS FROM THE SKIES

Her body floated fluidly with the sparkling Sea, as if she herself were the water. The tensions of her body and mind were no longer, as she was no longer consciously stirring mad with the unease of not knowing. Like the water that engulfed her, she was simply *being*, now—she simply *was*. Free, and open—just floating.

Perhaps she drifted along for minutes within several hundreds of seconds, or perhaps she sailed along for many hours—however many hours are considered hours in a time and space such as the Seas of Time and Space.

However long long can be, her mind and all its worries were set free. Soon her mind was able to reach the places it needed to be. Slowly, she awoke within her new and clear mind when suddenly and seemingly from nowhere—though nothing is ever from nowhere—the face of the Coyote came into her mind, followed by the sound of his gallant voice, "Fully afloat now... going where the wind takes ya, Girl."

"Fully afloat..." she repeated the words inside and out of her mind.

"But remember," the Coyote continued, "worry and fear dim the lights, Girl."

"Worry and fear dim the lights..." she repeated his words in her head once again, and in those words she was reminded.

She was awake, though her eyes still closed. She took a deep breath in, avoiding the sweet and salty waters of the cosmic sea slipping past her lips. She knew it was time to take control of the fears that had once grasped her mind. She knew in an infinite sea of stars—with nowhere to swim to—her only option was just that. Still being pulled by the forces of the cosmic waters, she tried to focus on the rhythm of her new, clear mind, instead—no longer crashing like the water, as she knew she had to take control. She knew now that she could. She knew she was ready.

She focused on the feeling of the shut of her eyes, releasing some of the tightness from her lids. Thoughts of the Wild Child came into her mind. She breathed in deep and smiled, upon crashing against the ripping waves. She pictured the Wild Child running barefoot through the woods, hearing the sound of the child's laughter within the realms of her mind. This laughter carried her to the memory of sleeping on the softest moss next to two other beating hearts, and she could feel the warmth of her heart rising in the Sea of Cosmos.

As the waters of the Sea splashed her face, her thoughts traveled to memories of the rain washing over her skin, and the feeling of running free through the wet, muddy forest. This led her to wonder about walking with the Coyote, splashing in the lagoons, playing with the stars. She thought of the strange stardust and the falling stars.

She thought about the wild creatures of the wild woods. She thought of the ones she'd met, her interactions with each of them. She thought of that strange bat that made her laugh, and the menu that bat had spoken of, and glimpses of the giant fruits from the forest filled her mind, so much so that she could taste the sweet juices. She thought of the Gypsy's towering pies, and the smell of sticky mangos. She thought of the Coyote. She thought of the many, many cats and the sound of the Cat Lady's laugh.

She thought about the feeling of dancing with the Gypsies, who perhaps were the Crows—she still wasn't sure if she knew what she'd always known. She thought about the Crows, and the way that they flew, and that one Crow with the strange blue eyes. She wondered if they could fly to her up there where she thrived in the bright starry sky.

She thought about the old woman's story of the Gypsies who change to Crows... or the Crows who change to Gypsies. As her mind moved faster and she became consumed in her sweet reveries, she thought of the morphing Wild Child. She thought of the spinning colors of light and magic that was the essence of the little girl. Thinking of the little girl's spinning web of colorful light led the images of her mind to the wild colors of the wild, wild, Wild.

There in her mind, she reflected on the beauty of the skies and the glistening forest. Visions of sparkling water flooded her mind. The thought of the water soothed her. She took a deep breath. She focused on that. She had a love for the Sea, and she was starting to think that perhaps this sea was no different from the rest.

With her eyes still shut, though not as tight, she started to feel the way the Sea of Cosmos felt then and there—calm, that is. She felt still. She felt peace. She felt joy. Her lips curled into a smile, her face softer now. She felt the choppy waters release their grip. She felt the swell and the surf simmer and soften.

Her body was no longer being agitated and tugged on. She opened her eyes—everything was lit again. The Sea of Cosmos was calm and sparkling once more. The stars were brightly set and shimmering. The Gypsy Moon was shining, brighter than before, radiating a heat hotter than any sun. The celestial seas glowed through the Heavens, and she remained right there, in the center of it all.

She looked up and around to where she saw the masquerade of shooting and darting stars that were once coming at her, and when she saw what she saw, she started to understand something which she had not quite understood before. She realized now that the things that seemed so daunting at first were in fact quite harmless and small. The things that seemed so big and scary at first sight, were really no more than rains from the skies—a storm passing by—and that's all it ever was.

She saw the clear picture of what she'd once feared. The showers of stars that had been plummeting down toward her were now beginning to rain into the sea around her, as the storm set forth to pass by. Like any rain shower, the shimmering specks of light fell like raindrops, splashing into the water and becoming a part of the bright Sea of Cosmos... or perhaps falling right through it, wherever that would lead to.

She laughed loud with a roar as she watched the stars hit the sea. She felt like a girl in a pond getting caught under a midsummer night's rain. How silly she was, she thought. This was nothing—scared of nothing, once again. But how was she to know it was nothing? It could very well have been something. The unknown could always be anything... perhaps it could be anything one perceives it to be.

The stars rained down and kissed her forehead, her cheeks, her hair, her shoulders. Each drop splashed into glitter upon hitting her warm skin. She rejoiced as the rain washed over and replenished her. Swimming under the showers of her emerging mind, becoming the light and the sparkle of the stars, of the sea. She was becoming the light and the sparkle of time and space, and all that's in between—she was in it. She *was* it.

Star-drops hit the Sea of Cosmos with a splash. Within the confetti of the showering stars—diamond-like rocks fell into the sea. She reached for one with her sparkling fingers.

Fresh thought from the skies.

"Marbles...!" she whispered in delight, knowing this meant she was starting to see the light.

The marble dazzled between her fingers unlike any of the ones she had seen on the path. She held the marble up to her eyes and looked within at her reflection. A mirror of stars and brilliant light shined back at her.

She was the light. And every star in the sky.

She twirled the marble in her fingertips and it slipped right through, falling to the bottom of the cosmic sea—wherever that would be. Perhaps it fell to her previous path. Perhaps it found another sea.

She watched it drop til out of sight and howled in excitement and delight. As she howled, the Sea of Cosmos rippled out from her. You see, she could rumble the infinite seas of life with just one single laugh.

"Marbles fell from the skies... and the Tamer's minds..." She splashed her hands into the water, recalling what the Cat Lady had told her. "If ever you see marbles falling from the sky... you'll know somewheres some Tamers or a... Tamed one... also lost the marbles in their minds..." She grabbed her head, planting her sparkling palms on each side of her marble-less mind. "My marbles! *I lost my marbles!*" Laughter and tears flooded over her.

Finally, she was free.

One by one, the infinity of stars shined brighter, as if someone switched on the lights. She laughed in wonder and revelation. She cried in relief and liberation. She wailed at the moon and showering stars.

"YEE-YEE-YEEW!"

Her sparkling body dressed with the luster and drops of space and time, in the center of the sea of all that ever could be.

She sighed in relief and fondness of all that she was seeing—all that she was being a part of, all that she was feeling, all that she was becoming. She was okay. Everything was going just right. She surrendered once again. She put her trust into the Sea of Cosmos, like she'd always done in the seas she knew from down below.

Her body sailed along with the harmless passing storm. After some time which was no time or much time, the heavenly rains subsided. The storm moved along, as it always does. Once more the stars rested like blankets above her in the skies of space, and sheets of sparkling diamonds rippled like before, this time only brighter.

She laid her back against the sea and let herself float. No longer was she being swept up by the vibrations of the commotions of the infinite skies. No, now it was much more than that. Now she was being swept up by something greater, more powerful. Now she was being swept up by the perpetual rhythm of every heartbeat that's ever been.

She felt the cadence and pulse of all that was—all that ever was—all of creation. In sync with all of it now, she was riding on the current of all things alive—all things being and blending—all things expanding and becoming. She smiled, looking up into the infinite and unknown.

"I'm home."

"You're getting it." She heard a soft, yet amplified voice speak to her. "Soon you'll see who you really are..." the voice told her.

"Who I really am..." Yes, she thought, it's time. She wanted to know, then and there, without wasting another beat of her heart.

"And when you do, then you'll know that you are powerful enough to tame all of the choppy waters, and turn on all of the lights," the voice replied, "for, you are a conductor, after all."

"Me...?" The stars of her eyes shined brighter. "A conductor...?" She thought back to what the Cat Lady had said about wild women... wild women were conductors. Was *she* a conductor? Was she a wild woman? The marbles had fallen from the skies. Which can only mean that marbles had also fallen from her mind.

She had been untamed. She was wild, once more. She was a conductor.

"Mm-hmm, 'at's right..." Boundless amplified voices answered her. She knew she was speaking with the stars now, but their voices sounded familiar.

The stars above her formed into a giant sparkling Coyote.

"Aha! Ya got it, Girl... the gift of buoyancy," the Coyote spoke from the stars.

She looked at her shimmering giant friend in the sky. "You're in the stars..."

"'At's right, Girl. 'At's right. How's the water, Girl?"

"It's... it's... glowing!" She splashed. "It's... sparkling!" She splashed again. "It's... it's making *me* all of those things too..." She held up her arms, revealing that she, too, was glowing and sparkling just like the Sea of Cosmos.

"'At's right, Girl, you certainly are those things... always have been."

"Coyote... is this what you mean by, traveling in circles?" She spun circles in the sparkling sea of diamonds.

"'At's right, Girl. Ya been here before, that's for sure."

"I have?" She splashed the sparkles and they rippled back onto her.

"'At's right, Girl. It's where ya come from."

"*I come from here?*" Same as the stars...

"We all came from here, Girl. All of us alike, come from the same place." The Coyote ate a stray star. "And ya know something, Girl? All of this, it's alive in ya."

"Because I'm seeing it... so therefore it is?" The stars in her eyes were aglow.

"Maybe it's because it is, so therefore you're seeing it," the Coyote suggested. "This is all a part of ya, Girl... it's where ya from." The Coyote shimmered within the stars.

"Home..." She was home. She knew it. "I feel alive here, Coyote, I really feel alive..." She felt the forgotten parts of herself coming back to life. "And... you were right, Coyote... Worry and fear... I let it dim the lights, just like you said. I dimmed all of the lights... *all of them!*"

"'And then ya turned 'em back on, Girl. You know what to do. And now you're remembering what ya *can* do." The Coyote kicked a star to her, and when she caught it, it fell from her hands like sparkling sand. "Remember... *you* control the switch, Girl."

"I control the switch..." Those words felt right—she believed them as she spoke. She watched as the Coyote paced a circle in the sky, a train of stars trailing around him. "I never thought that all of *this* was alive in me..."

"Yeah ya did, Girl... ya just forgot. Ya needed some fresh thought." The stars of the Coyote glistened as he shook his oversized tail of sparkling diamonds.

Fresh thought... new marbles.

The stars of the Coyote danced and shimmered, shifting out of his form and into something else... someone else...

"And what do you believe a proper reflection of *you* to be, Dear?" the stars questioned in the voice of the Cat Lady. They gathered together to reflect the old woman in the skies—and all of her cats too, of course. "Is it rippling in the water?" the starry Cat Lady asked. "Is it flying in the sky?"

The stars whirled out of the Cat Lady, and into the shifting colors of the Wild Child, who asked, "Do you see your reflection in *me*, Silly?" The little girl in the stars laughed—and her laughter rippled through the entire Sea of Cosmos.

She floated through the little girl's ripples, and created her own as she laughed along with the child of the stars.

"Or perhaps, Butterfly, it is me in which you, you see," the Gypsy of the stars spoke in the sky.

"Gypsy!" She flung up her sparkling arms, and a piece of the Gypsy fell into her hand—dispersing into dust.

"Hi Butterfly, the simple truth—your reflection is in *all* that surrounds you."

She gazed into the abyss of all that surrounded her, all that she was fully saturated within, all that was a part of her. "Is *all of this* a reflection of me?"

"I wouldn't say it quite like that. "The stars of the Gypsy spun into a celestial frenzy and returned to Gypsy form. "I'd say it more like this, to see yourself at all, is to see all that does exist. And in the time that passes by, sweet Butterfly—time, time, what is time? Is it not just a melody that plays in your mind…? And with that in mind, Butterfly, is not everything a melody that plays in your mind?"

"*Everything?*"

"You are the orchestrator, Butterfly, of what plays in your mind… I will say it more like this—with every vision in your mind that twists… faith and a wish in your consciousness—a reality exists. And only you, and the conductor of the stars, can create all of this." The Gypsy of the stars sprinkled cosmic glitter down to the girl. "Whatever is, Butterfly, comes from something stirring in your mind."

"Then… is it all real?" She spun under the Gypsy's sparkling shower.

"Oh very much, Butterfly, very much indeed. Your mind is real, don't you agree?"

She did agree. Her mind was real, indeed.

"Then everything your mind creates is as real as real can be. After all, Butterfly, you live in The Land of Thee!"

"Yes... I *live* in The Land of Thee..." She was no longer from that other world she'd escaped—she was home now, home in the stars, in The Land of Thee. Where she belonged.

"Welcome to The Land of Thee... Welcome to The Land of Thee... Welcome to The Land of Thee..." the Gypsy sang the song and danced the dance in the sky. "Where things may seem—"

"—how you choose to see...!" The words of her note spilled from her mouth as her memory struck. She lived in The Land of Thee—where things may seem how you choose to see.

Her memory was beginning to come clean.

"*That's it,* Butterfly!" The Gypsy clapped. "Welcome to The Land of Thee... Welcome to The Land of Thee... Welcome to The Land of Thee..." The stars of the Gypsy scattered into a murder of shimmering crows who seamlessly continued on with the song. "Where darkness lights up mystery... and all the pathways that you seek..."

The Crows of the stars recited the words of her note to her, and she realized that they truly had been reciting to her, all along, just like the Cat Lady had told her.

They led her to the very place she was—*home.*

She clapped her arms and spun herself around, calling out, "YEE-YEE-YEEW!"

"See, there ya go, remembering what ya always known..." The Coyote stood in the stars once more. He pawed at the Gypsy Moon and chipped off a crescent sliver from the side of it, dropping it down to her in the Sea of Cosmos.

"Go on, Girl, hop on."

She swam through the celestial waters and climbed onto the floating sliver of moon. She rested her back against it, letting her legs hang off the sides into the sparkling water. "Thank you, Coyote..." She watched her cosmic friend in the sky. He was her family. He was a part of her home.

"'At's right, Girl. Relax. Sit back. Let yourself flow... float with the stars."

"Now, would you say I've sent you far enough, Birdie?" The Colossal Ocelot filled the sky as he spoke from the stars, and the Coyote was no longer.

"Further than I could have imagined..." Her starry eyes shimmered.

"Oh but it is not. You cannot go any further than you can imagine, Birdie... You got as far as you wished to get. And how do you feel, now that you are here?"

"I feel... very much like the stars..." Just like he said she was.

"Hungry, Butterfly?" The stars spun themselves once more into the shape of the Gypsy of the Night. "This is not quite pie, but a treat more suitable for this night of all nights..." The Gypsy swam through the sky and plucked tangerine bits from the Gypsy Moon, dropping them down to the sparkling girl on her crescent in the Sea of Cosmos. Little moon rocks fell from up above, and one by one she plopped them past her lips. New, wild flavors erupted on her tongue, her nostrils flared, her cheeks flushed. Her tongue danced with the heat and the sweetness of the cosmic candy as a new kind of warmth took over her body.

"Thirsty?" the shimmering Gypsy asked, tipping a starry teapot of glowing moon milk. "Open up, Butterfly..."

She parted her lips just in time for the Gypsy Moon tea to hit her tongue and slide to the back of her throat, warming her to her core and providing the comfort of a mother's milk. The hot milk of the moon settled in her stomach with the butterflies, and swam through her body and mind, bringing light to the pieces of her she'd once left behind.

CHAPTER 24

SAME AS THE STARS

S he basked in the Sea of Cosmos on her crescent of the Gypsy Moon, floating into the feeling of the warmth and comfort of the treats and potions of the sky. The wild creatures in the stars continued to shift before her eyes as she felt her body, her mind, and her soul uniting with all the hidden memories of her infinite mind.

She felt herself unifying with everything in the sky, everything in existence. One within the Sea of Cosmos, a ripple within the rest. Her hands melted into the sparkles of the sea, everything surrounding her was the rest of her, the parts she had misplaced. She was everything. Everything that ever was, and is, and will be—that's what she was.

Intertwined in the commotion that life is derived from. Swallowed whole by the divinely cosmic sea of life. Floating atop the milky dew of the ocean in the sky. She felt like liquid—as if her skin had spread across and over the surface of the ocean, and her body encompassed everything now. She was not *one* thing, she was *all* things. She was not one beating heart, she was *all* beating hearts.

Soaking entirely in the rapture of the Wild and the infinite—she dipped her hands in the waters of space and time. She licked the sparkling brine from her fingers. She was alive—she was aglow, and so was everything else. She saw the light between her and her mind—the light between her and space and time—the light between her and everything. She saw the light of life connecting all things.

The webs of life spun before her eyes—shining threads like that of a spider's silk—holding and intertwining all of existence together. Tangled lines linking all the fibers of life flashed beyond the stars of her eyes. Looking through the layers and dimensions of life, and the false concept of time, and everything that ever was—she saw the entire composition of life, alive and breathing all around her, and within her. She was a part of it all.

She was a part of the delicacy and brilliance of life that lived above everyone's heads. She was not only a part of it all, no—she was a *fundamental piece* of it. A part of the equation of everything. Every movement that she made in the Sea of Cosmos rippled throughout every part of creation. Every breath that she breathed, every beat of her heart, every round of circulation within her body, everything her eyes and mind would see, poured into the sea and altered everything that ever was, ever is, and ever will be. She was a part of it all. She was everything. She was a conductor within the conductor.

"Story time!" The Babes in the stars scattered themselves across the sky, whirling this way and that, and when they came back together they shifted into a playback of memories, a film of what she'd lost, a teaser of what she'd been seeking. She was shown glimpses of her true self—flashes of memories of who she may have been, and the parts she'd played in particular puzzles. From beginning as pure light, to falling from the skies, to shining, and flying, and soaring up high—the stars reminded her of moments she had lost and forgotten.

The images in the skies played back to her as she was beginning to see them in her mind— muddled and scattered and overlapping as they slowly came to light. The brief flashes in the skies of many lives and moments and breaths and heartbeats—reminded her she had always been a part of everything that has ever been.

With the help of the stars and the skies, and beyond the confines of space and time, she was beginning to slip into the understanding of who she truly was. The stars showed her where she came from. She was from this place. This place was from her, she and this place were one in the same. She was the same as the stars. She was home.

She was not a lost girl. She was not a girl running from anything. She was not a scared girl. And no longer was she tamed. She was a woman of the Wild. She was a woman made of the luster and dust of the stars. She was a woman with a fire burning inside of her and a beast roaring and running wild in the light of the Gypsy Moon. She was a Wild creature.

"I really am *everything*... with the eyes of a girl..." she melted deeper into herself, "with stars inside of my eyes." Perhaps she had not yet remembered *everything*, but she remembered the feeling of who she truly was. She remembered being wild.

"Try to catch me!" The Wild Child came to life above her within the stars. "But first, dream!" The child of the stars sprinkled stardust down to her eyes. She softened further into the sea craft of the sliver of moon, watching the Wild Child disperse back into a blanket of scattered rippling stars.

She yawned and did not fight her swift slip into her sudden slumber. For, when a Wild Child sends you off to sleep, there must be a reason—don't you think? She closed her eyes, enraptured by the sparkling waves, the moon milk, the true bliss. She drifted into dreams with the slight knowing of what she now slightly knew—what she'd always known. She slipped into a celestial sleep that was hundreds of thousands of stars from where she was when she had first woken that morning.

She floated into dreams of drinking up all of the oceans and eating from the stars and the moon. She dreamed of a time when there was no moon in the sky, and she dreamed of a time when there were two moons in the sky. She dreamed of being chased and hunted down by Tamers in the dark night, and she dreamed that she could fly. She dreamed of black wings and white wings and she dreamed of being things she'd never seen. She dreamed of the Crows singing songs with her, songs she hadn't yet heard but already knew. She dreamed of spiders and bees, and owls and bats, and coyotes and cats. She dreamed of glowing like the Gypsies and the moon, and spinning in a web of light.

But is a dream really a dream when it is dreamed in the Seas of all things?

She dreamt through thirteen-hundred and thirty-three breaths, dripping salty tears from her eyes, releasing perhaps millions of marbles from her mind. Soon she was shaken from her stupor. Her body jolted atop her quaking crescent sea craft. The sparkling water splashed over her. She opened her eyes in the middle of space and time, to see that the Sea of Cosmos was not choppy or calm—but rather in between. The water was not angry, and yet it was not still. It was perfectly alive. She smiled in delight, for she felt no fear—she felt as if she were in the hands of a trusted friend, once more. Regardless of where she was, she felt ready. She felt thrill. She felt bliss. She felt connected to everything. She was fully aware that everything was going just right, as it always had been from the start.

She looked ahead as her sliver of moon sailed to the edge of a celestial waterfall. Though she was aware of the butterflies in her stomach, she did not panic. Her heart beat softly, her eyes sparkled. She felt something rising inside of her, but it was not fear—it was life, it was love, it was faith that she would be alright. It was excitement—excitement for the unknown, excitement for what was next to come, excitement for being alive, and knowing that everything was going just right.

There was nowhere for her to go except over the edge and into the unknown. She knew she was going places, and she wasn't going to push against the forces of nature—she wasn't going to resist the momentum that was sending her to the next phase—she was going to enjoy the ride.

She was ready.

The moon slid over the crisp sparkling edge of the waterfall. She slid off the crescent slide—gripping the end of its pointed tip with one hand. She glowed and glistened, and her fire burned brighter, as she slipped down the cosmic waterfall with the falling luster of the sea—holding onto the sea craft above her head. Falling up or flying down, depending upon perception, she was sent through the mist of the stars and skies once again. She felt elation. She felt trust. She felt love. She did not feel fear.

She did not know where or when her fall would end, and she did not concern herself with pondering over such things. This time she embraced the feeling of flying or falling or floating or flowing—whichever it was. She embraced the feeling of the confusion of the fluttering butterflies within her body. She embraced the distant unknown and the ride she'd have to take to get there. It was all okay now. She knew that everything was going just right, regardless of free-falling through the sky.

She fell like stardust, awakening the memory within her refreshed mind of how she'd once fallen from the skies. Once more, she was a part of the shift in the colors in the sky—bleeding and pouring into each other, marrying the radiant embers and tangerine glow that enclosed her and the moon at her fingertips. She lit up the sky as she moved through those colorful lights and layers of infinity. Shooting like the stars—blending into the movement of time and space, as time and space blended into the movement of her—surging through it all.

She was returning to the Wild, to the Land of Thee with a deeper knowing of what she was. Returning with the freedom of her burning fire and her roaring beast within. Returning with her shadow, returning with her light. She was returning to the Wild out of the darkness that lurks in the night, and from the light that creates all things in sight. She fell from the stars and with the stars. Like the Gypsies, like she'd done once before—she fell from the stars.

Would anything be different in the Wild upon her return? With a marble-free mind and fresh thought from the skies, perhaps she would see things a bit differently through the stars in her eyes.

She fell faster toward the Wild as she watched the stars fly into the form of the murder of Crows. The starry birds flew in circles around her as she darted through space and time.

"Ah, Beast," that one particular Crow called out.

The Crows flew above her head to the moon piece in her hand, and grabbing onto the other end of it, brought it to her other hand. She gripped her fingers around it, holding on to each tip of the moon with both hands. It filled with air and pulled against her descent, slowing her speed and lowering her down like a parachute. A falling orb of light in the sky—she and the moon went down soft and slow through the layers of life, as the birds of the stars flew circles around her.

"Do you know what you have found, Beast, now that you have found it?" The blue-eyed Crow flew before her face and spoke with its familiar voice.

"My memories... I found my lost memories! Ones I've always had, ones I had forgotten... like the Gypsy said..."

"Revelations take time, Butterfly..." the Gypsy of the stars danced around the falling girl. "Time, time, what is time?"

"Is it not just a melody that plays in your mind?" she eagerly answered the Gypsy, as she descended into a deeper understanding of the concept.

"Yes, Butterfly! Yes, indeed! Time, time, what is time? Is it not just a melody that plays in your mind? And through the layers of space and time—time, time, is not a straight line." The Gypsy poured from the starry teapot of wild moon milk tea—glowing liquid slipping beside the girl in the sky.

"Who is that for?" she asked the Gypsy.

"Some beast will find it... whichever beast wants it... So tell me now, Butterfly, are you aware that your story here is only just beginning?"

"Well, no offense, Gypsy, but that's what you told me when I first saw you on the path..." she reminded the dazzling wild woman.

"Indeed, I did, sweet Butterfly." The Gypsy sparkled in a twirl, and continued, "And I will tell you why—when I saw you on that night—you were only just beginning, isn't this right? And now you see, I say—you are always beginning, in every which way. You are never not beginning, always."

"I am always beginning?" She realized the Gypsy was right—she was just beginning. Like a child with a fresh slate—she was just beginning. "I'm wild now... I'm new..."

No one could stop her now. No one could tame her.

"Always beginning, is what you are, Butterfly. There is no end, no finish line. There will always be more to seek and find... just when you thought you saw it all—" The Gypsy clapped her stardust hands in front of the girl's face—her hands dispersing into the falling sky. "Surprise! It's all in the memory of what never dies—imprints across space and life. Your light burning bright inside... where everything you've ever known resides... remember?"

"Yes, I remember... Those memories that I saw in the sky... I've lived those another time..."

"Of course you have, Butterfly!" The dispersed stars from the Gypsy's hands returned to the Gypsy as feathers.

She watched the wildest woman, her sister made of stars, fly through the sky with wings. She knew her sister carried the light, and every answer of the night upon her wings.

Did she have wings to gain?

She wondered what she was destined to be in The Land of Thee, now that she was once more wild and free. Would she fly like the Crows? Would she grow her own wings? "It's blurry and mixed up... but I can feel the memory of who I am. Where I came from. I felt myself falling from the stars, from my home, just like I'm doing now... with you..." The stars in her eyes gleamed as bright as the stars of the Gypsy. "And I know... although I can't remember it all clearly yet, I know I've always known you..."

"And I have always known you... And now *you're* getting to know you, too."

"I'm not tamed anymore, am I?" she asked the Gypsy, bating an answer to what she already knew. "I'm a Wild Woman, aren't I?"

"YEE-YEE-YEEW!" the Gypsy called out in confirmation.

"YEE-YEE-YEEW! I am wild!" she screamed into the night. She wanted to be heard. She wanted to scream so loud that the Tamers would hear, and they would know that they could never tame her again.

"Yes, Butterfly! Yes! You're even more than you give yourself credit for. You still have so much more to remember. First and foremost... the stars are your home... the moon is your throne..."

"My throne?" She looked up at the moon parachute in her hands.

"'At's right, Girl." The stars shifted back to the Coyote who sat by her falling side as she sparkled through the night.

"What does that mean—the moon is my throne?"

"You're bound to find out, Girl..."

"You mean as I travel 'round in circles?" She laughed and spun, falling through the sky.

"Revolving and evolving, Girl. Seeing things through different eyes each time."

"Seeing things *very* differently... or perhaps seeing unfamiliar, familiar things the same..." She looked down at the Wild below her. "My memories... those flashes of life and things in the sky... They've made me remember feelings... feelings inside of me that I had forgotten, feelings that feel like home to me."

"You are home, Girl. No matter where ya are... you're home."

"No matter where *you* are, feels like home, Coyote..."

"I am wherever you are, Girl... haven't ya figured that out?" The Coyote ran circles around her.

"There was so much I didn't see at first... I didn't remember this feeling... but I do now... I see so much now..." She spoke as the stars of the Coyote scattered and whirled into the Wild Child.

"No one can catch me!" The star child ran from the falling girl in the sky, laughing. The stars returned as the Coyote once more.

"So, Girl, do ya still wanna play chase?" the Coyote asked her. "Still gotta find us in the forest..."

She looked at the approaching Land of Thee. She was ready for anything. She was ready for everything.

The Coyote shook his starry fur and the diamond dust shattered into the murder of Crows. "Have you forgotten what you were hunting when you arrived, Beast?" The blue-eyed Crow flew shimmering circles around her head.

A note made of the stars floated past her face, the words seeping from it as diamond dust, quickly dissipating into nothing. "My note!" She reached her hand out, releasing one side of her parachute and quickly plummeting toward the Wild. The piece of moon in her hand flapped in their windy descent, her gown flew up toward her face. She pulled it back and the Crow of the stars flashed its blue eyes at her and flew up. She felt the other end of her lunar parachute slide back into her hand, and she was sailing once again.

"See how quickly things come your way when you let go, Beast?" The bird flew in front of her face. "Ah, but your note... looks like you've lost it again..."

She watched the rest of her starry note dissipate in the sky, every word was nothing more than stardust glinting in the night. "Can't you just tell me what it said?"

"Do you think *we* are the penmen of your note?" The Crow stopped flying circles around her. "We need not write the words, Beast, we deliver the message."

"But if you didn't then... who did?" Who wrote the note, if not the very ones who had been harboring it from her?

"Beast, where is the fun in this?" the Crow snapped. "Perhaps we make a game of it?"

She wanted to play the game. She knew she could win. Eventually, she could win.

"Perhaps along the way in this game, you'll find more of what you're looking for... answers, that is..." the Crow cawed like a woman. "We will meet upon your landing, in the right place at the right time. In some way or perhaps another..."

"That's it? Can't you tell me more?" She wanted to know what kind of game it was. She wanted to play a fair game—whatever such a thing as that is.

"Yes, Beast, as you'll have it..." the Crow yielded to her complaint. "Once you spot us after your landing, then you can begin."

"How do I begin?"

"You must first find the key... Beast. You must first find the key." The

Crow rolled its starry blue eyes.

"The key!" She was winning. "The key to what?"

"The key that reveals to you a hidden door... though never truly hidden, as nothing ever is." The Crow blinked at her. "Beast."

"How do I find the key?"

"Are you trying to remove *all* of the fun, Beast?" the bird of the stars snarled.

"Just a little hint?" She was winning, she was winning... in her descent with the stars.

"Beast, down below there is much, much more. You could open up a whole new door, that is, if you find the marble that is yours."

"Oh... the marbles... a gift to the wild creatures... and the Gypsies..."

"And the Beasts, Beast."

"I lost my marbles..." she whispered to the night.

"Only the ones that were weighing you down... the marbles you intended to lose. Congratulations, Beast." The Crow laughed wildly. "Now the real fun can begin!"

"I danced with the Gypsy Moon and lost my marbles... just like they said I would!" She laughed and kicked her legs in delight as she fell through the sky. Once afraid that this very thing could happen—now she was dancing in the skies because it had.

"And listen, Beast, when those that have been tamed lose the marbles from their minds, fresh marbles fall down from the skies—"

"And those are the ones that are mine?" She wanted them. All of them.

"All the ones that you can find, Beast. Start with one, if you want some advice. But the first one you find will be the key." The Crow of the stars flung its starry wing against the girl's cheek, and the feathers dispersed to dust against her skin. "Now, no more hints... a game's a game and it is much more fun my way."

"But, how do I find my marble?" She scrunched up and wiggled her nose to diminish the tickling of the stardust feathers upon her face.

"Oh, Beast, we cannot tell you how to play the game. Where is the fun in that?"

"Well, then, can you at least tell me… what's next… in the game?"

"Fine, Beast, fine. If you find the key, then you'll need to find the door. If then you find the door, Beast, it would be wise to go through… now, *that* is up to you."

"What is behind the door? That is, if I do go through?" she asked, already knowing what she would do.

"Beast. In this game, if you continue to play, your next destination from the door is to the bridge. That is your very last hint."

"The bridge? A bridge to where?"

"Up." The Crow flew up and back to her.

"How does a bridge go up?" she asked, her eyes following every shimmering movement of the bird.

"Bridges go all different ways. The wild ones go wild ways, Beast."

"So… I'm looking for a bridge going up…"

"You must first find the key." The Crow prompted. "And there is one thing more, Beast… You must also find the Queen."

"The Queen?" Who is the Queen? "Does the Queen have my note? Who is she?"

"She is a moon-maker," the Crow revealed.

"How do I find… a moon-making Queen?"

"Beast! Have you ever played a game before?" the Crow barked.

"Well, yes, of course, but I… I've never found a Queen…"

"How have you ever found anyone or anything? Is this not a game of finding things?"

"Yes—"

"If it is truly what you wish, then surely you will find it, Beast."

With that, the Crows of the stars pulled the parachute out from her hands, and she fell fast. She was quickly approaching the wild trees of The Land of Thee. She looked up at her lunar parachute that was now being held in the beaks of the mischievous starry Crows.

The butterflies in her stomach rose to her throat. Her spine was seconds away from colliding with the spearing tops of the trees. As the Wild grazed her back, she was swept into the glowing parachute. The Crows carried her above the treetops to The Land of Thee. She curled her body into the warm, moonlit sack—securely held in the beaks of the birds made of the stars.

As she melted into the comfort of the heat of her cocoon, the Crows flipped her out of the moon and she fell through the sky once more. She spun through her descent, until she landed face-front onto a carpet of fur. She pressed her hands down and lifted her chest, looking over the edge of whatever she'd landed upon. The large paws of a creature stood firmly on the ground... and she was on its back.

But this time she was not scared of her encounter with any big beasts. This time she was ready. This time she was aware. She knew she'd been returned to the Colossal Ocelot. Perhaps it was the wind of the Wild that sent her back there. Perhaps it was the guidance of her parachute or the guidance of the Crows. Perhaps it was truly where she wanted to go.

She wrapped her arms around the cat's fur, hugging him, pressing her face and smile into his warm coat, knowing now, that he was a part of her, her home, her heart, and she was a part of him—they were a part of the stars. She loved him as if she'd known him forever. Perhaps she always had.

She saw the Colossal Ocelot sipping from an orange, opalescent puddle on the ground. It was the moon milk, the tea that tastes of everything, the starry Gypsy's tea. He's the beast that wanted it, she thought, and she laughed, coming to the realization that everything is connected, everything goes around, we travel in our circles, and all is always provided.

She crawled behind the Ocelot's ear and whispered, "You're sipping from the milk of the moon..."

"Always have, little Bird," the Ocelot spoke between lapping his milk with his fiery eyes closed.

She rested her body between the Ocelot's ears and curled to one side, looking up at the sky. "I saw. I saw it all," she whispered.

"Same as the stars?" he asked.

"Same as the stars," she whispered.

"It's good to have you back, Birdie."

"It's good to be home…" She gazed up at the stars as the starry Crows flew overhead, still holding onto the glowing piece of moon that was once her sea craft, and then her parachute, and then her safety sack. They released it from their beaks and dropped it to her. It draped over her resting, sparkling body, covering her like a blanket. She clasped it in her hands and tucked it under her chin, letting her heavy, happy, starry eyes soften into a close. She drifted into sleep atop the Colossal Ocelot, under a bright blanket made of the moon, under the Sea of Cosmos and the stars from where she fell. She was home.

CHAPTER 25

LITTLE BIRDIE LOST HER MARBLES

S he awoke in motion, on the back of the Colossal Ocelot with her blanket of a moon wrinkled over her waking body. She opened her fresh eyes in a squint, acclimating to the brighter colors of the day that penetrated the strange morning light. The Gypsy Moon hovered over her, following her wherever she traveled. She stared into the moon that she'd come so close to touching, barely able to notice the missing sliver from it that now covered her body.

She and the cat brushed past the treetops coated in the gold sparkling dew of the morning light. "Good morning," she whispered to the trees as their leaves swept against her glistening body. They stretched their limbs—awakening with her, as she saw everything come to life again for the first time.

"Good morning, Darling. Oh, I do hope your travels were well." The white owl was perched upon the branch of a dancing tree. "And clearly you are *winning...*"

She looked at her arms. She slid the lunar blanket from her body. Her shoulders gleamed a new sparkle. Her arms, her hands, her legs—every inch of her body still wore the sparkle and shine of the Sea of Cosmos. She was cloaked entirely in the embodiment of the skies, the stars. She was the sparkling essence of the Sea of all Creation.

"I am!" She threw her sparkling arms up in victory, "I *am* winning!" She pulled the gleaming blanket back over her star-soaked skin.

"Indeed, you are, Darling. See you soon." The Owl closed its eyes, returning to its slumber as the girl and the Ocelot continued forward.

She felt as if she were floating. She had no more concerns weighing her down. No more worries stifling her. She had no more fear. She knew who she was, and she was allowing herself to just be. She was moving freely in the Wild. She *was* wild. She was a wild creature that flew up to, and fell down from the stars.

She didn't know where she was or where the Colossal Ocelot was taking her, but she knew that she was home. Wherever it was that she was, she was home.

She grabbed a fist full of fur, rolled over, and pulled herself up to sit on the back of the traveling cat. The piece of moon that had blanketed her, draped over her shoulders and she closed it around the front of her body.

"Good morning, little Birdie."

"Good morning, Ocelot." Her cheeks warmed as she knew she was saying hello to an old friend.

"Have you acquired many plans today?" he asked.

She looked around at the sights of the new day that surrounded her. She heard the faint zephyr whispering to her. She felt the trees wanting to dance with her in the fresh morning air. She sensed the stars wanting to be closer to her. There was a new vibration in the air, as if she herself was brand new, and all of creation wanted to greet her. Perhaps that vibration was always stirring in the air... perhaps she wasn't ready to tune into it until now. Now she was ready.

"I'm..." she thought of the birds of the stars, "I'm going to be playing a game. Not so much a game of chase..." She thought about her mission set by the Crow. "More so a game of hunting…"

"Ah, music to my ears. I am quite remarkable at both endeavors, I'll have you know."

"Oh, I know you are… I know *firsthand*…" She patted the top of the Ocelot's head.

"You were a perfect participant in my favorite game, Birdie, you always are."

The Crows swooped in front of her face and cawed like women cawing like crows. She looked up at them, their luminous eyes shining down at her. She knew their game had begun. She cawed in return—a declaration of their game commencing.

"And now we begin!" She drummed her hands upon the Ocelot and shouted her order.

"Allow me to guess, Bird… that was your cue, was it not?"

"Yes! The game begins!" She held up her lunar blanket and waved it through the air like a flag.

"It would be an honor to assist you in your game with the Crows, Birdie, if you'll have me, that is." The Ocelot rolled his eyes to the top of his head to see her as he walked. "I do suppose perhaps I owe you a bit of a helping paw or two, Birdie. Now, how do we begin?"

"We must first… we must first find the marble… the *key!*" She knew she was with the creature she was meant to be with for this part of her game. In her deepest knowing, in her memories—she knew he had walked with her many times before.

"Little Birdie lost her marbles…" the Ocelot teased.

"I lost my marbles!" She was proud. Finally, she had lost her marbles. Finally, she was wild. Finally, she was free. "And I must find the new marble that is mine… but… *how* do I find the marble that is mine?" She looked to the marble cloaked path.

"Are you asking, how do you find *your* one tiny marble within this mess of marbles?" the Ocelot asked, stepping over the mounds of marbles.

"There are at least a *million* marbles on this path…"

How was she to know which of those marbles was her marble? How was she to find the one special marble in a wild place filled with fallen marbles that upon first glance, almost all looked identical?

She thought about the first marble she'd found from that previous path, and the reflection of her starry eyes that she saw within it. She reached into her pocket, but she realized that everything must have slipped out when she was hanging upside down, or perhaps when she was flung into the Sea of Cosmos. She thought about the Sea of Cosmos, and all the marbles that fell from the skies. This brightened the light between her and her mind.

"I know!" She dropped the blanket and stood atop the Ocelot. "I know which one is the key!" She thought for a moment. "But... I dropped it from the sky—it could've landed anywhere..." She whipped her head all around, looking to the glistening trees as if they held the answers to the mysteries of her missing marbles.

"*Indeed*, it certainly did land somewhere." The Ocelot purred, rumbling the balance of the girl. "That's the exhilarating thing about losing your marbles—the new ones tend to make you look around, while they hide in plain sight." The Ocelot slowed down. "Often you'll fly right past them—like a blind bat. I Ia! Why don't we start right here, Bird?"

"The Crows *did* say to begin when I saw them..."

The Ocelot bowed his nose to the ground to let her slide off his head. She planted her feet onto the path of marble flooring, holding her blanket cape over her glistening shoulders.

Marbles filled every foot of the path—some had fallen from the skies, some had come from Tamer's minds, and some had fallen from the minds of those who had once been tamed. Some of those were her marbles, and she wanted them. It was her job to find her fresh marbles, her fresh thoughts that were scattered across the ground and mixed up with the ones that had fallen from her tamed mind. Across the Wild, across the Land of Thee—every marble collected the golden dust that fell from the wild skies, while she traipsed across them with her new, fresh mind.

As she searched through the mind marbles, she used the bottom of her blanket to wipe away the shimmer from her legs, but it did not wipe away. Perhaps this is because she was using light to wash away light, which simply cannot be. Perhaps it is because you cannot wipe away light at all, regardless of what you use.

"I'm... I'm still sparkling..." she continued to use the glowing blanket in the attempt to rub the glow from her skin.

"You wear it very well, little Bird," the Ocelot commented as the girl continued to wipe away at her gleaming skin. "You can never wipe away that which shines forth from inside of you. You can only let it shine. Otherwise, you are playing the game all wrong, little Bird."

"I can only let it shine..." perhaps this was a part of her now, perhaps she was a sparkling wild creature in The Land of Thee. Perhaps she was always meant to be.

The cat sniffed his wet nose at her glistening body, scrunched up his eyes and she watched in slow motion as he released a large sneeze, sending her flying across the path and onto the marbles, almost entirely covered in Ocelot snot.

The Ocelot shook his head, laughing, and pawed at her with his giant, soft feet. She wiped her stellar towel over her body, wiping the cat sludge away. When she wiped it from her face and looked at him—with his innocent eyes of amused concern—she erupted in laughter, straight from the butterflies in her belly.

There she sat, on a mountain of marbles, her skin soaked in sparkles, covered in the boogers of a monstrous, yet harmless cat—laughing together, from the warmth in their bellies.

She stood up and stepped onto the cat's paw, reaching up and tying her towel around the cat's large neck—now turning the piece of moon into a glowing bandana.

She scratched under his ear until he purred. "Ready?" she asked him. "Always," he told her.

She examined the cluttered ground and dropped to her hands and knees, beginning her search through the clusters of lost and fallen marbles. The colossal cat followed her lead, pawing around at the piles of marbles—both of them knowing that only *she* could find that one special key. Still, he searched with her—he hunted—for all wild beasts enjoyed playing the game.

The vultures screeched in their own game of hunt, and she flung her stare overhead, where they flew far above her, circling over their prey.

"They can't touch you, Birdie... *especially* when you're with me," the cat assured her, smiling with his large, sharp teeth. "So, tell me, Bird, what happens after you find your marble?"

She grabbed a handful of marbles and tossed them up in the air, "Take that!" she yelled, the vultures flying away as she and the Ocelot took cover from the drop of the marbles. She would never let herself be captured again, by any kind of creature.

She thought back to her conversation with the star Crows. "I am supposed to find... the moon-maker...? The... the Queen? After I find my marble," she grabbed a handful of marbles and dropped them back to the pile, "that is my next move in the game—find the Queen... the moon-maker. Maybe she has answers for me..." She looked to the Ocelot. " Do you know the Queen?"

"I know that there can't be a game without a Queen," the Ocelot told her. "Is a game really a game without a Queen?"

"Can you help me find her?" she asked, a spark of hope carrying her voice.

"Indeed, I already am, Birdie. Perhaps you could say I'm leading you right to her." The Ocelot let out another, yet much smaller, booger-less sneeze. "So, shall we continue?"

She believed the cat, and she wanted to win. "Okay! I'm ready."

She and the cat walked side by side on the marble-coated path for only several steps before she climbed onto his paw and hitched a ride. She leaned back against his leg as he continued forward for both of them.

"What do you know about the Queen?" she asked. "What is she the Queen of?"

"She is the Queen of The Land of Thee. She is the Queen of many things. Some may say she is the Queen of... Everything."

"Well, where does she live, this Queen of many everythings?" His answers seemed awfully vague. "Where is her home?" Perhaps they could cut right through the game—go to the Queen.

"Her home is on her throne," he casually told her.

"Her *throne?* Where's her throne?"

"Wherever she is."

"And where is she?" She felt as if she were chasing his tail, or her own.

"Always at home. You'll see, Birdie... you'll find her. Of this, I am certain."

A shimmering flash of light from within the marbles blinded her eyes for two or three giant Ocelot steps. "Stop!" She whacked the Ocelot's leg.

The Ocelot stopped. "Find something, Birdie?"

She stepped off his paw and dropped to her knees—searching for another flash of light to strike at her. She dug through the marbles before her, and there it was—the flash of light. She squinted her eyes and picked it up, holding it to her eyes as it illuminated in her fingers. She looked inside it to see her reflection, and just like in the Sea of Cosmos—a mirror of infinite stars and brilliant light shone back at her. She knew. This was her marble. This was the key.

"Got it!" She stood up and dropped the marble into the pocket of her gown. She was moving forward in her game, she was winning. Now it was time to find the Queen.

"Good hunting skills you've acquired..." The Ocelot hunched his face down to her level.

"When you let it go, it comes much faster..." She told him of her tricks she'd recently learned.

"Ah, yes, so it does, Birdie, you remember." The Ocelot flared his nostrils, sniffing at her pocket. "And, what are you going to do with what you have found now that you have found it?"

"Open up a wild door... if you find the marble that is yours..." she recited what the starry Crow had instructed.

"Wild door, you say...? I believe I know the door in which you speak of..."

"You do?" She stepped closer to his face. "Can you take me?" She rubbed the marble in her pocket.

The Ocelot brought his chin to the ground, and she tugged on the glowing moon-scarf around his neck and lifted herself up. She crawled to the top of his head and slid down his long neck to sit comfortably between his shoulder blades. Together, they continued to journey forward.

CHAPTER 26

THE QUEEN OF THE WILD

"To the... gateway!" she called out. "YEE-YEE-YEEW!" She called to the Wild—to The Land of Thee.

"OWE-OWE-OWE!" The Wild called back to her. Her cheeks swelled like the moon, and her eyes dazzled with more stars. She lifted her spine higher and looked out across the tops of the trees, opening her arms—embracing her home, embracing herself.

"You rang?" The Gypsy of the Night spoke from over her shoulder.

"Good morning, Gypsy!" She stood and turned to face the Gypsy and thirteen plates of towering pies balancing upon the colossal cat's back.

"*Bom Dia,* Butterfly! Oh, you look your natural self!" The Gypsy spun the girl around. "Your glitter! Your shimmer! Your shine! Your sheen! You're glowing, is what I mean!"

"Oh, yes! It's from the Sea..." She showed off her new look, proud it was her.

"Oh Butterfly, you see what you want to see! Perhaps your glow *is* from the Sea, perhaps it is from somewhere deep." The Gypsy walked halfway around the girl upon the cat's back. "Perhaps the Sea helped set you free and release your wild light—though, it's always been this *free,* and this *bright*—you just needed to shift your sight..."

She looked down at her shimmering, shining skin. She was her again, and she was new. She was free. She was wild. She was on fire like the moon.

"As I said, Birdie," the Ocelot chimed in, "you cannot wipe away that which shines forth from inside you, you can only let it shine..."

"To shine or not to shine, was always yours to decide, Butterfly. But—regardless of what one decides, whatever light's alive inside, will always break free and shine... now here, Butterfly, eat some pie!" The Gypsy grabbed two handfuls of pie, shoving both handfuls into her own mouth and the mouth of the girl, then picked up a tower of pies and flung it forward—to the mouth of the Ocelot, who caught the whole tower in one gulp.

"Gypsy, what can you tell me about the Queen?" The Gypsy knew all the secrets of the night. She knew the Queen, she had to.

"But, Butterfly, what can I tell you about *you?*" The Gypsy turned the question around.

"Well, I don't need to learn more about myself right now... I want to know about the Queen..."

"Butterfly! This is The Land of Thee! You will never know enough about you. You are... bottomless! You are... forever! You are everything!"

"I am... aren't I?" Once again, the Gypsy was right. "But... I'm interested to learn about the Queen..."

"The Queen is not something to be learned... The Queen, Butterfly, is one to endure. I see I say, I say I see... I will say it more like this in turn, the Queen has not yet fully returned, the Queen—"

"So I can't meet her yet? Where has she been? When will she return?"

"Butterfly, I enjoy your curiosity much more than your confusion... tell me, did you ever stop to think the word *return* is merely an illusion?" The Gypsy poked the girl's nose. "In order to return, one must have *gone*... but no one ever goes. For, what lives within, always lives on." The Gypsy pressed a palm against the girl's sparkling chest, and they smiled at one another in synchronicity with crumbs around their lips.

"The memory of what never dies..." she reminded herself.

"You've got it, Butterfly! Imprints across space and life... The beast, the fire, the light that burns inside, the shadow that never hides... living on forever, lives upon lives. Now, we eat more pie!" The Gypsy knelt down and slid each hand under a plate of a tower of pies, and placed the towers between the two of them. The wild women plopped down on the cat's back with their legs hanging off to each side, taking handfuls of pie from the towers and filling their mouths.

"I could divulge some tidbits of insight to you, little Birdie, for, say... another tower of delicious fruity pies..." the Ocelot announced to the ladies on his back.

"Is that so?" She stuffed some of the loose pie bits back into her mouth, and with both hands she lifted up one of the towers that sat between her and the Gypsy, flinging it over her head, where it landed into the colossal mouth of the now purring and well-fed cat.

"What would you like to know?" The Ocelot asked after gulping down all the pies in one swoop swallow and licking his chops.

She took a moment or two to swallow her mouthful of pie before answering, "Well, I don't know this Queen that everyone here seems to know... but I know it is essential to my game with the Crows that I find her... and now I know that she has not gone, yet not fully returned from some*where*, so... *where* do you think I could find her?"

"Surely through this walk with me, you'll get closer to where she dwells. A wild one in motion will always get closer to what she seeks," the Ocelot answered her without really answering her. "Don't doubt it, little Bird, you'll find her. You are a natural at winning the game. Enjoy playing it, my little Treat, and surely you will soar. With this knowledge, it is inevitable that you find all things you seek and need."

"You know, Butterfly... The Queen is not a *thing*... the Queen has to be *seen*," the Gypsy added.

"How do I *see* the Queen?" She leaned to the side to see the Gypsy past the tower of fruity pies.

"It is much easier than you think." The Gypsy stuffed her own mouth with an extra oozing handful of fruity pie.

"Is it *you*, Gypsy?" She studied the Gypsy with inquisitive eyes. "Are *you* the Queen?" Could it be? Was this Gypsy the Queen?

"Oh, yes I am the Queen of The Land of *Me*, but never could I be the Queen of The Land of *Thee!*" The Gypsy laughed with her mouth full of crust and fruity filling.

"The Queen of the *Land of Me?*"

The Gypsy swayed side to side, lifted her arms, and dazzled her fingers around her own body, her light growing brighter as she presented herself as The Land of Me. "That's right, Butterfly, The Land of Me. I am Queen of The Land of Me, the Queen of all things in which the way I see. That's the beauty... the beauty in everything. Seeing how I choose to see... seeing what I've seen through the eyes of a Queen."

"And what's that like? Seeing through the eyes of a Queen?" She wanted to know if it was much different from seeing through her own eyes.

"Oh, Butterfly, you tell me!"

"What do you mean?" She twisted her face with her question. "What do you see when you look at me?"

"I believe we've previously discussed such things..." the Gypsy reminded her.

"Yes, yes, but that was before I knew what I know now..."

"Butterfly, Butterfly... I see a wild thing. I see a light that shines brighter than you can even see. I see the stars in your eyes even when you blink. I see the imprints you make across space and life, even as you sleep. So, Butterfly, do tell me, what is it that you see when *you* look at thee?"

"Well, I was asking you," she took a bite of pie, "because you said you're a Queen..."

"And I say that you're everything. So, Butterfly, what do you see, when *you* see Thee?"

"I... I see a wild thing..." She nodded her head and wiped the back of her hand across her mouth.

"I see my sparkle, and glow shining from me..." She looked down at her body in amazement once again, as if she'd just discovered herself for the first time. "I... I see *me*."

"Don't forget the stars in your eyes!" the Gypsy added on her behalf.

"Right... the stars in my eyes..." She smiled at the Gypsy, a soft and sure smile—unraveling a lifetime of self-revelations, while eating from a tower of pies on the back of a colossal cat.

"So, Butterfly... Ms. Wild Thing with stars in her eyes, who are you, in the eyes of *you*?"

"Perhaps..." She stood up on the cat's back, lifted a tower of pies, tossed it over her head to the cat, then placed her hands onto her hips in front of the Gypsy. "Perhaps I am a beast, or a beaut, or a brute..." she declared with her chin lifted and her words certain.

The Gypsy stood up in excitement. "Perhaps you are all of those things! Perhaps you *yourself* are even a Queen!"

She laughed at the Gypsy's joke. "If I were a Queen, I think I'd already have won the game!"

"Indeed!" the Gypsy agreed.

"I'd already know where the door and the bridge and the—oh! The note!" She snapped her sparkling fingers. "If I were a Queen, I think I'd at least know who wrote to me..."

"Oh, Butterfly, you and your note! You've such a curiosity of words and how they were wrote. "

"Why would I have ever been sent here with it, if it wasn't of some sort of importance?" She was even more certain now, that that note held meaning... there was something about that note and its strange words.

"Notes are letters made into words that create worlds... see, it is only of the importance in which you give it, Butterfly—as is with all things—seen or unseen—it is up to *thee* to make out what anything means."

"Yes. It *is* up to me. And that's just what I'm going to do—I'll find it, and find what it means... to *me*..."

"And, Butterfly, you'll find down the line that it is the not yet knowing of things that leads you to what it all means..."

"And... the journey is the best part..." She reflected on the many steps she'd taken in that wild crazy place—all leading to where she now stood—atop a Colossal Ocelot traveling through her forgotten home, sparkling from head to toe.

"Oh, Butterfly! You are *truly* alive!" The Gypsy danced on the back of the cat, and sang, "Welcome to The Land of Thee! Welcome to the Land of Thee! Welcome to the Land of Thee!"

The words echoed within her and she joined in the song and dance with the Gypsy, "Welcome to the Land of Thee! Welcome to the Land of Thee, Welcome to the Land of Thee!" They sang together, and continued in sync:

> *"Welcome to the Land of Thee,*
> *where things may seem how you choose to see,*
> *where darkness lights up mystery,*
> *and all the pathways that you seek.*
> *Where the Wild live free,*
> *and the child sends you off to sleep.*
> *Where the tea is poured to sip and drink,*
> *and the beast finally breaks free.*
> *Where things appear differently*
> *depending on what you believe..."*

She sang the words of her note as if she'd known it by heart. Parts of the note that she hadn't yet read flowed from her lips so naturally as if she'd already memorized all of it. These words were alive inside of her, but where? How? All this time.

Time, time, what is time...

"Oh! My note!" She slapped her hand over her mouth as her mind overflowed with revelation, though still a bit mixed up—you see, revelations tend to get mixed and muddled during times of significant unraveling. This was one of those times.

"You're getting it, Butterfly!" the Gypsy cheered.

"Gypsy... was it you?" She looked into the Gypsy's diamond eyes. "Did you write that note to me? Did *you* send me here?"

The Gypsy laughed but did not answer. "Tell me, Butterfly, did you ever hear the story about the girl with the stars in her eyes?"

"I... I've heard a couple of stories... like," her mind sifted through the many stories she'd been told, and though she knew she'd always been lied to, she still did not know what the truth was, "*only a moon-gazer has stars in her eyes,* and—"

"Oh, no, no! The words certainly do read as this—only a *moon-maker* has stars in her eyes, Butterfly!" The Gypsy threw her head back and laughed. "Oh, do share—what other Tamish nonsense did you hear?"

"That only a woman with stars in her eyes—"

"*Can set the Gypsy Moon arise,* sweet Butterfly," the Gypsy interrupted.

"You mean *see* the Gypsy Moon arise?" she corrected the Gypsy, which was a silly thing to do—for the Gypsy of the Night was always right and true, and deep down the girl knew that she'd always been lied to.

"*Set,* Butterfly."

"The saying I've always known goes—"

"The saying you've always known? You mean the saying that the Tamers *wanted* you to know?"

"Sometimes I forget that I've been tamed..." she admitted, still adjusting to this new old world.

"The *real* saying goes, sweet Butterfly—*only a woman with stars in her eyes can set the Gypsy Moon arise.* The moon wasn't there *forever,* Butterfly..."

"That's right, I was told. In my memories... in the sky... I was shown..." She recalled her blurred memory of a moonless sky, and the tale told to her by the Cat Lady. "I remember... I saw the making of the moon in my memories..."

"You did more than just *see* the making of the moon, Butterfly." The Gypsy jumped off the cat's back, and walked beside them. "Only a woman with stars in her eyes can *set* the Gypsy Moon arise..." the wild woman repeated as they both stared into the bright Gypsy Moon. "Only a moon-*maker* can have stars in her eyes. And you, Butterfly, have stars in your eyes, more stars than all the skies."

The girl slid from the cat's back. "You're not saying..." Surely she'd remember such a feat as that.

"You know what I'm saying, Butterfly—*you* make the light. You control the switch—light or dark, you're the spark..."

She knew what the Gypsy was saying, but how could it be true? If she had the fire and strength to make the moon, then how could the Tamers have ever gotten hold of her? How could she have been tamed for so long? As she spun within the webbings of her mind, she remembered something the Cat Lady had revealed, about the one who stayed in the sky the longest, until the moon was complete. Her heart jumped into her throat. Was it her? Was *she* the moon-maker?

"I see your ruminations, Butterfly. You already know what you know." The Gypsy kicked water up at the girl as they walked through a puddle-filled path.

The girl wiped the puddle water from her skin and splashed more water over her body to wash off the glitter that illuminated from her skin. But again, the sparkle and shine did not wash off. As if her skin had soaked and locked it in for good—the luster remained a part of her.

The cat pulled the lunar bandana from his neck and dropped it from his mouth down to the girl, where it landed beside her in the puddle. She washed her face in the water, catching her reflection. She saw herself aglow, sparkling. She saw, for the first time with her feet planted in the Land of Thee, her true self. She saw the stars in her eyes. She saw who she really was. She was done trying to wash it away. Why would she ever want to wash away her sparkle, her shine? This was her.

She grabbed her sliver of moon from the puddle, still glowing bright like the moon, for, it *was* the moon—it was *her piece* of the moon. She

pulled it over her shoulders, tying it around her neck like a cape—a glowing, flowing, magnificent cape. She stepped forward with a sparkling radiance, draped in a glowing moon-cape.

"What did you see?"

"I saw... me."

"And tell me, Butterfly," the Gypsy grabbed her hand and spun her around, "who do you think is she, me, thee... who do *you* think is *you*?"

"As I said before, sweet Gypsy, perhaps I am a beast, or a beaut, or a brute..." she said with proud sureness, flailing her moon-cape out to the sides, and up and down, and in and out, and circled once around the Gypsy in a jovial dance.

"Perhaps, Butterfly, you are a cat, or a crow, or a girl, or a Queen..."

"Perhaps she is a birdie..." the Ocelot added to the list.

"Or maybe I'm a butterfly?" She spread her glowing cape out to her sides like wings, fluttering around the Gypsy and the Ocelot's giant legs.

"You, Butterfly, you are *everything*... and now you're really starting to see!" The Gypsy danced with her, and pointed to the ground. "Like this *here*, who is *she*? Is *she* not *thee*? Perhaps she too, is a *Queen*?" The Gypsy of course, was pointing to the prominent shadow dancing around on the ground.

"My shadow!" Her shadow spun and burst into hundreds of shadow-butterflies fluttering all around.

"That's mine! Those are mine!" She tried grabbing at them. Soon they gathered at the tip of her sparkling feet, forming into one large shadow-crow. It flew a circle around her and the Gypsy and the Ocelot until it disappeared over the glistening trees.

"What resides within will always shine forth, Birdie," the Ocelot reminded her.

"*Especially* the shadow!" the Gypsy agreed. "And the Crow! And still so much more than you think you know. Soon you'll see, sweet Butterfly, there is so much more for you to see..."

"So, then, show me!" She wanted to devour it all.

"Show you, Butterfly? You see I say—I've practically *told you* the answer to the question that presently you seek—though, it's always a matter of how you choose to listen to me..." The Gypsy grabbed hold of the sparkling girl and spun with her. "Needn't you worry, though, just as before—soon you will see—you will see so much more. And perhaps, Butterfly, perhaps you'll agree—perhaps you will see that you're much like a Queen."

"How could I be?" She stopped their spinning. "I'm not even married to a king, or anyone, or anything..."

"That's not what makes a Queen a Queen." The Gypsy spun herself around.

"Well, where I come from, that's what it means..." As she spoke the words she realized she *was* where she came from, and she was still adapting to her new found memories.

"Not in The Land of Thee. You see, Butterfly, the Queen you seek is *thee,* for, *this* is The Land of *Thee*, and the only *she* that could be Queen in The Land of Thee, is *thee*."

"But *I am thee...*" And definitely not a Queen, possibly...

"Oh yes, Butterfly, you are, most certainly."

The blue-eyed Crow flew over her shoulder, and landing atop the Gypsy's head, declared, "She's right you know, Beast, and you've more to go... it is your turn in the game." The Crow stared into her starry eyes.

"The gateway..." she reminded herself, hearing more crows singing the song.

She looked to them in the sky as they flew a halo above her and sang, "Welcome to The Land of Thee... Welcome to The Land of Thee... Welcome to The Land of Thee..." When she lowered her gaze back down, the Crow and the Gypsy were gone.

"Where'd they go?" she asked the Ocelot.

"Don't ask me, I saw not one thing... I'm just a tiny little cat..." the Ocelot whistled up to the sky.

She smiled at the ginormous cat, knowing he knew exactly where they went, and how, but she let it be. She had faith that she would learn everything, soon enough. She stepped onto the cat's tail and walked onto his back.

She sat on the big beast with her cape on, looking like a Queen of the Wild.

"Ready?" the cat asked her.

"Ready!" And she certainly was.

As I said, Birdie," the Ocelot chimed in, "you cannot wipe away that which shines forth from inside you, you can only let it shine..."

CHAPTER 27

THE WILD GATEWAY

S he and the Ocelot traveled together through the thicker parts of the forest. The further they traveled, the brighter the forest continued to grow, with star-dust glistened leaves larger than the ones on the previous trees. The Gypsy Moon swelled in concordance with her breath. She watched it continue to expand at the same pace that she was expanding. The moon was not only growing in enormity—it and the sky were also growing brighter—the moon in its tangerine hue, the sky all around it glowing, and golden.

From atop the Ocelot's back, she could look out to the distance through the amber air, seeing deeper into the unknown—deeper into the Wild—a wilder view of the Wild—a wilder view of herself. Everywhere she shifted her starry gaze, she witnessed more of not just everything, but how everything was connected. From the roots of the trees on the ground, to their big dusty leaves, to the warm sparkling breeze, to the snowflake stars, to the sky and its dripping colors, to the moon that mimicked the beating of her heart, to the *feeling* of the beating of her heart, to the warmth of the cat's back. She was seeing, with stars in her eyes, and feeling, with the wild in her heart and soul—all the details of life—every corner drenched in light, every little black line, every filled gap in the spaces of existence.

She was a part of it all, and she knew it.

There was still so much more to see, still so much there in the Wild that seemed to be calling her name. She knew it. She could feel it. You see, most wild creatures are correct upon first hunches. There was still so much of the Wild that was waiting to be seen, felt, tasted, explored, and devoured by her. There was still so much of herself to be seen, felt, tasted, explored, and devoured by her. Whether she was beginning, or revolving, or evolving—she was living, and therefore thriving—thriving in the Wild, like the wild creature she truly was.

The two wild creatures walked through the afternoon. Rather, the Colossal Ocelot walked through the afternoon, while she stayed seated atop his back looking out at the Wild, like the Queen of it. Or perhaps she was a bird, or a bat, or a girl. Whether she was a beast, or a beaut, or a brute, or a Queen, or a butterfly, or a bird—*she was she*—whatever she wanted to be. She was free. She was free to believe that she was anything she wanted to be—she was everything. She wasn't scared of anything. She was ready for anything. She was a wild one.

She sat up tall with her spine straight and strong. Her bright glowing cape draped over her shoulders, her sparkling legs dangled over the sides of the Ocelot's spine—she was a royal sight. One that her sparkling eyes had not fully seen just yet, but much like revelations—to see the things that are right before your eyes sometimes takes time.

Time, time...

She looked ahead and saw more mysterious land and crystalline streams. Gaps of land of different colors, and thick, golden stardust swelling in the air, hovering over land like dense fog. Past that fog she caught glimpses of bright turquoise water and shimmering mountains reaching to the heavens.

She caught several flashes of a long bridge crossing over the turquoise water—from the wild forest to a place so far, she could not yet see... aside from a soaring mountain here and there. It stretched so far she could not see where it ended. But there it was—it was the bridge. But, she thought, it couldn't be the bridge she was seeking, for this bridge did not go up—it went across, as most bridges do.

"Do you think that bridge leads to where the Queen is?" she asked the Ocelot.

"No, Birdie, I do not think that is where the Queen is at this time. I do believe she will be heading there, as she most usually does... but I do not think she is there, just yet."

"Where do you think this mysterious Queen is?"

"I think she is here, in The Land of Thee."

"So she's returned...? But *who* is she? Really?"

"Don't you suppose, stubborn Birdie, that in a land called The Land of Thee, the only Queen that could be is the one that is... *thee?*"

Thee, as in me? Pieces began to shift into place, like a puzzle beginning to take shape. Perhaps the Gypsy was not joking with her. Everyone seemed to know her there. Every creature spoke of her return. But, oh, it couldn't be. Could it?

"The Queen has not fully returned..."

She had just returned to her wild self. Could she really be a Queen? She had stars in her eyes, like the tales of moon-makers.

A rustling in the trees and branches caught her attention, shifting her thoughts. She glanced up and around, barely catching a glimpse of a wild one in the foliage.

"Bet you can't catch me!" the Wild Child interrupted them.

Captured by the excitement of finally spotting the little girl, she stood up on the Ocelot's back and said, "Oh, yes we can!"

The Wild Child swung across the trees and past them.

"Ready?" the Colossal Ocelot asked.

"Yes, yes! Let's go!" She sat back down and held onto the cat's fur. Her glowing cape flew up, trailing behind her as she and the Ocelot chased after the Wild Child, and the colors of the sky danced deeper into the day that began its shift toward night.

Riding on the back of the cat—she flourished in the middle of a game of chase within a larger game of seek. Her skin sparkling and bright, her cape flying behind, the wild air soaring past her hair and face, her lips curled to the tops of her cheeks—perhaps she *was* a Queen, she certainly felt like one then and there, that is.

The afternoon bled into the evening during their high-speed-chase, dark settling itself around them like a blanket. The ambers, golds, and yellows of the sky married the blues, purples, and pinks deeper in hue, though the air was still light with the mist and gold dust and the stars.

They traveled under the guidance of the moon. Through paths of wildflowers nearly as tall as trees, and paths filled with every kind of green, they came upon a crystal framed entrance in the thick of the wild forest.

That's where the Ocelot stopped.

"We have arrived, little Bird, this is the place you were looking for—we've arrived at your door... your gateway, as you say."

She stared at the threshold she'd been instructed to find. A thick screen of ivy hung within the entrance of this passageway—this gateway that would lift the veil to a new path. It was as tall as she was, atop the Ocelot's back, and it was made entirely of glowing tangerine gypsum and sparkling marbles. The crystals—reaching out from the ground like roots—entangled into one another, woven into an iridescent portal—hundreds of collected marbles filling all the gaps and spaces in between.

She reached into the pocket of her gown and pulled out her marble, her key.

She looked at her starry-eyed reflection within her marble, then studied the door. She lifted onto her knees upon the Ocelot's back and placed her marble in the gateway—right in the holding space of two gypsum crystals coming together at the highest point.

As she pulled her hand away, the gateway lit up from the top to the bottom—the entire portal brightened as if she'd poured golden light over it. The marbles and the gypsum glowed bright tangerine—the golden light drenched down into the ivy that dangled within the portal. When the light hit the ground, it did not stop—the ground below the ivy lit up, the ground below the Ocelot's feet lit up, the trees and leaves along each side of the Gateway lit up, and so did their eyes. You see, light does not stop spreading once it is loose, it runs wild—to every dark corner, every shadowy edge, every word read.

"Ready?" the Ocelot asked as they watched the Wild light up.

"Ready." She was.

The Ocelot took a few steps back and lowered his body to the ground. She slid down from the side of his back and stepped over his giant paw. She stood between his arms, in front of his whiskers and heart-shaped nose—his eyes shining in the light of the gateway and glistening at the twinkle in hers.

"There you have it, Birdie, your gateway that leads to so very much more..."

Where would this take her, she did not know. But she was ready. She was ready for more of the unknown. "Thank you, Ocelot. I couldn't have gotten here without you..." She wrapped her arms around the top of his head and hugged the side of his face.

"Perhaps, little Bird, you *could* have gotten here without me," the Ocelot blinked slowly, "but it surely would not have been the same, or nearly as much fun."

She pulled away from hugging his face, and looked him in the eyes as if she'd made another revelation. "You walked me to my destination..." Her starry eyes shimmered.

"I happily took part in it, yes... but, perhaps, little Bird, you've been walking me to mine, as well. I much do prefer walking with you over stalking you, Birdie. This has been quite enjoyable."

"I'm so happy I got caught in your trap, Ocelot..." she laughed at herself, "I never thought I'd hear myself say that. But... I'm so happy to have found you..."

"We've known each other for a long, long time, Birdie."

"For how long?" she asked.

"Since before the Gypsy Moon."

"Since before the moon..." she gasped, diving into her newly flooded well of memories.

"We came from the same place, remember Birdie? We are the same, you and me…"

"Me and you… the same as the stars…" She rubbed her hand along the bridge of his nose.

"Always, and forever, my Pet." He bowed his head.

"I'm sorry, Ocelot, I'm still trying to remember everything…"

"No apologies, Birdie, you're almost there. We've been walking you back to your memories… remember? You mustn't forget—you are everything, looking through the eyes of a—"

"A girl, I know…"

"The eyes of a Queen," the cat corrected her.

"Ocelot, I—"

"Now, go on through that entrance, little Bird. Go find the little girl that swings in the trees. Find who you believe to be the Queen. And then, perhaps, you will find that bridge of yours…"

"You're not coming with me?" she asked, realizing she was about to embark on a new journey—on her own once more.

"This is *your* game, little Bird. I do have a responsibility to keep up with my own games, and a large puddle of delectable moon milk to lap up, from that Gypsy in the sky—she is so wasteful. Ah, thank goodness for cats like me." The cat licked his chops. "Oh, but, Birdie, this is not goodbye—goodbye is no such thing. Forever I have known you, little Bird, soon you will remember that. And I will be with you forevermore… and quite soon, indeed, I will meet you on another path… perhaps for a different game."

"I would like that very much." She didn't want to walk away from the colossal cat, but she knew it was time to. She knew there was more for her to see.

The Ocelot dropped his head down, and pressed his giant forehead against her little one. She wrapped her arms around his head and squeezed him in a hug. She scratched under both of his ears until he purred so loud and so deep that he shook the ground under her feet.

"When I see you next, Birdie, perhaps you'll have found the Queen…"

"Trust me, Ocelot, I'm going to win this game!" She had no doubt in her mind.

"I haven't a doubt in my mind of that, little Bird. Now, go through that ivy and play and win the game. I'll be going this way—doing the very same."

She and the cat pulled apart, smiling at each other through every line on their faces and twinkle in their eyes. She watched as he lifted himself onto his four feet and walked down a path that formed at the discretion of his steps. She knew it was not goodbye, she'd learned that no one ever truly leaves her. Perhaps he was on his way to find that puddle of milk from the moon and the Gypsy of the stars.

She flung her cape and spun herself around, looking up at the glowing gateway. She took a deep breath into her lungs, and seven steps toward the door. She stood there—tall and sparkling—alone yet not alone at all, her cape only slightly rippling with the soft zephyr. Standing like a wild creature, before the gateway of the Wild.

CHAPTER 28

THE SHADOW QUEEN

S he looked at the falling stars, and the ones still in the sky shining bright with the Gypsy Moon. The moon swelling with the beating of her heart and each new breath, she curled the corners of her lips as high as they could reach... and continued closer toward the gateway.

She stood in the doorway where the illuminated ivy draped down, twirling it between her fingers. She pressed her palm against one side of the gypsum archway and felt a jolt of electricity permeate her body, her butterflies, her mind, her eyes. She gasped as if she'd just taken in her first breath of life.

She poked her head through the curtain of ivy, peeking into the other side, which, to her surprise, wasn't drenched with golden light like everything else. It was so dim on the other side she could barely see through the darkness. She looked to the ground that was lit no further beyond the tips of her toes. She shimmied her toes forward, poking them out from the curtain of ivy, and as she moved—the light on the ground followed beneath her feet.

She took in another deep breath, and still looking down at her feet, she walked completely through the wild gateway. She watched the light of the ground not only follow her steps, but now blaze ahead of her to the other side of the gateway—lighting up the entire path stretched out before her. She watched the night light up through a meadow of glowing wild flowers—every dark gap of the wild, every shadow filling with light. She laughed and smiled even wider.

"I control the switch…" she whispered to herself, continuing through the lights of the magical evening, atop the lit-up path, alongside the brightest wild flowers.

"Yeah ya do, Babe!" The Bat flew past her nose and she stumbled her stepping. "Ya also control the menu and what ya get, Doll!" He flew a circle around her and called, "Order up!"

As she watched him fly off into the night, she continued forward, thinking on what he said. That is, until she was distracted by the sight of nearby wild flowers moving and rustling around. Had she spotted the Wild Child? She jumped up and hopped through the flowers like a bunny, chasing after the little girl, following the sound of the Wild Child's laughter.

She played in the flowers until she saw a bushy tail sticking out from them, wagging from side to side. She paused, surprised, and laughed.

She took two leaps in the Coyote's direction, landing in front of his face. "Gotcha!" she declared, swinging her hips and cape from side to side.

"Ya got me, Girl!" The Coyote stood up and tackled her down to the ground, licking her face and yapping at her as they rolled around and laughed in the flowers. "Now let's go get that child…"

The Coyote nudged his snout under her arm as he stood. She rose with him, and together they walked through the field of radiant wild flowers. The Coyote nipped at them as they walked along, and spoke with a mouth full, "So, found what ya been looking for?"

"I think I've found much more than I was looking for…" She paused, recognizing the last worries that held space in her mind. "And Coyote… the Tamers… they can't ever tame me again, can they? They can't make me go back to where I came from, right?" She never wanted to go back there again. She wanted to stay where she was, where she belonged—her home.

"Firstly, Girl, you *are* back from where ya came, never forget. Secondly, Girl, don't you worry 'bout them Tamers," he ate some more, and continued, "They'll keep chasing after ya, but you just keep your eyes on the light... on your light. As long as you know who you truly are... you'll be just fine, Girl, just fine."

She knew who she was. She almost knew it all. They could never capture her again, she would make sure of it.

"So, what is it that ya seeking now, Girl?"

"I'm looking for the Queen... Do you know her? I think she's the one who wrote my note... I'm looking for the Wild Child too, but you already knew that!" She smirked and pat him on the back. "Oh! And... do you know of... a bridge that goes... up?"

"Ah, the bridge. And which Queen, Girl?"

"Which Queen?" What does he mean, which Queen? Was there more than one Queen?

"There are two queens, Girl, from the ones in which I figure ya speak of and might be looking for..."

The Crows had not told her she was to search through many Queens. But of course, she should have known—for the Crows play games their way. "But how will I know which one to find? Or which Queen is which?"

"The trick is that the two make one, if ya get what I mean... if ya find one of 'em, ya found both of 'em."

"Do these Queens travel together?"

"In a way, ya could say that, Girl, if ya want to."

"I want to find the Queen... both queens, rather..." She placed her order, as the Bat had instructed.

"BOO!" The Wild Child jumped down from a tree branch, and landed atop the Coyote's back as the two of them walked along.

She stumbled back, surprised to see the Wild Child fall from the sky. The Coyote, of course, was unfazed. The little girl laughed hysterically on the Coyote's back.

"I got you!" the child said in laughter.

"And I got *you!*" She squeezed the little girl's toes as her alarm turned into laughter. The three of them walked together in the lit up path, surrounded by the falling stars and glowing flowers, under the Gypsy Moon and an amber milky night's sky.

"Wild Child... who is the Queen... the *queens?*"

"That's the moon-maker," the little girl answered without hesitation. "And that's the Queen."

"But... but who is that?" she asked in accommodation of her own denial. "*Who* is the Queen?" As if she didn't already know, deep down.

"It's you, Silly!" The little girl and the Coyote stopped in the path and looked at her.

"No, no." She laughed through her words, continuing her incessant denial. "Really, who is it? Who's the Queen?"

"Really, really!" The Wild Child reached over to the girl, pulled the glowing cape from off her back, and spun it up and around in the air—turning into something much smaller. The Wild Child held up a crown of glowing gold. "It's *you! You're* it!" The little girl placed the crown onto the Queen's head, and said, "*You're* the Queen, Silly!"

She looked at the Wild Child and the Coyote through the refusal in her eyes, as if they had to be in on this wild tale. But what was a tale in The Land of Thee told by wild creatures and beasts, but a revelation of answered mystery and lost reverie? You see, she had only just begun to realize that she's always been a Queen, and she learned not long ago to trust the tales of the beast. After releasing her denial, she accepted what she'd always known.

She lifted her hands and felt the crown that now rested atop her head, made from the Gypsy Moon. The flashes of memories that she saw in the sky struck her mind once more, and she saw herself flying high, lit up with light, lighting the night. She saw herself falling from the sky, and then the images of her mind turned black. She looked back at the little girl and the Coyote. "If I'm the—"

"Now you gotta catch me!" the Wild Child called out as the Giant

Coyote took off running, "I'm going up, up, up!" the little girl shouted back to her.

"See ya in your circles, Girl!" the Coyote yelled to her as he ran further down the path.

She watched the two wild creatures run ahead and she continued to ask the Wild, "If I'm the Queen, then who's my king?"

"The Wild is your king." She heard the Wild answer her, in that familiar voice of the Crow. Just as she looked over her left shoulder, she felt something land on the right one. The big blue-eyed Crow sat tall atop her shoulder, staring into her starry eyes.

"The Wild is my king?" she asked, wondering what that means.

"Indeed, Beast."

"And *who* are thee?" she asked the Crow.

"I am *thee*," the Crow revealed. "Shall I show thee?" the Crow offered.

"Yes, please..."

The bird flew behind her, and when she turned to see where it flew to, it was gone, and in its place—her shadow stood before her face, taller than it ever had before.

"I am the Shadow Queen," the shadow introduced herself.

"The *Shadow* Queen?"

"That's what we said."

"The two make one..." she repeated the Coyote's words, "find one of 'em, found both of 'em..."

Now she understood.

"Yes, Beast. We are one, you and I... *we* are *thee*."

"So... you're a part of me?" She studied the shadow.

"Very much so, Beast. See, all that shines forth always comes from within." The Shadow Queen disappeared before her eyes and shifted back into the Crow, which landed upon the girl's head this time, hunching its face and beak in front of hers. They stared eye to eye, the bird upside down.

"How come you haven't spoken up until now? Why didn't you just tell me?" she asked the Crow.

"I *have* been since you've arrived. It takes time for you to hear what you already know. But, now you know, Beast... you know what you already always knew."

"So... *I'm* the Queen and *you're* the Shadow Queen... Were you with me while I was tamed?"

"I am the shadow... I am everywhere you are. I am everything. I've been here, and I've been there, the whole time."

"And the note? *You* wrote it to me?"

"*You* wrote it. You could say we wrote it together... after all, I *am* a part of you, Beast."

She wrote the note... to herself. Somewhere deep inside her wild beating heart, had she always known she would need guidance from herself, to lead her back to The Land of Thee? To herself, her home, her kingdom, her throne...

Fully returned.

"Why did we write it?"

"Aware that you could become tamed by the Tamers... and forget who you were and where you came from—you wrote the note to remind you," the Crow told her.

She wrote the note to remind herself—a map to return to her home.

"But... wouldn't you forget whatever I forget?" she asked.

"Beast, I am The Shadow Queen. Nothing can be forgotten within me. I am everywhere and I am everything." The Crow fluttered her feathers.

"Then why did you take it from me?"

"I do believe things are much more fun my way. Don't you agree, Beast?" The Crow flew off the girl's head and pecked at the girl's hand until she opened and lifted it, and the bird sat in her palm. She held her arm up high with the Shadow Queen in the palm of her hand and continued to walk the lit-up path.

"I never got to finish reading it, you know..." she told the bird.

"Oh... you mean this?" The Crow pulled out a small piece of paper from within its feathers. It was her note. Finally—she'd found her note.

"My note!" She stopped in the path, grabbing the paper from the Crow's beak. "You've had it this whole time?"

The Crow flew up from her palm and flew three circles around her—disappearing as the bird and reappearing on the ground before her as her shadow, who then shrugged in response to her questioning. She opened up the folded piece of paper, and read:

"Welcome to The Land of Thee,
where things may seem
how you choose to see,
where darkness
lights up mystery,
and all the pathways
that you seek.
Where the wild
live free,
and the child
sends you off to sleep.
Where the tea
is poured to sip and drink
and the beast
finally breaks free.
Where things appear
differently
depending on
what you believe.
Where skies will open
skies will speak
with rain that falls
from tears she weeps.
Where water rises
in the stream
and sweeps her to

a rocky beach.
Where vines dangle
from the trees
and pull her up
by her dirty feet.
Where she opens up
a hidden door
with the marble
that is hers.
Welcome to The Land of Thee,
where you'll find
your memories,
where you remember
you are the Queen,
where you'll travel
with the trees,
where The Wild
is your king,
and from the Crow
you'll read this thing
right beside
the Shadow Queen,
and once the bridge
has been seen,
you'll travel up to—"

The Shadow Queen shifted back into the Crow and snatched the note out from the girl's fingertips once more.

"Give that back!"

"Beast, my way is so much more fun—you have to admit!" The Shadow Queen flew off.

"Well, I guess your way is *my* way, since we are one...?" She pressed her glowing crown firmly onto her head, and ran after the Crow and

"Beast, I am The Shadow Queen. Nothing can be forgotten within me. I am everywhere and I am everything." The Crow fluttered her feathers.

her note, and the Wild Child and the Giant Coyote. She was aware now, that she'd been playing a game all along—a game with her mischievous shadow, a game with herself, a game with her other half, the Shadow Queen.

She chased after the bird, and the letter, and the child, and the Coyote until she reminded herself that she could stop running. She remembered that she wasn't in a hurry. She was free to go however fast or slow she pleased. She remembered that whatever it was that she was seeking—it would all find her, if it truly was meant to.

As she walked along the path—shimmering and shining—her toes caught a bump and she nearly tripped over something in the path. She stumbled forward a few extra fumbling feet, and after she adjusted her crown and turned around, she saw two small cats in the middle of the lit-up path playing with something shiny, something that chimed with the sound of bells.

These were the cats she'd kept crossing paths with along her journey. Both cats had eyes that glowed as bright as her crown—as bright as the Gypsy Moon. She took two steps to the cats and knelt down. "I'm sorry, I didn't see you there..."

The cats rubbed their fur against her shimmering hands, and elbows, and feet.

"Are you seeing who you are now...? Are you knowing who you are now...?" The Cat Lady and several of her cats rested in one of the low branches of a nearby tree.

"I am a Queen! I am wild and free!"

"Look at you, back on your feet! Flipped the other way around!" The wild old woman laughed up at the skies. "Remember this, Dear—all of what you are, and ever have been, is forever. Eternally stirred up in the winds and sweet breezes, Dear, in the whispers of the night, in the crashing of the waves, in the purring of the kitten, in every shade of light."

As the woman spoke, more cats continued to appear on all of the branches, up and down the tree. "If you listen closely, you can hear yourself sing and roar from miles away... So, remember, Dear Queen, to listen to the many rumbles of the Wild...”

Before she could respond to the Cat Lady, the cats on the tree had multiplied even more, and the Cat Lady was no longer in sight—all she could see were cats on a tree. She looked at the two cats playing in the path—each playing with a tiny bell, like those that the Cat Lady wore on her fingers and toes. She picked up the bells from the ground and wrapped each one around one toe of each foot. She smiled, looking at her sparkling, dirty feet, and stood up.

“I *am* the rumble of the Wild,” she declared.

She walked in a soft dance with a brightly lit crown garnished over her head and jingling bells adorned on her toes. She rambled under the Gypsy Moon and the Wild night’s sky that dripped of golden colors and dropped down many stars—stars that fell and danced around her and the two cats who followed along.

The many different wild flowers swayed with a breeze that wasn’t really in the air—they swayed with the breeze that she created—the sweet zephyr that *was* her. The trees enjoyed her moon-dance with the enchanted evening—their branches lifting higher as if they were limbs—moving and grooving to the rhythm that she made with her toes—the rhythm that *was* her.

For she was the rumble of the Wild—she was a Queen—a Queen of the Wild. A Queen of The Land of Thee—a Queen of the land of *she*—a wild, wild Queen, who could stir the energies of a magical night into a sweet breeze.

CHAPTER 29

THE WILD BRIDGE

She hadn't slept at all that night, and she wasn't the least bit tired. You see, she was a wild creature, a wild creature with certain intent—the intent of joy, the intent of enjoying winning—winning without resistance. The path of the least bit resistance is never an exhausting one. She was more awake, aware, and alert than ever before. She was alive and thriving, alive and shining, alive and winning. Winning—like she always had been.

She'd found herself out there in the Wild. She'd found who she'd once forgotten. She knew she'd find even more of herself the further she traveled.

The lights and colors of the sky shifted once again from the midst of night to the breaks of dawn. The golden night had danced and stirred and swept through the brightly lit field of wild flowers. A wild and new day was soon to break through—the air was lighter, brighter, and more golden—the golds and purples danced with the blues and pinks that dripped into the fiery skies of her next adventure. She was ready for a new day. She was ready for a new adventure.

She spun herself around the movements of the night, walking and marching forward fearlessly along the brightest path. She sang wild and loud as she traipsed on her jingling toes through the deepest depths of the all-telling twilight.

"Welcome to The Land of Thee... don't you get glum when you're missing the sun... Welcome to The Land of Thee... don't you get glum..." She walked and rambled with her arms out to the sides, twirling and balancing between the two cats that chased and batted at her jingling feet.

"You're not in a hurry, are you?"

She felt a tap on the middle of her back. She spun to find the Gypsy standing before her. Within the fingers of one hand, the wild woman held two hot cups of bright wild tea, and in the other hand was a large platter of a tower of fruity pies. Pies made of both light and dark, and all that's in between. Only the stars knew how the Gypsy could have tapped her on the back.

"I could always stop for pie!" The two women sat on the ground in the middle of the lit-up path, with the tower of pies by their side, and the two cats licking the edge of the crusts.

"I do love surprises, Butterfly... But it is of no surprise to me, I see I say, I say I see, that you wear the crown of the Queen..." The Gypsy adjusted the girl's glowing crown for her.

"You knew all along..." She smirked at the Gypsy.

"Of course, Butterfly, remember—revelations take time. Time, time, what is—"

"Gypsy?" she interrupted the rhyming riddler from her riddling distractions.

"Right! You already know. And now you know too—you are the Queen of *you*, of The Land of *Thee*—no one else could ever be." The Gypsy pulled a feather from behind her own back and grazed it across the girl's cheek. "It's always been you, and you've always known that, too..."

"That's the memory of what never dies..."

"Exactly right. Now, Butterfly, let's eat our pie." The Gypsy threw the feather to the sky and it disappeared. The two glowing women each took a bite of pie, then picked up their cups of hot, glowing moon-milk, clinking the cups together. "Cheers, Queen Butterfly!"

"Cheers, Queen Gypsy!" They sipped their cups of warm moon-milk.

"Now, may I see your crown?" The Gypsy reached over and pulled the crown from the girl's head and walked behind her, placing the moon-piece down to the ground—where it sat as a throne. "Her home is her throne, her throne is wherever she goes..." the Gypsy repeated the words she had spoken from the stars.

"Oh!" She looked behind herself and stood up. "*My throne...*" She recalled what the Ocelot had told her about the Queen. "Her throne is her home..." She was home.

"Have a sit! Have a sit in a seat made for a Queen! Have a sit in a seat made for *thee!* Have a sit in a seat made for a moon-maker, a Tamer-shaker!"

She sat on her glowing throne, and the Gypsy handed her a cup of tea. The wild women clinked their cups. "Cheers to us, wild Queen!" The Gypsy sat on the ground, leaning on the throne. "So tell me, Butterfly, do you know now, what you'll do with those stars in your eyes?"

"I'll be seeing things how I choose to see... I'll be seeing... *everything...*" She looked around with her renewed sight. "So... you and I, we're both Queens?"

"Everyone is their own Queen... or King, if they choose to be. It is all, always, up to thee." The Gypsy shoved a slice of pie into both of their mouths and said, "And... what is the next thing?"

"I'm revolving and evolving..." spitting cake as she spoke, "rambling on, floating... flowing where the wind takes me..." She swallowed. "Making my way to the bridge." She pointed ahead. "Catching up with my shadow." She nodded and adjusted her hair behind her ear.

"Oh, the bridge, Butterfly! Perhaps I'll see you on that other side."

"So you know where it goes?" she asked the Gypsy.

"So do you."

"Well, I still don't remember *everything...*"

"You will, Butterfly. Remember, revelations take time..." The Gypsy shook her head back and forth—her hair flying to the sides as black feathers expelled from her head and flew into the sky... as if the feathers themselves were birds. "Time, time, what is time?"

She watched the feathers fly off in a hurry, following their strange flight until she watched them dissipate into the stardust of the sky. Who was this Gypsy of the Night? *What* was she? She was different from the Babes, but how?

"Time—" the Gypsy was about to begin again with her riddle.

"Is it not just a melody that plays in your mind?" she answered the Gypsy before the Gypsy had to ask, again.

"You Queen, *you* are time," the Gypsy told her.

"I *am* time," she repeated the Gypsy's words, trying to understand them. "Time, time, what *is* time..."

"Time, time, is just a rhyme... don't get it stuck inside of your mind. Just eat your pie, and fly up high." The Gypsy plopped another handful of pie into both of their mouths, and pulled two more feathers from her back, stabbing each of them into the tower of pies.

She and the Gypsy sat in the wild garden of wildflowers, eating their wild breakfast—the tower of every kind of pie. The colors of the pie and the colors of the sky dripped in synchronicity. That is, until the screeching of the vultures sliced through the sky, interrupting the stardust from where they flew. Her eyes blazed up at them, she knew they were following her—flying a halo so high as if they were only stars. She remembered, reluctantly, they were all from the stars. They were all the same as the stars. But were the Tamers and the Vultures from the stars, too?

"So, Butterfly, are you still scared of the darkness that lurks in the night?"

As the Gypsy asked her this next question, she heard the Crows call out her name. She looked once more to the sky—the Crows ripped up through the sky, cawing like angry women, darting toward the vultures. Her sisters. Soaring through the sky to save their sister who had just returned from the grip of such beasts. They'd never left her. They'd always been right there with her.

"Watch out up there... I'll have you know we're a bunch of Tamer-shakers!" she yelled to the vultures and cheered for the Babes, "YEE-YEE-YEEW!" She watched as the minuscule vultures scattered far, far away deep into the skies.

When she brought her focus back to the land, the Gypsy was gone.

"I see I say, I say I see—it is of no surprise to me..." she said in her best Gypsy voice, feeding herself another bite of pie. With her mouth full of fruit and crust, she answered the Gypsy's question to herself and to the Wild. "I'm not scared anymore. I *am* the darkness that lurks in the night..." she took a small sip of her tea to wash it all down, "and I am the light that shines in every corner."

She stood up, ready for the day ahead, and declared, "I control the switch."

As she finished the moon-milk tea from her cup, she noticed the different etchings on the porcelain. She spun the cup around to see a ladder etched into it, hanging down from the rim. Surrounding the hanging ladder were birds and girls. She knew it was the bridge. When she looked inside the cup, she read the words: "The Queen will drink from this cup, and then she'll ramble up, up, up."

She placed the cup down, curled her lips, and laughed—aware at this point in the game that she could expect the Gypsy's teacups to be messages of what's to come. She did not know what was to come, and she did not worry about those such woes any longer—for why worry over woes when one can be woe-less, after all? She had found, by this point in this path, that most of the fun was had in the not yet knowing and with the least bit of woe-ing. All she needed was faith in the fact that everything was going just right.

She persisted on her journey forward, into her next adventure—wherever it was that that was.

She picked up her throne and it went limp—draping down like a towel in her hand. She shook it out, and it separated itself into three separate glowing strands that dangled to the ground. She continued onward along the bright path, braiding the three strands of moonlight between the fingers of her hands. The two cats chased behind her, attacking the dragging strands of glowing light and her jingling toes.

After she finished braiding, she wrapped the braid around her head, tying it in the back, letting the strands dangle for the cats to continue chasing after. She walked her golden path—crowned with a braided glow, her skin sparkling, shining under the Gypsy Moon—the moon that shared the heart and soul of the moon-maker—the moon that shared the heart and soul of *her*, the moon-maker.

You see, the light of the moon that shined down on her was her very own light all along. She *was* the light of the Gypsy Moon. She was the light of the falling stars. She was the light of the path. She was the light in the night. She was the light all around her, and she was the dark. She was the switch that controlled it all. She was the Queen—a wild woman—a conductor. She was all of it, she was everything. Now, she knew that. Now, she knew what she always knew.

The cats ran and played and chased the tail of her glowing braid. The Crows cawed and sang in the morning distance—somewhere she could not yet see. The stars shined brighter, fell faster, and multiplied. The trees woke to the waking day, coming to life more than any of the times she saw before.

She walked along, watching as the trees stretched their large, limb-like branches, interlacing their arms in different dances. They showed her their morning merriment—their branches wrapping around each other, pulling one another into dips and swift, soft backbends.

During this dance, one tree lowered a branch to the ground in front of her. She looked at the welcoming offer of the Wild, as the two cats went ahead of her in walking up the tree limb. She stepped onto the tree's friendly helping hand. You see, when a wild creature becomes aware of who she really is, and what she really wants, the Wild will provide for her in all the wildest ways.

The branch lifted her and the cats almost as high as the tops of the trees. She looked out ahead, and through her starry eyes and the treetops, she saw the sparkling water and the bridge that stretched across it. Crystal clear, turquoise water—calm, still, swallowing up all the stars that drifted into it. The bridge stretched beyond where her eyes could see—a path resting over the sea.

The further she traveled on the tree, she began to see faint formations standing in the sky, far off in the distance, past the bridge. Beams of light and glitter struck out from these formations—looking like massive dunes of diamonds. The longer she looked and the closer she got, she realized these glinting formations were mountains—dazzling, magnificent, monumental mountains with peaks so high, they couldn't be seen. But through their shimmer and their shine, they were surely calling her name.

As she looked out to the gleaming distance, she spotted a big black-winged bird flying over the water, flashing its blue eyes at her. The Shadow Queen.

"Aha!" She walked to the tip of the tree branch to see more of the water's edge. She screeched with laughter. She saw the Babes out there on the sand, swimming in the sea. But the Babes were not alone—they were blended with a murder of Crows.

"The Babes!" she said to one of the cats. "The Crows!" she said to the other cat. "The bridge!" she called out to the trees and to the Wild. "YEE-YEE-YEW!"

The branch carried them to another tree, further along the path. She and the cats stepped off from the branch of one tree and onto the branch of the other tree, which carried them to another tree and another tree and yet another tree.

In her tree-transportation, she looked down at the golden path and saw her shadow—her Shadow Queen. It was large and dark, and it waved to her and then spun around. She watched as it skipped ahead of her along the moving branch in its shadow form. The shadow disappeared and the blue-eyed Crow flew before her face. "See you soon, Beast!" The bird flew away.

The trees carried her and her mini-beasts through the golden path and meadow of wildflowers and stopped when she'd met her destination. She and the cats stepped off the tree and back onto the path, where the sand had turned ultra fine and soft, and smaller trees and leaves congested it.

She walked under the canopy of greens and after many sandy steps with her cats, she was released onto the beach. She waved to the Babes, who played in the light and the sea straight ahead of her. She noticed the Babes stood in a murder of only Babes—the Crows had once again vanished.

"YEE, YEE, YEEW!" the Babes called out to her with wide grins and open arms.

"OWE, OWE, OWE!" she called back, running to them.

She and the Babes met each other halfway on the sand. They crowded around her, embracing her sparkling body in several hundred hugs. They spun her, and she twirled and dipped them down. She passed her bright braided crown around for the other Babes to don, and it bounced from head to head. They danced together in the sand and with the Gypsy Moon. She watched all of them, and she smiled. She watched herself, and she smiled.

She knew the Crows and Babes were playing this game with her all along—helping her get to her destination. There she stood, right where she wanted to be, right where she belonged—with her feet in the sand, wearing the suit of a Queen, surrounded by a beach full of other beautiful Queens.

"She's returned!" the Babes called out and started chanting, "Welcome to the Land of Thee... Welcome to the Land of Thee!" They danced in circles around her.

"Are you ready?" One of the Babes grabbed her hands, pulling her closer to the water and the bridge.

"Ready!"

She stood before the water and the mysterious moon—staring at it, bigger than ever. It stared back at her as the wild bridge stretched between the two of them. The Babes walked onto the bridge ahead of her.

Before she stepped onto the bridge, she dropped her knees to the sand to pick up the cat of white and the many shades of dark and placed it into her pocket. Then she picked up the cat of black and the many shades of light and did the same. She stood up, brushed off her hands and knees, looked at the Babes on the bridge and asked, "Where does the bridge go?"

"It goes up," her blue-eyed Shadow Queen of a Crow answered her as it landed on her shoulder.

"Up?" She looked at the bird. "But—"

"Where the brights are brighter, the darks are darker... and the Wild is much, much wilder... Beast." The Crow almost flew from her, until it turned and revealed, "To the place where the Tamers are heading, to find you..."

They're still following her? She scrunched her brow, feeling a slight pit of fear stir within her where the butterflies once resided. Why did they want her back in that world so badly? Why did they need her tamed?

She took a deep breath. She listened to herself breathe. She reminded herself that her sparkle could never be tamed again. She kept her eyes on the light. Her light would not be dimmed, no matter who tried.

"Watch!" a Babe called to her, pulling her from her thoughts.

She looked to the bridge now filled with Babes, and she watched as each one of them jumped off the bridge and splashed into the sparkling, turquoise water. When they came back up, they were not the Babes that she saw splash down. The Babes burst out from the water—soaring into the sky as the beautiful, black-winged Crows, singing her song to her.

She jumped with the excitement of this remarkable sight, jumping only as much as one could jump when carrying cats within her pockets. She laughed wildly, she laughed ravingly, and she laughed some more. The Crows flew up and around her as she cackled hysterically, drenched in pure delight, shimmering with pure, shining light.

The Crows spun her around and her laughter roared even more. Tears began to drench her eyes. She laughed at the expansion of her perception—the knowing of what she'd always already known, and the not yet knowing of what she did not yet know. She laughed at the surprise in what she could see with her starry eyes. She laughed at the wonderment of where she was and what she was now seeing—in a place she hadn't expected to be, but was delighted to have found herself there, with wild creatures by her side.

You see, she was right where she belonged. She was right where she wanted to be. She was wild, and she was free. She'd found herself soaring to her highest frequency—a time in which laughter tends to take over—a simple symptom of the enjoyment and the thrill of life. A symptom that was sure to transition to other more fascinating things.

She laughed so hard that her laughter turned to hiccups. As the birds flew and sang all around her, she hiccupped, and she laughed and she hiccupped even more. As her hiccups halted with a roaring belch from the depths of her, the butterflies flew out from her mouth, fluttering from deep within her, out into the salty, starry air. Perhaps as many as a hundred butterflies flapped their wings from her mouth and past her lips. She watched as they flew all around her, and into the sky.

They were glowing like she was. They were bright and free, flying all around her, and within the flight of the Crows. She laughed even more, with sparkling stars in her eyes.

"Going up?" the blue-eyed Crow asked her as it flew by her face, and the rest of the murder of Crows flew up toward the sky.

"Yes please!" She watched as a handful of Crows flew over the bridge, and far, far away to wherever the other side of the bridge led to. She watched as they flew toward her from the unseen distance, growing larger with each flap closer. She squinted and gasped when she realized they were holding the other end of the bridge in their beaks—lifting it from above the water, and flying it toward her.

When they got nearer to her, she wasn't sure what they would do. What would they want with the other end of the bridge? How would she get to the other side?

The birds approached her, flying at her and fleeing upward before colliding with her face. They carried the bridge far up into the sky to where she could no longer see them. The bridge stood before her starry eyes—one end at the water's edge, the other end going straight up to the sky. The bridge stretched above and stood before her like a ladder for her to climb.

She looked at the bottom of the ladder, and up toward the sky. "Ready," she said to herself and to the Wild. And ready she certainly was. Perhaps she did not know what she was ready for, but she knew that she was ready.

She took three steps forward, grabbing hold of the bridge-turned-ladder, and she started to climb. She climbed, sparkling and aglow, with a cat in each pocket, bells on her toes, and wearing her crown of braided light that was made from the moon—the moon that was made by her.

As she climbed higher, watching the birds further up in the sky, she wondered if she too, could fly. Though, that is something she would never know, you see, unless of course, she gave it a try.

She thought, as she continued to climb, that whether or not she wanted to fly, whether or not she'd try to fly—as long as she had faith that all would be just right—it would be in the not yet knowing, in the getting there—that would be the thrill of her life.

ACKNOWLEDGEMENTS

I have spent countless hours over the last five years daydreaming of the day that I would be writing this page. And now that the day has come, it feels surreal and I find my thoughts overlapping one another with every single thank you that I want to give.

So, here we go... as my eyes begin to water, and that lump rises into my throat.

To my husband—my best friend, my biggest support, my rock, my soulmate, my everything. Thank you for always being by my side, for picking me up whenever I need, for cheering me on during this whole process and encouraging me every time I needed it. You are my dream come true, my fairytale, my magic-making partner in crime. I am so grateful that you stood by me, sat by me, stayed by me every night while I stared at all the words of this book. Now I can't wait

to take a break and watch a movie with my best friend. I love you infinitely.

Thank you for making me a mama to my littlest best friend, and for being the best dad to all of our little bears. We would be lost without you. Thank you for guiding all of our little men to be the best guys they can be. They have the best teacher.

To my Mama and Daddy for showing me what the sweetest, most unconditional love is. For showing me what a true best friend is, and for being my first best friends. For always supporting me in everything I've ever done. For always making me feel like your special little girl. For convincing me and guiding me towards becoming an indie-author—here's the proof that I took your advice! For showing me what it is to be a strong, loving team, even in the hardest of times. For not only being my best friends, and my cradling arms, but for guiding Byron and I in our journey as parents, and for showing us how to be the best we can be.

To my editor at Shadow Rain Publishing for being an absolute blessing and helping me perfect my book. Without you, this book would not be what it is today. Thank you so much for not only being an amazing editor, but for your immense support and endless guidance and help. And for literally always being there whenever I need an answer to a crazy or obnoxious question.

To my dear friend, Shannon, for not only reading my first draft, but for encouraging me to continue

forward with it. For your constant help in all things. For being literal sunshine. For always being there. Thank you.

To all of my friends and family. I love you all. To all of you and every bit of support you've ever shown me. You mean so much to me.

To my community, I am so grateful to be here with all of you.

To my friends in the writing and reading world—thank you. Thank you for being so supportive, so helpful, so accepting, so warm and loving. So many of you have changed my life and kept me hopeful on the days that I wanted to throw my computer out the window.

To every reader of my words, or anyone who ever holds this book—I love you. You are one of the biggest parts of my dream. It does not exist without you.

To Yahweh. And to all of my Angels. Thank you for giving me strength when I need it. For loving me. For guiding me. For granting me this story to share with the world. For always guiding me. For each new day and every miracle. For every breath. For all of the beauty of this life. Thank you. And thank you for wining and dining my mama up there.

I love you all. Thank you.

ABOUT THE AUTHOR

Missy Miller is an author, poet, mama, wife, and wild child on a little fishing island in New England. She spends her days running through her backwoods with her little bears, chasing the sparkles on the sea, dancing on the beach, making up songs about mundane daily things, cleaning her house, cooking family meals, feeding the crows, writing the many random passages that come to her mind throughout the day on anything she can find, trying to seek out the silver linings in all things and always getting giddy when talking about miracles and the magic of this life, sometimes playfully imagining that her life is a whimsical fairytale or an epic 80's beach movie, never wanting to miss a moment with her family...

which is why it took her five years to write her debut novel.

Under The Gypsy Moon: The Land of Thee is book one of the Gypsy Moon series.

You can keep up to date on any of Missy's works by going to:

www.authormissymiller.com